MARRYING MY BILLIONAIRE BOSS

NADIA LEE

Marrying My Billionaire Boss

Copyright © 2020 by Hyun J Kyung

All rights reserved.

No part of this book may be reproduced in any form or by any electronic or mechanical means, including information storage and retrieval systems, without written permission from the author, except for the use of brief quotations in a book review.

To Diane.

1

NATE

I hear the cuckoo clock in the living room go off seven times, and my whole body starts to tighten, like a dog that just *knows* it's playtime.

The security monitor beeps on my phone, causing my heart to skip a beat. That'll be Evie, walking into my Malibu home. Since she started as my assistant nine months ago, she's never missed a day of work or been late even once. I exit the bathroom, nothing but a towel around my hips as she comes into my bedroom.

She's tied her wavy golden hair loosely today, and I love the reddish color of her lipstick because her mouth looks so delectably delicious in that shade. Her pink dress flatters the soft swell of her breasts and the beautiful lines of her waist and hips. There isn't even a hint of anything inappropriate or flirty about the outfit —alas. I'm parading around practically naked in front of her, but her gorgeous cornflower-blue eyes never stray below my chin.

A lesser man would be crushed.

But I'm Nate Fucking Sterling. And dammit, I know I look good. Women fawn over me. They think they're so subtle, but they always cop a feel. Or at least a look.

Not Evie though. She's immune. Don't know why. She's not

blind, or a lesbian. I haven't done anything to repulse her as far as I can tell. I've been working my ass off in the gym to gain more muscle around my biceps and chest and put more definition on my abs. But even with everything on full display, I don't think she's noticed.

"Good morning," she says, walking into my gigantic closet.

"Morning." I sit down at the edge of my bed to watch. Just because she doesn't check me out doesn't mean I can't check her out. Her ass looks amazing in that dress. Actually, her ass looks amazing in anything. It would look amazing in a potato sack four sizes too large.

"You have a visit at the Sterling Medical Center this morning on your way to the office, so how about something conservative?" She picks out a charcoal bespoke suit and a slim silver-blue tie, along with a pair of polished loafers.

"Yes, that'll do nicely." She has great taste. I wouldn't let her pick my outfits otherwise, no matter how hot she was.

"Glad you approve, Mr. Sterling."

Mr. Sterling. We've been working together closely for the best part of a year, and she still refuses to call me Nate. So I started to call her Ms. Parker, just to show her how silly it is to be so formal. Which turned out to be a huge tactical error, because she seems to actually *enjoy* being called Ms. Parker.

Okay, so she's from the Midwest. It's probably more traditional than here in L.A., but people there must call each other by their first names. Why else would you give them to your kids?

And she calls *other* people by their first names, even around the office. It's just me who gets the Mister treatment. Do I look like I have a giant pole up my ass? I know I was born to money, but I try not to be a stuck-up douchewad. And based on how people treat me, I thought I was doing pretty well...until now.

But it's too late to ask for an explanation without sounding weird. I've gone through a hundred different scenarios I could use to broach the topic, and they all sound stupid.

"I'll get your breakfast started while you get dressed," she says, walking out.

My bedroom feels empty and sort of sad without her in it. But

Marrying My Billionaire Boss

apparently prepping my breakfast is also her job, even though I didn't ask her to do it.

Honestly, I don't need this much help in the morning. None of my assistants ever did this before. But when I first interviewed Evie, she acted like she'd do anything to work for me, and I decided to test her. Mainly because I'd had a string of shitty assistants who acted like they'd do anything required for the job, but then couldn't even locate a paper bag to find their way out of.

So now her job includes coordinating my outfits in the morning and getting me breakfast.

When I'm done putting on the clothes she picked out, I go downstairs. The open floor plan gives it an airy feel, with glass walls facing the Pacific and its waves. And there's one of those contemporary waterfalls in the sunken living room. But the most spectacular thing is Evie, standing in my ultra-modern kitchen, bright light around her like an angel's halo. I even hear a faint strain of heavenly chorus.

She looks at me over her shoulder, a small smile on her lips. Air sticks hard in my throat, and my brain goes blank, mesmerized by her mere presence.

"I made you your favorite—a kale and protein smoothie with fresh berries."

The moment's shattered as she offers up a tall glass of frosted purple-green concoction from hell. But I'm a gentleman, so I give her a grateful smile as I take the vile shit. "Mmm, berries!"

I'd rather die in my eighties with carcinogenically grilled dead cow floating in my veins than live to be a robust hundred with this antioxidant goo keeping me young and wrinkle-free. But she honestly believes I love this crap—it's a long story—so I down it with a huge grin that hurts my face even as the shake violates my palate like Atilla the Hun violated Europe. This should show her my appreciation—and ensure she returns to my place every morning.

And if I walk around topless long enough, maybe she'll notice I'm not just her boss, but a man, too.

Maybe you should accidentally drop your towel tomorrow morning. She'll definitely notice that.

Oh, please. That's so clichéd. I don't do clichés.

Because parading around in a towel isn't a cliché.

Doesn't count. That was an accident. I got up late one morning, and she came into the room just as I stepped out of bathroom. Maybe I should buy a transparent towel. Surely something like that is available somewhere on this vast planet.

While I'm guzzling down the supposedly life-recharging breakfast of champion rabbits, Evie rattles the day's agenda off her tablet. A meeting to be rearranged at the other party's request.

"Some people have no respect for my time or schedule," I say, mildly annoyed because it's the second time they've asked to reschedule.

"Or maybe they know you can afford to be flexible."

"Still kind of presumptuous. You didn't say yes, did you?"

"Not yet."

That's my girl. Always clear on where to draw the line. "Good. I hate it when people act like I enjoy being flexible or changing my mind. Once I make up my mind, I don't change."

"Of course not, Mr. Sterling."

When I'm finished with the veggie desecration, she hands me my coffee. *Finally.* I take as big of a gulp as possible to erase the lingering taste of kale. I should convince my brother Justin to buy up every kale farm on the planet, burn the shit to the ground and salt the soil.

Carrying the travel mug, I start to go out to the car that'll be waiting.

"Other way," Evie says.

"What?"

"Miguel's not here today,"

"He's not?"

"You gave him the week off."

Oh, that's right. His wife's about to pop their second baby out any day now, and I gave him a paid week off. Pregnant women apparently become needier and/or crazier around this time, according to Justin, who has a kid and should know. Plus Miguel is a great guy, and he deserves time off.

"Okay. Thanks for the reminder."

I turn and head to the garage, Evie following closely, her heels clacking quietly. As soon as I open the door, the lights come on. I step inside and peruse my collection. It's hard to decide what to drive out of the ten cars I have. I steal a glance at Evie. Instead of admiring the various examples of world-class mechanical engineering, she's staring at something on her tablet.

Well then. I choose the Bugatti. This gleaming black-and-red babe is a beaut. Very impressive, too. It better be, for a cool nineteen million. I've only taken it out for a spin twice, and not with anybody else. Evie should be flattered.

I open the door for her. "Get in, Ms. Parker."

She blinks as though startled. "Thank you, Mr. Sterling, but I'm afraid I spaced out a bit."

"You did?" This is very unusual.

Red stains her cheeks. It's really cute. "Yeah, I brought my car here."

Right, because Miguel didn't drive her. But she followed me into the garage because our routine is sharing a ride to the office. So. Disrupted morning routines can fluster even the unflappable Ms. Parker, huh?

And this explains why she didn't care what car I'm taking, because she thought she wasn't going to be in it. Well, she's about to be surprised. "Get in anyway. I'll have that taken care of."

She considers for a second, then nods. "All right. Thank you."

I smile with satisfaction. Who can resist a ride in this stunning marvel of European manufacturing? No one, that's who. The Bugatti was an inspired pick.

She moves past me and slides in. I inhale the lingering scent of her citrus shampoo and lavender lotion, then walk around, climb in behind the wheel and start the car. The engine roars impressively. I steal another glance, but she's tapping on her tablet, her eyes glued to the screen. Meanwhile, all I can smell is her in the car. The pulse in her neck is fluttering—and maybe it's my imagination, but I swear I can feel it more viscerally than the vibration of the engine, as though her throat's pressed against mine.

I shift, wondering why my pants feel so tight. *Maybe I've been squatting too much.*

We hit the road. It's not as satisfying in the morning because of traffic. But still, the Bugatti's damn nice, although from Evie's lack of reaction, we could be in one of those Ubers that Court likes so much. *Just what the hell is on that tablet? The winning number to the next Powerball jackpot?* We're in a damn Bugatti, not the boring Bentley that Miguel brings to pick us up in the morning. She should look up. Maybe check me out discreetly.

"So how was your date last night?" I ask casually, although I'm certain it sucked, based on the fact that she looks so fresh. No signs of fatigue or tiredness, which wouldn't be the case if I had a date with her. We would positively *wreck* the bed. And the kitchen. And the bathroo—

"It was all right." She's still tapping away. "The food was nice, and it ended on an interesting note."

Interesting good or interesting bad? Hard to tell from her neutral tone. And with a woman, it could mean anything. "Planning a second date on your tablet there?"

She gives me a frown like I asked her if she's on her period. "No. I'm going over your agenda for the week and making some adjustments. I also told Elizabeth you'd be more than happy to be auctioned off to raise some money for her new project."

"Okay." *Good*. If she's not planning a second date, the dude was probably lame. And I do want to help Elizabeth out. She's a good friend and very big on helping people less fortunate than her, which means practically everyone on the planet. And this project to financially support families of children going through chemo is a big deal and something I believe in.

"Also there's an email from the Ethel Sterling Children's Memorial Hospital. They want to know if you can fund-raise for the preventative medicine department's latest initiative."

"Again? How did they spend the money we raised last time?" I ask.

There was a problem with some creative accounting at the hospital. My great-uncle Barron went apoplectic and told me to fix it. So I did. Five people were terminated and charged with embezzlement. And since then I've had everything audited bimonthly. The hospital bears Barron's late wife's name. No scandal there is too small to overlook, and nobody—absolutely *nobody*—steals from the children the hospital was built to serve and gets away with it. If Barron had had it his way, those five would've been drawn and quartered in a public square.

"Productively," Evie says after a moment. "Your auditors confirmed the numbers submitted by the committee."

"Okay. Then I guess we can give them some more."

On the horizon, I see the familiar six-story building—the Sterling Medical Center. It was also built and is funded by my family's foundation. We're big believers in accessible health care, and it's fucked up that in our country, one minor illness can toss a middle-class family into a pit of financial hell.

"You know that it doesn't help to do announced inspection visits if you're trying to find dirt, right?" Evie says as I park.

I nod.

"So why do you have one scheduled for next month?"

"Because I'm going to do an *un*announced one next week." I grin. "They'll never see it coming."

Evie laughs. The sound is lovely and makes me happy. She's so pretty when she laughs, and all I can think about is kissing her. Except that's totally, one hundred percent inappropriate, because she's never once given me the slightest hint that she's interested, and I can't afford to lose an assistant this good over a kiss that won't go anywhere.

If she were some other, shallower woman, my ego might be dented a little. But it isn't even that. I wonder if I need to be a better person for her to like me. She hasn't shown any indication she's impressed with my money or my connections or my influence. But the problem with being a better person is that I don't know how. I am what I am, and I'm afraid I met her too late to change.

"Should we get going, Mr. Sterling?" she asks.

"I suppose we should, Ms. Parker."

We walk into the clinic together. It isn't luxurious, but it isn't spartan, either. Pleasant is how I'd describe it—pale plastic seats, clean linoleum floor, pale green walls, classical music on low volume and countless posters promoting ways to stay healthy on a budget. Everything is designed to be easy to clean and disinfect and, most important, to soothe. Just because it serves people who can't pay doesn't mean it's going to look cheap and pathetic.

The director is already in the lobby. Robbie Choi, in his early forties, gone prematurely gray. I put him in charge after half a year or so because I didn't have the time to manage it myself anymore. I wish he'd go back to whatever's more urgent—I'm sure he has a lot on his agenda—because I don't need him to babysit me as I look around. But I know he won't. I've already received reports, and my auditors are in the middle of checking the finances. Everything appears proper as far as the paperwork goes. I just need to see things for myself.

"Nate, it's so good to have you here," he says. "Hello, Evie."

"Hi, Robbie."

Fuck me. *Robbie*? And with a *smile*?

But I can't fire Robbie. He's good at his job.

I give him a miniscule smile. "It's good to see you, too." We shake hands. "I already reviewed the reports you sent. Everything looks good."

He beams. "I'm happy to hear that. There's something—"

"Oh my God! You're finally *here*! I was *dying* waiting for you."

A woman I've never seen before rushes toward us, her arms spread wide. She's practically naked, her wild black mane flying around like some dark miasma as she comes on in a tottering, breast-quivering run on ridiculous stilettos. And is that a...*fur bikini that she's wearing*?

Clearly, she's in the wrong hospital. The Sterling Medical Center does not have a psychiatric ward.

I'm about to tell her so when she hugs me, her limbs wrapping me up like tentacles. "Nate! I missed you so much!"

2

NATE

AN INTERNAL ALARM GOES OFF AS GOOSEBUMPS BREAK OVER my skin. I couldn't tell by looking at that hideous, flour-white Frankenface. I mean, it's obvious she's had a few too many plastic surgeries. But up close, that whiny, high-pitched voice is unmistakable.

Georgette the Psycho.

An ex-girlfriend. We broke up a year ago. She's a social climber whose family isn't anywhere close to poor. They have hundreds of millions of dollars in their coffers. But she wants more.

The Sterling fortune more.

"Georgette, what are you doing here?" I ask, desperately trying to unpeel her arms. I can feel Evie's gaze on us, and damn it, I don't need this spectacle.

"I missed you *so much*." She looks up, fluttering her fake lashes. "Did you miss me?"

As much as dysentery. "Aren't you supposed to be in rehab? And what *is* that you wearing?"

"Do you like it? It's *mink*!" she squeals. "I ordered it special from Moscow, thinking of you."

What the hell? I inspire mink bikinis now?

"And rehab is all finished." She clutches me tighter. "Nate, darling, I want you to know I'm clean now. I got clean for you. To be *worthy* of you!"

Oh boy. Maybe she didn't get the memo last year when I dumped her after she pulled a crazy fake-pregnancy stunt. Absolutely nothing this woman does is going to make her worth my time or energy. I mean, she thinks I like mink bikinis.

"I even redid myself. What do you think? I remember how you said you like Angelina Jolie's mouth, so I got it for you!"

"You got—"

"And Natalie Portman's nose, and those boobs you were eyeing when we watched that cheerleader movie that time." She pushes the enhanced mammaries against me, making them impossible to ignore. "I had my floating ribs removed, like Cher..."

I stare in horror. She piecemealed a face and body together out of random features I said were pretty? Is she insane?

Stupid question. She *is* insane. Certifiably. Everyone knows this. The only reason she isn't locked up somewhere is her parents. They're overly loving parents, and they've hired a great legal team to protect her.

"Georgette, I'm working. And this is a hospital. You need to let me get on with my job," I say, forcibly separating our bodies.

"*Work*ing?" she whines, stumbling back a step. "But why? You have *all* the money. Just tell Justin to take care of whatever it is."

I pinch the bridge of my nose. If she were a man, I'd punch her in the face, just to shut her up. Justin takes care of the profit-generating side of the family business, and I deal with the charitable portion. That isn't changing, not for her, not for anybody.

Evie steps closer to us. "You need to go," she says to Georgette.

I wince. Evie doesn't have to get involved in this madness, and Georgette is most definitely an equal-opportunity bitch.

"Who the hell asked you?" Georgette glares at Evie. "The hired help doesn't get to talk unless addressed first."

Evie's jaw drops. Red colors her cheeks, but this time it's an angry red.

"Georgette, shut up. If you aren't sick—and I mean *physically* sick—then you need to leave," I say furiously. I'm seriously embarrassed for her. And at myself for having dated her. I was young and stupid, thinking with my dick more than anything else.

"I'm not going anywhere without you!"

Her whiny voice makes me clench my teeth until it feels like I'm going to chip a tooth. Thankfully, security has finally arrived.

"Take this trash out," I say coldly, gesturing at Georgette.

The guards approach her.

"No, stay away! He and I are meant to be!"

She launches herself at me again, but I'm quicker this time. I sidestep, and Georgette flails, off balance. She screams when the guards grab her arms, but I don't hire donut munchers for security. They start to drag her away.

"Nate, don't let them do this to us! I'm going to have you, no matter what! We're destined! Fated, like Troilus and Cressida!"

Slapping my hand over my eyes, I grind my teeth. Georgette and her degree in classical literature. Are our attorneys good enough to get me off on a technicality if I kill her? It wouldn't even be murder, just self-preservation. She's a soul- and money-sucking monster who'll drain me of life if I let her.

Robbie clears his throat. "I apologize. That was... um...unfortunate."

"Yes. Very," I say tightly. My schedule isn't exactly a national secret, but how the hell did she find out that I was going to be here? When I find out who told her, they're fired, effective immediately.

I inhale deeply and force myself to relax. "But it's done now. Let's continue." I'm not letting Georgette derail my agenda.

The rest of the visit is uneventful. Everything is as described in the reports. Robbie runs a tight ship. Doctors and nurses—at least the ones we see—treat patients with compassion and patience. We screen them carefully to ensure that they're dedicated to helping people, rather than just fattening their bank accounts, although the center pays well.

I thank Robbie for his time, commend his staff on a job well done and leave with Evie. She didn't say a word after Georgette got dragged away. But she must have a lot on her mind. She's never been this quiet during an inspection before.

When we're back on the road toward the office, I say, "You can tell me what you think, Ms. Parker."

She looks at her tablet, as though needing to consult her notes. "I'm thinking the Sterling Medical Center is in good hands."

"Really? That's all?"

She shrugs. "You don't think Robbie's good?"

Oh, for fuck's sake. She knows that's not what I mean. "Of course he's good. I picked him. But I'm wondering..." I don't know how the hell I'm going to ask this without sounding ridiculous. I just want to know if she was disappointed or disgusted that Georgette made such a spectacle. But it's ludicrous for me to expect Evie would have a reaction. To have one, she would need to feel something for me. But she thinks I'm just a guy who makes her do things for money. Okay, that sounds a little dirty, but that's basically what a job is.

"You're wondering...?" Evie prompts when I don't continue.

"Never mind. Nothing."

"Okay." She returns her attention back to the infernal tablet.

I fantasize about chucking it out the window. It's company issued. She wouldn't miss it. And it would give me at least several hundred dollars' worth of satisfaction to Frisbee the damn thing into traffic.

But I don't do that. I don't want her to think *I'm* crazy.

I park the Bugatti in the underground garage of the tall, contemporary Sterling & Wilson building. It's our new second headquarters here in L.A. The original HQ is in Chicago, but Justin moved to L.A. to be with his wife, Vanessa, when he got married. And the hub of Sterling & Wilson is basically wherever he is. I followed, partly to hang out more with Court, who was studying at UCLA at that time, and also because L.A. has better weather.

Evie and I walk into the executive elevator. She hits the button for the thirtieth floor, where my office is.

"Mr. Sterling?"

"Yes, Ms. Parker," I say, my voice tighter and more proper.

Like I have a stick up my ass for real. Ugh. I shouldn't be like this with Evie when the morning's embarrassment has nothing to do with her. I should apologize and—

"An email just landed in your inbox. I think it's from that woman in the medical center..."

I'm going to run Georgette over with my Bugatti. Actually, no. My baby cost nineteen million bucks, and Georgette isn't worth it. *Obstacles, obstacles...*

I know. I'll call Uber and have *them* run her over. They can do it with a Prius, in an environmentally friendly way. "Just delete it. She's a sociopath."

Evie tilts her head and blinks up at me. "You don't want to know what she said?"

"It isn't like I have to read it to know what she wants."

"She isn't asking for money. In fact, she says she's going to pay money to get you."

"What?" That's so unlike Georgette that it makes me wonder if she got part of her brain surgically replaced as well.

"She plans to attend Elizabeth's auction and bid on you." Evie purses her mouth, a frown pulling her eyebrows together. "She says she intends to win."

Oh, holy fuck no.

The elevator door opens, and I walk out on autopilot, my mind whirling. Why did Elizabeth invite her? Actually, she probably didn't. She invited Georgette's parents, maybe, and Psycho Girl got one of the tickets.

Georgette's parents would never give her money to bid on me. They know how I feel about her, and they're embarrassed and worried about pushing me too far. I might have a rep for being nice, but I'm still a Sterling. Barron has made it clear more than once that he worries about gold diggers trying to snatch me up, since I'm the only unmarried man left in the family.

But Georgette has a decently large trust fund. She can win me without their help.

Others are undoubtedly going to bid on me, but not with the level of mindless zeal that she has. I need a plan if I want to avoid her clutches.

And that means...

My gaze slides over to Evie, who's following half a step back. My trusty assistant. The one who makes me a kale shake every morning. Surely she wants me to live a long, happy life, and that won't happen if Georgette wins me at the auction.

"My office, please, Ms. Parker."

She takes one look at my face. "Yes, Mr. Sterling." She follows me in and shuts the door.

I pace for a moment, then stop and turn to face her, my mind made up. "I need you to go to the auction and bid on me."

Evie blinks a few times. "I'm sorry, what?"

"If you don't, Georgette will win me. So you have to do it."

She bites her lip. "I'm sure you can ask somebody else to do it for you. Vicki, perhaps?"

"Vicki...? Doesn't ring a bell."

"Last Wednesday? That sudden lunch meeting?"

"Oh. No. Definitely not." Vicki is fifty-six years old, goes to bed by nine and loves children. I met her to screen her for Justin for a nanny position because he had an emergency meeting in Chicago that day.

"How about Melinda? Or London?"

"No, no, no. None of them will work. They're all going to want something."

The look she gives me is dubious. "Like what? The date they won?"

"Like a ring on their finger. Like to become Mrs. Nate Sterling." I shudder at the very idea of having a missus.

"It could go that way. There are all sorts of possibilities when you're dating someone." Her tone is patient, like a kindergarten teacher explaining the way life works to a toddler.

"Hah. In bed, maybe," I say before I can stop myself. "Commitment strips you of choices. And why settle for *one* when I don't have to?" I put my hands on her shoulders. "Evie, listen. You're the only person who can save me from Georgette. You saw how she was back at the medical center. She won't just want to marry me; she'll want suck the marrow out of my bones."

Evie makes a face. "She can't be *that* bad..."

"Oh my God, worse," I say, desperate to convince her. "She punctured our condoms. When that failed, she faked a pregnancy to trap me into marriage, then 'miscarried' when she realized she couldn't hide the fact that she wasn't pregnant anymore." The shit she put my family through was criminal. The only reason Barron hasn't buried her and her family is because her parents are nice people and apologized profusely. And she was crazy enough to accuse me of dumping her over her "pronounced nasolabial folds."

"Nasolabial...?" Evie says faintly. She takes a moment, then clears her throat. "Well, even if I wanted to, I can't help you. You understand that I don't make enough to go to an auction like Elizabeth's and bid, right?"

I smile, sensing a victory. It's cute how she worries about such an inconsequential aspect. I pull back, dropping my hands from her shoulders. "Bid to your heart's content. Better yet, bid as high as possible so I'm not embarrassed. I'll take care of the cost."

She presses her lips together. *Oh, right!* She said she doesn't make enough. That must've been one of those famous female hints. "And you'll get a pay raise and a bonus for helping me out."

That earns me a frown. Does she want a company car? If so, I can arrange—

"I really don't have anything to wear to an event that fancy," she says.

Ah, she wants an expense account. "Not a problem. Buy yourself a new dress and send me the bill."

Her frown only deepens, which is definitely not the reaction I was expecting. I think for a moment, then snap my fingers. Of course a woman can't simply *buy a new dress*. "And get matching shoes, purses, clutches, jewelry and whatever else you need to complete the look." Magnanimity is a cardinal virtue.

"That's very generous..."

Hah. I have her now.

"...but I'm afraid I can't do it. I'm sorry, Mr. Sterling."

"Why not?" What more does this woman *want*? A new watch, maybe...?

"It really does go beyond my job description. And what would people think if I were to bid on you?"

"People? *People?* Why would either of us care about

that?" The only thing she should care is what *I* think! She works for me, not for "people."

She continues, "You're better off finding a friend to do it. There must be at least one female friend who can help you out."

"But I don't have—" I say, then inwardly wince at how bad that sounds. "I mean, all my female friends are married or engaged. I can't ask them."

"Hmm. Well, there's always Craigslist. If you want, I'll put up an ad there for you."

What the hell? I said I wanted to be saved, not have another sociopath after me! The Internet is full of psychos!

Then she leaves the office, closing the door quietly. Somehow the fact that she'd rather foist me off on a random stranger hurts more than the fact that she can't do it herself.

3

Evie

By the time I arrive home, it's almost eight. As promised, Nate had my car waiting for me in the office garage. Thoughtful of him to remember, because I totally forgot about it. But then, he's a very considerate boss.

I tried to ignore his mood all day long, but of course he's upset that I refused to bid on him at the auction. He never said anything, but he seemed a bit...broody, I guess, is the word to describe his mood for the rest of the day. He even shot me a few resentful glances while I worked on my tablet.

But I'm not going to bid on him at the auction. No way.

I walk into the apartment, and there's Kim in a tank top and boxers, stretched out on the couch. She's a stunning brunette with the most beautiful caramel-brown eyes I've ever seen. There's a small, jagged scar on her jaw line that she can't hide, even with concealer. But instead of diminishing her allure, I think it adds to her mystery. How did the super-efficient assistant to a man as wealthy and important as Salazar Pryce get a scar like that?

I've never asked, not wanting to be nosy. I'm lucky to have her as a roommate, because this place isn't far from Nate's house, has two lovely suites and is way out of my price range. Not to mention, she's been mentoring me. There's no way I could've survived in my job for nine months without her help and advice. As a matter of fact, she's the one who referred me into my current position.

"Hey, you're finally home," she says. "I left you some Thai chicken and rice."

"Yes, please." I kick off my heels and dump my purse on the dining table before rushing to the kitchen. "And thanks. You're a goddess."

She waves airily. "I bestow my Thai chicken favor upon you."

I microwave the food and bring it over to the couch with a glass of Merlot. She sits up, and I plunk down next to her and dig into my dinner.

"Didn't Nate feed you lunch?"

"He offered, but I opted for having my PB&J at the desk." It was obvious he was going to try to wine and dine me into changing my mind about the auction.

"Why? Is he becoming too irresistible for you? Was he extra hot today?"

I almost choke on the rice. "Shit. Not like that."

Kim raises an eyebrow.

"I mean, yeah, of course he's hot." *Oh my God, sooo hot.* "And he did greet me in nothing but a towel again today."

My hormones start to stir at the memory. I can't decide if he walks around half-nude on purpose. I don't think he does, though, because A, he does whatever he wants all the time anyway, and B, I haven't done anything to discourage or encourage him. The first time it happened, I used every ounce of willpower and kept my eyes on his face, even though my traitorous peripheral vision told me his shoulders are super-wide and his chest is lean and totally made to lay my head on, among other things.

I check him out when I'm pretty certain he isn't looking. His back looks freakin' amazing. Defined. Powerful. Muscles rippling smoothly as he reaches for whatever shirt I've picked out for him that morning.

"I think he's been working out more recently. He's gotten even more muscular," I say. If he were lying down, and you slowly poured a glass of Merlot—like, say, the one I'm holding—over his stomach, you'd end up with six little islands surrounded by dark red channels like rivers in a miniature landsca—

"The man's in his prime. Of course he's getting more muscular," Kim says. "I'm telling you, he is totally into you. That's why he keeps showing off his body. It's like the mating dances those birds do. He's displaying himself so you'll say yes."

"Oh, for God's sake, stop." I wave my hand, embarrassed and confused over her insistence that there's more to his parading around topless than him just...parading around topless. "I don't know why we have to have this same conversation every week. No matter how hot he is, he's off-limits. Good for admiring from afar, but that's it."

"You never kno-ow," she says with a little singsong lilt. "He's young, rich, handsome and *definitely* single. Perfect for you, and I know you think about him in the most carnal way."

Crap. Am I that obvious? "I do *not*. That's just your little fantasy."

"I bet he fantasizes about you calling him Mr. Sterling in that prim voice while he rams into you." She does a breathy Marilyn Monroe voice. "Oh, Mr. Ster*ling*. You're so *big*."

Oh lord. My face turns hot. I bet he'd feel solid and amazing on top of me. And he's *built*. Those broad shoulders, the pecs...

Bad hormones, bad!

I gulp down the wine. I started calling him Mr. Sterling because I wanted the formality for a little distance between us. He never corrected me, and called me Ms. Parker in return. But when I told Kim a couple of months later, she said he was probably having boss/assistant power-dynamic wet dreams. *Ugh.* I then immediately thought about switching to "Nate," but it seemed stupid after being all "Mr. Sterling" for so long.

But regardless of Kim's imaginative interpretation, Nate's never hinted he was interested in me. His "display," as Kim labels it, is just him being comfortable in his home.

Besides, even if he really were interested, I'm not doing anything with Nate Sterling except my job. Date a boss? Oh, no. Been there, done that, and basically had to flee my hometown because of it. I've learned my lesson.

"Look, when I left Dillington, I made a plan." I tick the points off on my fingers. "One: go to L.A. Two: get a job. Three: find the love of my life. Four: live happily ever after.

"I've done the first two, so I'm halfway home. Just need to finish up the last couple." And I have to remind myself that no matter how much my hormones wish it were so, Nate is *not* the love of my life who I can have a "happily ever after" with. The man was born to a staggering fortune and dates models, socialites and other celebrities, most of whom look like they should be models, too. I'm just Evie Parker. Nothing special.

"All that 'love of one's life' stuff is overrated," Kim says.

"Your friend Hilary has it."

"Yeah, but she wasn't looking for it. He came knocking." She looks at the ceiling. "It's very Zen. The more you pursue it, the further away it gets. Like a rainbow."

"Maybe mine will come knocking, too."

"Why? Did your date go well last night?"

I make a face. "If you call shit-tastic fantastic. He wanted to go to a steakhouse, but I told him no because I didn't feel like lingering over multiple courses, which are sort of inevitable at places like that. So we had Mexican instead. Casual, right? If we'd hit it off, we could've gone for drinks or something afterward, you know?"

She nods, all wise in *how things ought to progress,* even though she's single, just like me.

"He's a klepto. Napkins, salt and pepper shakers, knives. Even some chips."

"No way."

"Oh yeah. They *aaall* went into his knapsack."

"Oh my God. Really? Did the waiter see him?"

"I don't think so, but I'm not sure. I was too embarrassed to look around much. I just wanted to die."

"If anybody should die, it's him, not you."

That's a great point. I deserve to live. I don't steal restaurant utensils. "Anyway, that wasn't even the worst part."

Kim leans forward.

"He forgot his freakin' wallet at home! I mean, he said it sheepishly, but it's not like I'm stupid." My blood boils, thinking about the credit card bill I'm going to get for the month. I didn't budget for that particular dinner. "I should've known."

"So if you'd gone to a steakhouse..."

"Yup. The asshole had *five* drinks." And wanted more, but I stopped him, saying he needed to drive.

"Wow."

"He told me to send him an invoice and he'll cut me a check."

"Maybe you should."

"Why? So I can get charged a twenty-five-dollar bad-check fee?"

Kim shakes her head. "I'm so sorry. I can't decide if I should laugh or cry for you."

"Just laugh. That's what I did when I came home."

"Girl, you have the worst luck."

"I know, but what can you do?" I shrug, trying to brush it off. The fact that in the ten months I've been in L.A. I've met more losers than I can count is simply beyond my control. I could probably write an encyclopedia on bad dates, just based on my own experiences. But I have to go through this pain to find the love of my life, so I'm dealing with it. Mostly.

"Bet you *Mr. Sterling* wouldn't have forgotten his wallet," Kim says slyly.

"Would you stop? He's my *boss*. Besides, he's got too many crazies around him." I tell Kim about the furry-bikini lunatic at the clinic. And the determined desire on her part to win him at the auction.

"She must really want him, but then, a lot of women do," Kim says. "I doubt he'll let her, though. He's supposed to be the nicer younger brother, but he never struck me as soft, despite the friendly vibe he gives off."

"He won't. He asked me to bid on him at the auction."

"Whoo! Tell me you said yes."

I give her a look reserved for the mentally deficient. "Of course not. I turned him down."

Kim gapes. "Why?"

I can't believe I have to point out such an obvious reason. "Because I don't have the *money* to bid on him."

She waves it away. "Oh, please. He'll front it. Probably as a work expense."

It's amazing how she's giving me the same solution he did. "And I don't have anything fancy enough to wear to the event."

"So tell him! He'll let you expense it."

Argh. Did she and Nate share notes? "He has other friends who can help him."

"But did he ask *them*...or *you*?"

The question makes me stop. He didn't ask anybody else. He asked me.

Apparently my expression is answer enough. Kim straightens. "Okay, here's the deal. Some people might look at us and see glorified coffee fetchers or whatever. But we're not. We're managers. We manage our bosses. Some of these guys can't tie their own shoes without us around. Like Nate. He can't even decide what to wear without you to choose everything for him. And you have to take care of his breakfast, too. What does that tell you?"

That he needs me to bail him out of this auction thing. But what if people jump to the wrong conclusion? What if I lose my job over it or have to start over somewhere new again? "But does it have to be *me*? Can't it be somebody else?"

"Our bosses trust us. They need us to make them feel safe from people who want a piece of them. We're the ultimate gatekeepers. You bidding on him at the auction *is you doing your job*. Nobody gets to him so long as you're there, not even his family."

"But it's so complicated," I say, then shovel the rest of the chicken and rice into my mouth. "I don't want to go on a date with him after the auction."

Oh yes, you do! He's probably filled out the date plan for the auction already—about how he's going to whisk the winner away to a gorgeous private beach on Bora Bora. Hell, his family probably owns half the island.

"You don't have to," Kim says. "It isn't like anybody's going to be watching."

Hmm. That's true.

"And you can probably swing a pay raise out of it. I would."

I keep my mouth shut and don't tell her he already offered.

And out of all the things, that tempted me the most. I'd love a pay raise, even though it'd be a little early, employment-wise. I need to rebuild my savings, just in case. Sometimes financial security and independence are the only things that can help you start over. If I hadn't had any savings, I'd be still stuck in Dillington, enduring the whispers of people who believe the worst of me because of my ex. He thought I was good enough to fool around with, but not enough to keep. I was basically a box of Kleenex to him, and I deluded myself into believing it was more. Then, to add insult to injury, he told everyone I was the sleep-my-way-to-the-top type. As if! I worked my ass off at that job. But again, nobody believed me.

Obviously having taken my silence for incredulity, Kim adds, "You can totally get one, depending on how badly Nate wants you to do this. Negotiate, girl! It's extra time and effort, beyond the standard scope of the work. He should value you for that, and you should make sure he rewards you properly."

4

Nate

Saturdays are terrible. So are Sundays.

The cuckoo clock hoots seven times, but Evie isn't here. Just me in this damn big mansion and the perfect sapphire-bright Pacific over which the sun shines. I swear the orb is saying, "You're going to be alone. Alone. Alone. Alone," as it travels through the sky.

Bastard.

I wish I could be the kind of douchebag boss who made his assistant come in on weekends. But I just can't. She works hard, and she needs to recharge. I've seen people burn out, like my cousin Kerri, and I don't want to have Evie burn out and hobble around with a hand over her stomach. Or worse, quit.

After a shower, I go to the walk-in closet and look at the two outfits. Evie picked them out yesterday evening, saying I could wear one on Saturday and the other on Sunday. It's seriously cute that she worries I might actually wear the puke-colored flower-print shirt and pink shark pants that are hanging in my closet. They were a gag gift from Court, and I have no desire to put them on, although I think Evie believes she's the only barrier between me and them.

Regardless, she has good, utilitarian taste. A simple T-shirt and shorts because she knows I'm visiting my brother today for lunch. There's no point in wearing anything nice, because my young nephew has no respect for high fashion or the price of silk.

I go to the kitchen and open the fridge. As usual, Evie has left two kale shakes in the special vacuum containers. I told her I didn't know how to operate a blender, so she makes them every Friday evening before going home. Says she wants to ensure I get proper nutrition over the weekend.

She'd murder me if she saw me dumping them down the drain. Like now. Five days a week is plenty. I need a break, too.

I reach for my secret stash, buried deep in the wine cooler, behind the Beaujolais. Ah. Smoked ham, smoked salmon, cream cheese and bacon.

Yes!

I fry up the bacon, reveling in the life-affirming smell of grease and salted, smoked pork belly, smear an extra-generous serving of cream cheese on my toasted egg bagel, then pile ham and salmon high on the pure, unadulterated carb platter. Then, with a roar of triumph, I bite into my creation, a victorious T-Rex savoring his meal.

So. Good.

I wash it down with coffee. And not just any coffee, but coffee spiked with a good shot of vodka. As satisfying as the breakfast is, it still doesn't make up for Evie's absence. But it helps keep my spirits from flagging. Doing my best to undo the insufferable violation the kale shakes have inflicted on my system over the workweek is a good starting point.

I still haven't been able to change her mind about the auction. Yesterday I offered her the use of a company car—any model— because there's always a point where people break. I thought she was wavering, but she shook her head ruefully at the end. And I have no freakin' idea why.

Should I have offered to replace everything in her closet with something newer and better? Maybe made the pay raise more concrete and enticing? Ten percent would've been a good place to start. Or maybe I should've told her she could make use of the family's various vacation properties. We have them on the

Riviera, in Bora Bora, the Maldives...you name it. If she doesn't like any of them, I could book her a suite at whatever resort strikes her fancy.

But maybe I should just hire a mercenary to solve my problem, provided I can figure out where to look. I'm not going to have Georgette murdered. That's not how I roll. I simply want her *removed*...to some as-yet-undiscovered deserted island, sans laptop, tablet or cell phone. She can keep her mink bikini, though. I'm not a complete bastard.

I check my personal emails, which is something I do only on weekends. Everyone who has my email address knows I only answer on Saturdays and Sundays, and they text or call if something's urgent. I have a couple of unread emails—one from Mom and the other from Barron.

I decide to read Barron's first, because Mom's will be chatty and cheery and I can end on a high note. You never know with my great-uncle.

Nate,

I'm sending you a bronze statue Catherine purchased. It's quite unique and artistic, but I think it bothers Stella, mainly because the grandchildren are so young. But you're an adult, so you'll appreciate it. It should arrive Saturday morning. Make sure it's in pristine condition, then keep it that way.

B

Unique and artistic, huh? I wish I knew if those were Catherine's words or his. Or maybe Stella's. As Barron's art curator, Catherine's been busy padding his collection. She's good at her job, so whatever statue she bought must really be something for Barron's girlfriend to object.

On cue, the intercom buzzes. How convenient. It's like Barron knew exactly when the crew he hired would be arriving.

The crate isn't too big, considering. It can stay in the living room. Maybe by the indoor waterfall.

The crew brings the wooden box in, moving with exaggerated

care as though there's a live nuke inside it rather than a hunk of metal. They're moving so gingerly that it takes forever until they're done. But I guess they have to do that because the statue undoubtedly cost a fortune. Barron does not buy cheap art.

I sign for it, eyeing the thing, and the crew show themselves out.

Unique and artistic? Looks to me like it's just a rough metal frame around two people fucking. It isn't even that imaginative. Just plain ol' missionary. Not that there's anything wrong with missionary, but I thought it'd have be more inventive to be considered "art." Still, I can see why Stella would object if there are young kids visiting.

I fold my arms and slowly circle around to take the statue in from different directions, wondering why in the world Catherine bought something this crass and mundane. She has far better taste—

Then I see it. Depending on which angle you view it from, the position of the couple changes. The missionary position morphs into doggy style...and then some sixty-nine action. Yup, definitely unique and artistic. No wonder Catherine bought it. And of course Stella objects to keeping it in the house. This is X-rated art, and her grandkids are way too young.

I email Barron.

The statue made it safely. I can see why you're giving it to me.

Then I can't resist adding a little teasing: *But what am I going to do when I want to have a baby of my own?*

Barron's response arrives within a minute.

A baby? You don't even have a girlfriend.

I have to chuckle. The message is a remarkable show of restraint on his part. He didn't go into a long spiel about how he's getting old, how my mom's getting old, and how it's my duty to marry a nice, sweet girl and have some babies because old people like him and my mom need something to look forward to, like a giggly bundle of joy to bounce on their aching, arthritic knees. Or maybe his assistant is unavailable to type all that stuff up. Barron doesn't like to type. Says it's tedious.

I check my mom's email. It's nothing urgent, just some catching up. She's planning to spend some time in Los Angeles because Ohio is too cold this year, and the temperature is bothering her joints. To be honest, that seems like an excuse. Mom might be old, but she's healthy as a horse, and she loves her home with its huge garden and five-acre lot. My guess is she just wants to spend time with her grandson. And possibly hint at a second grandchild—from me. She's going to have to wait a long time for that, because she wants me to do things in the "proper" order: find the right girl, fall in love, get married and *then* have the baby. I'd like to become a father at some point, but I'm in no rush to find "the right girl."

Still, I'd love to see Mom, because she's been widowed for so long and I don't visit that often. But she lives in Harrisburg, Ohio, which is a pain in the ass to get to, as it's two hours from the only airport in the area. I email her back, letting her know I miss her a lot and can't wait to see her.

That done, I drive over to Justin's place. It's early, but lunch at my brother's place on a weekend isn't just a meal. It's pre-lunch drinks, then the actual lunch, then lingering over coffee and tea and cake. Vanessa won't have it any other way, and Justin lets her do whatever she wants.

Their home is a huge mansion with every real-estate-value-enhancing feature a developer could think of because my brother and his wife decided they need a good space for their family of three. Actually, I think Justin wanted to get it more than her. She wasn't exactly the most enthusiastic of brides, and he was paranoid she was going to disappear or change her mind about their marriage. And even with our vast wealth and connections, Justin would've been helpless to stop her because of who and what she is. Not only is she a Stanford-educated lawyer, but a Pryce as well. The Pryces are dysfunctional enough to fuel a decade's worth of daytime talk shows, but they always protect their own against outsiders.

When I reach the mansion after an hour of fighting L.A. traffic, I see a pearlescent pink-and-cream Cullinan parked in the driveway, past the gates. It can't be Vanessa's car. She's more the fiery red type, and Justin knows better than to get her something in pink, of all shades.

I park my Lamborghini and go inside. Vicki, the nanny I helped Justin and Vanessa hire, beams at me, coming out of the kitchen. "Hi, Nate. Everyone's here already."

"Everyone?" I echo stupidly.

She nods, like I should know.

"Nate!" A sweet, high-pitched voice is heard first, before I see the little blue-eyed, golden-haired angel dashing toward me.

"Hey, princess!" I pick her up with a huge grin, hoisting her up high and settling her against my chest like the precious bundle she is. Isabella is Dane and Sophia's child, which means...

That frothy pink Cullinan is *Dane's*.

Whoa.

I shake my head, trying to shove my world back on its axis. Vanessa's oldest brother, Dane Pryce, is cold enough to make Antarctica seem tropical. The image of him in the driver's seat of that girly car—even though it's a Cullinan—is so incongruous that it's sick.

Maybe he was high when he bought it. Or maybe not, because the man is never high, never drunk and certainly never out of control.

Carrying Isabella, I walk to the gigantic open space that is the living/entertaining/sitting room or whatever. It has the requisite TV hooked up to the best surround-sound system money can buy, and lots of couches and armchairs. There are enough throw pillows to stock a showroom.

"Hey, bro!" Justin says with a grin. Although we aren't twins, we're very much alike in our looks—the same dark hair and dark eyes. But everyone says I'm the softer one—probably because I've never had the expectation of carrying on Sterling & Wilson's vast business interests. Justin was always the chosen one, the heir apparent, the one groomed since birth for his position. And I wouldn't want it any other way.

His son, Ryan, is cuddled against him. He waves at me, his hand shiny with I don't even want to know what. It doesn't seem to bother Justin, though. He's gazing at the boy like the child just cured cancer.

"Hi, Nate! How are you?" Vanessa comes out of the kitchen with a huge pitcher of margarita and four glasses, and kisses me on the cheek. She's a stunner, her bottle-red hair pulled into a simple ponytail that swings with each step, every facial feature fine and delicate.

Motherhood hasn't seemed to faze her one bit. Energy crackles around her, but then, just because she isn't with her old firm doesn't mean the woman's sharklike instincts are dead. She is still a scarily good lawyer.

"Did you see Dane's new car?" I say, gesturing outside.

Vanessa laughs as she pours generous amounts of margarita into the glasses. I pass one to Justin and take another for myself, before sitting down in a plush armchair with Isabella eyeing my glass greedily. "That's not his car," Vanessa says. "It's Sophia's."

Something in her tone lets me know he's not here, which is a bit of a shock. The man refuses to be away from his wife if he can help it. "She's here? Just her and Isabella?"

Vanessa nods, then takes her drink and settles down next to Justin.

Whoa. Is he in the doghouse? That's just not how I imagined Dane would be. He's so pussy-whipped—er, in love with his wife that if she said cars run on water, he'd agree with her and eviscerate anybody who tried to say otherwise.

"He's out of town, and I thought maybe she should visit us."

"Why is he out of town?" Ever since he met his wife, he quit working overtime and weekends. Whoever pulled him away is going to end up dead.

"Oh, some emergency," Sophia says, coming from upstairs and taking Isabella from me, then plucking a glass from the table and settling in an empty love seat. "You know how it is."

She's a pretty blonde, petite and slim. She was a U.S. national figure-skating champion and was on her way to the Olympics when an unfortunate accident ended her competitive career. She's one of the warmest and most genuine people I know, and I still don't understand how she fell for someone as undemonstrative as Dane. I'm certain the pink diamond the size of a quail's egg on her finger isn't it.

"It was nice of Vanessa to invite us over," she says. "Dane was rather...umm...worried."

"Why?"

"He doesn't like to be out of town, leaving his wife and daughter behind, obviously," Vanessa says.

"Oh, for God's sake. It's only for a day or two, right?" You'd think he was going to be stuck in a Siberian salt mine for the next couple of decades.

Sophia smiles. "He'll be back tonight."

"You'll know how it feels when you meet the right woman," Justin says.

"Oh no," I say. "I'm never letting myself get pussy-whipped. It's embarrassing."

"Uh, language?" Vanessa says.

"Sorry," I say. Ryan does like to parrot what he hears.

Vanessa shakes her head. "You're being ridiculous, trying so hard to be un-whipped. Is that why you wrote in your bachelor auction date proposal that you plan to take the winner to Vegas and"—her gaze flicks over to the kids—"do bad things?"

I frown at her, surprise and annoyance tugging at me. "How do you know that? You aren't going, are you?" Justin would never let her bid on some other man.

"Not participating, if that's what you mean. But I am helping Elizabeth organize things. When I read it, I thought you had to be joking. But she told me you were actually serious when you sent that in."

"Yes. I take dating very seriously," I say, although my mood is deflating rapidly as I remember why I had to write such crap for my date plan.

"What's wrong?" Justin asks. There's no hiding it from my brother.

"It's Georgette."

He hisses, while Sophia and Vanessa wince.

"Didn't she die of an overdose? I thought I read that somewhere," Sophia says.

"No, she's alive. And out of rehab, and apparently clean, if you can believe that. She came to find me at the Sterling Medical Center...wearing a mink bikini."

Justin starts to laugh. "A *what?*" Vanessa says, sitting up straighter. "Okay, tell us everything. Start from the beginning."

So I do, including the part about Evie's refusal to rescue me from Georgette's gold-digging clutches. Laying it out like this makes my anxiety spike. This fucked-up shit with Georgette is too damn *real*.

Justin's the first to open his mouth. "Restraining order, bro. You need a restraining order."

"Doesn't do much if you're dealing with a determined stalker," Vanessa says.

"Do you think it would be self-defense if I accidentally threw her out of a window?" I ask.

Vanessa considers. "Nooo... I don't think that would fly."

"But *she* would," Justin says.

"Maybe Elizabeth can just ban her or something?" Sophia suggests.

Vanessa shakes her head. "Georgette's parents are huge supporters of the foundation. She'd never do anything to humiliate them like that."

That's the problem with being nice: caring about what others think. "I can't let her win me. I'd rather eat dog sh—uh, poop."

"Don't eat dog poop, Uncle Nate!" Ryan says. "Mommy said it's unsaintly."

"Unsanitary, Ryan," Vanessa says, over-enunciating the middle syllables.

"If your assistant won't bid on you, get somebody else to do it," Justin says.

"It sounds easy, but it's not," I say. "You know how hard it is to find a woman who won't be expecting more from me than just some money to do the job? Oh no, they're going to want to be my girlfriend. To get *involved*. Maybe more."

My brother makes a face. He never had to deal with this problem, but knows how it is.

I continue, "I asked Court to get his girlfriend to bid on me, but I don't know. He didn't seem too keen. For all I know, he never even told her about it."

He's pretty gooey-eyed over his girl, whose name I can never seem to remember. Although they aren't married or anything, I have a feeling he doesn't want her bidding on me. It was always "bros before hos" for Court...until now. Traitor.

I eye Isabella. "You think Isabella's too young to be bidding at a bachelor auction?"

Sophia laughs. "Not at all. But you'll have to convince Dane first."

I give her a dry look. "Yeah, that'll totally work. But if *you* ask..."

"Not doing that," she says. "It would only upset him."

"But what about *me*? Doesn't anybody worry about *my* fate?"

"Make Evie an offer she can't refuse," Vanessa says.

I thought I already did that. "Like what?"

She shrugs. "How am I supposed to know? She's your assistant. You figure it out."

5

EVIE

DESPITE KIM'S ADVICE, I DON'T BROACH THE SUBJECT TO Nate immediately. To be honest, I don't know how. The new statue that appeared over the weekend seems hugely accusatory. *This is what's going to happen to Nate because of you!*

And it's pretty horrific. It looks like the woman's trying to literally suck the soul out of the guy's body through his cock. I mean, maybe I'm overthinking this after Nate said the thing about Georgette and his bone marrow, but I'm pretty sure the statue is depicting Nate getting violated in more ways than one.

Then there's Nate himself. He seems distracted, irritated and anxious. I've never seen him like this. He must really be worried.

And he couldn't find anybody to help him.

Despite what I told him, I didn't put an ad up on Craigslist. What Kim said is right. Nate trusts me to take care of everything, and I can't just dump him onto some unvetted stranger off the Internet. For all I know, an ad might attract an even crazier person than Georgette, and no one needs that.

Besides, Georgette's becoming increasingly more disgusting. Or unhinged. Maybe she doesn't know Nate doesn't check his own emails, except for one very private account only a few of his family and friends know about. (Not even I know the address for that one.) She's been sending nude photos of herself in various twisty poses designed to show of what she can do in bed. Forty-six of them so far.

Every single one of them has the subject line: *Feel free to do what comes naturally with this.* ;) ;) ;)

Ugh.

She doesn't seem worried about the possibility that Nate might post them all over the Internet. Or that *I* might sell them to a porn site in exchange for hazard pay.

Actually, no amount of hazard pay would be enough to compensate for all the eye bleach I'm going to need. Since I'm a good assistant, I don't bother Nate with the crass porno shots. But they cement my decision to rescue him from this obviously disturbed individual from his past, popping back into his life like a genital wart that refuses to die.

Except I'm not exactly sure how to broach the subject after turning him down so firmly earlier. But like Kim said, it's my job to guard him from the likes of Georgette.

On the sixteenth day since he asked me to bid on him at the auction, I add broccoli to his kale and protein shake for an extra dose of antioxidants and vitamins, all the goodness he needs to fend off the crazy folks and help make the world a better place with the Sterling fortune. I know he enjoys nutritious food to keep himself healthy, and I give him mad respect for that, even though I could never drink what he does because it tastes like sewer every time I sample a bit. But *no pain no gain* is a real guidepost for Nate.

He comes down to the kitchen from his bedroom. His dark brown hair is carelessly styled, like he just ran his fingers through it, although he goes to this unbelievably expensive barber. He hasn't had a single drop of coffee yet, but his eyes are clear and alert. He's dressed in a pale cream shirt, the collar undone, and some black slacks I picked out for him. He looks fabulous, as usual—strong and powerful. Watching him is how I learned what men who work out look like with clothes on.

I hand him the shake with a smile. "Here you are, Mr. Sterling. I put a little broccoli in for extra folate."

"Oh, good. Thank you, Ms. Parker." He takes it with an appreciative smile, then drinks it like a champion.

When he's finished, I take the empty glass. Then I take a deep breath and start. "You know, I gave what you said a lot of thought."

"Which 'what I said'?"

"What?"

"I've said a lot of things since you started working for me, Ms. Parker."

It's been so long that he probably forgot what I'm talking about. "About Elizabeth King's bachelor auction."

"Ah. That."

"Yes. Have you, um, found somebody to help you?" Maybe it's presumptuous of me to assume he's been sitting on his hands. He might not be capable of picking his own outfits, but he's still a billionaire with more connections than the Internet.

He glances at the coffee on the counter, and I pass it to him immediately. He probably needs some caffeine now.

He takes a slow sip, his eyes on mine. "I asked Court's girlfriend to bid on me, although that annoyed Court quite a bit. So I owe him a kidney if he ever needs one."

Court is one of a very few people Nate counts as a true friend. So it makes sense he asked, and I feel bad that Nate feels like he's going to owe Court a huge favor later.

A kidney-level favor, Evie. All because you turned him down earlier.

Nate adds, "But maybe none of that matters, because they broke up."

Now I feel doubly bad. Both about Court's breakup and the fact that Nate is back to square one. But it also tells me I made the right decision. "Well, then. I'll do it."

"Do what?" he asks, then takes another sip of coffee.

The caffeine probably hasn't hit his bloodstream yet. Normally he's sharper than this. "Bid on you at the auction."

He goes still in the middle of lowering the coffee mug. A smile slowly breaks on his face. It's so radiant, so beautiful, like the heavens opening up, that air catches in my throat. Holy shit, I always knew he was gorgeous, but right now, he's stunning.

"Thank you, Ms. Parker. You're a gem."

You're welcome. My pleasure. If I can see you smile like this again, yeah. Sure. No problem.

"Ms. Parker?"

I realize I've been staring without saying a word. I clear my throat. *What the hell's wrong with me?* I've never spaced out like this before at work. "Yes, Mr. Sterling?"

"I was just saying you need to take a day off."

"I do? But why?"

He looks mildly confused. "Don't you have to get ready?"

"For what?"

"The auction. I distinctly remember you telling me you have nothing to wear. So you're going to need to shop."

Oh, that. I flush. "Yes, but I don't need to take any time off for that. It won't take long."

He shoots me a dubious look. "Are you sure? Don't you also need shoes and other stuff?"

I take a quick mental inventory of my closet. Yeah, I'm definitely going to need to buy everything else that goes with the new dress. "Yes, but I can do it on Friday after work."

"Well... If you're sure. But you can take comp time. It is work-related, after all." He reaches into his wallet and pulls out a black American Express card. "Here."

I stare. He said he'd pay, but I thought it meant I'd have to pay for everything myself first, then he'd reimburse me. I didn't realize it meant he's going to give me his credit card. A freaking black AmEx! How much does he think I'm going to spend? Or is this the only card he carries?

When I don't move to take it, he places it in my hand. His fingers are warm and gentle against my skin, and I shiver as a frisson of electricity travels up my arm.

"Put everything on it," he says. And there's that smile again.

"What's the budget?" I ask, my voice a little faint.

"Budget?" He looks at me. "Don't be silly."

6

Nate

Cha-cha-cha, cha-cha-cha. Oh yeah.

If I could, I'd tap-dance to the office, but it's too damn far. And I'm sure Evie wouldn't want to join me. The stilettos she's wearing are sexy, but probably aren't that great for tap.

I should've known she'd come through. She's never let me down since she started working for me. Well, she is obtuse about my attraction to her—and irritatingly immune to my charm—but that's personal, not professional.

So now I don't have to rely on Court's ex, who disappointed me by breaking up with him. I mean, seriously, what woman would break up with Court? If I were gay, *I'd* do him. The fact that she doesn't recognize his coolness makes her stupid. She would probably only bid like fifty bucks and think that was enough to win me. I'm better off in Evie's lovely, competent hands.

We might even have a real date. That's the least I'm going to owe her.

"You have a meeting with Elizabeth King to go over the May fund-raise for Ethel Sterling Memorial," Evie says, her soft blue gaze on the tablet.

Her gaze isn't the only thing soft on her. Her palm is soft too. I enjoyed touching it, placing my card into it. Maybe I should have her buy stuff every week.

She keeps talking, reading off the day's agenda. I watch her mouth move. She's wearing some kind of plum-colored lipstick, and her lips look scrumptious and extra juicy. I wonder if she *tastes* like plum? Some lipsticks are flavored—something I learned when I was thirteen.

But even if she doesn't, it'd be okay, because then I could taste her instead...

Kissing her will earn you a slap in the face and leave you at the tender mercies of Georgette at the auction.

Okay, stop. I have a meeting with Elizabeth at her office, and I don't want to go in there with a mushy brain full of thoughts about Evie's mouth.

Miguel pulls the Bentley SUV up in front of the Pryce Family Foundation building. It's tall and looks impressively expensive, all gleaming marble and glass. You can't do charity work out of a humble, low-cost office, not if you want the rich to open their wallets. They like to be seen, and they like to feel special as they give money they will never miss to people for whom it will be life-altering.

The floor the foundation occupies isn't ostentatious, but welcoming and trust-inspiring in neutral colors. The interior is minimalist, but everything's high quality and old-money, just like the Pryce family itself.

Elizabeth's "assistant," Tolyan, who looks like he's chewing on broken glass, grunts at me in greeting. Evie moves a little bit closer. *Don't worry, Evie—I'll carry you if we ever need to run from that serial killer.*

"She's waiting for you," a normal-looking person says to me. Rhonda is her name, if I remember correctly. A nice woman, and loyal to Elizabeth. She turns to Evie. "Would you like some donuts? Tolyan brought some."

Probably poisoned or full of blood jelly, but Evie looks so thrilled at the prospect of sugar that I can't bring myself to warn her. "Just...eat it with a lot of coffee," I tell her, and walk into Elizabeth's office.

She rises from her desk, and I smile with genuine pleasure, since she's one of my closest friends. A gray-eyed blonde with a model-perfect face, she's in a blue dress cinched with a thick white belt. One of my exes was of the opinion that white belts make you look fat, but on Elizabeth, it looks fantastic. Probably because she also has a model-perfect body.

Numerous tabloid writers have tried to link us romantically, but we never had those kinds of feelings for each other, even if we were seen in each other's company a lot. We do quite a bit of work together, since she manages the charitable foundation for her family. Unlike mine, hers does everything, not just health care. But accessible medicine is still a big deal to her, and she knows leveraging what my family has already built makes more sense than trying to start from scratch on her own.

"Nate, so good of you to drop by. I know you're busy."

"Not as busy as you. I'm just going to my office, while you're already here, toiling away." I grin.

She leads to me the sitting area with a love seat and two armchairs. "Want anything to drink? Coffee?"

"No, thanks. Already had mine."

I spread out on the love seat, and she takes an armchair, crossing her legs.

"Is your husband spoiling you the way you deserve?" He better be, or I'm going to kick his ass.

She smiles. "Terribly."

"Good. And before we start, I want you to know Barron appreciates your help."

Some women might preen or even have greed flash in their eyes at the mention of Barron's gratitude. Although my great-uncle is retired, he's still the head of the family and wields tremendous influence and power. But Elizabeth just smiles. "Tell him not to mention it. I believe in what he's doing with the hospital."

"He appreciates it anyway. And so do I."

"You're helping out too, by auctioning your prime, unmarried self off for the cause."

I gesture carelessly, utterly relaxed. It's the first time acid hasn't flooded my belly at the mention of the auction. I know who's going to win me, and it's not Melons of Troy in a mink bikini. "This prime specimen will undoubtedly fetch a handsome price."

She laughs. "We'll see. Your proposed date is rather... I don't even know what to call it. Crazy? Over the top?"

"You don't think it works?"

"If you're trying to develop a reputation for eccentricity. Or depravity."

"That bad, huh?" I lean closer, thrilled with her reaction. "Tell me more."

She spreads her hands. "What is there to say?"

"Would you bid on me if you were single?" *Say no.*

"You know I don't bid at my auctions."

"But if you were to break your rule..."

"No, I wouldn't. Flying to Vegas on your private jet and having a drunken orgy? Not my idea of a good time. No offense."

"None taken." I sigh with happiness. "Think I should put how many people are going to be involved in the orgy?"

"You're going to limit your options that way? What have you done to my friend, imposter?"

I laugh. "You're right. Why limit myself? I'm going to get a huge-ass suite that can fit at least fifty. That's probably more than Ryder ever had."

Predictably, she scrunches her face at the mention of her actor brother, who set the standard for *wild* until he settled down. "Ugh. I didn't need that image this early in the morning."

"Sorry, babe." The apology is so unrepentant that I might as well have not said anything.

"If you go unsold, I'm going to point and laugh," she says.

Oh, I wish. But Georgette is coming. She's a fucking nutjob, but she's a very consistent nutjob. If she says she's going to do something, she always follows through. I know she's going to be at the auction, and she's going to bid on me anyway, along with the other determined social climbers of our generation. "Wanna bet?"

"Bet?"

"I say I get sold for big money." I have Evie. I already asked her not to embarrass me, and she'll bid accordingly.

Elizabeth wrinkles her nose. "Weak. How about we bet you're the most expensive bachelor of the night?"

"Fine." I can pull that off. "If I command the highest price on the meat block, you owe me a favor. Within reason, of course."

"And if you lose?"

"A hundred thousand bucks to the cause of your choice?"

She gives me a look. "Deal."

7
———

EVIE

So I've got my boss's black AmEx...and no idea where to go to rack up the big bucks he's expecting me to spend.

It's Saturday, and the auction is tonight. Yesterday I went to the malls and other shops I normally hit, but couldn't find anything that would be acceptable at the kind of glitzy affair someone like Elizabeth hosts.

So it's eleven a.m., and instead of scrolling down my Facebook feed in bed or watching something mindless on Netflix like a normal, well-adjusted adult, I'm frantically hyperventilating because *where am I going find what I need for this evening?* I'm pretty sure the denim shorts and loose Disneyland T-shirt I have on won't cut it.

But Google isn't telling me where I need to go. *Why are you failing me now?*

Kim laughs at something on TV, then glances at me. "What's wrong? You've been on your computer for hours."

I shake my head slowly, resisting an urge to tear my hair out by its roots. "I just..." I bite my lip as Google shows me a local store with hideous "haute couture" dresses. More like a haute mess.

"Need some help?" She sits up straight. She takes her self-imposed position as my mentor seriously. She said Hilary Pryce helped her when she first got started, and she's paying it forward.

Although this isn't PowerPoint or juggling a calendar, maybe she knows a decent store or two. Doesn't she sometimes shop for her boss? And from what I've heard, her boss's taste runs from really expensive to super-ultra-expensive. "Yeah, um... I told Nate I'd help him with the auction thing."

"Hey, good for you!" She beams. "How come you didn't tell me earlier?"

"Because I told him on Thursday, and you were working late again. And yesterday, I was out shopping until I wanted to cry."

I don't think she heard the "wanted to cry" part. Excitement lights her eyes. "Ooh, ooh, what did you get?"

"Nothing! And I don't have anything to wear."

"Isn't the auction, like, today?"

"Yes!"

She frowns for a moment. "Did he at least give you some money?"

I flash the black AmEx at her.

"Now we're talking. Any limit?"

"No. He said I could buy whatever I wanted."

Her expression says she doesn't understand the problem. "So...?"

"Nobody has anything decent! This event is going to be *super* glitzy. And Nate specifically told me not to embarrass him." About the bidding amount, but I'm pretty sure he wants me to be presentable as well. Security might block me if I'm dressed less than perfect, like those snooty New York restaurants that turn you away if you aren't in your Sunday best.

"You can dress the man like a champion, but you can't dress yourself?" Kim asks, both eyebrows arched.

"His closet's full of prescreened clothes." Except for a hideously ugly green flower-print shirt and set of pink pants with magenta tiger sharks, but Kim doesn't need to know about that. "Mine does not. I have stuff that looks okay for work and all, but this?" I gesture in the general direction of the Aylster Hotel, where the auction's taking place tonight.

"You should've said something earlier."

"I tried every mall I could hit yesterday," I say.

"The *mall*? No! Oh my God. You need help, girl."

"I know! I just don't know where to turn."

Ask Nate, my subconscious says, but he can't even pick out his own clothes in the morning. No way am I asking him for fashion advice.

Kim holds up a finger, takes out her phone and calls a number. "Hello, Josephine? Sorry to bother you on such short notice, but it's an emergency... I know, I know, but it's for Nate Sterling... Yeah, Justin's cutie-pie brother. It's for that auction today... No, not a tux. It's not really for *him*, it's for his assistant. She needs to be dre—"

She pulls her phone away from her ear. Even I can hear the screech on the other side. Kim looks at me and holds the finger up again.

When the high-pitched screaming subsides, Kim puts the phone back to her ear. "Well, of course. Black AmEx. Unlimited. You can spend to your heart's content... Hold on, let me ask." She turns to me. "When was your last facial?"

Last facial? "I've, uh... Well, never."

Kim inhales like she's bracing herself to face a horde of pissed-off rhinos. "Never," she says, then immediately holds the phone away from her ear as another long screech comes from it.

When it dies down, she says, "Well, yeah, it is a challenge, but... I know you're used to dealing with people who... Well, but remember your roots, girl. Evie really needs you. How else is she going to outshine everyone else there?"

I shake my head frantically. I do *not* want to outshine everyone else. I just want to be presentable enough not to embarrass myself or Nate. The goal is to blend in.

Kim ignores me. "Yeah... Yeah... Okay. Got it. *Thank* you. Love you too." She makes a loud kissing noise and hangs up.

"Who and what was that?" I ask, still thinking about the "outshine" thing.

"My friend Josephine Martinez. She's going to personally dress you for the auction."

The name is vaguely familiar. "Isn't she a personal shopper or something?"

"Yes."

"I can't afford her!" Especially when she's going to try to make me stand out!

"Of course you can. You have Nate's plastic!"

"But he never said I could put Josephine on it too!"

"What do you think matters more to him? You coming to the auction looking great, or you not putting Josephine on the card?"

Well, when you look at it that way... But I still don't feel comfortable. Josephine has to be hideously expensive. Her help will probably cost more than the dress. "Let me just text him to make sure." I whip out my phone and quickly type, *I really need professional help, and Josephine Martinez is available. Do you mind if I put her service fee on the card?*

I hit send and wait. Nothing. Is he still sleeping? Nate never struck me as the late riser, but maybe he sleeps in on weekends. I bite my lower lip. "He's not saying yes."

"Did he say no?" Kim asks.

Kim Sanford: never lacked for comebacks will be written on her gravestone. "No."

"Then it's a yes. Josephine is mission critical. If you don't hire her, you'll never be able to bid on Nate. Evie, trust me. He won't care. At all."

She's probably right. Nate never cares about money. It's just me—I'm having a serious problem spending it like...like I have a credit card with no limit. Call it my blue-collar Midwest roots. My mother taught me never to take handouts and never take advantage of anything.

"Do I have to put on something different?" I wonder if I'm going to have a *Pretty Woman* moment with snotty shop clerks. Or maybe Josephine's going to be too embarrassed.

"You're fine."

Within half an hour, Josephine arrives. She's gorgeous—glossy, dark hair, perfect makeup that looks airbrushed onto her face and a pantsuit and shoes so stylish they strike me speechless. She and Kim hug each other, then she turns a critical gaze in my direction. I can feel myself whither a little.

"This is the client?" she asks.

"Yep. Meet Evie Parker. Evie, Josephine Martinez."

Right. I'm a client. I shouldn't be so nervous. *Think—what would Nate do?* I shake hands with her. Her nails are long and painted bright red and purple.

"Nice to meet you," I say.

"The pleasure's all mine. You look pretty. Now could you turn around for me?"

I turn, feeling self-conscious and slightly stupid. Is she judging me? Probably. Now that I think about it, I have a mustard stain on the butt of my jeans. Some jerk spilled a huge glop of mustard on a yellow chair at a restaurant, and I wasn't able to get all of it out.

"I presume you need the works?" Josephine says once I'm facing her again.

"The works" sounds like a scary verdict. Guess my having shaved this morning didn't earn me any bonus points.

"Yes," Kim says. "She does."

"At least you called me early enough. Otherwise I wouldn't have been able to help. You also need hair and makeup. Not sure if we can fit in a facial, but your skin's gorgeous. Exfoliate regularly?"

"Yes," I say with a smile, relieved that glamorous Josephine approves of something.

"Well, it shows. Okay, let's get going. And Nate's card?"

"Yes?"

She opens her palm.

I hesitate, unsure if she's asking me to hand it over. He never said I could just give it away to somebody.

"Sweetie, I can't make you shine if I don't have the money. I promise I won't lead you astray. After all, it's my reputation on the line."

I inhale deeply. I don't have much time left. And I have to trust her to make me over before it's too late. "Okay." I give her the card.

Her fingers curl around it, the nails glittering. Somehow the sight doesn't reassure me at all.

8

Evie

I should've known it wasn't going to be a normal kind of experience, like where you and your friends go to a store, try on prom dresses, giggle and share opinions. Not that I'd know anything about that, since I never got to go. My mom couldn't afford to buy me a dress—or anything else that a prom entailed—and I told her I couldn't go because I hurt my ankle and wouldn't be able to dance anyway. It was a ridiculous lie, but she didn't probe too much, probably because she knew why I was doing it.

Josephine doesn't give me time to change, saying it doesn't matter what I wear. I shoot a pleading look in Kim's direction, but she says she has to work because Salazar wants her to plan the most perfect getaway for his wife, no expense spared, and he's already rejected four of Kim's proposals.

So it's just me and Josephine in the Lexus as she takes me to a huge black boxlike structure. I don't think it's a warehouse, but it certainly doesn't look like your regular store either. It's a good thing Josephine is driving, because I'm pretty sure I would've gone right past it.

"Let's go," she says, stepping out of the car.

I follow, not really having much choice. I tell myself the place doesn't look like a place you'd dump bodies. Which isn't that reassuring anyway.

The door opens, and we step into a brightly colored interior. Lightly veined marble covers the floor, and the pale cream walls have recessed nooks with green plants.

A tall, slim Asian woman comes out. She's dressed to the nines, just like Josephine. Maybe there's a secret tribe of women who spend all day looking perfect.

Unlike Josephine, the woman has her hair cut diagonally, the slanted edge razor straight. She hugs Josephine and they exchange air kisses.

"What a surprise. I thought you weren't coming today."

"Wasn't on my schedule," Josephine says. "But there's an emergency."

The woman pulls back. "Ah. So this is...?"

"The emergency," I say, as though it isn't totally obvious. "I'm the emergency."

Josephine makes the introductions while I mostly stand there feeling grossly underdressed and awkward. The woman, Jun, makes some comments about having "just the thing" for me, and then leads us down a spotless, gleaming marble hall with four potted palm trees to a huge room at the end. Feeling totally out of my depth, I follow with my mouth shut so I don't end up looking like a complete hick. Aside from personal pride, I don't want to do anything that will reflect badly on Nate.

Other clerks who are just as sharply dressed as Jun and Josephine roll out several racks of dresses. One pushes a large sliding door to my right, revealing shelves of shoes, individually spotlighted and gleaming. I don't have to see the price tags to know they cost a fortune.

Another assistant brings out a tray of freshly cut fruit, cheese and two flutes of champagne. "Help yourselves," Jun says to me.

Damn. Just how long are we going to be shopping that she's serving those? More to the point, how much are we going to be spending?

Josephine's going over the selections hanging from the rack. "No. No. No. Too light. It'll make her look washed out. We need something to make her *stand* out." Her hands flutter around. "Something that will make a statement."

A *statement*? Goosebumps break out over my skin. "Actually, I, uh, prefer to sort of blend in." I smile weakly, trying to hide how much the idea of public attention is turning my stomach.

Josephine looks at me, then blinks a few times. Jun is frowning. They look at each other.

Josephine finally breaks the silence. "Evie, nobody dresses for Elizabeth's auction to blend in. You go there to be *seen*."

"Seen?" My voice is thin. "Like, by people?"

Jun nods emphatically. "By everyone!"

I'm going to die.

"Now this..." Josephine pulls out a fiery red off-the-shoulder dress. "Look at this. This has your name on it. In neon."

Oh. My. God. I'm going to pop in the crowd, like an angry zit on an otherwise pristine face. "No. No way. How about that beige?" I point at a more demure one hanging on the rack.

"*That?*" Jun looks horrified. "You might as well wear industrial carpet. The color's all wrong for you."

"I, um, kind of have a problem with getting a lot of attention." I can handle one on one or a couple of other people. But a crowd? No way. It makes me too self-conscious and clumsy. Just thinking about it makes my stomach roil.

Josephine purses her mouth. "All right. Maybe red is too strong a color. But that beige would be absolutely hideous on you. You need..." She taps her lower lip. "Why don't we try pink?"

I nod. "It's my favorite color." And it's softer. More...blendy.

She beams. "Great. You can put this one on." She pulls out a pink version of the red one she's holding. "Still, with your coloring, red *would* be more spectacular..."

"Especially with a red peony in your hair," Jun adds.

"I can put a pink peony in my hair," I offer in a compromise. I'm amenable to anything as long as I don't have to wear the red, spectacular or otherwise. I just want to be presentable.

"I suppose that's an option," Jun says.

"Underwear or no underwear?" Josephine asks, tapping her lip.

Is that even up for a debate? Of course I have to have underwear, especially in public!

"Better to go without," Jun says. "No lines."

No, no, no, no, no. "Don't you have some kind of thong or something that won't show?" I refuse to believe they don't have such underwear in this fancy store.

The look Jun gives me is full of pity. "Don't believe the advertising hype. Nothing is foolproof except going without."

"I don't want my nipples to show through!"

"Oh, that." Josephine waves it away. "The bust area is lightly padded. And it's not like people can tell what you're wearing underneath—or not—by just looking at your dress."

Jun nods. "Exactly."

"But *I'll* know," I say, feeling the all-too-familiar anxiety snaking around my stomach and squeezing until I feel like I'm going to throw up last night's Chinese.

"Are you going to announce the fact? No? So it'll be okay. Although if you do, Nate probably won't mind." Josephine winks.

Jun snaps her fingers, and her people start selecting shoes. "Now, let's see. Heels. Definitely stilettos. Open toe. Straps. Sexy." She taps her lips. "Silver or gold?"

Clearly in her element, she seems to be perfectly okay making the decision sans any input from me. I look down and see my old flip-flops. Okay, so maybe she thinks my input would be a waste of time. She's probably worried I'll pick a pair of industrial carpet shoes.

"Gold is glitzier, but silver has more class," Josephine murmurs in my ear.

In that case... "Silver." Glitzier is probably a code word for *showier*.

Josephine nods with a smile. "Excellent choice. Now. We need to do your mani pedi. And the hair. And makeup."

"Facial," Jun says.

I recall Josephine's compliment about my skin looking good. "I don't think that's necessary. I mean, I *do* exfoliate."

Jun looks at me like she would a confused child. "Yes, but that's not the same as a facial. We can probably do the facial and wax at the same time."

"I shaved this morning," I point out quickly in case she's thinking I forgot to shave my armpits.

Jun raises an eyebrow. "You used a razor down there?" She gestures toward my crotch.

What? My cheeks flame. "I mean, my legs and armpits."

"Well then. A Brazilian, obviously."

Every nerve cell between my legs shrivels with horror. "Why?" Is the dress see-through in the crotch area? Maybe I should've asked before I said yes. And if it is see-through, I'm putting on a pair of granny panties!

Josephine peers at me. "You're going to win Nate Sterling, aren't you?"

"Yeah..." Otherwise I wouldn't be having this ridiculous conversation with two people who have a great sense of fashion but no common sense. "What does that have to with waxing? And why am I discussing waxing with a stranger whose last name I don't even know?"

"Watanabe," Jun says with a friendly smile. "And I know yours—Parker. Do you feel more comfortable now?"

Hardly. I think I'm going to cry laughing. And I need a drink. Oh, that's right, Jun's people brought one out for me. I reach for a flute and down it fast.

Josephine takes control. "What do you think is going to happen when you win him?"

What is this? A trick question? "Nothing? He's going to thank me? I'm going to go to work on Monday, make him his shake and take care of his agenda for the day?" I shrug to hide my discomfort and an intense desire to flee. Now I wish I'd driven my own car here. And kept Nate's AmEx in my purse instead of handing it over to Josephine.

Josephine and Jun start giggling.

"You're going to go on *a date* with him," Josephine says. "Don't you want to be prepared? You have to baby your lady bits right after you get waxed, especially if it's your first time." Her expression says she knows I've never done it before. "So better now than later." Jun nods sagely.

Finally I realize what they're assuming, and put a hand over my mouth. "Oh, shit. You think Nate and I are..." I let out an awkward laugh. "I mean, you don't really think... We aren't like that. I don't have any intention of going there. He's my *boss*."

"Plenty of people date their bosses," Jun says.

"And marry them," Josephine adds.

"Yeah, well, not this one. And *Nate?*" It's my turn to laugh. "You know what he hates the most? *Commitment.* He doesn't like having his choices stripped away. It'll be years, decades maybe, before he even starts to think about getting married. If ever. Trust me on this."

"But you're going to bid on him tonight," Jun says gently.

I'm almost tempted to pat her hand. "And I'm going to win him, but that's as far as it's going to go. Trust me."

9

EVIE

MY ANNOUNCEMENT SEEMS TO DEFLATE THE J GIRLS. EVEN though they take away waxing from the list of things I "must" do before the auction, the mani pedi, hair, facial and makeup stay.

While a team works on me, Josephine orders up a little food because she doesn't want me fainting from hunger before the bidding starts. I'm grateful for that, because it takes forever to get ready. Do all the high-society people waste their entire day to look good? If so, I see why they all need assistants, because they'll never have enough time to get anything done. But I shouldn't be too judgmental. It's the reason I have a job. A good-paying job. And I know I'm lucky to hold the position when I only have an associate's degree and a crappy résumé.

Although I still think the facial's redundant, when the team is finished and I look at myself in the mirror, I totally see the light.

My skin *glows*. And it's not from the foundation. No foundation is this good. "Oh wow."

"Toldja," Josephine says.

"How much does it cost?" I ask, wondering if I can afford to do it again.

"Don't worry about it. Nate's paying."

I think that's code for "out of your price range." Besides, it's not like I'm going to get another one anytime soon. Maybe on my wedding day.

Josephine helps me squeeze into the pink dress. I'd rather do it alone, but it's quite fitted around the bodice and hips and sort of tricky to maneuver. The material is thin, though it feels very soft and expensive against my skin. Jun was right to call for commando. I'm not sure if there's any underwear high-tech enough to really be invisible underneath.

They also take my compromise to put a pink peony in my hair seriously. Their stylist puts my hair up in a loose bun and sticks the flower in. It adds to the ensemble, though. I look like I could blend in quite well at the auction and not appear to be the "hired help," as Georgette put it.

Josephine sighs wistfully. "Red really would be better."

"The client isn't comfortable," Jun says.

"I love pink," I say firmly, studying my reflection in the mirror. "And I think I look fine."

Josephine shakes her head. "No, honey, not yet. You need jewelry."

Jewelry. It didn't even occur to me. Guess this is why she's the expert.

"Diamonds and pearls. Rental or outright purchase?" Josephine asks.

"Rental!" I say before Jun can give an opinion.

She gestures lazily, and four huge glass cases appear, brought by her trusty assistants. Josephine picks out diamond and pearl drop earrings and a matching necklace and bracelet. I put on the earrings, while she hooks the necklace around my neck. A few tiny diamonds and pearl hairpins go into my bun as well.

"*Now* you look ready," Josephine announces.

Jun nods.

I have to admit, the jewelry really does complete the look. Josephine and Jun have great taste, despite their eccentricity, and I owe Kim one for hooking me up.

"There's a limo waiting outside," Jun says.

"A limo?" I ask blankly. "For what?"

"To take you to the Aylster Hotel."

What is this? High school prom? "I can drive my car."

"Unless you own a Bentley or something similar, no, you cannot," Josephine says. "A limo is an acceptable alternative."

"Listen to her," Jun says. "It's a cost of attending the auction."

"Okay, has it occurred to anybody that if people just skipped all this limo and high-fashion stuff and just donated the money they spend to get *ready* to donate, things might be much more efficient?"

"I'm sure it has. But then we would be out of work," Jun says.

"And women wouldn't get a chance to dig their talons into the eligible bachelors they've been salivating over." Josephine's tone is positively mournful.

I shudder at the gruesome imagery, telling myself it's not that bad. But then crazy Georgette and her mink bikini pop into my head, along with her endless nude pics. Maybe Josephine isn't exaggerating.

Josephine hands me Nate's black AmEx, which I put into my small clutch.

"Everything's taken care of, including my fee," she says. "No discount; Nate can afford it. Leave the jewelry with Kim when you're done with it, and I'll come by and get it. And your things will be delivered to your place later today or early tomorrow, depending on the courier schedule. Is that okay?"

"Yes." I check to make sure I have my phone and my own plastic in the clutch I'm taking with me.

"And if I'm right and you end up marrying Nate, you owe me a picture. Or better yet, an invitation." Jun fans herself. "I've never been to a billionaire's wedding."

"Oh yeah. Sure." *When the sun orbits the moon, maybe.* I laugh away her ridiculous fantasy and walk out to the limo.

Because the likelihood of my dating Nate, much less marrying him, is basically nil. Actually, that's generous. It's more like a negative number. A very large—or would that be small?—negative number.

All that's going to happen is me bidding on him tonight, I think as I climb into the limo. I wonder how much I can really spend. Nate and I didn't discuss that in detail, and now I wish we had so I'd know just how much I can throw out there. And he never responded to my text earlier. Wonder if he's been busy getting a facial of his own. There's nothing that says men can't get them, and he does glow so gorgeously all the time.

The limo seems to be proceeding at a snail's pace down the road. An arthritic snail. I check the time. Crap. The auction's started already.

"Can you go a little faster?" I ask the driver.

"Can't. There's some kind of accident ahead."

Ugh. I check the program I got from the auction. The bachelors are being auctioned alphabetically. Which means I still have time, since Nate is the last one of the night. Still, I don't want him to worry, so I text him.

I'm on my way. Traffic's bad, but I should be there on time to make things right.

My phone stays quiet. He's probably busy. I check the pins in my hair, pushing them into the bun more securely. They're real diamonds and pearls. I can't afford to lose even one of them.

Finally a response comes through.

I think I saw HER. You're the only one I can count on.

Oh damn. The weight of responsibility presses upon me. My phone buzzes again. It's an email.

I can't wait to win you tonight! I've been thinking of this since we last met.

And a picture of Georgette in that abominable mink bikini bottom with her mouth open and tongue hanging out in some kind of weird porno pinup pose. *Eww.* I don't know how she can wear that over her crotch. The ghosts of the dead minks are going to haunt her lady holes, making them close up. Or give her vaginal itchiness and a hairy ass, since she likes fur so much.

After what seems like an interminable delay, we finally make it past the fender bender. Traffic picks up speed, and I sit back with a sigh. Do people really *have* to pause and stare? It's not like accidents don't happen every day.

"I have to get to an event that's already started, so if you could step on it, I'd really appreciate it," I say to the driver.

"I understand."

And he really does understand. The limo stops in front of the

Aylster Hotel in less than half an hour. A smartly dressed porter opens the door with a flourish.

I hop out, then remember I should tip the chauffeur. I open my clutch and see only two twenties. Screw it. I give him both. "Thank you."

He smiles. "Enjoy your evening."

I run inside. I was here once before with Nate when he had to set up some kind of banquet eight months ago. The lobby seems almost to shimmer with all crystal and marble. I dash across the hard floor, wincing at the lack of support and cushion my fashionable but utterly impractical shoes offer. I stop abruptly when I realize I have no clue which ballroom is the right one. I turn to a woman in a hotel uniform and ask.

"This way, ma'am." She escorts me up to the second floor, where there is a huge and very expensively dressed crowd milling around. "You can show your invitation to the security team there."

I can hear an MC's tittering laugh as the women inside holler and hoot. I guess I'm in time. "Thank you."

Elizabeth's assistant is helping out with the security team. He looks surprisingly dashing in a tux, although it doesn't do a thing to soften his hard edges. I trot toward him because he's the only person I know in this sea of people. "Hi!"

He stares.

And I babble, "I'm here to bid on Nate Sterling."

He smiles, just a slight curving of his lips, although his pale eyes remain assessing. "Do you have a ticket?"

"Yes." I show him my mobile invitation.

He barely glances at the screen. "Hope you have a decent war chest. The competition is rather...fierce."

Bad enough that even he noticed, huh? But do the other bidders know that I have Nate's money to spend? "Fierce or not, I'm here to win," I say, and walk inside.

On the stage are a brunette in a golden tube dress and Nate, who has apparently just come out and looks great in a white tux. *Wait, white?* I could have sworn I picked out a black tux for tonight before I left his place on Friday.

Maybe he spilled something on it. Regardless, the white one fits his wide shoulders and trim waist immaculately. And it hints at the shape of his pecs and thighs underneath the pristine fabric. All in all, perfect. He probably had help from Elizabeth.

From the breathless way the MC is speaking into the microphone to get the ladies worked up, it seems like she's already finished with the intro and ready to move to the actual bidding.

Just in time.

I walk over to get to an empty seat while keeping my eyes on my boss, silently trying to communicate *I won't let you down*. Finally I reach an available chair in the back and sit down.

"My God, he's *so* hot," a redhead in front of me says.

"Scorching," says her blonde friend. "I've been dying to see this guy."

"The last Sterling man standing." The redhead sounds like she's about to cry.

"Seriously. That Pryce girl isn't going to let hers go." The blonde licks her lips and flexes her fingers as though she's about to dig into some nice tasty veal.

Poor Nate.

"Ten thousand!"

The sudden cry jerks my attention left, then all the way in front. And...wow. That's Georgette. She's in a bright red and black dress, thankfully made with just regular fabric rather than some kind of fur. Her makeup is cartoonishly ludicrous with red blush and blue eye shadow that I can see even from this distance. It's especially dramatic against her pasty white complexion. Didn't anybody tell Old Glory isn't a good look for someone's face?

"Ten thousand five hundred," the redhead in front of me says. Clearly, Georgette isn't my only competition.

"Eleven!" Georgette cries triumphantly.

Nate scans the crowd, an anxious frown on his face. He's probably looking for me but not having much luck since I'm in the back, nicely blending in in my pink. Since the redhead isn't stepping up, it's my turn.

"Eleven five," I say.

"Did somebody say something?" the MC says from the stage.

I wince. Do I have to yell too? A quick clearing of throat. "Eleven five!" I say more loudly.

"Twelve!" Georgette says.

"Twelve five!" says the redhead.

"Thirteen!" *I won't let you down, Nate.*

"I know that voice!" Georgette hops on an empty chair, then sees me in the back. "You? The hired help doesn't belong here!"

The insult barely registers as everyone's gaze swings toward me. Each one pierces like a lance, and my mouth goes dry as my heart palpitates. I *do not* like attention. I don't like people staring. And I certainly don't like public assessment and judgment.

The bit of food I ate at Jun's boutique spins in my belly. Acid floods my mouth. *Don't throw up!* That would definitely get me all kinds of attention, staring and judgment.

"Fifty!" Georgette says, her nose in the air, an ugly sneer on her lips.

The MC repeats the amount with a breathless excitement I can't decide is faked or not, while the crowd starts to buzz. The redhead in front of me leans back in her chair, clearly done with the bidding.

Georgette laughs like a villain twirling his mustache and whips out her phone.

"Do we have fifty and five?" the MC asks.

My phone alerts me to an email. I glance at it, needing something—anything—to make me forget I'm being examined like an acne pimple when I'm supposed to be blending in like industrial carpet.

This is us tonight.

A picture pops up, and I almost yelp and drop my phone. It's Georgette, naked, and the position of her legs leaves absolutely *nothing* to the imagination. She definitely did the prep work that Jun recommended for me, and she's pouring white syrup all over her face and a hairless travesty nobody should have to un-see.

I'm definitely going to get sick.

A text pops up. Nate. *Don't lose or embarrass me. Bid big!*

So much palpable desperation and will in that single text.

I lift my head. The MC is ready to close the bidding. "Going once. Going twice—"

I take another nanosecond glance at the picture Georgette sent. I can't let Nate costar in that show. And I really don't want to have a bidding war with Georgette either and drag this out. That woman's unhinged, and I hate the way the people are all looking at me.

Screw it. "Five hundred thousand dollars!" I yell out.

A stunned silence falls for a moment. I squeeze my eyes shut to block out everyone's shocked gaze, because I just can't deal right now.

Georgette is the first to recover. "You don't have that kind of money!" she screams.

The MC fans herself. "Half a million dollars! Oh my goodness. Going once..."

Georgette points at me. "She's an *assistant*! She doesn't have that kind of money! It's illegal for her to bid when she can't pay!"

The MC looks at Georgette coolly. "If she doesn't pay, then you win by default."

"Make her show you her bank account *now*!" Georgette screams, spittle flying.

Nate leans over so he can speak into the MC's mic. "Let's not be crude. This isn't that sort of event." His tone is jovial enough, but I can sense the barest hint of steel underneath.

"No! I refuse! She has no business being here! She's just a working girl!"

God, I hate her so much that I want to rip her fake lashes off and stab her eyeballs with them. Not because she's being true to her condescending self, but because she's putting a spotlight on me, and people are staring. My skin crawls, and I swear if she doesn't stop, I'm going to run up there and puke on her!

Elizabeth's assistant appears and taps Georgette's shoulder, murmuring something. She turns around, then screams, "You can't shut me up! I have the right to speak my mind—"

He hoists her over his shoulder like a sack of flour and carries her out of the ballroom. He looks bored, while she screams a single high note the entire time. It's amazing that her vocal cords don't snap.

"Well." The MC smiles. "Now that the interruption's over... Going twice..."

The floor stays quiet.

"... *Sold!*"

The MC raises her free arm with a flourish. Nate beams. Everyone else in the room is clapping, but they're also staring at me.

Every drop of saliva in my mouth dries. Somehow I'm getting the feeling that maybe I shouldn't have bid so high, even if it is Nate's money.

10

EVIE

SINCE I'VE DONE MY DUTY, I START TO SNEAK OUT, shoulders rounded to make myself as small as possible. People are murmuring, their eyes on my retreating figure.

I. Must. Leave. Now. Nate will take care of the payment, since he knows I don't have that kind of money. But he was the final bachelor, so the crowd's milling around, talking and staring and pointing. Now I wish I'd worn a scarf around my face or something. This is just too much, because the people don't have anything—or anyone—on the stage to distract them.

When I walk past the doors to the ballroom, relief starts to unfurl. The scrutiny sucked, but *I did my job*. I bailed Nate out of his horrible situation. Kim should be proud of me. Hell, *I'm* proud of me.

Flashes go off, putting spots in front of my eyes. My vision seems to swim, and I raise my hand as more cameras flash around me.

What the...? Is there a celeb behind me?

I turn around, and through the spots I see Nate. Huh. *Doesn't he have other things to do? Maybe toast to his victory over Georgette?*

"Hello, Mr. Sterling," I say, since I can't think of anything else.

"Good evening, Ms. Parker," he says with the grin that never fails to make him look ten times hotter.

"I should get out of the way. I think they want to take your picture." Which makes more sense than them taking pictures of *me*. He's an important man.

As I start to move away, Nate's arm snakes around my waist. He pulls me to his side until we're flush against each other. "They're here to take pictures of the winners and their prizes."

"Uh... They are?" My belly flutters. Nate feels warm and solid against my bare arm, but I don't think that's the reason for the vibrating sensation in my stomach as more flashes go off. I really shouldn't have eaten anything at Jun's. I look up at him. "It wasn't in the program."

Nate frowns as though he can't believe I didn't know. "Photo ops are a given."

"Maybe for you." I sniff, then smell stale alcohol. Where is it coming from? There's nobody around us.

He beams, pulling me closer. "You won me. So you're part of the package now."

Oh. My. God. "You never told me that!"

The blinding smile on his face loses a few watts. "I thought you knew."

"No, because it wasn't in the fine—" I stop as the stale alcohol smell hits me again. "Were you drinking before the auction?"

"Yeah, last night." He winces. "Not that much, though," he adds. "Only, like, fifteen or twenty."

"*Fifteen or twenty?*" The words are entirely too loud, and I cover my mouth. "Nate, shouldn't you be in the hospital?" *We can leave here immediately. I'll even hold your hand.*

He looks at me, then looks at himself, then back at me. "What for?"

"For alcohol poisoning," I hiss at him. "You can barely have three drinks without falling flat on your face." It was a pain to drag him to his mansion when he was all but passed out. And he told me things he shouldn't have, things I shall not recall because he was drunk and had no idea what he was saying.

Understanding dawns on his face, although I'm not sure what kind of understanding is required for this. *Doesn't he know his limits?*

Actually, never mind. He's a man. Of course he doesn't know.

"You should've called me last night," I say.

"It's okay. Court was there to...er...take care of me." He coughs into a fist.

"Speaking of which, I didn't see his girlfriend bidding on you." The redhead with the blonde friend definitely wasn't Court's girl. "I guess he still hasn't made up with her?"

"You missed it. She bought him for fifty bucks." Nate shakes his head.

Holy shit. "Fifty bucks? Like five-zero?" No wonder she's not part of this photo op. What's that girl's secret?

"Fifty. Only one zero behind the five."

"Ouch." I wince on Court's behalf. "Wasn't he in high demand?" Although Court isn't as loaded as Nate, he's still an extremely rich bachelor.

"Long story, but he was happy with the outcome. And that's all that matters."

A reporter shoves her way toward us, somehow bypassing security. I see Tolyan's missing, which explains why.

"Tell me what it's like to bid on one of the world's most eligible bachelors!" she demands, almost knocking my teeth out with a recorder. "Did you know you'd win?"

My stomach turns to ice. There's no way I'm going to give her an interview or comment. Nate pulls me closer, and thankfully her attention switches to my boss, like a high-strung Chihuahua on four shots of espresso. "What does it feel like to be the most expensive bachelor of the night?"

Nate gives her a charming smile. "Well, what can I say? The ladies love me."

And I love you too, for taking her focus off me.

I practice deep breathing as she throws a few more questions at him. In fact, I pretend I'm not here. I'm in my room. In my pajamas. Surfing the net. This is a scene from a very badly scripted Netflix show, not a slice of *my* evening...

"And you?" The reporter swivels, jamming the black thing

back in my direction. "What does it feel like to win one of the most eligible bachelors in the world?"

The question shatters my calm-inducing imagery. The cheese from earlier pushes upward, and my feet tilt sideways as my knees turn to butter.

Nate tightens his arm around me. "Ms. Parker?"

Oh thank God. I guess I won't end up on my butt with him holding me up.

"I only need one quote!" the reporter says, obviously not getting the hint that her need for that quote is the problem here.

"Gonna be sick," I say weakly, and then throw up on her shoes.

11

Evie

My defiling of the reporter's shoes makes the front page of numerous gossip rags and tabloids. Along with photos of me and Nate together that were taken before all the hurlage. What happened at the Aylster Hotel even becomes a topic on commute-time radio talk shows for a day or two. I can't listen without feeling shivers run up my spine, so I have to click away or turn off the radio every time it comes up.

Talk about embarrassing. At least radio doesn't have pictures, just a bunch of snarky commentary, which I unfortunately sometimes catch when I'm late switching the station.

Some claim I was nervous. *How overwhelmingly astute*, I think. Some say I became sick over the prospect of having to pay half a million bucks for Nate, which of course is totally off the mark. Nate himself seemed to think the puking was okay as long as it wasn't on *his* shoes.

I thought he might become a little upset after he managed to flush all the alcohol out of his system. But no. The man actually preens reading headlines declaring him the most sought-after bachelor of the auction. Pettily enough, I wish I'd spent more money at Jun's boutique. And maybe gotten two facials.

I text Mom to let her know I'm fine and ask her to ignore the articles. She asks me if any of them are true, and I tell her most of those papers are writing fiction. Lying without lying. I hate this, but I don't want to worry her. She's going to have a heart attack if she thinks I'm repeating the same mistake I made back home by actually dating Nate.

For a brief moment, I wonder if anyone in Dillington saw the articles and recognized me. I can't decide how I feel about that. Are they going to feel a twinge of guilt they drove me away? Or are they going to whisper, "Oh, look, that girl's latching on to another boss. Guess she'll never learn"?

At least Nate is ten billion times hotter than my ex, Chadwick.

And a trillion times the gentleman.

After laying out several outfits for the day and the weekend for Nate, I walk downstairs to the kitchen to make his shake. It's been three weeks since the auction, but the hideous Georgette-violating-Nate statue is still in the living room. Does he really want this reminder of a nightmare that never happened? Maybe I should be more proactive and ask him how he wants to dispose of the postmodern monstrosity.

When I put the blender into the kitchen sink for the housekeeper to clean later, Nate comes down the steps. He's in a light charcoal suit, no tie. I hand him the day's healthy green concoction, and he takes it with a smile.

"So. What do you want to do with that...um...statue? I can have it removed today if you'd like." Then I frown as it occurs to me that somebody might pay good money for it. Art collectors have the weirdest taste. "Or maybe it could be auctioned off to raise money for something?"

Nate doesn't answer. Instead he chugs the entire glass of vitamins and other goodness down. I immediately hand him his coffee, knowing he needs the caffeine to think.

After a couple of sips, he says, "Definitely not."

"Why not? To remind you never to let down your guard?" There's no way Georgette's the only crazy ex in Nate's closet.

"Remind me to what?"

"I know Georgette surprised you, but you don't have to keep something that continues to remind you of the trauma."

He looks at the statue, then back at me. "What about the piece makes you think it's about her?"

The angular predation with which the female is devouring that cock? The look of absolute insanity on her face? "Isn't it?"

He raises both eyebrows. "No. It's a 'gift' from Barron. He couldn't keep it in his house because his girlfriend objected to it, what with grandkids visiting and all."

Well, at least the girlfriend's sensible. "No kidding. That thing's a horror."

"You think so?" The corner of Nate's lips twitches. "I didn't know you were into art."

"You don't have to be into anything. That woman looks like a damn succubus."

"A *what*?"

"You know." I clear my throat, unwilling to discuss specifics.

He looks over at the statue for a moment. "I...really don't."

I tilt my head and stare at him. Is he just messing with me? Or does he honestly not see it? Sure, the statue is sort of modern and slightly abstract, but I thought people who grew up buying stuff like this would know at a glance. "She's sucking his essence out through the...um...sausage."

Nate chokes on his coffee. I quickly hand him a napkin before he soils his shirt.

He places it over his mouth, then laughs into the white square. "Sucking his essence..." He stops, chokes, then starts laughing again. "Through the..."

"I really don't see what's so amusing." Maybe I should've just said "cock" like a mature adult, but that would have been totally inappropriate with my male boss, who is hot and has starred in a few of my more feverish dreams.

"I'm trying to imagine what Barron would say if he were to hear that. Or Catherine, who curates his stuff." Nate gestures at the hunk of bronze. "Oh man..." He wipes his eyes.

I scowl. "I'm sorry, Mr. Sterling. My taste is probably a bit plebian."

"Nothing wrong with plebian, Ms. Parker. Just makes you human and adorable."

He looks at me with a small smile, and my cheeks heat. His dark eyes are gorgeous in the morning, especially when he's in a good mood. And that mouth is positively *inviting*, like it wants me to lay my lips over it.

Get a hold of yourself, Evie! He doesn't mean "adorable" the way you think he does. He was probably trying to say "funny," but chose the wrong word because he hasn't finished his coffee yet.

I force a smile of my own. "I'm glad you find it acceptable." I have no clue what I'm trying to say. But I feel like I have to say something to break the effect he has on me.

Something flickers in his eyes, and he straightens. I let out a soft sigh of relief that he's back in boss mode.

We walk out together. I take another glance at the hideous hunk of metal. If the statue is from Barron, there's no way we can get rid of it. Nate's great-uncle has a certain reputation. The office keeps a fresh stock of Earl Grey tea and sugar cookies even though nobody really drinks it or eats them much—we're more chocolate chippers—because he likes them, and it's impossible to predict when he's going to visit. I think it's a waste, personally. He hasn't come to the office in the nine months I've been working there, but my thoughts on the matter are probably unwanted. All the older employees whisper his name with awe, respect and a tinge of fear. Sometimes I wonder if we're expected to kneel and prostrate ourselves before him.

We take Nate's car, which is a crimson Ferrari today. Apparently, Miguel is off again—and for the indefinite future. Nate told him to take as much time as necessary, and HR is going to pay his salary as usual. Nate's attitude is that all parents deserve to take care of their infant child together without having to worry about money.

Sometimes I wish my boss were just a little bit of a dick so I could safely put him in a "hot, but such a douche" box, which would make him less attractive. Of course, there are times when he acts slightly spoiled and too used to getting his way. But moments like this remind me he's a good person inside.

When we're halfway to the office, Nate's personal cell phone rings.

The Bluetooth speakers say, "Barron Sterling."

Geez! Did he somehow sense I was trying to get rid of his statue?

"Speak of the devil." Nate grins. "Must be calling to check up on his gift."

I shake my head at his irreverent tone. I'm sure Barron has better things to do worry about a bunch of twisted metal. Doesn't he?

"Yes, Barron?" Nate says cheerfully.

"What the hell is going on with the news these days?" a thunderous voice booms.

No greeting or anything warm. Grouchy. And will definitely demand prostration if we ever meet in person.

"I don't know, but I'm sure it didn't impact Sterling & Wilson," Nate says. "Or at least Justin will have done something to minimize its effect on the busi—"

"Not Justin. *You!* The gossip rags are claiming that Elizabeth's auction is a sham!"

That's a strong accusation, especially against someone like her.

Nate's jaw tightens. "Fuckers. What are they saying?"

"Well, you should know. You're the one they're talking about!"

Bewilderment crosses Nate's face. "*Me?* How—"

"And your friend, that Court boy, didn't help matters by getting auctioned off for fifty bucks!" Barron continues. "Highly irregular, when there were women who bid more."

"Well, yeah, but he had his reasons," Nate says.

"Oh, yes. Reasons. Much like Ted Bundy, I suppose. And then," Barron continues, "you got auctioned off to your assistant for half a million dollars!"

Oh, shit. Is that what this is about? Am I in trouble with Nate's great-uncle?

"I thought that was the least the Sterling name deserved." Nate's tone is entirely too droll. "Did you want her to bid higher to preserve our repu—"

"This is a serious matter! Donations are falling off, and some people are starting to question Elizabeth's ethics!"

"Oh." For once, Nate looks slightly chastised.

"Now, did you take your assistant on that date?" Barron asks ominously.

Nate's gaze slides toward me. "Uh, no... Not yet."

I give him a smile that I hope is supportive and reassuring. I don't need a date with him. As a matter of fact, I don't *want* a date with him.

"Nathan," Barron says gravely. "People are placing bets. They're saying Elizabeth's auctions are rigged, all the big bidding is just a publicity stunt and that you aren't going to follow through on your proposed date."

"Oh, come on!" Nate says, shoving a hand into his hair. I have to agree.

"I'm very fond of Elizabeth. You'll have to fix this for her."

"I'll have a chat with Ken Honishi," Nate says.

I make a note on the tablet to arrange for a call with the Sterlings' retainer as soon as possible.

"That won't be enough." Barron's tone is cool. "So it's true you had your assistant bid on you. Don't tell me you didn't."

"Fine. I won't," Nate mutters.

And I won't either. I don't think I can lie to the man, even over the phone. There's something about the crackling authority in his tone that's cowing.

"And you haven't had the date yet," Barron states.

"No." Nate steals another glance in my direction. "The fact is we didn't plan to."

Yes. Exactly. The whole thing was over and done with the moment I saved my boss from his mink-bikini-wearing stalker maniac.

"Well, change your plans. Follow through on that date, and make sure you appear together in public, where people will see you." There's a tone of hard-edged command that makes me shiver.

"Barron, we—"

"I trust it'll be taken care of by Monday." Barron doesn't bother to add "or else."

The line dies.

12

NATE

EVIE IS STUNNED INTO SPEECHLESSNESS. I'M PRETTY stunned, too, even though I manage to get us to the office without having an accident. I didn't realize Elizabeth's foundation has been under attack. *Shit.* She's a good friend, and I should've been more aware, especially since I'm at least partially responsible.

But who the hell is attacking her? Although it isn't what Barron asked for, I should have Ken sue every single one of those fucking tabloid scribblers.

I cut through the Sterling & Wilson lobby, my strides eating up the ground. Evie has to trot to keep up, her trusty tablet held tightly to her chest like a shield. I don't blame her. Everyone feels this way after dealing with Barron. Even I'm not one hundred percent immune, and I grew up around him.

"Ms. Parker, see what Ken's schedule looks like today."

"Yes, Mr. Sterling." She nods and immediately starts working at her station once we arrive at my office.

The second I'm seated at my desk, I call Elizabeth. "I hear you're having problems," I say when she picks up. "You should've said something."

"Well, hi. Thomas was a little fussy last night, but I didn't realize you were so interested."

I grind my teeth. It's so like her to act strong and unperturbed, no matter what happens. As much as I admire that quality, right now, it's really irritating. "You know what I mean."

"Actually, no. You have to be more specific."

"People are saying shit about the auction."

"Oh, that?" She laughs softly. "Amusing, isn't it?"

"You're *amused*?" Is she deliberately doing this to make me feel silly for being this upset on her behalf?

"It's just people who lost out on their bidding being petty. It'll blow over."

"But it's your family's reputation." And as dysfunctional as her family can be, they take their reputation seriously.

"Nate, if I got worked up every time somebody said something about me or the causes we champion, I'd never get anything done."

"But nobody says shit about you!"

"Not openly, but that doesn't mean they don't say it. Trust me. I hear things."

Or maybe it's her assistant who hears shit and passes it on. That man is an unfeeling freak. "Okay, well, don't worry. Barron's on it, and so am I."

"Barron really shouldn't bother himself," she says mildly. "He should enjoy his retirement."

I snort. "He's never going to really retire. I bet he gets reports on how each little part of his empire is doing every morning, so he can read them over with his Earl Grey and sugar cookies." And if he didn't, I'd be worried and send a doctor to check him over.

"Be that as it may, please don't feel that you have to do something. It's my problem, and I can fix it. But thanks for your support anyway." Her voice is warm and full of sweetness.

We end the call, but somehow I actually feel worse. It really *isn't* her problem. It's mine because I rigged things to avoid being won by Georgette. Otherwise I would've just let somebody win me, then suffered through the date for a good cause.

I eye Evie's shadow on the other side of the frosted glass wall. She heard Barron, and she's probably amenable. If not because she's afraid of Barron, then because she cares about Elizabeth's cause.

There's really only one course left for us to take: go through with the date. That's the fastest and surest way to shut people up.

I hit the button on my desk. "Ms. Parker, a moment, please."

She walks in, carrying her tablet. "Ken is set to speak with you today at three. That's the earliest he can manage."

"Okay. But we need to talk about us."

"Um...us?"

"The date. We kind of have to do it."

She clears her throat. "I see. Okay." She worries her lip, then firms her mouth like she's come to a decision. "Do you want me to make a reservation at a restaurant? I'm pretty sure I can manage one at someplace exclusive either today or tomorrow. The kind of place a half-million-dollar bachelor would take his winner."

Oh, Evie, Evie. She obviously doesn't realize we actually have to stick to the date I proposed, not this eating-out thing she prefers. "No. You need to go home and pack for an overnight trip."

"Excuse me?" She looks at me like I just asked her to strip naked and do a backflip.

"We're flying to Vegas."

"Vegas? There are plenty of acceptable restaurants in L.A."

"I agree, but we can't do that to quiet the gossip. We have to go to Vegas."

She takes a quarter of a step backward, her cornflower-blue eyes full of wariness. "And then...what? Gamble? That's not really romantic, if you ask me."

I stare at her. Why is she asking these ridiculous questions? She's normally sharper than this. "Obviously not. Everyone's expecting us to stay at the biggest suite imaginable. To follow the plan."

"Okay..."

A sudden possibility crosses my mind. *No. Freaking. Way.* Everyone knows what the date is supposed to be. *Vanessa* knew, and she wasn't even going to the damned auction. But the way Evie's reacting... "Ms. Parker, did you see what I proposed for the winner's date?"

"I didn't even know there *was* a 'proposed date.' I thought the bachelor and his winner would decide together."

"That's not how the auction worked. The bachelors came with a preplanned date for whoever won them. It was printed on the programs."

She thinks for a moment, then shrugs. "Sorry, but I didn't bother to check. I was running late."

I lean back in my seat. I hate to have to spring it on her like this, but I also can't wait to see how she'll react when she finds out. Is she going to be scandalized? Maybe even shocked enough to call me Nate again? I didn't miss the way she used my name after the auction, when she thought I was about to keel over from alcohol poisoning.

I force my expression into utter somberness. "Ms. Parker, the plan is to fly to Las Vegas on my private jet. And then we're going to have a drunken orgy."

She sputters, then starts coughing hard into her hand. I rise to pat her back, but she pushes the tablet out like a shield to fend me off.

Wheezing, she finally stands straight. Her face is red, and there are little beads of tears around her eyes. "We're going to *what*?"

So I've finally shaken her composure. "We're going to Vegas, on my jet."

"Yeah, yeah, the other part. A *drunken orgy*?" She shakes her head. "That's a terrible joke. It's not funny."

"It's not a joke." I ready myself to catch her in case she faints...or jump back fast if she decides to punish me by throwing up on my shoes.

She gives me a look sharp enough to cut, then swipes her tablet and taps away. Finally she finds whatever she's looking for and inhales sharply. "Oh my God. I can't believe you actually made that your plan! Why were people even bidding on you?"

"Because I'm really good at orgies?"

Her face turns red. Probably out of annoyance or a murderous rage, because she isn't laughing. I'm probably safe from murder, though. She needs me to pay her.

"I'm not going to be part of this idiocy," she says finally.

"But you won me," I point out, secretly amused and pleased that her main objection is to the orgy, not the rest of the date. Does this mean the invulnerable Ms. Parker is softening toward me?

"Only because you asked me to help! What was I thinking? And what were *you* thinking? A drunken orgy, when you can barely stand up after three drinks?"

It takes all my willpower to keep my mouth shut. It isn't her fault she thinks I'm a lightweight. I sort of misled her into thinking that when she first started working for me. I was trying to figure out how she really felt about me and pretended to be out of it with alcohol so she could openly share how she felt.

Unfortunately, she didn't. The woman's harder to crack than a bank vault.

"That's why you need to be there to keep an eye on me." I smile. "I'll double your bonus." There. I'm not entirely unreasonable. "And I'll give you overtime pay for the Vegas trip."

Her face is pinched. I see a very large *no* being placed into a catapult, ready to be hurled in my direction.

My ego twitches as her impending rejection prickles. Women love me. They spend money to be with me. But here's Evie, who's actually *pissed off* that she has to spend the weekend in my presence in Vegas! Which I'm going to pay for!

She inhales harshly. "Okay, I might be out of line here, but we shouldn't have to jump just because Barron said so."

"Yeah. But believe me, it's better to jump now than have him show up in person." The old man is much more difficult to reason with face to face. Especially when he sets his mind on something. He doesn't understand why everything he wants didn't fall into his lap yesterday. "Unless you want to tell him you're the reason we aren't going to Vegas like he asked us to?"

Are you fucking kidding me? is etched on her face. "But he probably doesn't know about the date plan. I mean, the details... Right?"

"I wouldn't bet on that. He probably knows everything." You don't become rich and powerful by lacking information.

She levels an accusing finger at me, her eyes narrow. "You did this on purpose."

"I didn't know that Georgette was—"

"There will be no orgy, drunken or otherwise."

"Okay." It's an easy point to give up. I don't even really want an orgy. I want the eminently adorable Ms. Evie Parker.

"And I want my own room."

"That won't do. It's supposed to be a date, remember? Who gets two rooms?" And why would I want her to have her own room anyway?

Her eyes go into slits. "You owe me *triple* the bonus!"

Ha, she's giving in. "Of course." She's selling herself short. She should've demanded ten times the bonus.

"Along with hazard pay."

I throw my head back and laugh. She kills me. "Sure. Just pack an overnight bag. Despite what you think, we're going to have fun tonight."

13

EVIE

"I don't know why Barron asked us to do it. Or why Nate feels like he has to do exactly what Barron said when we could just go out to dinner and be done with it," I complain loudly as I pack a bag for the overnight trip to Vegas.

Kim's voice is tinny on the phone speaker. She's still in the office. "Because it's Barron who asked. You do not say no to that man. Unless you want to end up worse than dead."

"What could be worse than dead?" I demand, my mouth going slightly dry.

"I don't know. But I kind of want to find out, so why don't you just ignore him and see what happens?" Kim's tone is half serious, half sarcastic.

"An *orgy*! Nate proposed a drunken *orgy*!" I wave my arms around in frustration and outrage even though Kim can't see me.

"Thankfully, Barron won't ask about that. Not even he wants to know about his grand-nephew's sex habits."

"Oh, stop. I'm going to throw up."

"You don't have to have sex, Evie. Although you could take one for the team if you feel up for it."

Yes, Evie. Take one for the team. All indications are that Nate can give you a great orgasm or twenty. Just look how the man's built.

Stop agreeing with Kim. "There'll be no sex, drunken or otherwise. And no more dating. This is the first, last and only time I'm doing this. Ever."

"Uh-huh. Look, I have a meeting, so I gotta go. Just relax and enjoy the trip. Nate is a gentleman boss with a bangin' body. Things could be worse."

Kim turns out to be right about that. It could be worse. And I realize that from every angle when I'm on Nate's jet.

Holy cow. I can see why Nate proposed flying on it to start the date off, even if he does plan to end it with an orgy. The thing is luxury defined. It has a bedroom with a real bed with a mattress —not chairs that morph into lie-flat "beds"—a shower with a dressing room and a lounge complete with a fully stocked bar. There's a library and a swanky office where you can work. There are vases with fresh flowers, secured for takeoff and landing.

The food isn't just edible, but amazing. For the short flight to Vegas, we're served champagne, pâté and caviar with freshly cut fruit, including some odd things I've never seen before called mangosteen. The white, juicy flesh inside the deep purple rind tastes like nothing like I've ever had. Nate casually mentions it costs about five bucks a bite, which promptly makes me choke.

When he just chuckles, I decide he must've been messing with me. Who the hell pays five dollars a bite, anyway? Mangosteens taste amazing, but not "five dollars a bite" amazing.

My unhelpful tongue disagrees.

Once the snack service is over, Nate goes over some reports on his laptop while tapping his temple the entire time. The cabin attendant tries to ply him with alcohol, but I stop her, since alcohol is supposed to hit you faster at high altitudes.

Since I don't have anything to do, not even a meeting to rearrange before the weekend, I fiddle with my phone, then read Kim's text again.

There's absolutely nothing to be done about it. If there were, I would've told you. It's only one night. Think about the 3x bonus, hazard pay, plus overtime. Besides, people like Nate travel in style. You'll be pampered and spoiled. Trust me.

It's true that the extra pay is something I can really use. People who say money doesn't buy you happiness have obviously never been poor. Or else they have a rich relative or friend to bail them out.

Mom already spent money she shouldn't have to because she knew I had to leave Dillington after the disaster with Chad. I can pay her back by being successful, and part of that is being financially secure.

The pilot announces we'll be landing in ten minutes. I breathe out hard. I'm not ready for Vegas, even if the drunken orgy *is* off the agenda.

Shoulda had the Brazilian, cuz you never knooow...

Shut up. Nothing's going to happen that will require ripping out all my hair down there.

Nate puts his laptop away.

"We shouldn't have cut the working day so short," I say. "We could've left at, like, midnight."

"But then there wouldn't have been enough time for the orgy, and the assholes would win their bet." He smiles his thanks at the cabin attendant as she takes away his empty glass.

The woman doesn't bat an eye, like discussing orgies is what people like Nate do on their jets all the time. I wouldn't know, since I've never ridden on one until now. Nate never asked me to travel with him, and I never volunteered, since traveling means hotels, and hotels mean...

It's best I don't let my mind wander too far. Besides, I have more urgent matters to consider.

"Can we not talk about *that*?" I hiss under my breath. "Besides, how many hours do you need to do one anyway?"

"Oh, at *least* twelve hours." His tone is grave—like we're on the topic of the annual budget for the Sterling Medical Center.

I put my hands over my ears. I don't even know why I'm trying. It's probably because even though he's obscenely rich, he acts like an everyday Joe from time to time. Fools me into thinking he's normal.

But he isn't. Not even close.

After this, I'm never going to get involved with his personal drama again. If a Georgette Number Two should happen to pop up, I'm definitely getting him somebody off Craigslist.

Focus on the triple bonus. Think about how your bank account is going to fatten up.

Yes. That's the only reason I'm doing this. For the security it represents.

A white limo is waiting on the tarmac as we touch down and deplane. It's flashier than I expected, but maybe that's what Nate likes in Vegas.

A smiling driver comes over and opens the door. "Mr. Sterling. Ms. Parker."

"Hello, Mario. Good to see you again. How's Amie?"

"A pleasure seeing you again as well, sir. She's doing great! Off to a magnet school this year."

"Good to hear. I'm sure she'll do well."

"Yeah, she's sharp. Like her mom."

I watch the exchange. Somehow it's surprising that Nate has had the same driver enough times to know about his kid. And that he knows and cares enough to remember the kid's name and ask after her.

Our overnight bags are delivered into the trunk as we climb inside. And the limo takes off. Mario drives as though he's transporting a fragile Ming vase. The engine is so quiet, the ride so smooth, it's almost like some kind of magic carpet.

Vegas is flashier than Los Angeles. Well, the Strip is, anyway. Lights are everywhere, and we drive past at least three Elvis impersonators walking down the street. And there's something I've never seen anywhere else: instant wedding chapels. One even has a sign that says, "Open 24/7." Do people really elope 24/7?

When we reach our hotel, Nate thanks the driver and tips him. My eyes widen. Did he just hand over a couple of hundred-dollar bills?

It's the same with the doorman, the bellhop and everyone else who does us a service. Nate greets all of them by name, asks about their families, then hands out money like candy on Halloween. Not crassly and overtly; sometimes it's a folded bill enclosed in a handshake. But always with a warm smile.

My mind whirls. I'm pretty sure I've been with him when

he's tipped in L.A., but I never really noticed because I always had my face buried in my tablet. I've seen him plenty of times before, but this is the first time I'm really *seeing* him.

By the time we reach our suite, my mental total on the money he's passed out is north of two thousand dollars. Even though math wasn't my best subject, I *can* add and subtract.

And as soon as we're alone, I whirl around to face him and point that out. "I understand you knowing everyone's name because you come here so much, but did you realize you were passing out hundred-dollar bills to everyone?"

He looks puzzled. "Of course."

"Why?" I ask, genuinely curious. Nate isn't the type to show off his wealth. I've been around him long enough to know he finds it distasteful. "You know that's a lot of money, don't you?"

"Well, Joe had his first baby last month, and Linda's kid just went off to college. And Bruno's son's started piano—the boy's talented..." Nate lists all the life happenings of the people he tipped. "They can use it. And it's not *that* much." He shrugs like it's really no big deal to him at all.

And knowing him, I have a feeling he's going to tip them again tomorrow. It never occurs to him not to care or be generous.

It's weird, but my earlier determination to do the bare minimum to get this farce of a date over and done with has kind of...evaporated. Nate really is the sort of man whose gorgeous face and body match what's inside his soul.

A soft feeling wells inside my heart. It's totally justified...but I can't afford it, not when it comes to my boss. So I forcibly turn my focus to something else. I let my eyes wander around the suite—taking note of the lively city on the other side of the windows, the elegant seating area, luxurious rugs and beautiful arrangements of fresh flowers. But they're not enough. I need something else to change the subject...and allow me to bury the emotions swelling inside me.

Finally I discover a leather-bound room service menu on a desk by the window. "I'm hungry," I say. "What do you want for dinner?"

"Can't eat here, remember?" He waves the menu away. "We have to go out. I made a reservation."

"You? But you should've said something," I say, slightly flustered. It's *my* job to take care of details like that. This isn't like our normal routine, and it's throwing me off.

"I couldn't let you do that for the date. Besides, it's actually the concierge who made the reservation."

I give him a sidelong glance. "You aren't going to pick up orgy buddies at the restaurant, are you?"

He laughs. "No. We just need to be seen."

A shudder goes through me. "'Seen'?"

"Yeah. People are saying that we aren't doing this for real, so we're going to show that we are. I even had a few paparazzi tipped off, just to be sure."

"There are going to be photographers?" My voice is slightly shrill. "Can we just skip that part? Barron didn't say we needed to be photographed or anything."

"Nope. Barron won't rest until everyone's satisfied the auction was real. But don't worry, the vultures won't be able to follow us in or anything. It's an exclusive steakhouse. They won't get past the door."

That's a minor relief, I guess. "But what about between the hotel and the restaurant?"

"We'll probably get some attention when we leave the hotel here, and definitely once we arrive at the steakhouse. But I go there every time I visit Vegas, so they're expecting me and they know what to do." Nate puts his hands on my shoulders. "Trust me, Ms. Parker. I won't let anything happen to you."

I look into his beautiful eyes even as my mouth goes dry, and my stomach churns. I really hate the attention, but like he said, nobody's going to be able to get inside to take photos or ask me ridiculous questions.

Besides, I trust Nate. If he says he won't let anything happen to me, nothing's going to happen to me.

I nod. "Okay."

14

Nate

I take a quick shower, then let Evie have the bathroom. There's still an hour until dinner, which will—hopefully—be enough time for her to get ready. I put on black slacks and pale blue dress shirt, then roll up the sleeves. I read somewhere that women find forearms sexy. I don't know why. They really aren't that special as far as male body parts go. Abs are much better—and a more logical choice. You have to work your ass off to get decent abs. Use them more during sex, too.

I put on a Rolex and study my forearms. They're looking extra defined, since I've been doing a lot of wrist curls and farmer walks. Tonight will be a good time to test them on Evie. Maybe they'll imbue her with such lust that she'll leap across the table and rip my clothes off.

Of all the fantasies I had starring Evie—and I've gotten pretty creative over the past few months—none of them had Barron making us go out. I wasn't going to press her about the date she won because I knew she wasn't going to get involved beyond helping me out with Georgette. Besides, I want her to go out with me because she *wants* to, not because of the auction.

What I still can't figure out is who the hell is behind all the asinine speculation and ugly gossip. I'm not the only one who hired somebody to bid on them. It's inevitable if you don't want to go out with any of the potential winners. Or if you don't want to bother with a date but want to help the cause anyway. The auctions aren't just about raising money, because straight donations would net just as much and be a lot easier. They generate publicity and awareness as well. They let the world know there are a lot of people who could use some assistance. Every time Elizabeth does an auction like this, charities see an increase in donations—mostly in money, but also in time.

But until now, nobody gave a damn. And certainly nobody badmouthed Elizabeth. My mind conjures up Georgette's furious face when she realized she lost, but not even she would go this far. Besides, she's probably back in rehab or whatever now. Her parents must've heard about the scene she made at the auction. And losing her bid to get me probably caused a relapse.

Regardless, when I find out who's been fucking with Elizabeth, I'm going to rip them a new one. Or two.

About five minutes before we have to leave, Evie comes out. My breath catches in my throat. She's gorgeous in a pale cream cocktail dress and a pair of nude pumps. The outfit is modest, but gives her an air of innocent allure, like a fresh bloom waiting to be discovered and admired. Her makeup is light and barely there. I love that she isn't hiding her beautiful face under layers of foundation and colors. But most of all, I thank the stars that she's let her hair down. It looks so soft and touchable that my fingers itch with the urge to tunnel through the golden mane.

She flushes. "Do I look okay?"

"Perfect," I say. "You look perfect, Ms. Parker."

"I'm glad. I wasn't sure." She looks down at herself. "I'm not very good at this sort of dress-up stuff. And don't want to embarrass you."

I don't tell her that she'd look beautiful no matter what she was wearing. I also don't tell her I'd make the restaurant let her in even if she were in a tattered potato sack, because I'm Nate Fucking Sterling and I won't let anybody make her feel bad. "You could never embarrass me, Ms. Parker. On the contrary, I'll be the envy of every man in the city."

The flush on her cheeks deepens. *God, why isn't this a real date?* If it were, I'd tease her, then kiss her. The hell with *being seen*; we'd spend all evening and the rest of the night right here in the suite.

But it's not, and she's already going above and beyond to bail me out. "I know you're nervous about the whole orgy thing, but I promise I'm not going to do anything you don't want," I say, offering her my arm. "We'll just have a nice dinner—you can order anything, not just what's listed on the menu—and then spend the rest of the evening doing whatever we both feel like doing."

She lays her hand in the crook of my arm. It feels warm and right through the thin fabric of my shirt. I wonder if she's noticing and admiring my forearms until I realize she's busy studying the rest of the suite.

Goddamn it. "Shall we get going?"

We walk out together.

"I've never been to Vegas," she whispers like she's confessing a grave crime.

"Well, we've rectified the 'never been' part. Ever gambled at a casino?"

"No. Never."

"We can rectify that, too, unless you don't want to?"

"I'd love to see one. But I don't know if I want to gamble." She wrinkles her small nose.

It's cute. And I can read her thoughts—the money. Evie is incredibly frugal. She brings a packed lunch every day, and never drinks those fancy concoctions from cafés around the office. I suspect everything she owns came from a clearance rack, and she drives a modest car.

"We can play a few hands." The casino is going to be disappointed, but they'll live. "You'll enjoy it. You know how to play blackjack?"

"Yeah… But nothing too high stakes."

"You'll change your mind when you start to win," I tease.

"The house always wins. Otherwise nobody would be operating casinos."

"Over time, yeah. But short term, who knows? Besides, it's an experience you should have, especially since it's your first time in Vegas. I'll front it. Part of the date package."

15

Evie

The restaurant is fantastic, totally fancy and expensive. I pretend not to see the prices on the menu so I can actually order something to eat. Nate is relaxed and, again, greets the maître d' by name while slipping him some money.

I watch him peruse the wine list, liking his semi-casual look. It still amazes me that the man can't pick out his own clothes, but wears them so well. He's rolled up his sleeves, exposing his arms almost to the elbows. They're muscular, defined and utterly hot. I watch them flex every time he turns a page on the list, picks up his water glass, adjusts his napkin. It's really too bad men don't know how sexy forearms are. Forearm and hand pics would get them so many more women than dick pics.

In my peripheral vision, through a huge bay window, I can see photographers lurking outside. A few took photos, but they weren't too obnoxious. Probably saving the obnoxiousness up for later. When I'm stupid and relaxed, they're going to pounce, I'm sure of it.

Shouldn't they be hanging out at that chapel across from our hotel? I'm sure some drunk and/or high celebrities are getting married there even now. That's gotta be more newsworthy than me and Nate eating dinner.

Regardless, I do my best to ignore them and enjoy the moment. I've never had a chance to eat with Nate one on one like this, even though I've been working for him for months. It's mainly my doing. I bring my own lunch, and Nate eats out. He asked if I wanted to have lunch together a few times, but stopped when I declined. I don't know what billionaires have for lunch, but I'm pretty sure it's something fancy, and I didn't want to impose.

Although it's a fake date, the company is fabulous. If Nate weren't my boss, I'd definitely be open to more with him.

Yeah, because a girl like you runs into billionaires like him all the time.

Okay, maybe not. But still...a girl can daydream, even though the kind of women he's usually seen with are the exact opposite of me—wealthy, extroverted, classy and model gorgeous. It's a pretty sure bet that none of them ever puked on a reporter's shoes.

While we're dining, Nate amuses me with stories about him and his family. And the horrible pranks he pulled in college.

"You never got into trouble for that?" I ask, laughing at one particularly clever practical joke he pulled on an "asshole stats professor." The nerve it took to shred everyone's midterm and turning the resulting confetti into a gummy-worm-filled piñata is... Wow.

"Nope. He could never prove it was me."

"But didn't he try to flunk you?" Some teachers can be petty.

"How? I aced every test." He winks.

"So if you're good at business and data analysis, why didn't you go into the main business at Sterling & Wilson? I mean, if I'm not being too presumptuous by asking."

Nate sips his wine and smiles. "Nah, it's fine. Somebody had to take over the charity part of the family fortune. Justin was chosen to lead Sterling & Wilson's for-profit side. He's great at that, and there isn't room for two top dogs. Big egos, you know?"

"You? Ego?" I ask, surprised. Not to say that he doesn't have a bit of healthy self-regard, but he could be utterly insufferable, given his background.

"We all have it. We just don't pound on our chests or anything because, you know, it hurts the ribs. The thing is, I enjoy my work, so there's no reason to try to run the for-profit side. I don't have to make any big decisions that affect meeting a profit target." He shudders like it's the most horrible thing that he could be doing. "The most complex thing I have to do is come up with a budget and make sure we're spending the money responsibly. Like I told Justin, all the benefits of the family fortune with none of the responsibility." The grin on his face is boyishly charming.

Except he's downplaying what he does. He might call it "none of the responsibility," but he takes his work seriously. And what he does is just as important as what his older brother does. I wonder if it's the laid-back attitude that makes him so compassionate and good, even if he doesn't like to advertise the fact. To him, the world is full of abundance, and there's no reason not to share the bounty with everyone.

After the final course of port and cheese—which taste like pure heaven—Nate charges the dinner to his credit card and tips the server with cash. I used to waitress when I was in Dillington, and I appreciate the gesture.

"Casino time!" he says with a grin as we head back. His eyes are lit with contagious excitement, and I laugh.

"Are you sure? It's my first time. I might suck," I say.

"No, no, no, wrong attitude. It's beginner's *luck*, not beginners suck."

I grin. "Okay. But only blackjack, and only a few games," I remind him.

"Whatever you want, Ms. Parker. Told you it's your night."

His carefree tone makes me feel ten times lighter. I can't remember the last time I felt this good and confident, even if the pesky paparazzi do jump out to snap a few more shots. It's just for one night, and I can grin and bear it, although the attention is probably going to give me hives.

It's for a good cause. After this, nobody will be able to call Elizabeth's auctions "fake."

And she does do a lot with the money raised. This one was for pediatric oncology, but her foundation routinely helps struggling single moms trying to raise kids, like my own mother used to.

The casino's overwhelming. My grip on Nate's arm tightens as I look around at the bright lights, the loud cries, the jangling slot machines and clapping at a few tables where somebody must've won big. Skimpily dressed waitresses walk around with trays laden with drinks, weaving like slippery fish.

A guy comes over and smiles at Nate. His teeth are straight and white, blinding against his smooth, dark skin. The light reflects off his hairless head, but the bald look works for him. "Mr. Sterling!"

"Hey, Tiny. What's up?"

I blink at the name. There's nothing tiny about the man. He doesn't even have a discernable neck. His black suit stretches over his giant muscles, and I'm afraid he's going to rip the seams if he flexes too hard.

"Haven't seen you in a while," Tiny says.

"Been busy."

"This your date for the evening?" He grins. "She's pretty."

I can feel myself flushing at the attention. *Do not hurl...*

"Yes. Evie Parker. This is Tiny Tim."

I extend a hand. Tiny Tim holds it as gingerly as he would hold a snowflake and shakes gently. I like him immediately.

They exchange a few jokes about gambling and probabilities that go way over my head. Then Nate takes me past several crowded tables to an empty one set up for two, plus the dealer. Nate gestures at me to take a seat, and I realize the casino has prepared this just for us. His chips are already stacked high. This must be how it is when you're a regular with deep pockets.

A waitress comes by for our drink order. "You already had three at dinner," I whisper to Nate, not wanting him to lose his head at the casino and do something he'll regret tomorrow.

"Yeah, but that glass of port was tiny." He holds out his thumb and index finger with a microscopic distance between the two. "One more won't hurt. I promise."

I mull that over. I only had one glass of wine and the port, so if I must, I think I can manage him. And there's always Tiny. "Well...okay. But just one."

"You're so strict."

"I still remember what happened." The most heart-fluttering

moment of my life— and the most awkward, because I knew all the sweet things he said were alcohol-induced. *So not doing that again. Ever.*

A wince passes over his face. "You're right. Champagne good?"

"I'll have a mimosa."

He orders our drinks and the waitress disappears. Nate tosses a few chips, and the dealer slides a card toward me, then another to Nate.

I check what I got. A ten of hearts. Not a bad start. I glance at Nate and the dealer. Poker faces. I lick my lips, nervous and excited at the same time.

The waitress hands us our drinks. I clink glasses with Nate while the dealer gives us our second cards.

"For luck," he says.

"For luck." I down the mimosa, which is amazingly refreshing. I feel a vague disappointment I won't be having more. But I know if I do, Nate's going to feel left out.

Besides, I didn't come to Vegas to drink. I came here to...

My vision blurs for a second. Whoa. Weird. I've never felt this woozy before. Maybe the mimosa's stronger than I thought— maybe more champagne than OJ? Don't casinos want you drunk so you get stupid with betting?

I lean against Nate. Damn, he feels so good—solid and warm. But I really need to get my crap together, because I'm betting good money here, even if it's not my own.

The last thing that crosses my mind is I really need to get the hell out of the casino before I do anything crazy.

16

NATE

OW, FUCK.

My head feels like a marching band on crack is banging away. Heavy on the drum section.

What the hell? Am I hung over? Really?

I don't remember drinking much. I think I had maybe...what? Three...four weak drinks? But I can easily knock back ten shots of tequila and stay sober.

I sit up in the dark. The room does a slow spin, and I put a hand on my head so it doesn't fall off. Then, carefully and with great effort, I take stock of my surroundings.

I'm in the hotel. The suite. My bare ass is touching the mattress. I'm missing my shirt, pants and shoes. My socks are still on, and my boxers are stuck at mid-thigh. What the fuck? I didn't even take off all my clothes before falling in bed? I push at my ridiculous boxers, then kick them off to the floor.

The gears grind s-l-o-w-l-y...

Where's Evie?

I turn my head gingerly, so my brain doesn't spill out my ears. I spot her on the bed, next to me and facedown. Is she dead? Oh, *shit*. My heart stops. Some people choke on their vomit and die, and I'm certain she can't drink like I can. I start to put a hand on her shoulder, but then notice her torso moving slowly up and down. *Okay, so she's not dead. That's good.*

A question pushes through the relentless throbbing in my head. What the hell happened? Evie and I are on bed together, and I'm more or less naked. And as for Evie...

Her dress is a mess. Her skirt is pushed up around her waist, and her underwear is missing. Or maybe she never wore any. That makes my dry mouth even drier, but I'm in no condition to do anything except pray I don't die. And I really have no business admiring the stunning curve of her ass when she probably doesn't mean for me to see it.

Although it is a really nice ass...

I gently tug the hem lower, covering her. There's no reason to add embarrassment to the raging hangover she's going to have. Then I roll her on her side, putting a pillow under her head. Shouldn't be able to choke now, even if she does vomit.

One of her shoes is still on, and I take it off and toss it on the side. That should make her more comfortable.

Moving carefully to avoid falling and breaking my neck, I lurch toward the bathroom. I need a shower. And lots and lots of aspirin.

Aspirin.

The minibar.

I change directions and stagger out to the main room. Ah, yes. A small bottle of aspirin. Oh, how I love thee. I could kiss the guy who invented aspirin, even though he's on the wrong team and likely long dead.

I down four pills, then leave the rest for Evie. The cold water from the fridge couldn't taste better.

That done, I teeter to the bathroom and turn on just the LED light on the magnifying mirror attached to the wall, so my eyeballs don't explode. I step into the shower and turn the knob. Hot water comes out instantly, thank God. I stand under the spray and pray to begin feeling half human. Or even a quarter human. I'm willing to go that low right now.

As more and more water sluices down, I start to think... *What the hell did I drink last night?* I don't remember anything after the champagne, which is weird as hell, because I normally don't black out like that. The last time I binged—well, I was trying to be a supportive friend to Court, who was depressed over being dumped, so that doesn't count.

And I can't imagine having much last night. Evie's fanatical about my "limit" and would never let me have more than three... maybe four if I give her a puppy-dog look. I'm ninety-nine-point-nine-nine percent certain she didn't leave my side at the casino. She knew the whole point was to be seen...

Ugh. Annoyed, I start washing myself. Evie's going to want the bathroom when she wakes up.

When I step out of the shower, dry myself and put a fresh towel around my waist, something flashes, reflecting the dim light from the mirror. Something on my left hand...

All the blood drains from my head. Or at least it feels that way.

Holy fucking mother of God! *What the hell is this?*

A golden band sits on my ring finger. Not just sits, *is shining*. I try to flick it off, like an unwanted spider, but it stays. Shit.

Where the hell did it come from? And how the fuck did it get on my finger?

And if I have this...

Oh, shit. Who the hell did I marry? Was Evie there too? Why didn't she stop me? It's her damn *job* to stop me from doing stupid shit! She's my assistant, isn't she?

I rush out fast. Well, as fast as I can without killing myself. Evie's still on the bed, her face on the pillow. I reach out to shake her until I see something glinting on *her* finger.

A golden band. Just like the one on my finger. I reel back, a giant, invisible ice pick spearing into my head.

No fucking way. Did I...? Did we...?

I shove my hands into my hair. I don't remember anything, but there's no way this wedding is valid. We didn't even consummate it. If we had, I would remember that *for sure*. I wouldn't have sex with a woman I've been lusting after for months and forget all about it the next day—what would be the point?

And I'm certain there weren't any proper witnesses. Who the

hell can find witnesses that fast? And even if you could find them, how would you know they were sober, legally binding witnesses?

I fish my phone from the bedside table. At least I had enough brain cells left not to lose it. I pull up a browser and start Googling: *Is a wedding legit without proper witnesses?*

Results pop up. They're all over the place, though. Some say yes, some say no, some say it depends.

Fuck you, Google. If I wanted a *yes—no—maybe*, I would've asked myself.

Who can I ask then? Not Ken. He's the family lawyer, and this would go straight into Barron's ear. Not Vanessa. She has no secrets from Justin, and I do *not* need my brother ragging on me.

Court! He probably knows. Or he can ask *his* lawyer.

I step out of the bedroom, close the door behind me and call.

"Hey, man," Court says. "How's the date?"

It's so like him to ask. Normally I'd be more social, but it's awkward to have to lie about it, so I try to keep it short without sounding too weird. "It's...good. Great. Nothing goes wrong in Vegas." I clear my throat. "Hey, listen, is a wedding ceremony valid without proper witnesses?"

A moment of silence is the answer. I hope he isn't wasting his time trying to Google.

"I don't know," he says. "Don't you have lawyers on retainer for that sort of question?"

"I'm not asking them." Does he not know who they really answer to? "Google didn't help, but I thought you might know."

"Uh... Nate? Are you okay?"

No! Would I be asking you this crazy question if I were okay? But I can't talk about it right now because I still have no freakin' clue what the hell happened. "Yeah, I told you that already. Hey, can you ask your lawyer?"

"I don't have a lawyer. Percy is Dad's lawyer."

It's like Court to get technical. On the other hand, he doesn't want to owe anything to his dad, so there's no way he's going to ask Percy. "All right. Never mind."

I hang up, my brain working overtime. Or at least trying to, because it's damn hard for a brain to function while floating in alcohol.

I have another bottle of water, then call down for two more pitchers, plus a thermos full of strong coffee and six dry pieces of toast. I need to fortify myself, get rid of this hangover and figure out just what the hell happened.

While I'm waiting for room service, I get a call from Justin. Probably checking up on me per Barron's orders. Sighing, I answer it.

"What's up?" I say with extra cheeriness. He doesn't need to know that Evie and I are wearing wedding bands. Or that I have partial amnesia about yesterday.

He doesn't waste time with a greeting. "Are you really married?"

I almost swallow my tongue. *Shit.* "What the hell kind of question is that?"

It would probably be good enough for someone else. But not my brother. "Oh, hell. What they're saying is true, then."

"Who is *they* and what are they saying?" Most importantly, what the fuck does he know in L.A. that I don't in Vegas?

"The tabloids. They're saying you eloped with your assistant."

I run a hand over my face, doing my best to kick the panic away. *Stall. Give yourself time to regroup.* "You read tabloids? Since when?"

"Ryder's PR people keep an eye on things and happened to notice, and they let him know. He called Vanessa."

Oh, shit. Ryder Reed is both Elizabeth's brother and Vanessa's cousin. *Just my fucking luck.* And if his people saw it, it means the article isn't on some obscure nobody-knows-about-this-site-dot-com. "Send me the link."

I hear some rustling in the background.

"Sent. Now... You didn't answer the question," Justin says.

How much should I say? On the other hand, what's the point of lying when he's going to find out everything soon enough anyway? "Why don't you ask Ken if a wedding is valid if I don't remember any of it?"

Justin swears. "How much did you drink?"

"Only three!"

"Bottles? At least tell me they were whiskeys."

"Three normal drinks. Four, if you really want to count a port, but the glass was *tiny*."

"Man... Bro." His tone is full of pity and something else I can't identify. "Three lousy drinks and you're married?"

"Hold on a sec." I need to see the damned article. I'm at a distinct disadvantage here. "Lemme check my mail."

Pinching the phone between my shoulder and ear, I dig through my suitcase and find my tablet. Email from Justin, email from Justin...

There.

I click on the link. It takes me to *The Hollywood News*, which has pictures of me and Evie at the restaurant. Going to the casino, laughing. So far, so good. The plan was to get those out there.

But then there's more. Shocking pictures of us going into the chapel across the street from the hotel. Then coming out. There are flowers in Evie's hair and a bouquet in my hand.

I stare, absolutely dumbfounded. No fucking way these are real. They've gotta be fake. Photoshopped. Mother*fuckers*. I'm going to sue their ass until there's no ass left, because this is an injustice! I'm a nice guy, but not *that* nice.

So who the hell put the ring on your finger, then? And on Evie's?

Shut up, logic.

"Barron doesn't read *The Hollywood News*, does he? It's not really his thing." He's more like the *Wall Street Journal* type. Or used to be, while he led Sterling & Wilson.

"He might. Stella likes celebrity gossip."

Crap. Why, Stella, why? Why can't you be a *New York Times*-reading lady who likes to lunch?

"You think Mom knows, too?" I say, a sinking feeling in my gut.

"Oh, yeah."

17

EVIE

My head feels like it's about to split in half. Or maybe it's already split in half, based on the pain radiating from my skull. My brain seems mushier than instant oatmeal.

But my bladder seems to be working perfectly, and is signaling that it's full and I'd better empty it unless I want to embarrass myself.

I get up—very slowly—and move toward the bathroom, praying my head doesn't explode or really, honest to God, split like a watermelon. All the while, I'm trying to think.

What the heck happened last night?

I was at the table, playing blackjack. And then...

...then...

...what?

Crap. Did I lose so much that I erased it from my mind?

But then how come my head feels so terrible? And why is my mouth so dry? And I'm sore all over, like I was brutalized by a treadmill.

I put my hand on the hem of my dress. At least I'm in the same one from last night, so that means I made it back okay. Nate probably helped.

Then I realize I'm missing *my underwear*. Sudden shock and dread knock in my chest. Where did it go?

But I need to take care of a most urgent bodily function before I can think about anything else. I make it to the toilet, manage to seat myself and then bury my face in my palms and groan as nature takes over. *What happened to my underwear?* Wait, I'm also barefoot. Did I take off my panties for some reason?

But *why?* And why in the world would I keep my bra on if I was trying to get comfortable last night?

I flush the toilet and wash my hands. Then...

Oh. My. *God!*

What is that thing on my finger? I bring it closer to my eyes just to make sure I'm not imagining it. Nope. It's a plain golden band. Like the ones you see at weddings.

The thing is, it isn't mine, even though it fits my finger perfectly.

Panic erupts. Did I marry somebody? Who? How? Where? What was I thinking?

Why didn't Nate try to stop me?

Actually, never mind. He can't hold his liquor at all. He probably passed out somewhere in the casino and wasn't even aware I vanished with some stranger to get married.

Moaning with intense self-loathing and recrimination, I cover my face with my hands, praying this is some nightmare. *Come on, wake up! Wake up!*

I slap my cheeks a few times. A couple of loud knocks at the door pull me out of my utter state of panic.

"Are you all right?"

Nate. He doesn't sound like he just came in from the casino. I open the door and see him standing in nothing but a towel. I take in the gorgeous lines of his broad shoulders, strong chest and defined, lean abs. There's a trail of hair that leads you down to... I'm not even going to look. I force my gaze up to his face.

This is so surreal. I feel like we're back in L.A., at his Malibu home. But it's definitely not Monday, and this is most definitely not his mansion.

"Where were you?" My voice is raspy from my throat being so parched.

"On a call with Justin in the living room. We just hung up." He hands me a glass of water and a bottle of aspirin. "Here."

"You went to the drugstore like that?"

"What?" His handsome face clouds with confusion. "No. It's from the minibar."

The pills probably cost ten dollars each, but I'm too desperate to care right now. I shove four into my mouth and chug down the water. A few drops trickle down my neck. I'm so hung over that I can't even drink without spilling. I run the back of my hand across my mouth and chin, like I've been sloppily swilling beer.

Keeping it classy. Yeah, that's me.

"What happened?" I ask, hoping against hope he remembers something.

"Not sure, but..." He scrutinizes my face, then a realization dawns on him. "You know."

"You mean *this*?" I lift my hand to show him the ring. "Yes. How could I miss it? It's a foreign invader parasite wrapped around my finger. Who did I marry and where is he?" I grab a fistful of hair in despair. "I need to get an annulment. Hopefully it can be done without a lawyer. I'd like to keep all my organs."

"Well." Nate clears his throat. "Uh...yeah. It's a bit complicated."

"How?" And why is he looking at me like...like he's torn between panic and mild gratification?

He holds up his left hand. *There's a ring just like mine on his finger.* Then he hands me his phone. I look at the screen. I've never, ever understood what people meant when they said they felt their heart drop to their feet. Now I do.

Because if the pictures are correct, Nate and I are now married through some ceremony I don't even remember! And if that's not bad enough, it's plastered all over the Internet. My face isn't even blurred in the photos. Everyone's going to recognize me when I walk down the streets.

"This is slander!" I shriek, tossing the phone back to Nate. I can't look at the lies anymore.

"Actually, it's libel. Because, you know, it's printed..."

"Argh! Do you think I care about that?"

He wisely says nothing.

"I don't want to be married to you, and you don't want to be married to me. We can just annul the whole thing. Nobody has to know, right? We'll deny everything!" I say, coming up with various ways out, since my boss isn't even trying. But that's okay. I'm not going to be resentful, because this is what he pays me for.

"Actually...it's not that simple."

"Why not?"

"My brother called me this morning..."

"So?"

"...about our marriage."

Oh no. Justin. Did he also call the rest of Nate's family? "You denied everything, didn't you?"

Nate clears his throat. "Well, that's the thing. I kinda didn't."

"Why not?" I ask shrilly.

"Uh. Hangover? Couldn't think fast enough."

I inhale and exhale slowly. *Okay. Okay. This isn't a total disaster.* I can fix it. There's gotta be a way.

But before I can come up with a solution, there's a knock at the door.

Nate sighs. "*Finally.* Damn room service. I need coffee, don't you?"

"*Yes,*" I say. Caffeine should help me think better and faster. Might help jog Nate's brain too.

I follow him, anticipating the coffee. Afterward, I'll shower and get myself more back on track.

But when Nate opens the door, it isn't room service. It's an elderly gentleman in an expensive-looking navy suit. Trim and stylish, he has wide shoulders set straight, his spine admirably vertical. Everything about him appears expensive except for the watch on his wrist. That looks...ordinary, something anybody could buy anywhere.

Something about his face feels familiar, but my caffeine-deprived brain can't seem to process what I'm seeing.

"Good morning, Nate." He walks inside, his steps measured and stately. "I don't believe we've met," he says to me, his tone surprisingly avuncular. "I'm Barron Sterling."

I feel like somebody just kicked me in the face, and my stomach shudders and churns like a broken washing machine in a spin cycle. My brain refuses to process for a moment, then finally starts working again. Oh, crap. Is this *the* Barron Sterling? He doesn't seem like the "prostrate before me, unworthy shits" type.

"Hi," I squeak. "I'm Evie Parker."

He gives me a mildly chiding look. "Tsk, my dear. You are Evie Parker no longer."

I'm not?

"Evie *Sterling* has such a lovely ring to it."

What? How does he know already? Nate didn't call him, did he?

"Congratulations on your nuptials." Barron pulls me into a tight embrace. "And *welcome* to the family."

18

Evie

For a man with his cutthroat reputation, Barron is a great hugger. If I could make myself forget that I'm being embraced by the head of the Sterling family and the fifth or sixth richest person in the world, I'd say it was even warm and sweet. And really welcoming.

But right now, all I can really focus on is the fact that I'm hung over, I haven't showered yet, and I'm *without my underwear*. My ass feels extra bare and exposed under the dress. It's a thousand times worse than going commando at the auction. At least then I wasn't trapped in Barron's unmovable arms.

Still, I have no choice but to return the hug and pray I don't smell like a dead skunk. Now I wish I'd at least brushed my teeth in the bathroom. Some first impression I must be making.

"You should've called," Nate says, his voice extra friendly and casual.

I realize Nate's still in his towel. I should've put out something for him to wear before Barron showed up.

Technically it isn't your fault because you didn't know Barron was coming.

True, but it's still my job, even if my head is so fuzzy and throbbing that two plus two is beyond me at the moment.

Barron finally pulls away and arches an eyebrow. Nate pastes on a smile, but it's so obviously fake that I feel bad for him. "I'm just saying we would've been more prepared. Or what if you missed us? We could've checked out."

"Ha!" Barron snorts. "Who gets up early and checks out the day after their wedding night?"

Wedding night? Oh, shit. The pit in my belly is turning into a sinkhole. Now if I could just disappear into it...

"I'll go ahead and order some Earl Grey tea and sugar cookies," Nate says.

Yes, *great* idea! Let's prolong the visit! On the other hand, there's no graceful way to kick Barron out. The glint in his eyes says he's staying. I smile the smallest smile I can get away with. It still hurts my cheeks. "Why don't you have a seat and enjoy your tea, while I go freshen up?"

"Of course," Barron says like it's the most natural thing in the world for him to just barge in on our "wedding" night/morning, and starts moving toward the seating area.

Nate turns on a lamp by the couch, and that's when I see my white thong on the seat of one of the armchairs.

Oh, shit!

It sort of blends in with the ivory upholstery, but I really don't want Barron noticing it. *And how did it end up there last night?* I don't remember that either. I doubt Nate and I had sex. We couldn't possibly, not when we were so out of it that we have no recollection of anything. Aligning the right body parts would've been beyond us.

You could've blown him, my unhelpful subconscious offers, sending electric shivers along my spine.

My throat would feel different, I argue with myself, half relieved and half sad nothing happened.

Doesn't your throat feel a little sore? The perverse shit is positively gleeful.

From drinking alcohol!

Regardless, I don't need the old man speculating about my and Nate's nonexistent sex life. And I need to stop internally debating the never-happened blowjob. *And he's getting closer to that chair!*

"Barron, would *you* like to freshen up?" I say, trying to sound as normal as possible. "The flight must've been long, and you know how planes are."

Barron gives me an odd look. "I don't know how Nate keeps his, but mine are clean."

Nate, too, gives me an odd look from behind his great-uncle, probably wondering what the hell I'm doing.

Desperate, I tilt my chin, then waggle my left eyebrow, hoping he gets the hint about the armchair. But he merely frowns in puzzlement, wriggles both his eyebrows wildly, then runs his index fingers over both and shrugs.

Telepathy fail. Shit.

Barron adds, "In any case, it wasn't that long of a trip. And I showered en route."

Of course his plane has a shower. Naturally. But he really shouldn't be moving toward the thong, like the *Titanic* gliding toward the uncrackable iceberg.

Yeah, except it isn't Barron who'll be sinking when he sees the underwear.

Come on, Evie. Think!

I smile harder. My cheeks are going to need Botox at this rate. "Would you like something to drink while we wait for room service?" I gesture at the minibar, hoping he'll go over to take a look at the options, so I can snatch my underwear from the seat.

"Thank you, dear. It's very sweet of you, but I'll be fine with just Earl Grey tea and some sugar cookies." He waves at me. "Go ahead and freshen up if you like. Don't mind an old man."

I think that's his polite way of saying, "Wash up, stinky!"

Before I can utter a word, he lowers his butt on *the thong seat*. I bite my lower lip. Is he going to feel it through the hideously expensive silk of his pants?

He sighs and leans back, his legs stretched out. Okay, maybe not.

Still... Is there some way I can make him move his butt and retrieve the underwear without him noticing? My foggy head can't come up with anything. Left with no choice, and praying he doesn't feel the thong now or later through his pants, I go to the bedroom. Nate joins me.

"What was that about?" he says quietly. "I thought you wanted to leave him alone so we could strategize."

"I was trying to *tell* you—" I abruptly swallow the rest. I'm not discussing the whereabouts of my underwear if he didn't get my silent message earlier. And I doubt Mr. I Can't Handle My Liquor can come up with a decent plan to retrieve the thong without alerting Barron.

"Tell me what?"

"Nothing." My thong is definitely off the agenda now. "You need to be dressed properly before we can face him."

I go through his things and pull out a dress shirt and a pair of coffee-colored slacks.

"Here you go. I need to shower." Then, eyeing the closed door, I lower my voice. Just in case. "And please make him leave!"

Nate shrugs helplessly. "I can't make him do anything. He does what he wants."

I was afraid of that. "Then don't let him get up."

"Why not?"

Closing my eyes, I quickly offer a prayer: *Dear God, if you wake me up now, I'll give you my left ovary and the small toe from my right foot.* I pour all my heart in it, squeezing my hands together as hard as I can.

Then I open my eyes again. *Crap.* God isn't listening. If there's broadband between us and the divine, it's more broken than my cable. "Just... Never mind. Let me shower in peace."

I slip into the bathroom, run the water and furiously brush my teeth and gargle with a small bottle of mouthwash provided by the hotel. Then I strip and hop into the stall for the fastest shower in history. I need to be out there to make sure Nate doesn't say anything to Barron that's going to get us deeper into this mess.

I put on a fresh white T-shirt and jeans. My hair's wet, but there's nothing I can do about that, since it takes forever to blow-dry, and I don't think Barron is the type to sit around patiently for that long.

Before going back out, I take a moment to inhale. *Calm down.*

Relax. You can do this. Barron is just here to say hello. Form a unified front with Nate. Tell Barron it was just a mistake. The end.

When I open the door, I see a huge room service tray with coffee, water, toast, tea and sugar cookies. Nate's munching on the toast and having coffee, while Barron's enjoying his cookies.

"...should've thought of your mother," Barron is saying. "She only has two children, and now both of you have eloped without any warning."

Because we were never planning to elope. Besides, we're going to annul the whole thing soon enough, and she'll get to attend her son's *real* wedding. So she shouldn't be that sad.

Tell him that, Nate!

But instead, my boss looks properly chastised. "You're right. I should've said something to her."

What?

"I know Blanche has been a bit impatient about babies, but she probably wanted to be part of the ceremony, even if it was a Vegas elopement."

"Of course." Nate nods like a dutiful nephew, then pours a cup of coffee and hands it to me, barely meeting my gaze.

Is he avoiding me?

Barron turns his attention toward me, his glittering, dark eyes pinning me like a lance. "Do you have any siblings, my dear?"

"No," I say, not ready to have this conversation with Barron. I quickly start drinking the coffee. The quicker the caffeine hits, the better I can handle Barron's questions.

"Then I feel for your poor mother as well." His tone is positively funereal. "You both need to buy her something extravagant and thoughtful to make up for this."

I choke, then spit the coffee all over my white shirt. Crap. Now Barron's going to think I'm a drunk and a klutz.

"Get your wife a napkin."

Wife. I start wheezing.

Nate does one better. He blots my chin and shirt with the napkin. Why, oh why is he trying to be extra solicitous *now*, when normally he doesn't even bother to pick out his own socks in the morning? I bet we look like a caring, loving couple. At least, it seems that way from the satisfied expression on Barron's face.

"Actually, it can't just be your mother," Barron says when I finally recover.

I brace myself, making sure nothing else is in my mouth. I'm not letting him ambush me twice.

"Your father missed a chance to give you away. Should make up for that too."

The mention of my dad deflates my mood. It would be nice to have him around at my *real* wedding—if Mom could ever find him. They broke up before she realized she was pregnant because he got a job in another state. She couldn't reach him because he didn't have any family, and it was before Facebook or Instagram. She always told me that my dad was a good man, and he would've done the right thing—if he had known about me—and loved me to pieces. I tried to find him myself, but it was impossible. There are just too many Bradley Browns in the world.

Nate looks chagrined, obviously sensing my mood. "Barron..." He shakes his head at his great-uncle.

For once, Barron no longer forges on like an unstoppable train. "I'm sorry. Did I touch on something sensitive?"

And that makes tears bead in the corners of my eyes. I sniffle. "No. It's just...my father's not around anymore. My parents lost contact with each other before I was born."

Nate squeezes my hand. The gesture is so unexpected that I almost flinch, then let him hold my hand, appreciating the contact and comfort. "It's okay. Really. I've gotten used to it."

"Nobody should have to get used to something like that." Barron purses his lips. "Regardless of how the actual ceremony went, I expect a small party to welcome Evie into the family. Justin should hold it. Say, two weeks from now at his home. He *is* the head of Sterling & Wilson now."

"Why not sooner?" Nate asks.

If we were alone, I'd smack him for that question.

"Unavoidable, I'm afraid," Barron says. "I'm going to be out of the country for a week. We can't have the party until I'm back."

Obviously.

"Do you want to tell Justin?"

"No, you should." Barron sighs. "You're right. It'd be better to do it tomorrow, but it'll take time to make travel arrangements for

Evie's mother. And I'm on my way to see Kerri and Ethan and my adorable great-grandson." His eyes soften until they're like melted chocolate.

"But they're in Virginia," Nate points out.

Barron shrugs. "Vegas isn't much of a detour." He stands. "I should get going."

Thank God he's finally leaving.

"I'll see you in two weeks," Barron adds.

"Yes, of course." Nate smiles.

And I do the same, because "No, you won't" isn't even an option when he's looking at us so expectantly. And with a hint that if we fail, we'll all die a horrible death.

Barron pats Nate's shoulders like he's single-handedly discovered a lost Shakespearean manuscript, kisses me on the cheek like we're real family and walks out.

I down the rest of my coffee. It's lukewarm, but I'm too wrung out to care. "We need to tell him the truth before the party."

"Actually, it makes more sense to play along," Nate says.

"*Play along?*" I blink a few times, wondering if he's still too drunk to think rationally. "As in...lie? And act like we're married for real?"

"Well...yeah."

The terror of school plays returns in dizzying vertigo. I hated —*hated*—being on stage, having to say the right things the right way even though they weren't at all what I *wanted* to say.

"He called you my bride and wife," Nate says thoughtfully.

Why is he talking like we're married for real? "We could tell him we changed our minds and got an annulment."

"Did you see how he was talking about Kerri's kid?"

"So? What does that have to do with us?"

His look says, *How can you be so slow?* "He's been hinting for a child...from me."

"But not from *me!*" I say, in case Nate has forgotten that I wasn't anywhere on Barron's radar until now. "He won't be too disappointed. And it isn't like he expects you to marry only once."

For some weird reason, talking about remarrying reminds me of my thong. I turn and go to the now-empty chair to grab it...

Except it's not there anymore.

"Where did it go?" I say shrilly as my heart freezes.

Nate jumps to his feet. "What? Is there a roach?"

"No! My thong! From yesterday. It was *right here*." I point at the cushion. "Barron was sitting on it."

Nate's jaw slackens. "You let my great-uncle sit on your underwear?"

Why does he have to say it like it's totally illicit and dirty? My cheeks flame. "Not *on purpose*! I tried to let you know, but you just waggled your eyebrows!"

"Oooh... Was that what...?" He points at the now empty seat, devoid of my underwear.

Wait a minute. I narrow my eyes. "Did you take it?"

"What, your thong? Me?" He actually puts a hand over his chest, all innocent. "Of course not."

"Then who took it? Not Barron." *Or did he?* Oh my God. Why the hell would he do that? He didn't seem like a perv. Then again, perverts don't have "I'm an uncaught sex offender" tattooed on their foreheads.

"You probably just imagined it out of panic," Nate says. "Even I thought I was seeing things when he showed up like that."

"I am *not* imagining—" But hold on. Maybe I am. I mean, you *do* see things when you freak out, right? I put my hand to my forehead, breathing hard. Then I look down at my finger. The gold band winks at me.

19

EVIE

I INSIST ON LEAVING VEGAS AS SOON AS POSSIBLE. WE accomplished more—a lot more—than we intended. Nobody's going to call Elizabeth's auctions fake or staged anymore. And I need to put some distance between myself and Nate, and pretend everything that supposedly happened after I got my ten of hearts didn't happen. I just can't think or talk about it and make it seem even more real when I'm still hung over from yesterday.

While I supervise our luggage being loaded into the waiting limo, Nate, in his usual fashion, stops in the lobby to say goodbye to Tiny Tim, probably giving him all the tips the man won't get because of our early departure. They chat for a few minutes and then shake hands.

I schedule an Uber pickup for when we get back to L.A., then pretend to be asleep the entire time we're flying to avoid talking to Nate. He doesn't try to talk to me, either. He may not be able to dress himself, but he's not entirely stupid.

When we land in L.A., I don't wait for Nate's fancy car service. The instant the aircraft door opens, I run straight to my Uber, taking my overnight bag. If there are paparazzi, they're being awfully discreet. They probably don't want to get kicked out. Or maybe—hopefully—they found something juicier to gossip about.

"Bye, Mr. Sterling. See you on Monday!" I say with a wave, and jump into the car before he can stop me.

I have four missed calls from Mom. I can't talk with her right now because I don't know what to say. Marrying my boss is already crazy enough. Staying married to him is inconceivable. I just need to think of a way to get out of everything gracefully and still not lose my job.

The second I walk into my apartment, Kim pounces. I feel like a mouse that just stuck its head out of a hole.

"Tell me everything!" she demands. "And you owe me ten million apologies for ignoring my texts! I texted you, like, nine *billion* times!"

"I know, I know!" I say, dumping my stuff on the floor because it's beyond me to care right now. "But I couldn't text you because I was hung over, and then there was Nate, and then Barron Sterling, and—"

"What?" Her eyes go wide at the mention of Barron. "Start from the beginning."

So I do, and tell her everything I can remember. Well, except for the mysterious vanishing thong, because I'm still not sure who took my damn underwear. I'm hoping that talking the events out will jiggle something new loose from my memory.

But nope. Nothing more comes to me. And now Kim knows everything she ever wanted to know about my time in Vegas.

"By the way, you can never tell anybody what I just told you," I say, needing to make sure every humiliating detail stays secret.

"Puh-*lease*. I'm your friend and my lips are sealed."

"Sorry. I'm just freaking out. I didn't expect things to get out of control so fast. Or for Barron to show up, acting like this whole wedding deal is real."

"That man does whatever he wants. He's worse than Salazar." Kim shakes her head.

I don't doubt that, especially having met him now. He's a human bulldozer. Once he's on a path, he goes. If something's in the way, he just runs it over.

"Anyway," I say, "I'm going to have to find a way to undo all this. Get a quiet, discreet annulment. This is the twenty-first century. I'm sure Barron expects Nate to have a string of wives. People get divorced all the time."

"Uh, you might want to rethink that." Kim says. "I'm sure he *doesn't* expect a string of wives. Barron Sterling is very traditional."

I put a hand on my belly. There's a vile, gnawing bug inside it, eating away at my stomach lining. This entire day has been a nightmare. Actually, this entire weekend.

"Didn't you say he wanted to have a party to welcome you to the family?" Kim asks.

"Uh-huh."

She grows serious. Like career-advice-giving moment serious, and the damn bug is gnawing faster. "Well, then...yeah. It's final."

Every cell in my body bristles. "That's positively *medieval*. He can't make me stay married to my boss."

"Then what are you going to tell him? 'Sorry, Mr. Sterling, but your grandnephew and I got so drunk, we got married without realizing what we were doing. And when you showed up, we were too hung over to tell you the truth. Hope you don't mind.'" Kim adds a fake smile and a cute little shrug.

"That's not helpful," I say, annoyed she is agreeing with the little voice in my head.

"What? The smile?" She sobers. "I was trying to imitate the kind of expression you'd be wearing, telling him all that. I call it the Doomed Yet Hopeful Fool."

Normally I'd laugh, but my head is still achy, and really, nothing about being married to Nate is funny. "Thanks. What would I do without you cheering me on?"

"Look, there are only three things for you to consider here."

"And they are?"

"One, is the marriage certificate legit?"

Oooh, good question. I didn't check, and I doubt Nate did either. We just assumed, like the tabloid writers. But you know what they say about "assuming." Immediately feeling better, I decide Kim can still be my friend.

"Two, did you have sex with Nate?"

What the hell? "You know the answer to that one."

"If you'd asked me yesterday, yeah, sure. But you married the man. Things are different now. It's a commonly accepted practice for a woman and her husband to fuck each other's brains out on their wedding night, especially when the woman's been lusting after the husband's hot, topless body for months."

I take it back. She can't be my friend anymore, not when she says stuff like—

"And three, did you use protection?"

My jaw hits the metaphorical floor so hard that I'm surprised it doesn't break. She knows I'm not on anything—no matter what I use, it messes me up—and I have no idea if Nate carries condoms around. His pants pockets are definitely empty when I hand them to him…but maybe in his wallet? Anyway, she knows I don't remember. And even if I did, it wouldn't matter, because *we didn't have sex.*

I would've definitely remembered it if I had it with someone I had dirty fantasies about for months.

"You're fired," I say.

An eyebrow goes up. "From what position?"

"Friend."

"Whatever. The day you start paying me is the day you can fire me. Besides, you'll want to keep me around when I tell you there's a very easy solution to all this."

"There is?" I lean forward eagerly. Kim always has an answer.

"Just go along with it for a few months. Then quietly divorce, citing irreconcilable differences. It happens. You two got married suddenly, plus you were drunk. So nobody's going to be surprised."

"Why can't we do that *right now?*" I cringe at how whiny I sound.

"Because you have to convince everyone you tried to make it work. If you divorce immediately, who's going to believe you? Most people expect you to know Nate's quirks because you've been working for him for almost a year. So a few months are necessary for you to convince the world there's a huge difference between dealing with Nate the boss and Nate the husband."

This is *not* what I want to hear. But I can't argue with her logic. Besides, I recall Barron's face from this morning. He'll probably accept the failure of Nate's and my marriage with grace if we fake some effort.

And there really doesn't seem to be any other way forward.

I clench my hands as grim determination courses through me. I can do this. It's only a few months.

My phone rings—a call from Mom. I've put her off long enough. She deserves an answer.

"Hi, Mom," I say, my voice warm. Even though I'm about to tell her something I'm too embarrassed about—*Hello, yeah, um, I don't quite remember getting married*—I don't want her to think I'm upset with her or don't appreciate her. She's the one constant person in my life—my rock, my best friend, my everything. She sacrificed everything for me, including her dream of becoming a nurse. Even though she never brings it up, I can never forget it. Or appreciate her enough.

"Evie, hon, what's going on?" she asks, the words tight and hurried. "Suzy told me you got *married!*"

"Well, uh, yeah. About that—"

"Apparently it's all over the news. Not that I really believe her, because she's such a nosy woman, but I just had to make sure. She said there were pictures, but you know how people can doctor those nowadays."

"Right." I wince. Mom hates it when her next-door neighbor is right. And I feel the same way, because Suzy was one of the most vocal gossips when the situation with Chadwick went south. "Well, it's sort of complicated." I swallow a huge ball of knotted nerves stuck in my throat. "My boss and I are, uh, married."

A loud gasp hits me harder than a punch. "But you never said! Never even *hinted*. It's such a big decision."

There's so much confusion and hurt in her tone. This must be how Catholics feel when they confess.

"It was, well, very sudden. And maybe a little too impulsive."

"I understand he's a billionaire. The nephew of *Barron Sterling*."

I clear my throat, embarrassed at hearing the concern in her voice. "He is. Grand-nephew."

"Oh my goodness. Evie, hon."

A lot of people might sound thrilled, even greedy, at learning their child married into a family like the Sterlings. Not Mom, though. She's just anxious for me.

"People like that aren't like us. And from what you've told me, he's nothing like you. You're too independent, too sensible for him. He's going to want somebody he can boss around so he can feel better about himself."

"Mom," I say, slightly uncomfortable with how she's denigrating Nate. He's really not an asshole...although, given his background, he probably should be.

She isn't finished. "A full-grown man who can't even pick out his own clothes? Who ever heard of such a thing? And can't make his own breakfast?"

"Well, he's an important man. His time is better off spent managing all the nonprofit hospitals and stuff his family funds." There. That should elevate her opinion of Nate.

"You mean his family gave him a job."

That sounds so full of judgment that I don't know what to say for a moment. But then I gather myself. "*He* gave *me* a job when there was nothing much on my résumé. He pays me better than most people with my kind of experience and education, and he's always treated me fairly."

Yes, especially the topless parade every morning.

"Well, I just don't want to see you hurt because of some slick city suit," she says. "You deserve better."

"Mom, try to be open-minded." But even as I say it, a bit of guilt pierces me. She had to help me the last time when things went bad. "I know the whole thing with Chad turned out badly, but I'm not as naïve as I used to be. I promise, I'll be careful. I'm not making the same mistake again."

20

NATE

NO MORE BACHELORHOOD.

I think about that as I step into my home and toss myself on a long couch, strategically positioned to face the waterfall. Which means my eyes land on the statue from Barron. From this angle, the statue couple is back to good old missionary. Not creative, but classic. You can see the woman's face as you drive into her, get to appreciate the moment when the orgasm breaks over her.

Wonder what Evie looks like when she comes. Flushed cheeks? Maybe a bit of sweat? But wait: does she sweat...or does she glow? And is she a screamer or a whimperer?

My cock says, *Let's find out!*

My brain says, *Stop having fantasies that aren't going anywhere soon. It's going to hurt your dick more than it hurts anybody else.*

It's unfair. I'm married to the woman I've been lusting after for months, but here I am sitting alone in my Malibu mansion. Actually, the hell with "unfair." It's like some Greek tragedy revenge of the gods. What have I done that was so wrong?

Maybe I should've insisted she do her wifely duty... Okay, maybe not. But at least come move in with me.

But from the way she ran, that would have made her quit on the spot.

The intercom buzzes, and a security alert pops up on my phone.

My heart beats a little faster, hope stirring. Maybe it's Evie coming back to say she was wrong to abandon me the way she did. Maybe she'll offer to have sex with me to make up for it. After all, there's nothing stopping us from indulging in our more carnal inclinations. We're *married*!

But no. My phone shows Court's familiar mug. What the hell is he doing here?

"Dude! Open up! I know you're in there!"

I consider pretending I'm not home, but change my mind. He's a persistent SOB, and when he sets his mind to do something, he does it. That's why he kidnapped his girlfriend's sister from her own wedding—he's just that focused on getting what he wants. The fact that he abducted the wrong girl didn't set him back much.

I hit the "open" button on my phone, then go back to being prone on the couch. Court isn't worth getting off my ass for.

Ten seconds later he's inside the house, and one second after that he's shouting, "Hey! You're really married?"

He's in a purple T-shirt that says, "I gave my heart to Skittles," and blue denim shorts. For a second I wonder why the hell he's professing undying love for a candy, until I remember that's the nickname he gave his girlfriend.

"What happened to your Southern gentleman manners?"

"Screw manners. Dude! Married? What the hell? I couldn't believe it when Yuna told me."

Of course she knows, I think with an inward sigh. The woman knows everything. "She's back in town?" I ask, trying to steer the topic away from my impossible-to-recall wedding.

"Will be tomorrow, because her mom's sending her back. Apparently Mrs. Min thinks Yuna needs to be around Ivy more so she starts to realize what she's missing in life."

Yuna's mother's life goal is to have Yuna married. And then pregnant. In that order, no variation allowed. Of course, it isn't easy to find a groom, because he has to be as wealthy as Yuna's family, which owns a giant conglomerate in Korea. Although Yuna has never specifically said as much, I'm fairly sure the groom also has to be tall, handsome and Korean. Gotta keep the family line pure.

"Tell her I can maybe hook her up," I say.

"How? Are you going to tell her to elope with the first billionaire bachelor she meets?" Court goes to the kitchen and helps himself to my wine. The bastard never brings me anything.

"You're welcome," I say pointedly, staring at the wine in his hand.

"Hey, you owe me for hiding shit from me all this time. I just got engaged to Skittles—"

"Whoa, seriously? Congratulations," I say, genuinely pleased for him, because he's crazy about the girl, and I think she makes him happy.

"—and here you are, already married! You never even hinted you had feelings for your assistant. You just said she was good at her job."

What the hell did he expect me to do? Recite a sonnet? "Because she *is* good at her job." Although there is a major downside: she always has to act so damn fucking professional around me, no matter what I try. It's almost embarrassing, really. "And unlike you, I don't go crazy with my affections. I'm a civilized person. So is she."

"Civilized, my ass." Court snorts, then parks that same ass in one of the chairs. "If you're so civilized..." He trails off as his gaze lands on the statue. "What the *hell* is that?" he says slowly.

"A gift from Barron."

"He sent you an X-rated statue for your wedding?" He runs a hand across his mouth. "Shit. That's like..." Squinting, he leans closer. "Can a woman really bend that way?"

"I don't know. All I see is missionary from over here."

"What?" He glances over at me, then understanding dawns. He gets up and walks around the statue, eyeing it from various angles. "Your great-uncle sent you a sex manual. What does he know about you that I don't?"

Gross. "Nothing. I'm quite experienced in bed, thank you. No woman's ever complained."

"How could they, when they were too busy fantasizing about becoming your wife?"

I should probably have a great comeback to this. Normally I'm capable of it. But right now, my head is still foggy from last night, and my focus slides back to the fact that the woman who really *is* my wife has never had sex with me. If we had, the suite would've been trashed. I have a list of things I want to do to her, and even a quarter of them would've absolutely ruined the room. Plus neither of us would be walking normally.

"Well, none of them *are* my wife," I say eventually. "And since I'm married now, they'll never get a chance to fantasize about it again."

"You know what? It's unjust that you didn't ask me to be your best man, even if you were eloping."

Yes. Let's focus on the most important point of my Vegas "wedding." "You don't need a best man for an elopement."

"Could've been a witness."

"Could have, but it was kind of spur of the moment. Besides, you were too busy with Skittles. Proposing to her, apparently. I am going to be *your* best man, right?"

"I don't know," he says with a touch of asperity. "Maybe I'll ask Edgar or Tony."

"Your brothers? Come on. Edgar's about as much fun as a wet towel. And Tony..." I try to come up with something, but it's hard because the man owns one of the hottest clubs in L.A. "Tony's already married and will probably be stodgy and boring by the time your wedding comes around."

Court scoffs. "You're so full of it. Anyway, are you going to introduce me to your wife or what?"

"Yeah, of course. But she's not here right now."

"Where'd she go?"

I sigh because there's no avoiding an answer. "Her apartment."

Court frowns. "She hasn't moved in with you?"

"Not yet." No real way to hide the fact that there's no trace of her living here. I should've tried to find the damned thong she was harping about in Vegas. Then I could've pretended like she was living here by leaving it draped on the edge of the kitchen counter. Or on the head of the statue dude. "I told you, we're civilized."

"That's *separated*, not civilized."

"Semantics." I close my eyes, hoping he gets the hint that I don't want to talk about it.

But Court is about as perceptive as a charging rhino. "Come on, man. This is weird. What really happened?"

That's the billion-dollar question, isn't it? Much to my endless frustration, I have no freakin' idea. Then I wonder if Court might be able to help me piece it together. His parents are pretty fucked up, especially his mom. So maybe he'll be better than me at thinking of ways things can go south.

I try to gather my thoughts and tell him what I can recall, winding up with my conversation with Tiny Tim as Evie and I were leaving the hotel. "You know him, right?"

"Sure. Big security guy, always smiling?"

"Yeah. He was done with his shift, and he asked me if I was all right."

Court leans forward. "So he saw something wrong?"

"He said Evie and I were looking pretty trashed the night before, so he made sure we stopped playing because he didn't want to take advantage. Then he said he had one of his guys keep an eye on us until we went to our suite. Apparently we actually went to the chapel across the street to get married. His guy witnessed the whole thing." I stick a hand into my hair. "The problem is, I don't remember anything. For all I know, I could've run down the street naked."

"I'm pretty sure you didn't. If you had, *that* would've made the front page of the all the tabloids." Court tilts his head. "What does Evie remember?"

"Nada. She's just as freaked out about it as me, and she's frustrated we can't just annul the whole thing."

"Why not?"

"Because of Barron." I'm frustrated too, but not for the same reason. It's more to do with the fact that I lost control and that the woman I want is my wife, but seems to have zero interest in having sex with me.

"That's weird about the memory loss. Evie being a lightweight, okay, fine. But you? After four lousy drinks?"

"I've been wondering about that too. There's no way I had more and forgot about it. Plus, Tiny said they cut us off when we started acting strange. It doesn't make any sense."

"You think your drinks were tainted?"

I laugh at the idea. "They'd never. The casino is aboveboard."

"Doesn't have to be them. Could be somebody else who wants to come at you."

"Then why drug Evie?" The possibility of somebody coming after me doesn't bother me too much, but them hurting Evie...

Court frowns. "Maybe they didn't know which drink was yours? Or maybe they needed to have her out of the way. If they wanted to kidnap you or drag you away, she wouldn't have let them, right?"

"Yeah, okay... But then why am I here, not kidnapped or dragged away?"

Court nods. "Yeah."

We sit and think about it for a few minutes. Finally, I say, "I need to look into it more closely."

"Not you. Me."

"You? Why?" I ask, surprised. He knows I'm capable of handling this myself.

"Whatever they were trying to do, they know they failed. Now they're probably expecting you, or maybe Justin or Barron, to make the next move, and they're likely ready for it. But me? They won't see me coming, and by the time they figure it out, it'll be too late."

That's a solid point, and I appreciate that he's going to do this for me when he's engaged and would much rather spend more time with his girl. "Thanks, buddy."

"Eh, I owe you one. Skittles told me about the phone call you made."

I nod slowly, although I have no clue what I said. I only remember calling her, shit-faced, after twenty-some shots.

"And you have to be my best man," he says.

I smile. "Wouldn't have it any other way."

21

NATE

"Cuckoo, cuckoo, cuckoo, cuckoo, cuckoo, cuckoo, cuckoo."

Exactly seven times. My body tightens with anticipation. Evie and I haven't spoken since she sprinted to her Uber, but it's okay. She's too professional to call in sick. She's going to be here in three, two, one...

And there it is. The sound of the security system alerting me to her arrival.

Very casually, I step out of the shower with nothing but a towel around my hips. This Monday is starting out like any other Monday, but it's going to end differently.

I've given a lot of thought to my and Evie's situation. And Court's right to call our living arrangement "separated." That won't do at all.

It isn't just that I've been lusting after her body and still get blue balls thinking about her. If we try to annul the marriage now —or if certain members of my family notice something's off— they're going to think that maybe the reason I don't want to keep her is that she took advantage of me in Vegas. Barron isn't the only one who worries about gold diggers coming after me. And no one in my family forgives easily.

The thing is, I don't want Evie hurt. What I want is her, in my bed, and distinctly *un*hurt. More like orgasmic and glowing. Then... Then we'll take it day by day. No need to get too serious, trying to plan every moment of our future. Because laying it all out like that simply isn't me. Justin's the one who's had his life completely planned since he was four.

Then what? Keep her? Because she sure doesn't seem to want to be kept by you.

My mood sours.

Divorce her and give her some consolation money?

Of course not. I bristle at the rude voice in my head. I've never treated my previous girlfriends badly, and I'm not planning to just because Evie is no mere girlfriend, but my wife. I'm not one of those worthless asshole playboys with too much money. My parents taught me better, and beyond that, I grew up watching my dad. Real men have manners, protect and help people who are weak and vulnerable and stand up to bullies and assholes. *Especially* if they have money.

And I intend to be a real man, just the way my dad showed me.

Evie comes into my bedroom wearing a fitted pink dress that molds to her trim, curvy body. Her breasts look extra enticing today. I wonder for a moment if she pinches one of her nipples when she fingers herself. Or maybe she's a grabber. Some women like to have the whole boob in their hand when they...

My cock perks up, letting me know that it, too, is amenable to being grabbed. Just as long as it's Evie's hand doing the grabbing.

Stay the fuck down. It's not time yet.

It's been almost twenty-four hours. She must've come to a decision—accepted our situation. People always adapt to new circumstances, and Evie is a smart woman.

And that acceptance means she'll acknowledge that we're married. Husband and wife. No more "Mr. Sterling" or "Ms. Parker." No more living apart.

And to confirm my thoughts, I glance at her ring finger. The gold band is still there. Ha! I knew it! I clench my hand, feeling victorious as my own gold band shines.

She smiles. "Good morning—"

Anticipation vibrates through me as I wait to hear my name on her luscious lips.

"—Mr. Sterling."

What did she just say?

"You have a teleconference with the head of the Kerri Wilson Lloyd Women's Health Center in Chicago," she says. "Then you have a meeting with the auditors who just came back from San Francisco. So for today, I think maybe something powerful and conservative." She walks into my closet.

Out of habit, my gaze drops to her hot, perfectly shaped ass. But that doesn't mean I've forgotten about the outrage of her still calling me Mr. Sterling. We shared a bed—albeit drunk and passed out. She should know I don't have a giant stick up my butt by now.

As though she sensed my baleful glare, she turns to me. "Is there something else, Mr. Sterling?"

Listen to her. *Mr. Sterling.* "My name is Nate."

"I'm aware of that, Mr. Sterling. After all, I've been working for you for over ten months." She gives me a sweet smile, the kind you might reserve for a curious and needy child.

My blood pressure skyrockets. I want to shake her, but that's really not the way to start off a marriage.

She lays out my outfit for the day. "I'll be downstairs preparing your breakfast." She turns around smartly and leaves.

The bedroom feels as barren and desolate as a Mongolian desert. Why is she doing this? Just to be perverse? Trying to needle me?

Fine. If she doesn't want to change the way she addresses me, I'll change the way I address her. Problem solved.

My mind made up, I put on the dress shirt and slacks she selected. They're both gray, although the shirt is so pale that it's almost white. I knot the burgundy tie into a prefect half-Windsor, put on my jacket and head to the living room.

She's already finished prepping my cup full of palate-despoiling green hell-slime. I take it from her, making sure our fingers brush. Simultaneously, I hear a small sharp intake of breath over the gurgling of the coffeemaker.

Yes!

If I were alone, I'd do a cabbage patch dance. *She's not immune.* Not anymore. It's like being married—even if we don't remember the actual ceremony—is making her less impervious to me. I can work with this.

I down the vile shit that tastes like cow fart, while maintaining a stoic expression. She watches me chug it down.

When the last drop of the green goo has slithered down and hit my belly, I can feel my system give a shudder of relief. I hand the empty glass back to Evie. "Thank you, Mrs. Sterling."

She sputters, almost dropping the glass. "*What* did you just call me?"

I pat her back, full of husbandly solicitousness. "Mrs. Sterling." Innocent. Matter of fact.

She pushes my hand away, the gesture gentle but firm. "That *isn't* my name."

Inwardly, I gird my loins, but outwardly, I give her a placid smile. "Normally when a woman marries, she takes her husband's name. Unless you want to hyphenate? Parker-Sterling, perhaps?" Her jaw drops open. I put a finger under her chin and close it for her. "I mean, it's a bit of a mouthful, but I guess we can manage."

Finally she recovers. "That is completely unnecessary. I'm happy with just Parker."

"So, Nate Parker? Hmm... Not bad, but it might cause some extra paperwork." I take the keys and start toward the garage, since Miguel's still on paternity leave.

"That's not what I meant, and you know it!" she says, her feet slapping the floor as she comes after me.

"Actually, I don't."

I select the Bugatti because it's a Bugatti kind of day. I open the door for her, and she climbs in, looking daggers at me. We've agreed to share my car while Miguel's on leave, for the good of the planet. Must reduce our carbon footprint. It doesn't hurt that she smells awesome, either.

By the time I'm settled behind the steering wheel, she has her tablet out like a weapon. She waits until we're on the road before she begins.

"I've given this a lot of thought."

"Good. I'm all ears." Undoubtedly she took notes on the tablet. That's her habit. I'm curious how she envisions our future as a married couple.

"I understand that Barron's traditional and all, but that doesn't mean we have to play into his fantasy of how things are. I also understand you don't want to upset him. And honestly, neither do I. So we'll pretend to be married for eight—actually, let's say six—weeks, then quietly divorce."

"Really? What's going to be the cause?" I ask, amused that this is what she considers the best solution.

"Irreconcilable differences. You know."

It's hard not to laugh when she's being so earnest. She's incredibly cute. Still, I make thoughtful noises. "Child support? Alimony? And what percentage of my money do you plan to take with you?"

The sound she makes is halfway between outrage and shock. "*Mister* Sterling. I would *never*. There won't be any children. And it's only for six weeks. Of course I don't expect alimony or anything like that. I just want to be able to continue to work as your assistant."

What the hell? Does she really think we can go back to being boss/assistant after a hypothetical divorce? I'm not sure if that's possible. It would be awkward...wouldn't it? "But why? *Irreconcilable differences* makes it sound like I'm an asshole boss-slash-husband you can't possibly tolerate."

Her gaze is fixed on the tablet. "There's a huge difference between a boss I can tolerate and a husband I can tolerate," she says, sounding like she's reading her notes.

I frown. Why does that feel like a small needle going into my belly?

"And you plan to live where during the six weeks?" I ask—the most important question, the one I've been dying to get an answer to. There's only one logical place, and I'm hoping she'll see it without me having to point it out.

"I don't understand. I'm not planning on moving. The lease

on the apartment isn't up until next year."

I cough, unable to decide if she's being purposely obtuse or just this clueless. "People are going to wonder if we don't even live together."

"I can drive to your place, then you can drive me to work, then back to your place, and I can drive home. Very simple. No one will know."

"Ha. The paparazzi will. They'll follow you around."

"Really?" She makes a big production out of looking around, craning her back behind us. "Because I don't see any."

"Because they haven't gotten mobilized yet. But they will, especially once it gets out that Barron's throwing us a party."

"Damn it. I should've known the Vegas thing was trouble." Her chin firms. "You know what? It doesn't matter if they try to say that we live separately. I can just explain I was visiting my friend."

Oh, man. Evie can't lie for shit. How does she plan to fake living together, fake being married and fake everything else? "Every day after work? And on weekends?"

"Kim and I are very, you know, close. It happens."

"And I become jealous of your *close* relationship with Kim, and you end up divorcing me," I say, writing the scenario for her.

Her expression brightens. "I hadn't thought of that, but sure! Exactly!"

Doing my best to suppress a smile, I put on a grave expression. "But that means there are going to be speculations about your and Kim's relationship."

"So? Even if they dig, all they're going to find as that we're just friends and roommates...or ex-roommates."

"Yeah, but think about it. You're spending more time with her than with your new husband. What does that tell you?" I don't bother to wait for her to come up with the inevitable conclusion everyone's going to reach. "You and Kim are lesbians. Or at least you, Evie Parker, are bi and doing both of us." I put on a sad expression, the kind a cuckolded husband might, and place a hand over my chest. "How could you cheat on me like that?"

Evie puts both palms over her face with a loud groan.

I finally let myself smile. Every obstacle can be overcome with patience and finesse. It's only a matter of time before Evie sees the light.

22

Nate

Once we're at the office, I don't let anything distract me. And the same goes for Evie. She understands as well as I do how important our work is.

The meeting with the Chicago head goes swimmingly. The women's health center is a critical component of what we do. Every woman who shows up is treated, no questions asked. It isn't our place to judge or probe. If they bring their kids, the kids are also given care. We have a pediatrics department specifically for that, and we do a lot of work with shelters, through a partnership with the Pryce Family Foundation. The most vulnerable people in our society are always the ones least able to take care of themselves. It's our mission to ensure that they're okay.

When I have a thirty-minute break from meetings, I lean back in my seat and stretch my arms. The issues in Houston were regrettable, but I think my solutions scared the shit out of the remaining medical centers. So many wealthy families aren't on top of their nonprofits the way they are with the income-generating portion of their business. But nobody in my family is the type to let anything slide.

The door to my office opens, and Justin walks in.

"Took you long enough," I say. "I half expected you to barge into my place yesterday." Good thing he didn't, though, because I don't think I could've handled another interrogation, especially when I was still hung over.

He sits down without waiting for an invitation. "Ryan was acting up, and I didn't want to leave Vanessa alone to deal with him. She's expecting a detailed update when I get home tonight, though."

"Yes, well, hey, take a seat and make yourself comfortable. It isn't like I have anything to do."

"I already checked with Evie. You have a little downtime."

I give him a resentful look. It's wrong how easily he says her name.

You could do the same. What's stopping you?

Because she isn't calling me Nate like she should. For some bizarre reason, it's a point of pride. Besides, her reaction to being called Mrs. Sterling was amusing enough to soothe my ego for the moment.

"So. You two are really married?"

I nod. "Looks that way."

"Then why is she here?"

What is this? *The Justin Is an Idiot* show? "Because she's my assistant?"

"Well, now she's your wife."

"She wants to work," I say, remembering what she said about wanting to keep working, even after the "divorce."

"But as your assistant?"

"Hilary works as an assistant," I say, referring to one of his brothers-in-law's wives.

"Yeah, but not for her husband."

I wave the inconsequential detail away. "Because she *never* worked for him. But Evie's been with me for almost a year now, and she's fantastic. Why should we have to change anything at work just because our private relationship has changed?"

Justin's eyes narrow, which is not a good sign. He didn't take over Sterling & Wilson by being stupid. If he hadn't measured up, Barron would've tossed him out like trash and taken me under his wing. The notion makes me shudder. Justin's shoes are not ones I ever want to fill.

"You said you don't remember anything, but that isn't true, is it?" He regards me over steepled fingers. "Tell me everything. No bullshit."

"I'm not. It's the truth." And I do tell him everything. There's no point in trying to hide anything anyway. If he thinks I'm holding back, he'll get the family's PI involved. And that would be bad, because Pattington always manages to find embarrassing details.

"It's a setup," Justin says after I've finished, his gaze flicking toward the door.

"What the fuck? You don't suspect Evie, do you?" I ask, slightly stunned.

"I trust no one. And you have a history of dating crazy, hot chicks."

I shrug, since I can't argue. Even if I wanted to, he has Georgette to fling in my face, and I couldn't block that with Captain America's shield.

"You're so careless at times," Justin continues. "Try to remember how much you're worth."

"I'm more than my balance sheet," I say, even though I know it's something that'll always follow me around.

Justin's expression softens a bit. "I know, but does the world know? They don't look at us and see people. They look and see money. Or greedy fuckers who have too much. Entitled assholes who don't deserve any of what we have."

What he's saying isn't wrong. But that doesn't mean I'm okay with it. He doesn't know Evie, so how can he brush her with a broad stroke like she's the same as everyone else in the world? "Evie isn't like that."

"Who stands to benefit?"

"Still. Evie isn't like that."

He gives me a long look. "I just want you to be careful."

"I am. And Court is looking into the whole thing for me."

"Court?" He looks vaguely annoyed. Probably his ego is bruised I didn't ask him.

"Yeah. Because if you're right, and it is a setup, whoever did it will be expecting me or you to come after them."

Justin thinks for a moment and then nods. "Okay. That makes sense. And I know he's actually pretty competent, even if he did steal the wrong girl at that wedding." He shakes his head. "But listen. You tell him to call me if he needs anything. I'll provide whatever's necessary to get to the bottom of this."

I nod, mildly mollified.

"And we have that party next Saturday at four thirty to welcome Evie into the family."

"Yeah, I know. Miles texted everyone. But why so early?"

"Kids. They can't stay up too late. It's going to be small—or I'm going to try to keep it that way to avoid overwhelming Evie. But Barron might invite some extra people. Make sure to show up on time. You know how Barron is."

All this talk about the family makes me realize that our mother has been awfully quiet... I didn't realize how quiet until just now. "Hey...is Mom okay?" She lives alone. She doesn't have anybody around to check on her, make sure she's taken care of, the way Dad used to.

"Of course." Justin's eyebrows pull together. "Why wouldn't she be?"

"She didn't call or text me. Not even once." And that isn't like her. I pull out my personal phone and check. Not even an email.

"Oh, that." He smiles. "She's on her way to Los Angeles. She wants to see you and Evie in person and hear all about your secret romance. Act surprised, though, because she wants to surprise you."

"She's already on the plane?"

He nods. "Should be." He checks his phone. "It took off an hour ago."

Oh, lord. Evie and I need to sit down and get our stories one hundred percent straight, because my mother is overprotective of me and is going to probe and wonder and question. No detail is too small for Blanche Sterling to overlook. "And where is she staying?"

"With us. She doesn't want to bother the newlyweds."

An idea strikes—a solution to one of my immediate problems.

Trying not to grin, I say, "Tell her I'd love to host her at my place. Actually, I insist."

"Are you sure?" Justin asks, raising both eyebrows.

"Yeah, there's plenty of room. And no reason to have Ryan running her ragged. Especially if she's coming out to hear about me and Evie."

He shrugs. "Okay, if you're cool with it. Just so you know, though, she *is* expecting to have dinner at your place tonight."

"That's not a problem," I say airily.

"Try to have it catered, so it doesn't look like your usual Chinese takeout disaster," he says dryly.

23

EVIE

THE MOMENT JUSTIN LEAVES, NATE ASKS ME INTO HIS office. I go in, my tablet ready.

"Yes, Mr. Sterling?" I ask, in an extra-prim voice I don't care for and would normally never use. It's just that I feel like I have to in order to ensure we maintain a proper professional distance.

"My mother's coming to Los Angeles. Right now."

"She's *what?*" I thought I wouldn't have to meet anybody from his family until later, at the party Barron was talking about. I was planning on figuring out a way to gracefully get out of it somehow. Maybe smearing my face with radioactively glowing biohazard material the day before.

"She's expecting dinner tonight. So call a caterer, and tell them to make it something fancy. Maybe rack of lamb or something."

Oh, no, no, no, no, no. I'm not ready to meet Nate's mom. Not even a little. And dinner? At home?

"Is she going to stay with you, too?" I ask, my voice thick with panic. I can't act like we're living together when we're not if she's actually going to be there.

"Yes."

No, no, no! "Did you tell her we'd like to have some time to ourselves? That's what newly married couples do."

"She hasn't seen me in a long time, and I think she wants to make sure I'm okay."

"You're *okay*?" *What does the woman think I'm going to do to him?*

"I have a history of dating women who are a little, uh, unstable." Nate scratches his chin.

Oh. My. God. I guess his mother must know about Georgette. But really, does she have to stay with us? Doesn't she know most new wives don't want to share a roof with their mothers-in-law?

Before I can vocalize my objections, Nate adds, "You should hire some movers and get your things over to the house. At least your clothes and daily stuff."

"Right now?" I run a hand over my hair. Can we hire movers so fast? But I don't have that much stuff. Most of the furniture is Kim's, and my bed would look out of place in his Malibu mansion. "What about Kim? I can't abandon her. She's my roommate."

"I'm not saying you should abandon your roommate. But do you want my mom to walk into my place with none of your things around? She's going to wonder, and believe me, she doesn't miss much."

Of course not. A woman doesn't marry into this family and raise two boys by missing things.

"I'm not sleeping with you," I blurt out. "She won't be spending her time in the...master bedroom."

Nate closes his eyes briefly. "No, I don't think she will. But sex is something we need to discuss."

My face flames. I'm so not ready to discuss this out loud—in his office, of all places—when I can barely wrap my head around the fact that we're married! "We already did."

He raises both eyebrows like he can't recall this discussion actually happening.

"In the car. On the way to work," I remind him. "Obviously I'm not going to do it with you if we're going to be finished with each other in six weeks."

"Even if we are only going to be married for six weeks, you can't possibly expect me to go without for that long."

Oh, please. Of all the... But then I remember the statue in his living room. In the pose I saw—the sausage one—the guy's face is twisted, as though he's in some intense agony. Well, I guess having it turgid for too long *would* be uncomfortable, but...

"Can't you just...um"—I swallow, debating how to say it without feeling awkward and embarrassed—"...self-serve?"

"Self-serve? What am I? A gas station?"

"You know what I mean." I curl my fingers and move my hand up and down, just enough for him to get the hint. "Like, in the shower or something?"

"You want me to cheat on you with Rosie Palm and her five friends?"

I nod, my face heating. He's making it sound like holding his hard cock in the shower in his own hand is the ultimate dirty act. And instead of being mildly offended, the mental image is making me want to squirm. I suddenly realize my nipples are hard and aching. *God, I'm a mess.* An emotional and sexual *mess*.

"For six in*ter*minable weeks?" he says.

I clear my throat. "I won't hold it against you. Besides, it isn't really six weeks, because even if we were married for real, we couldn't do it every single week anyway."

He looks puzzled. "Why not?"

I give him a withering look. "Think about it." I am *not* discussing my monthly cycle with my boss. Aunt Flo is coming in less than two weeks, and she always stays for a week.

"I don't know about sticking with Rosie for that long. She's a one-trick palm."

"You do actually have *two* hands..."

He shakes his head. "Same thing."

Hmm... I guess doing the same thing for six weeks can be tedious. The most logical solution would be to tell him to do it with other women. It's not like we're really married, but somehow, my tongue refuses to form the words. There's a huge, burning knot in my throat, like it would cause me physical damage to suggest he should just...seek some variety with someone else.

So I just say, "Well, I'm sure you can survive that long. After all, you've been drinking the same kale shake for nine months."

Guilt pricks at me. I haven't been cruel enough to make the *exact* same shake every morning. I vary it by adding broccoli one day, spinach another and artichoke hearts the next, and cycle them throughout.

"I see," he says finally. Is it my imagination, or does he sound slightly disappointed that I haven't done better with his shakes?

He opens his mouth, but I don't want to talk about sex or veggie shakes anymore. "Look, I'm going to go and grab a few things from my place. And I'll make something for dinner."

He looks mildly surprised. "You don't have to. We can cater."

"I know, but it's your mother's first meal with her 'daughter-in-law.' There's no way I can cater. Or do takeout." I certainly wouldn't do that to my own mom.

"But like you said, we aren't even married for real."

"Yeah, but she's your mother. She deserves that much. So what time is she going to be there?"

24

EVIE

I DRIVE TO MY PLACE FIRST TO PACK ENOUGH THINGS TO look like Nate and I live together. It isn't a lot—just toiletries, underwear, pajamas, a few T-shirts and shorts. Some work clothes. *Oh, and shoes.* I put everything into my two suitcases.

I've got Kim on speakerphone the entire time. Partly because I need somebody to talk to and partly because I need my friend's distraction and support.

"Wow. His mom. That's serious. Blanche Sterling is really reclusive, from what I've heard. Doesn't travel much, just stays out in her house somewhere in Ohio. Her husband died a while back. Anyway, it's a big deal she's coming out to L.A. to see you. She didn't do that for Vanessa."

Shit. Does this mean I should change into something better? Maybe my black cocktail dress? I've never met Nate's mom, but if she's anything like Kim's boss's wife, she's going to be expensive and fashionable, with hair the same color as when she was in her twenties. And she'll be in designer stilettos and a beautiful haute couture dress.

"By the way, do I need a new roommate?" Kim asks. "Not that I want to get rid of you or anything, but I don't feel right asking you to pay for your portion if you aren't even living with me, you know?"

"I don't mind. It's only for a month and a half. And I'll need a place to stay once the divorce proceedings start."

"Okay."

"Now, tell me more about Nate's mother. Do you know what she likes to eat?" *Please say it's something I know how to make.* If not, I'll have to look up a recipe online and hope for the best.

"No, but make her something you'd make for your own mom. I would, anyway. Shows how you really are, you know?"

Right! That's great advice. It's bad enough Nate and I are lying to Blanche already. And who doesn't like a good roasted chicken? "Thanks, that's a perfect idea. Okay, gotta go. I need to pick some stuff up from the store."

"Good luck!"

Feeling like I'm on a reality cooking show, I rush through the grocery store and grab a whole free-range chicken, a few herbs, a locally grown lemon, a bag of rice, butter, bacon, whole-wheat bread, a pre-made pie crust and two pounds of peaches—all of them organic, fresh, locally sourced and hideously expensive. I can hear my bank account screaming as I swipe my credit card at the cash register.

It doesn't matter, I tell myself. I need to prep the right kind of food for Nate's mom. We aren't married for real, but she deserves a good effort from the woman who's supposed to be her son's new wife.

I drive to his place, then let myself in and take stock of his kitchen. I've never used it like I'm about to now, but I'm grateful it's fully furnished, with double convection ovens and a giant gas stovetop. I dump my suitcases in the living room for the moment, then start the chicken and the peach cobbler. I need to hurry or I won't have enough time to make sure everything's done by six. As it is, I barely have seventy minutes to prep and cook everything.

While the chicken and the peach cobbler are going in the ovens, I drag the suitcases up the stairs. The master bedroom is empty, and it's weird to go in there without Nate around...like I'm invading his privacy or something. I can't believe I'm supposed to share this space for the next six weeks. He doesn't even have two beds. Just one giant California king. I wonder if we can discreetly install a rollaway cot.

Come on, Evie. Think of it like an extended sleepover. Just like in junior high and high school.

Yeah, except my girlfriends weren't hot like Nate. They didn't have his lean, gorgeous arms or eyes bright with humor or a killer smile that makes my heart feel funny...

Ugh, whatever. I can be professional about this. I *am* a professional.

I start to unzip one of the suitcases, then stop when I realize I'm going to have to put my stuff in his closet and bathroom. That just feels too...intimate. Maybe I should just take stuff out on an as-needed basis. That way it doesn't feel too permanent or anything. Yeah. I mean, who unpacks when they're only staying for a little while? Not me. Six weeks will pass by in a blink. A blip.

I shove the bags into the walk-in closet and shut the door. *Need to get the rice started or it's never going to be done in time.* And stop thinking about Nate's bedroom. Focus. I want to make sure Nate's mom feels properly welcomed.

I cook the rice on the stove with some butter, herbs and spices. Then I fry the bacon until the slices are crispy. I blot them with paper towels and check on the chicken and the peach cobbler. Both are coming along nicely.

Now, what else? *Salad.*

Wash, dry, chop the lettuce. Tomatoes, check. Avocado, check. Croutons, check. I then cut the bacon into small bits and toss them on the salad. That done, I quickly whip some balsamic vinegar, salt, pepper and extra virgin olive oil into a dressing.

The place smells nice. Homey and replete with the aromas of dinner. A bit of pride surges inside me. This should do for a proper welcome. Who doesn't love a freshly prepared, home-cooked meal?

With a few minutes left, I re-powder my face and put on a fresh coat of lipstick. I should be just as presentable as the food.

At six, I take everything out and set the table. Chicken. Rice. Salad. Peach cobbler. Some bread if she wants it. Butter.

It isn't too bad, considering how little time I had. But the longer I stare at it, the more it looks...lacking and sad. It's too ordinary. Like it's really made for *my* mom—a high school janitor single mom from Dillington—not someone like Blanche Sterling.

Maybe I should've catered something fancy. Multi-course fancy, with caviar and that five-dollars-a-bite fruit. What was it called again? *Mangosteen.*

Sudden frustration and shame spike through me, and my chin trembles. I sit at the table and bury my face in my hands, clenching my jaw and doing my best not cry and ruin my makeup. It's all just too overwhelming. I'm not cut out for this kind of stuff. And Nate really needs somebody who knows exactly what to serve his high-society mom.

Maybe I can still cater. Or is it too late?

I close my eyes. *Of course it's too late,* unless I plan to serve nothing but cold items. And really, dinner should be served warm.

I seriously consider texting Nate and telling him the oven has broken down. *We need to take your mom out to a restaurant. Whatever she wants to have.*

But before I can pull out my phone, I hear the security system beep and Nate's voice.

"Come on in, Mom."

Oh my God. *They're here.* I clench and unclench my shaking hands.

"Thank you, dear," comes a soft and clear voice. "I'm really looking forward to meeting your wife."

I stand up, hoping I don't faint. My mouth is so dry that I don't think I can speak.

I hear them moving and see their blurred shapes through the indoor waterfall. Then, abruptly, they stop.

"My goodness. Is that...*The Kama Sutra?*"

Oh, crap! *The statue!* I should've put something over it. What is she going to think, seeing it in the living room like that? Who the hell would consider it an acceptable piece of art to display when you have your mother-in-law coming over?

"Barron sent it," Nate says quickly.

"He sometimes has the *oddest* taste."

Yeah, I agree.

"Doesn't he know it's totally inappropriate?" she says.

"You know him. He does what he wants."

She makes a sound of disapproval. I wonder if I'm going to hear it again when she sees me and the dinner I made. My palms sweat copiously, and I wipe them against the back of my skirt, hoping they don't leave wet spots.

Nate and his mother make their way around the waterfall, and I finally come face to face with Blanche Sterling.

25

EVIE

THE FIRST THING I THINK WHEN I SEE HER IS THAT SHE looks nothing like Kim's boss's wife. If it weren't for Nate's solicitous hand at her elbow and calling her "Mom," I would've never realized she's Blanche Sterling.

Her hair is silver. I don't think it's seen dye in months, if ever. It frames her face like a cloud, and her skin isn't unlined from Botox or fancy creams. There are fine laugh lines fanning from the outer corners of her eyes, and her cheeks and mouth also have wrinkles that say she smiles a lot and enjoys her life.

The white T-shirt and jeans on her aren't designer items. They're stuff you can pick up from TJ Maxx or some similar store. Her feet are encased in a pair of gray New Balance sneakers.

Blanche walks toward me, her hands stretched out. "You must be Evie! I'm so glad to meet you in person."

I hold her hands and smile, the knot in my belly loosening a bit. "Hello, Mrs. Sterling. The pleasure's mine."

"Don't start with that Mrs. Sterling stuff. That's so formal, and we're family now. Feel free to call me Blanche. Or you can just use Mom, like Nate."

No way. That's not something I'm comfortable with. It's already bad enough I'm lying about being married to her son. So I keep my mouth closed and smile.

She continues, "I wish I'd been at the wedding. It's very inconsiderate of my son to elope, and in Vegas of all places! Nate can more than afford to give you a nice wedding."

I keep smiling, since I can't quite agree or disagree with her.

"Mom, aren't you hungry?" Nate says.

"Of course." She looks at the table, and her dark eyes light up. "Oh, this looks amazing. You shouldn't have." She smiles at me, and I can finally relax. "I would've been more than happy with Nate's usual Chinese takeout."

Nate groans. "Mom. It was just that one time."

"And the one before, and the one before that," she says. "You'd think your last name was Chen."

I laugh, amused by her dry tone. "Chinese takeout *is* very convenient, and we have a lot of great places. But I wanted our first meal together to be home-cooked."

"Well, it smells absolutely divine. Thank you, my dear. You're so kind. I know my visit's unplanned."

Her graciousness banishes the last bit of my tension, and I smile with relief. Maybe this is going to work.

She and I sit down. Nate brings out a bottle of chilled white wine from the cooler. I'm glad he picked it, because he undoubtedly knows how to pair the right type with the food I've made.

He pours three glasses, and we toast to a happy marriage, hahaha. I bring my glass to my lips, then pause. Somehow the wine smells really off. But Nate and Blanche seem to be enjoying theirs, so maybe it's just me.

Stress and adrenaline? Who knows, but I don't want to make a big deal about it, so I just tilt my glass and wet my lips without actually drinking any of it. I place my glass back on the table with a smile.

As we dine, I realize Blanche genuinely appreciates my cooking and the food, and wasn't just being gracious earlier. She asks me questions about my family, but never in a way that makes me feel like it's an interrogation.

"Your poor mother," she says. "I know what it's like not to be a part of your children's weddings. I'm sure we'll find a suitable way to make it up to her." She looks at Nate pointedly.

I pull my lips in, doing my best to look guilty, since that's what Blanche is expecting.

Nate gives an appropriately grave nod. "We will."

"I appreciate your concern, but it's really not necessary," I say. "I already spoke with my mother, and she said it was all right." When I have my real wedding, Mom's *definitely* going to be there.

"Nonsense. We will do what's right by her. Even though we're family now, we need to be respectful and show we care." She takes a bite of the peach cobbler. "This is *very* good."

"Thank you." Today's cobbler came out well. The peaches are exceptionally tender and sweet.

"So." She dabs at her mouth with her napkin. "When can I expect a grandchild?"

A chunk of fruit goes the wrong way, and I cough and gasp. Meanwhile, Nate is looking at his palm in a contemplative manner...then down at his crotch...then at my belly.

So. Unhelpful.

"Not that there's any rush," Blanche says. "I'd just love to have another one to bounce on the other knee. I'm not sure when Vanessa's planning to have a second child. She's so busy."

I take a couple slow sips of water. I need to sound like I'm humoring her without actually committing to anything. Who knew helping Nate out with the Mink Bikini Psycho was going to be this complicated? "Well, we're not sure, either. I enjoy working, and I don't want to put my career on hold just yet."

"Your career?" Blanche looks confused.

I bite my lip. Does she think that because I'm not a super lawyer like Justin's wife that I don't have a career I care about?

"She wants to keep working as my assistant," Nate says. "I'm grateful, too, because finding a good assistant these days isn't easy."

Blanche nods. "Very true." She turns to me. "I'm sorry. I thought you'd quit already."

"Why would I do that?" I ask, shocked and slightly annoyed with people's assumptions. My coworkers were looking at me funny too, like they couldn't believe I've continuing to show up at work.

"A working relationship—as a boss and his assistant—can be complicated if you're married. What if you're upset at home? Will that feeling bleed into your professional life? Or vice versa?" She shrugs. "I know times are changing, but it's cleaner and simpler if you don't mix things that way."

Ah. Not an unreasonable assumption, especially when she has no clue how things really are between me and Nate. "I'll do my best not to. But if I feel that it's going to happen, I'll look for another position."

"It *won't* happen, since I intend to be a paragon of consideration and love in both my roles of husband *and* boss," Nate says, not even batting an eyelash.

Despite myself, I'm impressed. He's good.

"I'm glad to hear that." Blanche finishes her wine, then points at my still-full glass. "Is it not to your taste?" She turns to Nate. "Do you have anything else you can offer your wife?"

Nate starts to stand, but I shake my head. "I'm fine. Besides, tomorrow's Tuesday and I have to get up early."

"Speaking of getting up early, I got up earlier than usual today. I was so excited about the trip. And now that my belly's full of delicious food and wine, I'm getting sleepy." Blanche turns to me. "Thank you, Evie."

"My pleasure," I say.

"Good night."

"Let me show to your room, Mom." Nate gets up, then takes her suitcase up the stairs.

Left alone in the dining room, I sigh. Things went remarkably well. Blanche genuinely seemed to like my food. And I didn't embarrass Nate or myself. I stand up and start to put away the leftovers.

A few moments later, Nate comes back. "Thank you. You made her feel so welcome," he says, then helps me clear the table.

I look at him with surprise.

"What?" he says.

"You. Clearing a table. Just seems...out of character somehow."

He laughs. "There really isn't that much to it."

"I know, but didn't you have servants and housekeepers growing up?" He still has a housekeeper come by to clean his place while he's at work.

He snorts. "Ha. Don't let Mom hear that. She's very Midwest and very middle class. She managed the household on her own, and Justin and I had to do chores if we wanted an allowance growing up."

"Wow." That's the polar opposite of what I imagined his childhood to be like. I assumed people like him had platoons of staff to take care of everything, up to and including tying his shoes.

"Barron didn't care for it, and he sent ridiculous gifts and money for our birthdays and Christmas. They used to argue about that all the time."

My respect for the woman goes up a hundred notches. It takes fortitude to argue with someone like Barron. "Did she win?"

"A lot of times, yeah. You know, my house, my family, my rules. Barron was always so annoyed." He grins. "And we were disappointed, like all little brats. But now that we think back on it, she was right. Without her, we would've grown up into insufferable assholes."

"I doubt it," I say, remembering his attentive kindness to people whose jobs are to serve him. He never takes them for granted. Or thinks he's entitled to their time and energy just because.

I open the dishwasher, but he shakes his head. "Hey, you cooked. And did a bang-up job. I can clean up."

He loads the machine, dumps in some detergent and runs it like he's done it hundreds of times. Then he grabs a brush and scrubs a couple of pots and pans that couldn't fit into the dishwasher, having them sparkling clean in no time. He also knows which cleaner to use with the copper pan, and not to use any soap at all with the cast iron skillet. Yup, definitely grew up with chores. Oddly enough, it makes him seem more human. And more touchable, like we have something more in common.

Still, I wander into the living room, pretending to check something on my phone, because I don't know how to approach the bedroom situation. With Blanche in the house, I can't have a guest room. She would wonder. But sharing the room?

Come on. You put your suitcase in his room.

That was before I saw this incredibly normal, approachable side of him.

He comes out of the kitchen, drying his hands on a towel. "Want to get some sleep?"

It's already ten. I should be in bed by now if I want to get up on time. On the other hand, I don't have to drive here from my place, so maybe I can sleep in just a bit.

Sleep in, my ass. Stop procrastinating.

I swallow. "Um... Sure. Do you want to use the bathroom first?"

"Nope. Ladies first."

I nod tightly and go to his bedroom. After taking out what I need from the suitcase I packed with my toiletries and night things, I change quickly into a pajama shirt and shorts, then floss and brush my teeth, erase my makeup and smooth some moisturizer on my face. I hesitate at the door. It's awkward to be doing my nightly routine in Nate's home. It isn't like I've ever done it before with him. In Vegas, I fell into bed without even changing.

I inhale. I need to be an adult about this, especially if I'm going to be repeating the routine for the next six weeks—or until Blanche goes home, whichever comes first.

When I come out, Nate's already in his boxers and lying on the covers of one side of his gigantic bed. It isn't any more indecent than how he normally is in the morning. After all, at least he has an actual article of clothing on, rather than just a towel. But this feels much more familiar and sexual. Alarmingly so.

The soft light from the bedside lamp spills over his wide shoulders, sloping pecs and ridged abs. And his long, well-muscled legs. My hands curl with the itching need to touch, and see if they're as warm and hard as they look. My mouth waters with a sudden urge to run my tongue over the hard contours of his body and steal a taste.

God. I'm acting like a horny teenager. Maybe it's the fact that all those male goodies are spread out like a banquet before me.

How long has it been since I had an orgasm from a non-battery-operated partner?

Over a year.

Think of something other than sex!

"The bathroom's all yours now," I say, gesturing behind me.

"Thanks, but I used the guest bathroom."

"What about your mom?"

"She's already out cold. Traveling tires her. Plus there's the time difference."

I'm feeling guilty now. And I cling to the feeling, because that's better than being turned on by my boss. "I'm sorry to hear that, especially since she came out here for nothing. Maybe we should've told her the truth."

"Actually, she was planning to visit anyway, so it doesn't matter," Nate says. "Our stuff just pushed it up a bit."

Bye-bye, guilt. Hello, more intense libido.

"Tomorrow's a busy day," he says.

"Yes." *Tomorrow's agenda! Right!* Any port in a storm. "You have four meetings, three with auditors and one with your lawyers."

"Uh-huh. Okay." He pats the empty space next to him. "Well, good night."

There's no way I'm sleeping there. What if I do something really stupid during the night? Like gradually migrate toward the center...toward him?

"I'll just take this love seat." I move toward the small couch in the seating area.

He jackknifes up. "Absolutely not."

"Why not?" Is there something wrong with it? Actually, now that I think about it, I've never seen him sit there.

"Because I'm a gentleman."

"And?"

"I can't let you sleep there while I take the bed." He swings around and stands up. "You take the bed. I'll take that one."

I study his six-foot-plus frame and the couch, which is barely big enough to accommodate *me*. He isn't going to be comfortable there. And really, there's no reason for him to give up the bed, when it's only for six weeks.

I press my lips together and think. There's an easy solution to this.

"Do you have some more pillows?" I ask.

"Uh, yeah. In the closet. Why?"

"Let's go."

I walk into the closet with him. He points out two huge drawers on the bottom, and I see six more pillows.

"Geez. Why so many?" I ask.

"I had trouble finding one I liked."

"So why didn't you toss the ones you didn't like?" Nate never struck me as a hoarder.

"Ah," he says, holding up a finger. "Because then they would not have been available to you tonight."

I laugh at his faux-wise tone. "Yeah? You could see into the future?"

"I just felt guilty about throwing them out after only sleeping on them a couple of times. I was thinking about donating them, but couldn't figure out where. I mean, who wants used pillows?" He shrugs.

Spoken like a true billionaire. I take them to the bed and line them up in the center. He watches with interest.

"Is that like a border?" he asks. "Will I need a visa to cross?"

"Ha ha, very funny. It's not a border. It's the Great Wall." I point to his side. "You stay there." I point to my side. "I stay here. We do *not* cross the wall. Ever."

"What if the wall moves? Or gets damaged?"

"'If the wall moves'?" I give him a stern look. "Mr. Sterling, why would pillows move on their own?"

"Well, Mrs. Sterling, the world is full of mysterious happenings." He leans toward me, and he smells of a hint of cologne and minty toothpaste. "Haven't you seen *Ghostbusters*?"

"That's a movie," I say firmly, ignoring the way his breath tickles my skin and my nipples go hard. "Mr. Sterling, you have to promise you'll stay on your side of the bed, or I'm sleeping on the floor." As threats go, it's pretty lame. But I have a feeling he would never let that happen.

"Fine, have it your way. But just know that *I* won't complain if *you* cross the border. *I* allow visa-free entry because I'm open like that," he says magnanimously.

I do my best not to snort a laugh. I refuse to encourage him. Then I slide under the covers, very carefully unhook my bra under the shirt and put it on the night table. I should've taken it off in the bathroom, but I didn't want to be without my bra around him any longer than I had to.

He stares at the bra for a few moments, then slides under the cover and turns off the light.

We lie in the dark. I pull the sheets closer. His scent wafts from the cotton. *Oh my God.* My body starts to hum with electricity. Holy shit, he smells so, so good, especially when it's mixed with a hint of laundry detergent.

Burying my nose in the sheets, I inhale some more with the desperate neediness of a glue addict. This is like...*scent porn*. I'm actually getting wet, and my nipples are impossibly hard and aching. If I were alone, I might finger myself to sleep. It wouldn't be the first time I've fantasized about Nate.

Evie, you are a sad, sad woman.

Squeezing my eyes shut, I will myself to sleep, but it doesn't work. My senses are hyperaware. I can hear the soft sound of his breathing, the heavy beat of my heart. The flesh between my thighs seems to throb, slick and oh so empty.

The hell of it is that I have a feeling this sensation won't be dissipating anytime soon. Certainly not in the next six weeks I'm going to be stuck with him.

26

NATE

"Visa-free entry? Ah hahahaha." Court actually slaps his thigh. "Did you also tell her you'd pay for a reentry permit?"

"You're such a dick. A loud but limp dick." He's being overly boisterous, which is drawing attention. Ugh. Bastard. I must've been nuts to ask him to lunch at Virgo, a bistro near my office, on Wednesday. And to bring Yuna, because she's in town, and she's usually cool. I was hoping to introduce Evie to them, but she turned down my invitation. Again. Apparently my being her husband hasn't changed her "no lunch with the boss" rule.

"You mean a hilarious dick."

Yuna kicks him under the table, making him wince and hiss. "You're being unsupportive."

"Thank you," I say. "The position of 'Nate's best friend' is going to become vacant anytime now. You interested?"

"We can do better than that. I'll be your soul sister." She grins, then giggles.

I laugh. She has a magical ability to make me laugh, and not with annoyance, unlike Court. She just flew in from Korea, but apparently isn't at all affected by jet lag. Her eyes are bright and clear, and she's listening with the attentiveness of a cat. She flips her auburn hair over one slim shoulder.

"I've missed you," I say.

"Missed you too. And the wedding! I wish I'd been here. I've never been to a Vegas wedding. Yours would've been perfect. It's awkward to crash some strangers' wedding, you know?"

"It wasn't that special," I say. She knows the truth about the wedding already. I trust her, and I wanted her as an ally, both for me and for Evie. I know Evie has friends of her own—like Kim—but I want her to have more. Some people from my circle, so she knows we aren't all ogres.

"You can have one yourself," Court says to her.

She ponders. "You think?"

"Most definitely not." I give Court a dirty look. "Unless you don't plan to involve your mom in the ceremony."

"That'd get me disowned." She leans closer. "Look, if your wife is being difficult, seduce her. Just show her your assets. No hiding."

"That means drop the towel," Court adds helpfully.

"Do you honestly think I've never thought of that?" I say. "But it's too clichéd."

"It's a cliché because it works," he says.

Yuna shakes her head. "Too obvious. Towels don't just drop to the floor on their own."

"Yeah, but subtle is too complicated." Court sips his drink. "Just pull a Hitler. Invade."

I choke on my soda. "I'm not going Nazi on her."

"Exactly," Yuna agrees. "Pulling an Attila is far superior."

I raise my eyes to heavenward and sigh. "I'm not pulling a barbarian horde on her, either."

"Look, bro, I hate to state the obvious, but...it could be she's just not that into you," Court says.

Yuna comes to my rescue. "Is she a lesbian? Because you're totally hot." Then she ruins it by adding, "If you were my type, I'd do you."

"Thanks, ex-friends," I say dryly.

"Look, she put up this Great Wall. What does that tell you?" Yuna asks.

Court squints like he's trying to multiply five-digit numbers in his head. "No nookie?"

"No! She wants you to smash it down. Or scale it. The Great Wall isn't impregnable. It didn't stop the Mongols. You can do this. Impress her. Give her something she wants. Appeal to her heart as well as her libido. And most of all, let her know she's safe with you. Women worry about that all the time, you know."

"Safe?" I ask, stupefied. "Why would she not think she's safe with me? I'd never do anything to hurt her." *And I haven't done anything to hurt her, have I?*

Yuna props her elbow on the table and rests her chin in her hand. "You're a billionaire. You're her boss. You're related to way too many powerful people. You have all the power, while she has none. That's a scary place for a woman to be."

27

EVIE

SOMETHING DEFINITELY HAPPENED TO NATE AT LUNCH. He's been pensive ever since he came back. And he's sighed seven times while looking at me. I counted. But I have no clue what's going on in his head. I haven't done anything out of character, as far as know, and the meetings were productive. I even double-checked today's notes, wondering if I made an error, but everything looks great.

He starts acting more normal during dinner. Blanche makes conversation like she doesn't notice anything off about her son, and wouldn't she know?

Maybe I'm being overly sensitive.

When it's bedtime, I change in the bathroom and do my evening routine. I brace myself mentally—and hormonally—for his tempting, gorgeous, nearly nude body. Although I've said very clearly that I don't want to have sex with him, there's a deep, illicit and perverse side of me that does enjoy looking.

Well. It's a spectacular view to go to sleep to, even though it gets me so hot and bothered that I stay awake a lot longer than I should.

Licking my lips, I come out of the bathroom. Then immediately stop.

Nate's on his side of the bed, the Great Wall fully assembled and erected. But instead of just boxers, he's in a white T-shirt and boxers. The shirt is fitted and molds to his stunning body, but there's something very wrong about having the precise definition and planes hidden from my view.

Except I can't tell him to take off his shirt. That'd be totally unprofessional. And wrong.

Well, you're married, so it's not *that unprofessional.*

Shut up if you're going to be unhelpful.

When did I start taking his nearly nude body for granted or use it to... I don't know. Fuel my lurid fantasies? Stoke my libido? Yeah, I've been having some dirty thoughts about him in bed. Impossible not to, when I'm enveloped in his scent. It feels like I'm surrounded by him, like his pheromones are settling on my skin, penetra—

Okay, stop. *I'm really relieved he's covered. Yes, I am.* I repeat that to myself as I slip under the covers.

Suddenly, Nate pulls his shirt over his head and flings it across the room. I should keep my head on the pillow with my eyes shut, but I can't. I lift my head just a little... Just enough to check him out.

Oh *yes.* Those muscles. The beautiful, lean, hard lines. The flexing of his abs. The powerful shoulders.

He starts to turn toward me.

Shit. I plop back down and shut my eyes. Then, with some effort, I inhale and exhale slow and deep.

Fake date. Fake marriage. Fake sleep.

God. My life is more fake than Georgette's breasts.

∼

Nate

It takes all my willpower not to cross the Great Wall and invade her like Court suggested. Actually invade her like the Huns and plunder that gorgeous body hidden underneath the prim shirt and shorts.

I only put on the shirt because of what Yuna said. I thought maybe my being topless was making her feel awkward or threatened. Well, technically Yuna said it was my money, position and relatives and family that make it threatening for Evie, but I can't do anything about that. But *this*...

I always thought Evie never noticed or cared what I wore or didn't wear. But no. There was definitely a hint of disappointment in her eyes before she stoically controlled her expression and walked to her side of the bed. It was all I could do not to start jumping up and down on the bed, arms in an overhead victory pose and screaming, "Yes! Yes!"

Instead, I waited for her to say something. Anything. Hell, all she had to do was smile or crook a finger, and I'd take off my shirt and more. Then eat her out until she rips the bedsheets, my name —my *first* name—on her beautiful lips as she comes again and again and again.

I bet she's tasty. Hotter than lava. And when I drive into her sexy little body...

But she just slid under the covers. Then inhaled deeply and let out some small sighs.

Oh well, then. I can be generous. I'm an accommodating guy.

The expression on her face when I stripped off the shirt... Ah yes. Priceless. Her eyes flared, interest sparking. I don't know if she realized it, but her little pink tongue swept across the seam of her mouth like she was hungry.

She said no entry. But all I need is a yes from her lips to change that. And now that I know she's definitely interested in me—or at least in my body—I plan to launch a full assault on the Great Fucking Wall.

28

EVIE

NATE IS ACTING STRANGELY. ALTHOUGH MIGUEL'S SUPPOSED to be back, Nate gives him even more time off, saying he deserves it. He insists on driving me to and from work. He also insists on having fresh flowers delivered to my desk every morning.

Except the flowers don't die immediately, so I have more flowers than a funeral home, and twelve oversized vases. I tell him, but he just says, "If I can't buy *my wife* flowers, who can I buy them for? Rosie?"

I grind my teeth at the continual personification of his palm, but say nothing. My coworkers also say nothing, not even super-chatty Melissa, who occupies a cubicle a few feet away. They don't seem to know what to make of my new position as Nate's wife. I don't say anything either, since I also have no idea what to make of my new position.

Mornings are the worst. He's topless, as usual, but his towel is now perched so low, the fold so loose, that I swear it's going to slip right off his hips any second. Sometimes I can see one hipbone, and more and more of the goodie trail is getting revealed. But somehow the towel manages to stay.

I can't decide if I'm happy or sad about that. And every night

I fantasize about him losing his towel and me unceremoniously replacing Rosie. Taking his cock in *my* hand. Then in my mouth. Then in—

I need some serious therapy.

Much to my guilt and horror, Blanche has started to make breakfast and dinner. She insists, saying she's entitled to cook for her son and new daughter-in-law. I'm going to go to hell for sure. And then there's the matter of the morning shakes. Nate eats the bacon and eggs his mom makes with an outward gusto, but I can tell he's hurting for his blended kale and antioxidants.

The day before the welcome party, I work like a demon to clear everything off my to-do list. I'm certain I won't be allowed to do any work. Not with Barron around. I take a quick look at the stack of papers on my desk. Must plow through them before Nate's done reviewing the reports on his desk. The floor's already empty except for us because everyone else left already. They took advantage of the generous policy of letting workers off at three on Fridays, except when we're on a deadline.

My cell phone rings, and I answer it automatically. "Hello?"

"Evie, babe!"

The voice sounds familiar, but I can't quite place it. I frown. "Who's this?"

"It's Chad! Remember me?"

Irritation and annoyance surge in equal parts. I do not have time for this. Or him. "How can I ever forget? What do you want?"

"When I saw the news, I couldn't believe it's really you. I had to look into it to make sure it really is the Evie Parker I know."

The nerve of him, calling me out of the blue like this! I never, ever wanted to hear his voice again. I just never expected that the fake marriage also comes with having to talk to the ex I hate more than mold on my favorite chocolate. The bastard did his best to ruin my life! "Well. He is very handsome. And a gentleman." *Unlike you.*

"I'm sure. I'm so glad you married well. I really am."

The egomaniac is clueless. Why am I wasting my time with him? "I have a meeting to prep for. Bye."

"Just give me thirty seconds. Look, my team is bidding on a

project at Sterling & Wilson. It's really important we win it, so could you put in a good word with the family?"

I pull the phone away from my ear and stare at it. Is he serious? He not only dumped me, but told everyone that I was crass enough to use sex to get ahead. He's the biggest reason people in Dillington were so nasty and I had to leave.

"My husband doesn't like it when I try to use him that way," I say coldly.

"Look, I know you don't have good feelings about our whole... thing. And honestly, I can't really blame you. But think of my team. They're *good* people. They deserve this job."

Is this the best he can come up with? If so, he needs to do better. "What they are is bullies. I haven't forgotten the message they left on my desk the day after we broke up. 'Slut' was the kindest word they used."

"Well, okay, they were a little harsh. And I guess you're right to be angry. It's just, you know, a lot of them have kids and all. But I guess I could still tell them..."

Oh, fuck him and his manipulation. I can't believe I never saw how he really was. On the other hand, I don't want to rehash our past. It's not worth it, and he'll never admit he wronged me. I need to make him feel so small that he won't bother me ever again.

What would Barron do?

Finally inspiration strikes, and I turn my voice cold and hard. "Never call me Evie again, *Chad*. It's Mrs. Sterling to you."

"But—"

I hang up, then block his number. I thought I'd already done that, damn it.

Claps come from the door to Nate's office, and I turn around with a start. He's standing there, one shoulder propped against the doorframe.

"Bravo," Nate says. He's smiling, but his eyes are frigidly controlled. I haven't seen him looking like this since the time he had to make an example out of the embezzlers in Houston. "Who was that on the phone?"

"My former boss," I say, wondering how much he heard.

Then I decide I don't care. I didn't do anything bad. My only crime was being young and stupid.

"Let me guess. He wants something from you, now that you're married to me."

I nod jerkily, feeling a little awkward about the circumstances. It surprises me for a second that he guessed correctly, until I remember he's probably used to people trying to use him and his connections.

Nate considers. "I haven't given you a wedding present."

Ooooo-kay. What's up with the sudden change in topic?

"I'll give you one. Well, the first of many." He smiles sweetly.

Somehow this is scarier than a threat. "What would that be?"

"It's a surprise."

I jump to my feet. "Wait. Don't beat him up, if that's what you're thinking. It's not worth it."

"I'd never dirty my hands that way. He'll simply be bankrupted. He'll never be anybody's boss again."

My jaw slackens at his cool, matter-of-fact tone. I'd love some revenge, but do I want Chadwick ruined forever? "Can you really do that?"

"Oh, quite easily. Nobody hurts you and gets away with it."

My heart flutters, and emotions I can't name grow in my chest. I can't remember the last time a man made me feel this protected and cared for. Well, no man has ever made me feel like this before, period. Then I remind myself not to read too much into it.

"Right," I say, sitting down. "It wouldn't look good to have your wife be disrespected."

Nate pushes himself off the doorframe and comes closer. I stay seated, utterly mute and still, like a small bird eyeing an approaching cat, my heart beating rapidly.

The backs of his fingers brush against my cheek, the touch feather-light. "Nobody gets to disrespect you. Regardless of who you're married to." His voice is like granite, a tone I've never heard from him before. "Six weeks from now, six years from now, it doesn't matter."

My stomach is jittery. It's difficult to draw air into my lungs. So many thoughts jumble in my head, and I want to lean into him so bad, just lay my hand over his and gently kiss the fingers on my cheek.

Except that's way, way too intimate. And not part of my plan.

With great difficulty, I pull back, breaking the contact, and force a smile. "Well, thank you. Now, we have to go over the women's health initiative report from the Sterling Medical Center. Let's get started so we can go home," I say. All the while, my heart calls me a coward.

29

EVIE

"So. What do you think would be good to wear? Really formal or semi-formal?" I ask as I sort through the dresses in the suitcases. I'm so frazzled that I only had a single slice of toasted white bread for breakfast and haven't bothered with lunch yet. No time to think about that right now. I'm just grateful Nate is taking care of the details of Mom's trip to the party. I initially volunteered, but he said he'd do it like a dutiful son-in-law.

"Ideally? Formal," Kim says, her voice loud and clear on the phone. "Something a bit on the traditional side. Nothing too risqué or flamboyant. I mean, you can do that, but later, without Barron or the other old folks around."

"Right." I look at the black cocktail dress I bought two months ago on sale. It's very basic, but also classic.

"You can just ask Nate, if you're really unsure."

And have him suggest I dress in some neon-pink piranha dress he saw in Fashion-Fails-R-Us? No thanks.

But I don't want to badmouth his lack of taste. He can't help it, and it's a sign God is fair. "He's out with his mom."

For which I'm eternally grateful to Blanche. After that

Marrying My Billionaire Boss

intensely connecting moment in the office, he's been a bit weird, watching me even more speculatively. I don't think he's going to go murder Chadwick, but the scrutiny kind of worries me, especially because I don't know how to make him stop being so... different or deal with this new side I'm seeing.

"Doing what?" Kim asks.

"Shopping. Apparently she hasn't bought enough gifts for the kids."

"They're big on kids," she says, her voice growing a little sad. "Especially Barron. I heard he lost two grandsons when they were little."

Sympathy wells. I didn't know that about Barron. Learning about his loss somehow humanizes him. Even a man like him—so immensely wealthy and powerful—can't control everything.

Not that it excuses his terribly overbearing attitude, but—

Kim moans.

"Are you okay?" It sounds like she's in some serious pain.

"Yeah," she says, panting a little. "Just my damn period. Started three days ago. I ran out of Tylenol, and I'm cramping like crazy. Not even chocolate's helping."

I make a sympathetic noise, but then it hits me. *She's on her period.* Not just started it, but on her third day.

Where the hell is mine?

Kim and I are one hundred percent synched. And I'm regular. Like "if I'm ever lost on a deserted island with no calendar, you could create one based on my cycle" regular.

"Uh... Kim?"

"Yeah?"

"What makes a woman not have her period?"

There's a pause. "Didn't you take sex ed?"

"Humor me," I ask, feeling a nasty pit in my stomach.

"Pregnancy. Hysterectomy. Excessively low body fat. Those are the most common ones that I can think of. Might be more, though."

"Right?" *Oh, shit.* "I gotta go."

"Why? Didn't you get yours?"

"I'm fine. Gotta go do my hair and makeup. Otherwise, I'm

going to be late," I lie, as a cold knot of panic rolls through my system. I refuse to accept, especially out loud, that I'm not having my period, especially when I haven't lost my uterus and my body fat isn't anywhere close to single digits.

"Okay. Good luck and have fun! They'll love you."

"Thanks," I say automatically. As soon as our call disconnects, I pull up a browser and Google. Google knows everything. Surely it has the logical, scientific explanation I'm hoping for.

It's so unhelpful. It says basically what Kim said, plus a few more improbable things like undiagnosed diabetes or stress. But I doubt it's stress, since Aunt Flo still came on time in Dillington, and that was the most stressful time of my life. As for diabetes, puh-lease. It doesn't run in my family, and I don't have any symptoms.

But pregnant? I put a hand over my belly. No freakin' way.

In order for me to be pregnant, I'd have to have had sex in the past month or two. Except I haven't. Can a squiggly sperm merrily swim around in my vagina for a year, then finally decide to fertilize an egg? Oh, and before that, smash through an unexpired rubber like the Hulk?

Impossible. I'm more likely to have a Martian spaceship crash-land on my head.

Dazed and panicked, I put on the black dress and put my hair back into a loose ponytail. Then press some powder on my face.

Maybe I've un-synched with Kim. Is it not possible? We haven't lived together in almost two weeks. Then I check my calendar. *Nope. I'm late.* Three days late. That's half the period.

Hand over my belly, I stare at my reflection in the mirror, willing myself to start bleeding.

This isn't happening. I can't be pregnant through some sex act I don't even remember! Maybe Nate remembers something. Okay, he's a super lightweight, but he's bigger than me, so he could've recovered his memory faster. Or so I hope. Is that how it works? Who knows, but I'm desperate.

I don't know how long I stand in the bathroom, but suddenly Nate is there.

"You ready?" he asks me.

I turn to look at him.

Hey, do you remember having sex in Vegas? The question forms in my head, but I can't bring myself to actually ask it. I'm not just a coward. I'm a chicken of epic proportions.

"Yes," I say with rubbery lips.

"Great." He smiles, then takes my hand and squeezes gently. "Don't be nervous. My family doesn't bite."

He thinks I'm nervous about meeting his family? Well, I guess that's better than him guessing the truth.

But...I rein in my panic and take a few calming breaths. There's no proof I'm pregnant. I just think I might be, but what is this? Some kind of immaculate conception? That only happens in the Bible. And the Virgin Mary, I am not.

Nate drives one of his fancy cars. A bright red Ferrari. I stare out the window, thinking about when I can see my gynecologist. She's usually booked solid, but if I tell her it's an emergency...

"Wait! Stop!" I scream.

"What?" he says, pulling over fast.

"Go back." I twist around until I can see the bright red DRUGSTORE sign behind us. "I need to go to that drugstore."

He gives me a worried look. "Are you all right?"

"I will be, once I grab some, uh, aspirin."

"Should've taken some before we left if you don't feel well," he mutters. "But you do look a little pale. You want to cancel?"

"No! I'm not canceling." What would his family think? And Blanche, who saw me earlier today. "It's just a little headache. Nothing serious." I give him my most reassuring smile.

He gives me a dubious look, but turns the car around. Once we're parked in front of the drug store, I get out, then trot around to his side of the Ferrari before he can think about following me in. "Just wait here. I won't be long."

"Okay."

I dash into the store. Where the hell do they keep the pregnancy test kits? It's just for a little peace of mind, because if I don't know, I'm going to obsess about it all through the party.

Finally I find an aisle of pregnancy tests. The shiny boxes are piled high next to condoms and lube. I guess they go hand in hand.

Sex. Then pregnancy. That's how it works.

There's really no way I'm pregnant. I'm just late because... Well. Shit happens.

I grab one that promises to let me know fast, then stop. What if it's defective? I pick out another box from a different brand. This is one thing I need to know with a hundred percent accuracy.

I pay for everything and shove both boxes into the bottom of my purse so nobody can see them. "Do you have a bathroom?" I ask.

"In the back to the right." The clerk barely looks up.

I walk over quickly, then see the dismal state of the toilet. It looks like it hasn't seen disinfectant in a decade. There's no way I can put my bare butt on the yellowed seat.

Forget it. I'm sure Justin's bathrooms are clean. Sparklingly so.

I head back out. My heart is racing with guilt and twitchiness, and my palms are sweating. The pregnancy test kits seem to weigh a ton. Are they glowing too? It's like they're emitting some kind of "we're here" signal on a radio frequency everyone but me can hear.

Is this how drug mules feel, smuggling in contraband? If so, how do they do it?

When I climb back into the car, Nate says, "Want some water?"

"Water?"

"For the aspirin. I've got a bottle somewhere in here."

Oh, crap. How could I forget? I'd totally fail as a drug mule. "Um, no, it's okay. They were out."

Both his eyebrows climb. "*Out?*"

"Yeah. Not a single bottle anywhere in the store." I smile, hoping it looks convincing.

I don't think Nate buys it. "They've gotta have some in stock. I can go in and check—"

"No! No, don't do that. They're totally out. I even asked the clerk."

"O-kay," he says dubiously. "Let's get going, then. I'm sure Justin has some."

We pull out and I slowly exhale.

"You don't have to worry about it," Nate says. "They just want to meet you and get to know you, that's all. Just be yourself."

"Of course." That's what people say about dating too. And it almost always turns out badly.

30

EVIE

Justin's home is beautiful. Technically, it's a mansion with multiple wings, and it's bigger than Nate's place. Unlike my boss/husband, Justin has a real wife and a kid. The place features a gigantic garden, a water fountain and a lake, the last completely fenced off to ensure his kid doesn't wander into it. The only thing it doesn't have is the Malibu view.

Justin comes out in a casual green polo shirt and slacks, relaxed and looking nothing like he does in the office, where he's usually all stern and serious. He welcomes both of us into his home, all graciousness and personable charm.

A stunning redhead in a stylish blouse and cropped white pants waves at us from the kitchen. "Hi. The guests of honor are finally here!" she says.

"Are we fashionably late?" Nate asks.

"Yes. But we forgive you. More beer for us." She places an affectionate kiss on Nate's cheek, then turns to me. "Hi, I'm Vanessa, Justin's wife. I've heard so much about you, Evie."

From most people, it would be a purely social remark. From Vanessa, it sounds vaguely ominous. I paste on a smile. "Same here."

Marrying My Billionaire Boss

We shake hands. Her grip is strong, but cordial.

"Do you have any aspirin?" Nate asks. "Evie isn't feeling well."

"Oh no," she says with a sympathetic look. "Sure, we have some. Come with me."

Crap. I do not want to go with her. I want to stay with Nate, but I can't suddenly declare myself cured.

Next time, come up with a better lie. "Thank you." I force another smile and follow her up a huge, winding staircase. I spot one guest, but only see her back. I have no clue who she is. Or how many people have shown up.

Vanessa takes me to the large bathroom in the hall. She pulls out a bottle of aspirin from the medicine cabinet. "Here you go. Take as many as you need, with some bottled water if you like." She gestures at bottles lined up along the bottom of the mirror. "Sorry to leave you alone, but I need to get back down there and make sure Barron and Justin don't kill each other at the grill."

"Grill?"

"We're barbecuing. Barron's idea." She sighs. "I think he just wants to try out Justin's new custom grill. It's pretty fancy." She grins, then vanishes.

I wait a few beats, then put the bottle back into the cabinet. Barron Sterling is here. People are *really here* to welcome me into the Sterling family. My stomach twists, and I can feel acid sloshing around. I probably should've had more than a piece of toast today.

I glance over to my right, where the sparkling-clean toilet sits. And I have two pregnancy test kits in my purse. *Why wait?* Once I know for sure, I'll feel so much better.

I lock the door, pull out both boxes and set them on the counter. Drink more of the water. Then open the boxes and pull a stick out from each.

The instructions are basically the same for both. *Pee on the stick, then wait.*

Okay, fine. I pee, then set the sticks carefully on the edge of the sink. *That should do it.* I wash my hands and wait. And wait some more. *How long does this take?* Shouldn't the results be instant?

Maybe they aren't showing anything because I'm not pregnant. I pick up one of the water bottles and read the marketing BS printed on the label. Something about carbon and aquifers. What the hell is an aquifer, anyway?

Don't look at the sticks, don't look at the sticks...

I look at the sticks. One shows a double line, the other shows a cross.

Pregnant.

Oh. My. God. *Pregnant.* This is...this is... *What am I going to tell Nate?* Biting my lip, I pace. Maybe I should take the test again. It's not completely out of the question that I could get two false positive—

The handle on the door suddenly rattles loudly, starling me enough that I drop the sticks into the sink.

"Hey!" comes a small voice from the other side of the door.

Shit! Who's that?

Tossing the test sticks into the wastebasket, I open the door and come face to face with a small boy holding his groin and hopping. "I need to pee!" he says.

"Oh. Okay..."

He pushes past me, drops his shorts and jumps onto the toilet. "I'm Ryan!"

"Uh, hi. I'm Evie. Are you... Are you okay?"

"Yeah. I drank too much orange juice." He points at the two boxes, *which are still on the counter.* Shit! "What's that?"

"Oh, those? They're just, uh, sticks." *Damn it.*

Ryan grabs one of the boxes and looks at the pictures. "You *pee* on them?"

"Well... Yeah."

"Why?"

Dear God, why me? "They, um, make lines when you pee on them."

"Cool! I want to do it."

"I don't think it's going to work if you do it."

"It'll work. I still have more pee." Clearly a Sterling. There's no way a normal child could be this confident.

Ryan takes one of the sticks out of the box but has trouble getting the individual wrapper off.

Marrying My Billionaire Boss

"Okay, Ryan," I say, "I'm going to help you with this. But it has to be our secret, okay? We're not going to tell anyone. Right?"

He nods. "Okay."

So I take the stick out of the wrapper and watch while he sprays it with urine. He's amazingly neat about the whole process.

"So when do the lines show up?" he demands.

"Well, this one makes a cross. But I don't think it's going to work for you."

"Why not? I peed on it."

"Yes, but you're a little boy. Only girls can make the cross appear. And even then, only sometimes."

Ryan is done, so he hops off the toilet and turns to flush it. And, of course, sees the used sticks I threw into the trash. One is lying with the display showing a cross. "Is that one yours? Did you make a cross?"

I close my eyes briefly. "Yes. But remember, *this is our secret*."

His little eyebrows pinch together. "My daddy said that I can do anything if I put my mind to it."

"And your daddy is right. But there are some things that only boys can do, and some things that only girls can do."

"Even if I put my mind to it?"

"Even if you put your mind to it."

He looks at me like he wants me to explain, but nope. I'm not touching this subject. That's what his parents are for.

"Tell you what." I surreptitiously put the boxes back into my purse, talking all the while to keep the boy distracted. "Why don't you wash your hands? And then let's go downstairs. I'm sure your family is wondering where you are." I'm going to have to figure out what I'm going to do about the fact that I'm pregnant later. Hell, I haven't even fully processed the fact that I'm an oven with a bun inside. "And remember, this is our little secret, okay?"

He nods. "I remember."

He washes his hands and then vanishes down the hall, saying something about getting a toy to show Uncle Nate.

I grab a bunch of toilet paper and wrap the used sticks with it. There. Now it's impossible to see them, and who's going to go digging around in the garbage anyway? Most people will probably assume there's a used sanitary napkin or something inside.

I check around the bathroom, making sure there isn't any other incriminating evidence, then wash my hands again and go downstairs. Nate is outside, next to a gigantic chrome grill, holding a beer. I see two empty bottles in front of him and shake my head. I know he enjoys drinking, but he needs to be careful. He's already at his limit.

Meanwhile, Barron is hogging the grill, laughing at something Justin is saying. As he flips a burger, our eyes meet and he smiles and waves.

I wave back with a grin that hurts my face.

A petite blonde comes in from outside, carrying a girl who looks like herself, except for the stubborn set of her jaw. The blonde woman is in a white scoop-neck top and teal skirt that ends two inches above her knees. Her small feet are bare, her toenails pink.

A tall, dark man with piercing blue eyes hovers nearby, like he's afraid she's going to break. The scene is so incongruent to the cold aloofness in his general demeanor that I can't help but laugh inwardly.

"Hi. I'm Sophia. You must be Evie," she says. "Sorry I can't shake hands with you. Isabella can be a handful, and she wants to come down and chase after Ryan."

God bless Sophia. Otherwise I would've had to explain the workings of pregnancy test kits to both kids. "That's okay. Nice to meet you. And hi, Isabella."

The little girl ignores me.

"She's a bit of a princess. Her dad spoils her."

"I bet. She's really cute."

"I do not," the man next to her says emphatically. "I'm Dane. Sophia's husband."

"Hi. Nice to meet you." He doesn't seem interested in saying more, and I rapidly find myself hoping something will distract him from giving me this icy scrutiny. It's like he can see right through me...and X-ray vision into my belly.

"You want something to drink?" Sophia asks. "Vanessa makes great sangria and mimosas."

"Um, I'm okay." No drinking with a baby on board. The moment the thought pops into my head, I feel slightly dizzy. *I really am pregnant*. What do I do? How am I going to I tell Nate?

I note that my mom has arrived, too. She's dressed in her Sunday best—a beige dress with a pleated skirt and low pumps—and is chatting with a slim brunette by a huge flower arrangement near the fireplace.

Relief floods through me. Nate sent a plane and a driver, but I wasn't sure if they'd made it to the mansion yet. I feel slightly guilty that I haven't checked up on her even once today.

"Excuse me. I should say hi to my mom." I need to get her away from the crowd and get some advice. Mom will know what to do.

Justin comes inside, carrying a huge plate laden with hamburgers and hot dogs. Nate follows, his platter heavy with grilled corn on the cob and a few chicken breasts.

"Is Barron still hogging the grill?" Blanche asks from her armchair.

"Yes." Justin rolls his eyes.

"The man acts like he's never seen a grill before," Nate says, then looks at me. "You feeling better?"

"Much," I lie, because what else can I say? I can't tell him I'm pregnant, especially not in front of everyone. I haven't had time to process that bombshell myself.

"Daddy!" Ryan appears, running toward Justin.

"Hey, buddy!" Justin says. Someone takes his plate, and Justin sweeps his child up into the air. "How you doing? Having fun?"

"Yeah! Daddy, did you know that you can get a cross if you pee on a stick?"

I suck air in hard as the world seems to tilt. *That little shit!*

Justin looks at his son, utterly bemused. "Uh... What exactly were you doing outside?"

"No, not like that kind of stick. It's white. Has a rectangle."

Vanessa walks up. "Is he talking about a pregnancy test?"

"But I can't do it," Ryan continues, "even if I set my mind to it. But you said I can do anything I want if I work really hard."

Justin pulls his lips in, but his mouth is twitching. "Ah, okay. Well, you know, you *can*, uh, usually, although—"

Ryan doesn't want to hear about "although." He turns a triumphant face toward me. "See? You're wrong!"

Oh my God. My mouth goes dry.

"Wrong about what?" Barron booms, closing the door to the deck behind him. *Why couldn't he have continued to hog the damned grill?*

"She said I can't pee on a stick and get a cross, like she did."

A scream gets tangled in my throat. I don't think I can breathe. Or, at least, that's how it feels from the roaring in my head and the tightness in my chest.

"A cross...?" Nate's gaze swings toward me.

My heart racing, I stagger back a step, feeling like the world is collapsing on me.

Barron also turns fully in my direction, and somebody gasps. I think it's my mom.

"She made a cross on her stick!" Ryan says accusingly. "But when I peed on mine, it didn't work."

Why don't you say it louder, so everyone in Los Angeles can hear you?

Justin starts walking into another room with Ryan, who squirms around and maintains eye contact with me over his shoulder. "I *can so* do it!" he screams.

"Oh my goodness, are you pregnant?" Vanessa's voice seems to come from someplace far away.

I'm so not ready to deal with this. And I'm certainly not ready to talk about it in front of Nate's family when I haven't even told Nate.

I try to tell them it isn't the time for a group discussion, but my tongue isn't doing such a great job of making words. My vision dims, and then everything goes black.

31

NATE

My vision narrows, my heart accelerating like it's trying to win a drag race. The platter in my hands hits the floor as I dive for Evie's crumpling body.

Dane lunges forward as well, and I slam into his solid shoulder. The impact jars my teeth, and we fall on the floor in a tangle of limbs and testosterone. But at least Evie doesn't hit the marble. She lands in my arms, and I feel more victorious than a running back catching a Super Bowl-winning pass.

"Whoa. I've never had a fan faint at the sight of me before," comes Ryder's voice.

It's all I can do to not roll my eyes. I usually find him funny, but it's irritating as hell when I'm holding an ultra-pale Evie. "Who invited the Hollywood star? Now we're all going to need to clear out to make room for his ego."

"Somebody call a doctor!" Barron thunders.

Vanessa already has her phone out. "On it."

"I mean," Ryder says, looking around to see who else understands the significance, "she actually *fainted*."

I put a finger under Evie's nose. She's breathing shallowly, but her skin feels a little cool against my palm. Is she supposed to be like this? And is it normal for pregnant women to faint? I've heard of fainting goats, but never of fainting expectant moms.

Then my mind pulls me back to the bombshell announcement Ryan made. *Baby. She's pregnant.* I stare at her stomach, which is still perfectly flat. When did it happen? How?

In Vegas? But I don't remember, and I'm pretty certain Evie doesn't either, so how did it happen?

On the other hand, just because we don't remember doesn't mean we didn't do it. We don't remember vowing to love and cherish each other forever, either, but still ended up with wedding bands on our fingers.

Just what the hell really happened in Vegas?

And God, Evie and I need to be alone, someplace private, so we can talk. After she's finished with her fainting spell. How do you wake someone up, anyway? I'm pretty sure a kiss on the mouth isn't it, contrary to the fairytales.

Ryan comes running back into the room. "Am I in trouble?"

I turn my head and see him staring at Evie with his eyes big and shimmering with unshed tears.

"No," I say, standing up and carrying her to a couch so she can lie more comfortably.

Vanessa puts a pillow under Evie's head, and I arrange her on the long leather cushions.

"You did nothing wrong," Barron adds, placing a comforting hand on the boy's small shoulder. "She just isn't feeling well."

She hasn't been eating that well, either. I should've known something was up; she's barely even nibbled at her breakfast the last few days, while worriedly eyeing me gobbling up Mom's bacon and eggs. Why would she have done that, unless her stomach felt wrong and she was wondering how I could eat like an oblivious horse? Or maybe she had something to tell me but didn't know how to approach it while I was shoveling food into my mouth.

"So this is why you eloped," Sophia says.

Dane nods. "Makes perfect sense." He'd agree with anything his wife said.

"I can't believe this."

Looking up, I see Evie's mom. I introduced myself when my

driver brought her here because I couldn't find Evie. I can only imagine how it looks to Mari Parker. If I had a daughter and some boss of hers got her pregnant, I'd beat him to death, especially if he eloped with her. My daughter deserves a real wedding, damn it! And things need to be done in the proper order—first the wedding, then babies.

Everyone—every adult, anyway—is looking at me expectantly. Part of my brain says I need to make an announcement about the baby now. Play the happy soon-to-be daddy. Except I'm still trying to process the surprise.

At the same time, a wrong move here might bring the wrath of my family down on Evie. I'd rather lose an arm than to let anything happen to her. Talking with her and figuring things out can wait.

So I paste on a slightly abashed smile. "Yeah, well... We're expecting our first child. She was late, and I told her to wait to see her doctor, but I guess she just couldn't." Then I sigh and roll my eyes in a "what can you do when your pregnant wife's being crazy impatient?" way.

"Smart girl!" Barron says. "Why wait when you don't have to? I'm glad she found out now, Nate. Now we can celebrate not only to welcome Evie, but a brand-new Sterling as well!"

32

EVIE

MY VISION GOES FROM BLACK TO GRAY. AN IMPROVEMENT. Then the gray slowly becomes paler, resolving until I have a clear view of the faces above mine.

Lots of faces. I recognize Mom and Nate, then a few others. But even if I've met them before, my brain's overwhelmed at so many people hovering over me.

"Everyone, if you'd pull back a bit. Let's give the expectant mother some air," says a middle-aged woman.

"She's right. We don't want to suck all her air like some oxygen-stealing parasites," Barron says, gesturing for everyone to take several steps back.

Nate doesn't move away. He is still holding my hand, looking at me with anxiety twisting his face. For a moment, I have no idea why he's looking at me like that. Does he have something to say? And why am I lying on a couch? I didn't take a nap or...

Then I remember. *Oh, crap! No, no, no!* Ryan told everyone I'm pregnant. Okay, he said I peed on a stick and made a cross appear, but the adults know exactly what that means.

I squeeze my eyes shut. I need to go back to into a faint so I

Marrying My Billionaire Boss

can figure out what I'm going to say, how I'm going to deal with Nate's family now. And Nate... He really deserved to be told in private. We should've had some time to discuss how we plan to work things out with the baby.

Hell. I don't even know how this baby *happened*.

"Is she okay?" Nate asks the middle-aged woman.

"She's fine. Her blood pressure seems okay, although it's a little low. She's also slightly dehydrated. Low blood sugar, too, most likely, if she's been throwing up."

Nate's gaze swings in my direction. Barron makes a displeased noise, then glares at Nate like it's all his fault.

"I'm fine," I declare, sitting up to prove it. "I haven't been throwing up. I just didn't have much appetite today. My fault, really."

Mom holds my hand. "You need to take care of yourself better." *Instead of just your husband* is left unsaid, but I don't need to hear the words to know what's on her mind.

"Here." Vanessa gives me a tall glass of pee-colored liquid. "Sports drink. Helps with hydration."

"Thanks." I smile at her, then at everyone else. *See, I'm fine.* I down the entire glass for their benefit, too. Thankfully, it doesn't taste the way it looks.

"She should see an obstetrician," the doctor says as she starts to pack up her things. "I'm sure you want nothing but the most expert care."

An obstetrician? Oh lord. That makes the baby feel nine billion times more real than the result screens on the pregnancy test kits.

"You'll take her to one tomorrow," Barron says to Nate.

"Tomorrow's Sunday," I point out.

Barron looks at me like I'm slow. "And?"

"Doctors don't work on Sundays."

He gives a booming laugh. "My dear. They do for a Sterling baby."

My shoulders sag with shock as the words sinks into me. *A Sterling baby.*

I make a mental note to follow Blanche's child-rearing

method and make sure my baby spends as little time as possible with Barron. Otherwise the kid's going to end up as an insufferable and entitled little brat.

Barron turns to the others. "We need cigars and drinks! Justin, bring out your best."

"Already done," says a tall, handsome man in a carelessly cheery voice.

I squint, unsure if I'm seeing correctly. He looks remarkably like *Ryder Reed*. Actually, they look so alike, he could play Ryder Reed in movies.

He pours everyone—except me and the children—two fingers of something amber. Justin passes out cigars to the men, although Barron declares they shouldn't really smoke around me for the health of the mother and the baby.

Nate takes his glass and sits next to me, holding my hand like the most devoted expectant dad. Someone hands me some ginger ale.

"To Nate and Evie. May their marriage be happy and everlasting. And thank you for making my wish come true." Barron beams. "I really wanted another grandchild. Boy or girl, I don't care which. Well, actually, I'd prefer a girl this time, as we already have two male baby Sterlings. Add a little balance. But that doesn't mean I'll love a boy any less...should it be a boy."

I smile uncertainly, unsure if he's trying to will me into having a girl to make himself happy or if he's just rambling. We all toast, clinking glasses.

Nate starts to bring his drink to his lips, and I put a hand on his arm.

"What?" he says.

Now everyone's looking at us. I sigh. It's so hard to be the responsible adult in a relationship. He's old enough to know he talks too much when he's drunk. "You had at least three beers outside, right?"

"Yeah."

"So. This is going to be your fourth drink. And hard liquor, too."

Nate looks like he's torn between laughing and crying, and

now I feel like a party pooper. "I mean, maybe another is okay...if it's no more than three sips?"

"Are you *both* giving up alcohol until the baby's born?" Elizabeth asks.

"No. Um. I just didn't want him to over-imbibe."

The Ryder lookalike snorts. "He's no Pryce, but the guy can hold his liquor. Probably better than anyone outside the family."

What?

Nate shifts his weight. "Is that an appropriate thing to say in front of the kids?"

"It's the truth."

My dehydrated, low-blood-sugar, hormone-addled brain finally catches up. "You can have more than three?" And oh my God, *that really is Ryder Reed*.

Nate looks like he'd love to have a lawyer answer the question. "Well...something like that."

"The question is, three *what*," Justin says. "Bottles? Vats? Wine casks?"

I stare at Nate. Why would he lie about this? He's had me booze-block him for months...for what? He had to know the truth would come out and we would both look silly.

I look down, and my gaze lands on my belly. Nate's family seems to think it's just a normal baby Nate and I remember having made. But the thing is...even if I lie about it, the truth is going to come out soon enough, because who knows what kind of conclusions Nate is going to draw once we start talking? He'll have to think that it isn't the first time somebody used a baby to trap him. Didn't he say Georgette did the same thing with a fake pregnancy? Mine's not fake, but he might wonder whose baby it is.

If I were him, I would.

The right thing to do is come clean. My muddy brain knows that much.

"You know...I need to say something about this baby," I say. "I know it's awkward, but—"

Nate quickly tugs at my elbow and pulls me closer. "Honey, they already know everything." He smiles at me.

Honey? And what "everything"?

"No reason to go into detail," Barron says. "No matter how it happened, we're happy to welcome another child into the family. I'm a traditionalist, but not completely inflexible." He smiles and looks around the room.

33

EVIE

A MIASMA OF CONFUSION FOLLOWS ME AROUND LIKE MY own personal fog for the rest of the party. I wish I knew exactly what Nate said. It's hard to just smile and pretend everything's great. But what other option do I have?

Thankfully, Blanche decides to stay at Justin's, mainly because Ryan starts raging about wanting to have his grandma all to himself. For once, I'm grateful to a small child for pitching a fit. Mom will be staying with us instead. Barron generously offered to put her up in the Ritz or Aylster—the best available suite his assistant can book for her, of course—but Mom, slightly horrified, vigorously declined.

Since we can't fit my mom in the back of Nate's Ferrari, the scarily cold Dane decides to drop her off in his super-fancy cream-and-pink Cullinan. I had no idea cars came in those shades, but I say nothing.

I dread what *she's* going to say. We haven't had a chance to talk, although she smiled and played along with everything. But I know she's wondering if I know what I'm doing. Hell, *I'm* wondering if I know what I'm doing.

And although Nate's family is too happy and distracted with

the prospect of a new baby, Mom has undoubtedly latched on to the fact that I took a pregnancy test in the bathroom of someone else's house. Except I can't really tell her everything. I don't want her to have to lie for me.

Once we arrive at Nate's place, I put him off for the moment and take Mom to a guest room. The second the door closes, she grips my wrist. "Evie, what's going on? You're really pregnant?"

I sigh. "Yes." I gently lead her to the bed, and we sit down.

"But...this isn't what you said. This can't be good for you." Worry has put more lines on her face. Unlike some of the older women at the party, Mom's face shows every bit of her life. All the hardship and struggles she's had to overcome. Little wrinkles fan from the corners of her eyes and below. They make gorges along her cheeks and around her mouth. The three deep lines between her eyebrows are from fretting about paying bills, how to put food on the table and a roof over our heads. Her only jewelry is a beautiful golden ring engraved with flower motifs on the outside and "...till death do us part" inside in a swirly script. She told me my dad gave it to her the day he told her he loved her. Seeing it chokes me up, since it's obvious she wants me to find a man who loves me the way my dad once loved her.

I hate it that I can't tell her what she wants to hear, but I haven't even spoken to Nate yet. So I take a moment to gather myself, mentally casting around for a way to reassure her without promising anything I can't deliver on. "Nate's a good person. He always does the right thing, Mom. You don't have to worry."

"But what is 'the right thing'? For himself? For you? How about the baby?" Mom lowers her voice. "A baby changes everything, Evie. And from the way that loud old man was talking, I can just tell that family will run right over you to keep it if anything goes wrong."

A sliver of fear cuts through me like a shark fin in night water. I force a smile. "You can't think about things turning out badly, Mom. We just got married."

"Well, I simply don't trust him." Her mouth tightens. "Did you see what he thinks is tasteful 'art' in the living room? It's not my place to say anything, but my goodness."

That damned statue. I wonder if I can send it back to Barron.

"Mom, come on. You've never trusted anybody with me. You didn't think much of the boys I dated in high school, to say nothing of Chad."

"And I was right not to. There ought to be a law against having sex with a mannequin," she mutters.

"*What?* I have never had sex with a mannequin!"

"That Chadwick?"

"What on earth are you talking about? Chad's not a mannequin."

"Oh, Evie," she says sadly. "You were fucking that dummy for months."

I have to laugh. "Okay, so you turned out to be right about him and a few other times." But I refuse to be pessimistic about *all* my relationships. "I know you're tired from the trip. Why don't you get some sleep? I'm exhausted, too." I yawn to emphasize my point.

"Of course." Concern clouds her cornflower-blue eyes, the same exact shade as mine. "You go ahead and turn in. Pregnancy does take it out of you."

I hug her. "Good night. Let me know if you need anything."

"Night, hon."

Leaving her alone in her room, I go to the master bedroom. My feet feel like two big huge chunks of lead as I drag myself along the hall. I honestly have no clue what I'm going to say to Nate or how he's going to react. There's no way he remembers having sex with me in Vegas. Otherwise he would've hinted at something. Is he going to wonder who the real father is? Insist on a discreet paternity test? That would be sensible for a man in his situation, even though a small part me would be slightly hurt that he couldn't just take my word for it.

It'd be monumentally stupid for him to take anybody's word for something like this, I tell myself. Maybe Mom knows this too, which is why she's so worried, even though she isn't saying anything out loud. How does a relationship work if one party has to prove to the other that they aren't lying all the time?

I open the door and quietly step inside. Nate has already changed into his boxers and T-shirt. The expression on his face is serious. Like, corporate bankruptcy serious.

"You know," I say, "I had no idea I was pregnant until today, because I was talking with Kim, and she said something that made me realize that I was, uh"—God, this is embarrassing—"three days late. So I had to check, even though I have no recollection of having had sex with anybody, and I'm sorry I didn't tell you, but I didn't want to say anything right before the party when I wasn't even sure, you know? I mean, I could've been late because of stress or because I'm in a new home or because...something. Sometimes, you know, a woman can be late for no reason at all..." I'm babbling. I need to stop, except my mouth keeps going. Nate stands up and walks slowly toward me. "I'm *seriously* regular, though, like, you could program a calendar app off my cycle, but—"

He puts a finger over my lips. "Evie. Breathe."

My mouth is parted, and I can almost taste him. It's all I can do to not flick my tongue against the pad of his index finger.

You're one messed-up woman. You're pregnant unknowingly, and you're worried about sampling his finger?

Then I realize something else. "You called me Evie," I say, almost stupidly, against his finger. It feels so good to move my lips against it. My mouth tingles.

He doesn't move the finger away. "Well, yes. It's weird to keep calling you Mrs. Sterling, especially when we're about to have a baby and all."

"Don't you have any, you know, questions?" Why is he not asking about the baby?

He finally drops his hand, which I follow like a puppy watching a strip of bacon moving farther away. "Like what? About Vegas? Do you remember anything?"

I shake my head, wondering if he's disappointed I can't answer that last question with a yes.

"Well, then, don't worry about anything. I already told my family it's mine. They won't question the paternity. Ever."

Shock sweeps over me. "Why did you do that?"

"Did you have sex with anybody since your last period?"

"No!"

"Hey now, calm down. That's what I figured too."

He gently puts his hands on my shoulders and has me sit

down on the edge of the bed. His no-visa-entry side of the bed. I'm so stunned that I let him lead me, then perch my butt on the edge of the mattress. He crouches down in front of me, holding my hands in his, and says, "I trust you, Evie."

Emotions I can't name quiver inside me. "Just like that?" My voice is shaky.

"Just like that. You would never lie to me about something like this, or pretend the baby was mine if it wasn't. You're too honest."

"You don't even want to do a paternity test?" I ask, just to be certain.

His eyebrows snap together. "That'd be insulting. To both of us."

His trust in me humbles me, overwhelms me. I know that with this man, I'm always going to be safe. I'll never have to tiptoe around, trying to prove myself, wondering if I'm enough.

After the whole clusterfuck with Chad, I felt like I had to build sky-high, broken-glass-topped walls around me to keep me safe. But they're falling around me...around my heart.

And I know without a doubt I love this man. Not for his billions, not for his looks, but for the amazing heart that beats in his chest, for the sweet tenderness shining in his eyes.

Hot emotion swelling in my chest, I lay my hand on his cheek and lean down, pressing my lips against his. They're softer than I thought, and the contact ignites my nerve endings.

A low groan tears from his throat as he rises, then moves until I'm lying half on the bed with him over me. I lick his mouth, taste him—all that amazing, brilliant, hot male who's been driving me crazy with lust these past months.

"You're so sweet," he whispers.

"So are you."

He gives me a mock frown. "Men are supposed to be manly."

"You can still be sweet. Sweetly manly."

His forehead touches mine. "Evie, make sure you're sure. Don't let your hormones cloud things here."

I can feel his hot, heavy erection against my belly. There are tight lines around his eyes and mouth. The offer is costing him a great deal.

And for that, I want him even more.

"Nate," I say, loving the sound of his name in my mouth, the gentle intimacy of it. "If I weren't pregnant and hormonal, I'd still want you. You've been the star of my dirty fantasies for a long, long time."

"Oh, thank God," he says with a shudder.

And then his mouth claims mine. It's hot, wild and unrestrained. I vaguely feel the Great Wall pillows get shoved away as Nate makes one strong sweep with his hand.

I entwine my arms around his neck and kiss him back, like I've always wanted. Our tongues glide past each other, then tangle, as we greedily savor each other, stoking the heat between us. I move my legs restlessly against his muscled thighs, reveling in the strength of his frame.

Everything about him makes me hot. I could kiss him forever. Stroke him forever. Feel his cock grinding between my legs through the underwear forever.

His mouth seeks the sensitive skin behind my ear, then the pulse point on my neck. I tilt my head, giving him room, wanting him to have all of me. His hot breath fans against me, and *God* I'm so turned on, electric pleasure making my spine arch.

"I have a *very* long list of things I want to do to you," he murmurs against the swell of my upper breast.

I wriggle, helping him get rid of my dress, then my bra. His eyes darken to near-black when he sees my bare breasts.

"So pretty." He buries his face between them and licks the skin there. Each flick of his tongue goes straight to my clit, making it ache, my thigh muscles tight.

"So which one do you want to do first?" I ask breathlessly.

There's a pause. "I can't remember any of them now that you're here. Where to start..." He looks at me, his expression full of searing hunger.

My lust burns hotter. "How about we start with what that damn statue was doing?" The position I saw had the woman sucking off a man on his back. It'll be amazing to do that...pull him deep into my mouth and see the pleasure break on his handsome face...

His breathing roughens. "I think that's a brilliant idea." Then he takes my nipple into his mouth, sucking and rolling the sensitive tip with his tongue.

I clench the sheet underneath, my back bowing. He seems to know exactly how much pressure I crave, what kind of stimulation to maximize my pleasure.

"Nate," I whisper, my voice soft, raw, pleading.

He releases the breast. "Say it again."

"Nate."

"God. I've waited forever to hear that. I want you to say it all the time."

My eyes prickle with tears. I thought I was just putting a professional distance between us, nothing personal. But his tone says it was totally personal.

He pulls the other nipple in his mouth, his hand traveling south and pulling at my thong until it slides down my legs and lands somewhere, in some other country. Anticipation quivers through me as I'm completely exposed to him.

"You have too many clothes on," I say, in a husky voice I don't recognize as my own.

"Damn right." He grins. "I've been working *hard* for this body." He yanks the shirt over his head, then slips off his boxers. They, too, vanish into the background.

Oh my. His cock is stunning. Hard. Long. Thick. Ending in a plum-shaped head. The thick veins throb on the shaft, and I push myself up and lick the tip, needing to taste him—slick salt and Nate at his most basic.

He lets out a low groan. "Damn, Evie, you have to stop. My control is pretty good, but not right now."

What? "Why not now?" I demand.

"Because I haven't come in the last two weeks. Rosie just wasn't going to cut it."

The admission is sexy. Hot. Desire pulses through me, but more potent is the love I feel for him.

I cradle his face between my hands and kiss him with all the adoration in my heart. All the warm, soft, gooey emotions welling inside me. Our mouths fuse, the contact lushly erotic. I part my thighs, so there's no doubt whatsoever in his mind that I want him —that I crave this intimacy between us.

One hand crushes my hair, keeping me close as though he's afraid I might vanish. The other traces the curves of my body, exploring and learning the sensitivity and texture of my bare skin —every square inch.

I moan, letting him know without breaking the kiss that I love his touch. And that he's making me so, so wet.

His fingers brush along my hips, then move closer and closer to the flesh between my legs. My breathing quickens, anticipation coiling. The pad of his thumb glides down my slick folds, starting from the clitoris…all the way down to the opening of my pussy and back up again. I shudder as pure bliss spreads through me. The taste of him, the feel of him is the only thing saturating my mind, my senses. I cling to him, my nails digging into his hard muscles. My God. He is magnificently male.

And all mine.

Thumb over my throbbing clit, he pushes a finger into me. The friction is sweet, but light. I clench around it, wishing it were his cock instead.

"Fuck, you're so tight," he says.

"It's been a while," I say breathlessly. Whatever happened in Vegas doesn't count, since we don't remember it. "And I'm dying to feel you inside me. Can we do that now?"

The muscles in his jaw bunch. "I need to get a condom."

"Why? You can't get me pregnant."

"Rubbers are for other things, too, and it's different from Vegas, where we were too drunk to remember. I'd love to go bareback, but if you aren't comfortable…"

I've never been with a man who'd think of my comfort and protection so much so that he'd forgo raw sex. If I'd ever had any doubts, this would decimate them.

I lay a tender hand on his cheek and brush my thumb over the intense frown on his face, the one he wears when he's trying to focus and control himself. "I trust you, Nate."

His Adam's apple bobs. "I'm clean."

"I know. So am I." I smile, so incredibly touched.

When he enters me, our fingers linked tightly, it's like every light in the universe has come on. It feels so good to have him stretch and fill me. Better than anything I've ever had. Nothing else in my life ever made me feel this intimately connected to somebody. Or cared for. Or adored.

He watches my face as he drives into me, each thrust slightly different, and incredibly pleasurable. He changes the angle of his hips, and as he pushes forward, he does a grinding motion against my clit that makes me see fireworks, whimper and gasp and pray for more.

And he gives me more. His dark eyes glitter above me, and I open myself wider for a deeper penetration. I want to feel him all the way.

Blissful pleasure builds, runs through me, begins to ravage me. My eyes squeeze shut as I lose myself on a tide of ecstasy, and the orgasm breaks.

"Nate!"

His fingers tighten on me. Not hard enough to hurt, but enough to know he's never letting me go. His movements are no longer controlled. The drive of his hips is harder, faster and wilder. I love it. This passionate, crazed side of him is a turn-on.

A second orgasm rips through me with shocking intensity. I arch my back and clench my teeth so I don't scream loudly enough to alert Mom down the hall. Nate stiffens, pushing into me one last time. I feel the hot warmth spilling inside, and I hold him to me, my heart glowing with happiness.

34

NATE

I flop onto my back so I don't crush Evie, then pull her close, needing to feel her warmth. It took so damn long—I worked harder to win her over than I ever had to for anybody else—that it almost seems like this is just another of my fever dreams.

But the solid feel of her head on my shoulder and the silken hair on my arm say it's real.

It takes a while before I can breathe normally again. Damn. I'm in good shape, but loving Evie took everything out of me.

But it was worth it. *She's* worth it.

I run my gaze over her beautiful face. It's soft—her blue eyes hazy with afterglow, her lips curved into a slight, satisfied smile.

I bring her hand to my lips and kiss the back of it. "You're amazing," I say.

"So are you," she says, still a little breathless. Then she flings her free arm out. "The Great Wall is no more."

"Yeah. I'm burning it down. We can do s'mores over the bonfire."

She laughs. "Whatever you like. I just want your hot body all to myself." She waggles her eyebrows, giving me an exaggerated lascivious look.

Marrying My Billionaire Boss

"You only want me for my body," I joke.

"I want you for other things, too." She grows a little more serious. "Can I ask you something?"

"Sure," I say, feeling extra indulgent and generous. She could ask anything—even to drive my precious Bugatti—and I'd say yes.

"Your family's right about your alcohol limit, aren't they?"

Naturally. She doesn't ask about a car that would get any other woman excited. I sigh. *My damn family. They talk too much.* Hopefully she's not too peeved about my little white lie. "Yeah. I can drink quite a bit."

She shifts until she can look at my face straight on. "So why'd you pretend to be totally soused after only three drinks?"

I run my fingers through her hair idly, wondering how I'm supposed to explain my rather ridiculous plan.

With honesty, obviously. And maybe you should come clean about your "inability to coordinate outfits" and obsession with green smoothies. You know you just made those things up to get her to come to your place in the morning, hoping you could seduce her with your body.

Yeah. But one thing at a time. I don't want to overwhelm her in her delicate condition. It'd be terrible if she fainted again...even if she is lying on a bed at the moment.

"Well," I begin slowly, picking my words with care. "I originally hired you because Kim said good things about you. I mean, partially."

"Partially?"

"Yeah. You being hot was the other part."

She snorts.

"Hey, it's true. You're hot. I've been lusting after you since the interview. Anyway, you were impossible to get close to, so I decided to pretend to be drunk. I figured, you know...maybe you'd tell me things you might not otherwise." If I were standing, I'd be squirming. It sounds even worse spoken out loud.

"Really?" She props herself on my chest. "Were you disappointed when I just brought you here, then said you were a great boss?"

That memory is the worst. Mildly humiliating, too. "Of course. You didn't take anything I said seriously."

"Who takes that kind of praise seriously? I thought it was sweet, but you were drunk." She tilts her head. "Why didn't you try to tell me the truth later?"

"Because the whole thing was stupid, and I didn't think it would come back to bite me like this. It's a bit annoying when you tell me to stop after three drinks, but it isn't like I *have* to drink. It was more important you didn't think I was an idiot." The moment the admission leaves my mouth, I press my lips together. I didn't mean to say quite this much. But Evie has the power to strip me down, make me feel vulnerable and exposed, the way nobody else ever has before. It's as though my subconscious knows she won't trample on me or break my trust.

"I think it's kind of adorable. I won't think badly of you. You're brilliant." She smiles, then kisses me. "We should do something else now."

"Like what?" I ask, wondering if she wants to talk about the baby. Pregnant women care about that kind of things, don't they? Maybe she wants to make a list of names she likes. We should decide on it before Barron decides for us. He'll probably want us to name the child after him.

"You didn't see just missionary in the statue, did you?" A naughty gleam sparks in her eyes.

My body reacts instantly, my cock going hard. "No, but maybe we shouldn't do too much. You're pregnant, and we need to be careful until you get checked out by an obstetrician."

She frowns. "You think?"

"Yeah. Definitely. A baby is a serious business. It's better these days, but women used to die all the time."

"You're so morbid." Her tone is surprisingly gentle.

"It's just that I'm involved with health care. I know a lot about it, including its history. Even today, things can go wrong." The hospitals and clinics my family funds treat so many cases like that. They're heartbreaking, and I can't let anything happen to Evie or our baby. "Besides, you fainted this afternoon. You don't know what it did to me to see you just collapse like that." I put a hand over my chest. "Unless you want to take a decade off my life, don't do it again."

"I'll try not to." She sighs. "As for the other fun stuff, I guess we can ration it out."

"Yes. Trust me, this is frustrating my dick more than it's frustrating you."

That makes her laugh, as intended. "But only until tomorrow. I'm definitely going to see my doctor, no matter what kind of bribe I need to offer."

NATE

Some random sound pricks me awake. I open my eyes, listening and wondering what time it is. The bedside clock says it's barely three. Evie's sleeping, curled next to me. She breathes so quietly that it takes me a moment to realize she really is inhaling and exhaling.

Another bump outside. Tension grips my body. The security system in my house is top of the line. It shouldn't let intruders in.

No. Wait. Is that Mari out in the hall? She might need something. I should go check, make sure she doesn't trip and hurt herself in the unfamiliar space.

I slip out of bed and put on a robe from the closet before padding downstairs. *There*. She's standing in the kitchen, holding a glass of water. Her gray hair is pulled back into a messy ponytail. There's something about her that's tough, but fair and down to earth. Honest. It's obvious Evie took after her mom a lot. Then I note the threadbare pea-green pajamas on her thin frame and make a mental note to get her something nice and luxurious.

"Mari, you finding everything you need?"

She slowly turns her head toward me. "Yes."

No smile. A small frown forming. Okay. She's the disapproving mother-in-law. I thought it was the fathers-in-law who didn't care for their daughters' choice of husbands. On the other hand, I shouldn't stereotype. Just look at Court's mom.

I should get everything out in the open, smooth over whatever issues she has with me. I want Evie happy, and getting along with her mom is going to be a factor. "You know, we didn't get to talk at all, even at the party. I'm sure you have a lot of questions."

"I'm wondering what's going on with my daughter. She's not the impulsive type."

I laugh. "Tell me about it."

"And yet I had to learn about her wedding from a gossipy neighbor. It's clear Evie married you out of impulse—or maybe because she's pregnant. And obviously it's been stressful. She passed out at the party."

"Yeah. I feel terrible about that. I should've been more attentive." For a second I debate telling her we were likely already married when we got ourselves pregnant, but decide against it. That would sound even worse, especially if she ever learns that we don't remember either the wedding ceremony or the wedding night.

"I care about Evie very much," I say instead. "I respect her brain, admire her beauty and love that she's hardworking and honest. I plan to make her happy." And I mean that. Every time I make her smile, I feel like the most accomplished man ever.

Mari's expression doesn't change. "The scariest man of all is the earnest jerk. They hit you when you least expect it."

I stare, stunned. What makes her think I'm a jerk? And not just any jerk, but a Class-A, Sneaky as Fuck Jerk?

"I've read articles about you," she adds. "I'm sure there's some journalistic exaggeration, but where there's smoke..." She purses her mouth.

Tabloids. "They are so much worse than the reality," I say. "You know how it is."

"Actually, I don't. I've never had to deal with anyone like you. And I worry about Evie. She's too innocent and trusting."

"Her trust isn't misplaced, ma'am."

"It isn't?" She smiles, but it doesn't reach her cool eyes. "Do you know the origin of the term 'con man'?"

"No," I say, wondering where she's going with this. Is she trying to warn me somebody's about to fleece me blind?

"The 'con' in 'con man' comes from 'confidence.' Using lies and deception to gain someone's confidence and then betraying them in the end. And I'm not sure how honest of a man you are."

My throat closes. I still have those two lies I haven't fessed up to Evie yet. Yeah, so they're minor ones—the one about my smoothie and my inability to pick out my own clothes—but they're still lies. And they're like a double garrote around my neck, choking me, especially when Mari's sharp gaze is pinning my face.

She lets out a sudden sigh, her shoulders drooping. "Maybe you don't mean to hurt her now. Maybe you think it's not going to be like your previous relationships. But it's my job to worry anyway. She's everything to me."

I cringe inwardly. If she'd seen some of the crazy shit that I've done, of course she'd think I'm a good-for-nothing, lucky-as-hell bastard who happened to be born to a rich family. Hell, *I'm* embarrassed about some of it.

But her disapproval is coming from the fact that she loves her daughter, and I can't fault her for that. "Then I'll simply have to prove myself—do everything in my power to keep Evie happy. All I ask is that you withhold judgment until—actually, make that *unless* I screw up."

For a brief moment, Mari's expression softens. "That's...acceptable."

35

EVIE

I'M THE FIRST TO WAKE UP. OF COURSE, I'M USED TO getting up earlier than Nate anyway. I roll on my side, prop my head on my hand and look down at his face. He looks so relaxed and peaceful. His mouth is soft—and just slightly curved upward at the corners. Must be having a great dream. *Maybe a sex dream about me.*

I wish he were just a little more selfish about his needs. But his refusal to go for a second round last night meant a lot to me, especially when he explained why. He's been managing so many hospitals, and I'm sure he's seen and heard about all the things that can go wrong with a pregnancy. I lay my hand over my belly. Besides, it's good to be on the cautious side. I'm sure my doctor's going to clear me for sex and every other normal activity I can think of. I'm healthy as a horse. The fainting yesterday was a total aberration.

Quietly, I sneak out of the bed, then out of habit, I walk into the closet and pick out a sky-blue polo shirt and jeans for him. He doesn't have any appointments, but it's always best to dress him somewhat nicely. Just in case.

That done, I put on my night shirt and shorts, then make my

way downstairs. I'm hungry and need to take better care of myself. No more eating only a single piece of toast all day or any of that stuff. I go check the delivery chute. There's a cooler full of fresh greens for Nate's shake. He hasn't had one for so long, basically since his mom's been here, and we have a huge pile of kale. I should toss out all the wilted ones.

At the very bottom of the bag is a head of broccoli. It's a deep green and extra firm. I inhale it. Smells *incredible*. I never knew a smell could be so tempting.

My mouth starts to water as I wash the veggies like I routinely do in the morning. I put everything into the blender, let the appliance work its magic, then dump the concoction into a glass. The thick smoothie rises, a frosty, glistening column of forest green. The smell somehow isn't pungent like usual. Instead, it's alluring, seductive, a cruciferous siren calling my name.

Unable to help myself, I swipe a finger around the inside of the blender and taste it.

Oh. My. God.

The flavor explodes on my tongue, the taste sweet and refreshing. *How can vegetables be like this?* The last time I tried a green smoothie, it was like licking sewage. What's going on? Did the delivery service change the type of kale? I check the leftover leaves. They look the same. Is it the broccoli? No...can't be.

I look down at my belly. *Is it the baby?*

Quite possibly. He—I decide to settle on he, because he and/or she is mouthful and I'm not going to have a girl just because Barron says he wants one—could've gotten his taste for the green goo from Nate.

Saliva pools in my mouth, and suddenly I feel like I'll die if I don't have a shake for myself. I make one using the remaining kale and broccoli.

Just then, Nate walks in, wearing a plain white shirt and shorts. "Good morning."

"Good morning." If words could bounce, mine would be hitting the ceiling. It's so exciting we can actually share his favorite breakfast! "Look, I made you your shake again!"

He looks at me like he can't decide if he should cry or hug me. *I knew he would be touched.*

"Um. I thought we'd make something else for your mom." He clears his throat.

"She doesn't really eat breakfast. Just coffee is fine."

"Uh-huh." Nate eyes two servings of shake on the counter. I can see some internal debate fleeting through his gorgeous face.

Finally, he says, "Look, Evie, you don't have to drink one just to suit me. I don't even really li—"

"Nonsense! It tastes amazing! I love it!" I hand him his glass, and take mine. "Cheers!" I clink our glasses.

Nate smiles brightly—probably thrilled I'm doing a better job of ensuring that I get sufficient nutrients—and starts drinking.

Pleased with myself, I chug mine down. I can feel all the antioxidant goodness and hydration coursing through my veins, infusing me with super health. Okay, maybe it isn't happening *instantly*—it hasn't even been digested—but it's lovely anyway.

"I can see why you insist on this every morning." I put a hand over my belly. "I think the baby's taking after Daddy."

"I'm..." Nate's smile is even wider now. "I don't even know what to say."

"You don't have to say anything. Just be happy."

"I'm happy. Very, very happy." He clears his throat. "Can we have some coffee?"

"Actually, I can't. I don't think I'm supposed to."

"Oh." He looks concerned again. "Are you sure you don't want anything else, though? Maybe yogurt? Berries?"

I beam at him. "I'm fine. Really."

He nods slowly. "Well then. Let me get the coffee started."

"I can do that for you," I say out of habit.

"It's okay. Really, you don't have to be like my assistant here." He goes to the coffeemaker and makes enough for two.

"But I am your assistant."

"Sure, at the office. But we're at home, and this is the weekend."

Ah. That's sweet, I think with a smile, although there's no way I'm letting him select his own clothes.

"I can make my own coffee." As soon as the brewing is done, he downs his quickly.

I don't know why he's in such a hurry. I don't mind if he wants to take his time and enjoy his java.

"I'm going to shower," he says.

I grin. "Let me go with you."

Just then, Mom comes down, and I realize that Morning Shower Fun isn't going to happen. I should spend some time with her, especially since she doesn't look any less worried. She's trying to hide it, but I know her too well not to notice.

"Actually, you go ahead," I say to Nate.

He looks at me, then at Mom, sighs slightly and goes upstairs.

Mom's in a white T-shirt and soft jeans. She takes a stool by the counter, and I serve her the rest of the coffee. She takes it black. Says it's better that way, but I also suspect she likes it that way because it's cheaper—no need for cream or sugar.

I take a stool next to hers, running my sweaty palms on my shorts. Why do I feel like I'm back in high school and got caught sneaking out late? "Hi, Mom."

"Morning, Evie." She's quiet, almost too calm. It's the voice she uses when she wants to talk about something I might not want to hear.

"Did you have a good sleep?" I ask, even though I'm sure that isn't what she wants to talk about.

"Yes." She takes a couple sips of her coffee. "This is good."

"Nate likes to indulge."

She looks at the dark brew, then at me. Her gaze is so penetrating, I'm afraid she's reading every thought in my head. "You really care about him."

I adore him, but I don't want to say that to Mom yet. Nate should hear it first. "He's a great guy."

She nods. "He seems to be nice to you."

"Hang around a little while, and you'll see." And I really do want her to spend time with us as a couple. Besides, I want to take her shopping and buy her something nice. Maybe new clothes or shoes. Maybe a mani pedi. She hasn't splurged on herself in ages.

"I can't. I need to go back."

The announcement hits me like a slap, and I suddenly feel like crying. I thought she'd be spending at least a week. Maybe I should've asked and made sure, but I was so stressed and frazzled about meeting Nate's family that I never did, just assumed. We haven't seen each other since I left Dillington, and surely she has enough vacation days saved up. If not, I can make it up for her. I have savings now.

Guilt rears its head. I didn't contact her—no text or calls. I was too wrapped up in maintaining the happily married couple façade. And I didn't know what to say to Mom about that, so I just told myself I'd talk to her later...later...until...

I put a hand over my eyes. "I'm sorry."

"No, baby, it isn't your fault. Betty's been out sick." She sighs. "Breast cancer."

I gasp. "Oh my God. Is she going to be okay?" Betty was one of the very few who stood by me through the Chadwick ordeal.

"It's treatable, but it won't be easy. I just want to be in town. Help keep an eye on her, make sure she's okay."

"Of course. I'm sorry to hear it," I say, wishing I could be there for Betty too, after all she's done for me. "Is she getting good care?"

"The doctors are doing what they can. She's going to beat it. She's a fighter."

"Yes, she is." I squeeze Mom's hand. I know cancer treatment is expensive, and I can't help but think maybe I can ask Nate if the foundation can do something for Betty. "If you or Betty need anything, just call or text anytime. I'll do everything in my power to help."

Mom gives me a small smile. "You're such a sweet child. Always were." She smooths my hair from my face, tucking tendrils behind my ears. "Your husband is a very wealthy man. A powerful man. He has a lot of powerful people around him, too. His friends. His family."

She isn't being too obvious, but I don't miss the subtle emphasis she puts on "his." "Mom, what are you trying to say?"

"I'm just saying you need to be careful." She bites her lip, something she does whenever she's debating how much to say. "People who never treated you well might come out of the blue to be friendly. There are so many who want to take advantage."

Oh. Maybe she heard about Chad's rather pointless call.

"Mom, I'm not a kid anymore. I can tell the difference between people being genuine and people trying to fake a friendship."

She gives me a slight smile, patting my hand. "I know you're smart, Evie. I'm probably fretting over nothing."

I shake my head, not wanting Mom to feel bad about it. "Probably, but I love it that you still worry about me. It means you still love me." I turn my hand over so I can squeeze hers. "Besides, Nate is used to dealing with people with, let's say, less-than-genuine intent. So he's not going to let anybody use me like that either."

Something like relief flickers in her eyes. "That's true. Yes, you're right." She looks up the stairs. "He would know how to handle something like that."

36

EVIE

NATE AND I TAKE MOM TO THE AIRPORT, WHERE NATE'S JET is waiting to take her back. I hug her tightly, asking her to come back anytime. Nate says the same.

Mom jokes that no husband wants to put up with a mother-in-law, but he says it's because none of them has Mari Parker as their mother-in-law with his most charming smile. Then he tells her few amusing anecdotes from his childhood and eventually has her laughing, the sound light and easy.

I stare, wondering when the last time I heard her sound like that was. And the answer is: never. She's always been serious. But then, our lives were hard, just one tiny misstep away from missing a meal or even homelessness. We've been extraordinarily lucky that neither of us ever got seriously sick or injured.

"Thank you," I say to Nate as we step into our home. It still amazes me that this beautiful place is mine too.

"For what?"

I turn around and hold his hands in mine. "Making my mother laugh like that. She's sacrificed so much for me, and I didn't realize how much until now," I say quietly, slightly embarrassed at how selfish I've been.

He puts a hand on my shoulder. "Don't make it sound like you've failed somehow. She adores you. She lived and worked hard for you, and she's proud of you. And you know what? How about if we send her and her friend on a nice cruise for Christmas? A suite with a butler, concierge service, the works. They can cruise the Caribbean. And get pampered."

His offer is generous, and I feel my heart grow warm. Smiling, I hug him. "Thank you. But..." I sigh. "I don't know if she can. Do you know why she had to leave early?"

"She got tired of the porn studio?" He tilts his chin toward the statue from Barron.

It makes me choke and laugh at the same time. "Ah, no. It's actually a friend of hers in Dillington. She's sick with breast cancer. She lives alone, and Mom wants to make sure she's okay."

All the light humor leaves his face. "Is her doctor any good? Is she getting the treatment she needs?"

"Yeah. I think so."

"I don't want to presume, but you know you and your mom can ask me for anything, right?"

"I know." I also know that he'll move heaven and earth to make it happen because he's just that generous and caring. "Thank you."

He places a soft kiss on my forehead. "Anytime. It's about time you get used to being my wife. And none of that six weeks, then get divorced stuff. The baby needs its father."

I smile at him because that's the right response, but I don't miss the fact that he didn't say anything about love. But it's clear that he trusts me one hundred percent. Otherwise he would never have told his family the baby was his. I should be happy about that. Love can't happen without trust. I'm at least ten steps ahead.

"So about *your* doctor visit..." Nate begins.

"Let's not do that on a Sunday, even if doctors *will* come out for a Sterling baby. If they're working on a Sunday, it's for emergencies. And I feel fine."

"Hmm. How about your regular doctor?"

"I, uh, don't really have one. I haven't had a chance—or a reason—to go to one." Besides, gynecologists are right up there with dentists on the list of specialists I'd rather not see. I know I need to do pap smears and all that, but the visits are always so awkward, and the doctor examining me down there with clinical efficiency and a glob of cold lube? I can't think of anything more embarrassing.

"Well, you have to see somebody. How about someone from the Sterling Medical Center? The doctors there are first-rate, and they can probably fit you in as a favor. And look, no kidding: if I don't call Barron and give him some news, he's going to show up with an obstetrician and one of those weird pink medieval sex-torture chairs."

I snort a laugh at his description of stirrups. He's seen them at the center, and they do come in pink. "Okay, okay, fine. How about Dr. Wong?" I remember working with her a few times, and I like her. Most importantly, she has a friendly demeanor that never fails to put people at ease. "Tomorrow."

"Yeah, she's very good. But are you sure you want to wait until tomorrow? Because—"

"*Tomorrow.* Monday."

He doesn't like it, but finally says, "All right."

"Let me text her and see when she's coming in," I say, grabbing my phone. Thankfully, she'll be working and she says she can see me, if I drop by on the way to the Sterling & Wilson Los Angeles headquarters. I check Nate's schedule to make sure he doesn't have any meetings, then say okay.

Nate insists on coming with me.

"Won't you have to review some reports or something?" I ask.

"All that other stuff can wait. I want to be with you every step of the way."

I nod with relief. I'm glad he wants to be as involved as possible. I want our child to know he's loved by *both* his parents. He should never have to experience the achy pang of sadness at seeing other kids with their dads while he doesn't have a dad to talk to or play with.

～

EVIE

• • •

On Monday, I get up, shrug into a dressing robe and go to the closet first, to pick out his clothes. I want him in a power suit. Not because he has meetings, but because he looks hot as hell in it.

I sense his presence behind me and turn around, smiling. He's in nothing but boxers, and for a moment, I can't remember what I need to tell him. He looks utterly touchable: his hair slightly messy, dark stubble shadowing his chiseled cheeks. And his shoulders look extra broad today. I never appreciated how sexy broad, strong shoulders could be until I met him.

"Good morning," he says. "What are you doing in the closet so early?"

I notice the hanger in my hand and pull myself together. "Just picking some stuff out for you. What do you think?" I show him the navy pinstriped suit.

He gives it a cursory glance. "Nice, but I prefer a shirt and slacks."

"I know—" I swallow the rest of the words abruptly. *Did he just say he wants something other than what I picked out?* "I'm sorry?"

"Just a shirt and slacks is fine. No need for a suit. I don't have any meetings today."

I stare at him, trying to process what just happened. *He vetoed my choice.* He's never done that before. What's going on? Does he not like what I've selected for him? And by shirt and slacks...

My gaze drifts toward the back of the closet, where I hid the hideous puke-green shirt and pink shark pants. *Oh, good God no.*

"What's wrong with the suit?" I ask.

"Nothing. It came from my closet, so of course it's fine."

A small shudder runs through me. He thinks everything in his closet is great. *Not everything, Nate.* "Let me pick out the shirt and pants, then."

"Evie, really. I can dress myself."

I inhale deeply. "If you're doing this to lessen my workload because of my pregnancy, it isn't necessary. I'm perfectly capable of picking out your clothes as usual."

"So am I. I've been dressing myself since I was four."

His poor mother.

"I only said I couldn't and needed you here every morning because..." He clears his throat, looking slightly abashed. "Look, I just wanted you here every morning. I thought that if you saw, you know, my body in its most, uh, natural form—but without crossing the line, if you see what I mean—you'd be, well..."

"Yes?"

"...overcome with, uh, lust."

Men. "So. You actually can pick out clothes that won't embarrass you or the people who see you?"

He nods.

"Then what are the green shirt and shark pants for?" I gesture toward the back, needing to be sure.

"Those? They're gag gift from Court. He thought it'd be hilarious to put me in them. Too bad for him that he can never beat me in poker or blackjack."

I press the heels of my hands against my temples, unsure if I should be annoyed or glad that he isn't colorblind and has decent taste. I decide I should be a little bit of both. "I can't believe this. Do you know I had to get up an hour and a half early to come over here and help you get dressed?"

He looks a little guilty—but only a little. "Yeah, I know. And I'm sorry about that. But I didn't think you'd resist for so long! I thought you'd give in within, you know, a month or two...and then I could tell you the truth." He shoots me an angelic smile, the kind that I'm sure has granted him every get-out-of-jail-free card he's ever needed.

"You're incorrigible. Absolutely terrible," I say, doing my best not to let my twitching mouth curve into a smile. Damn it, even though I know he's being ridiculously manipulative, I just can't help myself from softening. He's too irresistible.

"I am, I know. But I'll make it up to you. How about I buy you a pink Cullinan for Christmas, like the one Sophia has? It's a pretty car."

Just the thought of such a crazy extravagance is almost

enough to make me faint again. I just haven't gotten used to this mindset. Not yet, and maybe not ever. "No! That thing probably costs a kidney and a lung."

"I think the new ones are only, like, a little finger."

"Still a no. And since you just confessed to your crime, you can pick out your own clothes. I'm going to shower. *Alone*."

I sashay away and step into the bathroom. But I don't lock the door, because I don't really want to shower alone. I toss my dressing gown on the counter and purse my lips. If Nate doesn't get my hint—hello, there was no sound of the lock clicking into place!—I'm going to be very disappointed.

I step into the glass stall big enough to host a foursome. The tiles feel slightly grainy, like fine sandpaper, against the bottom of my feet. I start the shower. The water—which comes out of the rainfall faucet above my head and twelve pulsing jets on three vertical chrome pipes—is instantly hot. I sigh under the spray. Now *this* is a perk I can totally get used to. Until I moved in here, I didn't know water could come out hot without having to wait.

The door opens. My heart beats faster. *Nate doesn't disappoint!*

He steps into the stall, having already discarded his boxers. His cock is hard and thick, the head almost touching his tight six-pack. My God, the man's magnificent. Perfect. If he hadn't been born rich, he could make a fortune as an underwear model.

"I don't feel right, not making amends after what I've done," he says lightly.

His gaze skims over my wet body from face to breasts to the flesh between my legs and below, then back up to my eyes. I feel the perusal like a physical touch, and my nipples pucker and my clit throbs. Hard.

"Oh yeah?" I say, slightly breathless now. "What are you going to do then?"

"Atone."

Raising an eyebrow, I eye his impressive erection. "I don't think a morning quickie is really a proper form of atonement."

"Depends on the quickie."

He steps toward me. Lust thickens my blood, need

hammering in my chest. He wraps my hair in his fist and kisses me hard.

I part my mouth at the masterful plundering of his lips and tongue. He pushes inside, then pulls back, then again and again and again, imitating the sweet friction of his cock sliding into me from yesterday. But instead of pushing into my pussy, his cock is pulsing against my belly.

His other hand slides down my wet body, tracing my shoulder, then down my arm until it hits my wrist, then jumps to my hips and rises back up. He cups my breast, holding its weight in his big, warm hand, circling his thumb lazily over my wet nipple.

Thick pleasure courses through me, sending one electric zing after another until my toes curl against the ribbed tiled floor. He pinches my nipple between his thumb and index finger, then tugs gently. A cry gets strangled in my throat.

"Love your body," he whispers, his voice rough.

I love what you do to my body, I think. But before I can tell him so, he takes the other nipple into his mouth. Gasping, I lean against the wall, my hands not finding any purchase against the smooth glass wall behind me. I grab the closest water pipe, then tunnel my fingers into his wet hair, holding on to him as my knees start to shake.

His mouth glides down, his legs bending. Then finally, he puts one of my legs over his shoulder and looks at my vulnerable pink flesh with bright, lustful avarice. "Gorgeous."

He runs a finger along the folds, and I bite my lip. I can feel the slickness sliding down my thighs. It's an incredible turn-on to have a powerful man kneeling between your legs, ready to give you pleasure.

"I want to hear you scream when you come," he growls deep in his chest. "I've been wanting to spend a morning doing this to you for a long time."

My face flames even as excitement sparks through me. He moves in and devours me like a starving man. His mouth pulls at my clit, making it throb until I think I'll die from the sharply blissful sensation. He's relentless, his fingers penetrating me, two at first, then three. I clench around them, sobbing as pleasure builds, pull by pull, breath by breath.

I start to get close. Nate curls his fingers just so, driving with just enough force to give me exactly what I need, as he tongues my clit with more lustful abandon than pure skill.

My vision turns blinding white as an orgasm shatters me. I scream his name, my back arching, my pelvis rocking and my whole body shaking.

He holds me tightly the entire time, his tongue lapping at me. When I finally stop trembling, he looks up at me with the same angelic smile he gave me earlier in the closet. And I feel my heart melt.

"How was my penance?"

I laugh breathlessly. "Very good."

He kisses my belly. "Am I forgiven, then?"

"If you atone like this...?" I hold his hands and raise them. He comes up until he's standing before me. "I suppose you are."

37

EVIE

NATE DRIVES US. I ASK HIM WHEN MIGUEL'S COMING BACK, and he says he isn't sure but doesn't care.

"You honestly don't know?"

He clears his throat. "I might've given him six weeks off. I was planning on changing your mind about the divorce."

"Why?" I ask. "I thought six weeks was the whole idea."

"It was not. And I didn't care for it. I don't like going about my life with a set outcome. That limits your options, and I prefer to not kill off possibilities. Life can really surprise you if you approach it with an open mind."

That's a wise attitude, I decide with a smile. Maybe I should adopt it. "Regardless, I'm sure his wife appreciates the paid leave."

"I deserve the Best Boss of the Millennium Award."

"Want me to alert the media?"

He gives it mock consideration. "Probably best if you do."

I smile. He might talk like that, but he doesn't really want it. If he were the type to want credit for every good deed he does, he'd make sure to advertise how much he tips, how well he treats his workers and so on. The charity portion of Sterling & Wilson has its own PR team. But Nate never seeks the limelight. The team only focuses on the good the medical centers and hospitals are doing with the Sterling & Wilson fortune.

I check my phone to see if there's anything urgent from the auditors or medical centers. I see a text from Kim asking to have lunch today, so I say yes because she's likely dying to know how the party went, and I want to tell her about the baby in person. I let her know she has to come pick me up, though, and she says that's fine.

That done, I confirm the day's agenda on the tablet one more time while Nate drives us to the Sterling Medical Center.

Once we arrive, we go up to Dr. Wong's office together. Her office is quite interesting. No frills, no nonsense. You'd think it should be sterile and creepy—in that *you're here because your body hates you and you're going to die* way—but it's actually comforting, because the place is just like the good doctor herself. I've never seen or heard her sugarcoat anything, but she's not unkind or cold.

Dr. Wong is a pretty woman in her mid-forties. Her glossy black hair is long and straight, and I envy how it sits around her face and shoulders like a sleek veil. My hair needs some serious spray help to stay neat.

I don't think she has any makeup on her face, but she has pink color on her lips. She smiles when she sees me and Nate. "Hello, Evie. And Nate. Congratulations."

"Thank you," we say together, and take the seats in one of the three examination and consultation rooms.

"Let's get you started. Pregnant already, huh?"

I flush, suddenly a little shy but also pleased and excited about the life growing inside me. "Yeah."

"Well, that's good. It's easier when you're younger. Try having a child when you're in your thirties. Your body just can't handle lack of sleep the way you used to in your twenties. Doesn't snap back"—she snaps her fingers loudly—"like it did before."

I laugh at her light, joking tone. Nate squeezes my hand. "I'll get Evie whatever help she needs so she can take care of herself, too."

Dr. Wong smiles. "I'm sure she'll appreciate it. Sleep deprivation can be hard, especially when your hormones are fluctuating. Anyway, that's all still to come, so let's make sure everything's fine with you now."

She does the usual—draws blood, checks my blood pressure, asks me about my appetite, any signs of nausea and so on.

"Are you going to do that ultrasound thing?" I ask.

"It's a bit too early for that. We can do it next time, if you'd like." She smiles. "And you should start taking prenatal vitamins as soon as possible. If you want, the pharmacy on site has some you can get on your way out."

Nate is tapping on his phone.

"What are you doing?" I ask, wondering if something critical at work just popped up. Maybe he should've just gone to the office. Or maybe I should've just waited until it was convenient for both of us, instead of jumping through Barron's hoops.

On the other hand, I still haven't forgotten the man's bulldozer-like ways or the way he commandeered the Vegas hotel. I had the disadvantage of being thongless, but I have a feeling that having underwear on wouldn't have made much difference.

"Making notes so we don't forget anything," Nate says.

I stifle a laugh. He's adorably cute. And usually it's my job to take notes.

A nurse hands Dr. Wong some papers, which she looks over. "You're in perfect health," she says, then explains what each item means.

I listen, but they don't mean much to me. All I know—all that matters—is that the results are good.

She adds, "There's no reason for you to restrict your activities, including intercourse, as long as they aren't overly vigorous or tiring. If you don't feel well, you should contact me anytime."

"Thank you." I smile, relieved. I didn't think there was anything wrong with me, but it's good to have a doctor confirm it. It should give Nate some peace of mind, too.

And he can lay off the one-sex-session-a-day rule, my lusty hormones whisper.

"Wait a minute, doc," Nate says, raising a finger. "If she's fine, why did she faint on Saturday?"

She turns to me. "You fainted?"

"I think it was the shock of realizing I was pregnant," I say hurriedly, hating feeling like I've been some naughty, information-concealing gnome. "I didn't even know I was, and before I could make an official announcement, Nate's nephew just blurted it out in front of everyone. Besides, the doctor who came by said it was just some dehydration."

She purses her lips. "I see. Well, avoid stress as much as you can, drink plenty of fluids and remember that you're eating for two now. A healthy mom makes a healthy baby."

"Yes, ma'am," I say meekly, even though I secretly think the doctor and Nate are being a little too coddling.

"But otherwise, really, you're fine." She turns to Nate. "She's fine."

Thank you.

She asks me to come back in a month, reiterating that I should call if I notice anything unusual or have any questions. I put it on my calendar, and Nate and I leave together.

"All clear," I say with a huge smile as we're talking toward the parking lot. "Now you don't have to worry about anything."

He nods once. "That's true."

"And we don't have to, you know, *limit* ourselves."

He laughs, the sound throaty and hot. "Yes, but remember what she said about no stress and eating well."

"You'll make someone a great mom," I tease.

Nate drives us to Sterling & Wilson's Los Angeles building. Although my body's still humming from the earlier orgasm and the doctor's good news, I try to focus on work once we're inside the office. What Nate does is so much more important than just making money. He is actually making a difference in the world. And I'm proud to be part of that.

While Nate's on a call, I get a padded envelope delivered to me personally from somebody named Miles Wellington in Arlington, Virginia. What's this about? There's a medical center funded by the family in Virginia, but I don't know anybody named Miles Wellington there, and his address isn't the medical center's either.

I open the package and a note falls out.

I thought it prudent to return this to you.

—M.W.

Thinking, *Return what?* I shake the envelope loose.

The thong that went missing in Vegas lands on my desk, and my heart stops for a moment. The underwear is sealed in some kind of clear plastic wrap, but it's obvious that it's been laundered, pressed and folded.

Oh, crap. How the hell did it end up with... Who is this guy again? Miles Wellington?

I lost the damn thong in Vegas. I just don't understand how it ended up in *Virginia*. And how did this man I've never even heard of know where to send it?

My face flames. *Did he sniff it?* Maybe wrap it up around his hot dog down there? Is that why he had to launder it before returning it to me?

No. That doesn't make any sense. Besides, why would a pervert return his plaything?

Then my brain finally kicks in, and I realize, *I have my thong on my desk at work.* Shit. I shove it back into the envelope and drop everything into the bottom drawer, then look around, wondering if anybody saw anything. Seems like I'm okay. Nobody's acting like they just witnessed scandalously embarrassing lingerie.

I put a hand over my racing heart. Okay, so it's not so terrible. My shame is safe. Just between me and this Miles Wellington person. *Who the fuck is he?*

When it's time for lunch, I gather my bag and get up. Nate comes out of his office with a smile that says he's satisfied with the world.

"Let's go get lunch," he says.

"Actually, I can't," I say, feeling slightly bad about it.

"Oh, come on. Don't tell me you're going to turn me down again. We're married. It's only right I provide you with lunch. Just because I don't pound my chest and hunt saber-tooth tigers doesn't mean I've lost all my caveman instincts."

I pat his pecs, not merely to soothe but because I just want to touch him. "I already told Kim I'd eat with her, and she's not going to feel comfortable talking to me if you're around."

He leans closer, the hot, woodsy scent of his cologne acting like a drug on my brain. "Are you ladies planning to talk about me?"

"Maybe." I give him a quick peck on the cheek, since we're in the office, and I'm not bold enough to do a kiss on the mouth when coworkers could be watching. "I'll have lunch with you tomorrow. I promise."

"Deal." His expression grows a bit serious. "You should probably consider moving the rest of your stuff from her apartment into our place, though. Mom's staying with Justin, and your mom's gone, so this is the perfect time."

"Oh." That's right. I left my things there because I didn't expect this marriage to last.

"You can hire movers."

"No, no, it's okay," I say quickly. I'm still traumatized and confused about Miles Wellington. My psyche just can't bear the idea of strangers pawing through my things, even if they're paid professionals.

"If you're sure. Then do you want to go do it today? I don't have any meetings for the rest of the day, and you can get it done. I don't know who might be visiting on the weekend."

I nod. "Okay. If you need anything, though, call me." *Still in assistant mode.*

Nate and I go down to the lobby together. He's holding my hand, and I let him, loving the skin-to-skin contact. Handholding isn't that much of a public display of affection. I just don't want to make my coworkers treat me differently because I'm Nate's wife now (or become hyperaware of my new status), and I feel like blatant PDAs are going to be like rubbing it in. We should limit ourselves to when we're alone or in the elevator—or in the lobby, if there aren't many people around.

When we step out of the elevator, I see Kim waiting. She's in a bright, form-fitting dress you just can't miss, and matching heels that are eye-popping. I start toward her, but Nate stops me. "Here. Treat yourselves to something nice and fancy. And take a long lunch." Handing me his black AmEx, he kisses me, full on the mouth, with all those people milling around.

His tongue flicks against me for a taste, and I lick him back, unable to resist. God, he tastes so good, as my body zings again. It's such a shame to do only one lick, so I go for another, then one more.

Finally he pulls away.

My cheeks heat, but embarrassment is no match for the heat he elicits in me. If I didn't know any better, I'd think he's really an alien from Planet Sex. NASA just hasn't discovered it yet.

"See you later," I say quickly, then dash toward Kim, who's been watching us with both eyebrows raised.

"Wow. That was something."

"That bad?" I ask, slightly uncomfortable, as we head toward the garage to get into her car.

"No, but girl. He's really into you. Everyone can see it."

Groaning, I place a hand over my eyes. There goes my attempt to downplay my marriage to Nate.

"Don't worry. You're married. Who's going to turn you and Nate into HR? Wannabe Unemployed 'R' Us?"

"You're not helping."

"No. I'm here to tell you the truth, the whole truth and nothing but the truth. Don't tell me you can't handle the truth."

I eye her. "Were you watching *A Few Good Men* last night?" After watching a movie or a TV show, Kim quotes it for days afterward. It can be a bit awkward when she's been binge-watching *South Park*.

"Yup. Tom Cruise was sooo delicious in that movie. He should've argued nude. More love from the audience."

We settle inside her car. She notes the plastic in my hand. "What's that?"

"Oh. Nate's credit card. He gave it to me. To treat both of us to a nice lunch."

Kim's eyes widen. "Wow. He gave you a Centurion Card."

"Eh, he's done it before."

"Yeah, to get you to buy clothes to go bid on him, not to treat yourself to lunch." She grins. "You know what this means. We should go to the bistro in the Aylster. I've always wanted to have lunch there, and I have the rest of the day off, so we can take our time and enjoy it. You don't have to get back early or anything, do you?"

"No. I have the rest of the day off too," I say. The hotel's probably on the pricey side, but Nate said we could treat ourselves. Plus, Kim and I haven't gone out like this in a while, and she was instrumental in my getting a job with Nate. Basically, if it hadn't been for her, Nate and I wouldn't be together now.

"So. What's your mom doing now that you're both at work?" Kim asks as she pulls out.

"She actually left yesterday. Got some stuff going on back home."

Even though I know she had to return to Dillington for a good reason, it does make me a bit wistful and sad that she isn't around. I don't know why I feel so down about it, because it isn't like I've been depressed the last ten months or so I've been in L.A. Maybe it's because I thought I'd get to spend more time with her, talk to her, catch up and see how she's doing. I also want to know if there's a way I can help her financially. The school janitorial staff doesn't exactly pay well, and I know she's gone without for a long time. When I told her I needed to leave town and start over, she didn't hesitate. She only asked how much I needed, then wrote me a check without a blink. I don't know how she was able to save up three thousand dollars, but that money didn't come easy. I want to do something nice for her to let her know I appreciate what she's done, although I'm not sure exactly what yet.

Kim pats my hand. "Maybe you can go home this Christmas. It'll be nice, you know?"

"Yeah... I don't know." I think back on her tiny one-bedroom apartment. Is Nate going to want to spend time there when he could be jet-setting around Europe instead? I know he went to Bora Bora last Christmas. I heard some of my coworkers gossip about it.

"Why not? You'll be a free woman by then."

I shake my head. How things have changed over one weekend. "It's complicated. Just park the car," I say, since we're pulling into the hotel. "I'll tell you inside."

Kim hands her key to the valet, and we walk inside together.

The hotel feels very different, now that I'm not here to bid on my boss. The lobby feels brighter, more relaxed. Even the doormen seem friendlier.

The bistro is named Nieve. The place is white, but not in an ugly, sterile way. I don't know exactly what the interior designer did, but the place looks wonderfully beautiful, like a proverbial winter wonderland. Or the North Pole in springtime, like I saw in a documentary once.

The maître d', crisp in a white uniform, comes over. "*Hello*, Kim. We haven't seen you in ages."

"I know. I've been busy, trying to please my boss." She grins. "Can you manage a table for me and my friend here?"

"Not for Salazar and Ceinlys?"

"Not this time. It's finally just me and my friend. I've always wanted to actually *eat* here, you know."

The man looks at me, and recognition flickers in his eyes. "We always have a table for you and Mrs. Sterling. This way." He leads us into the restaurant.

My mouth forms an O. "How did he know me like that?" I whisper in Kim's ear.

"It's his job to know."

"Sorta creepy..."

"Hey, price you pay for marrying a man like Nate Sterling. Don't worry. You'll get used to it."

I'm dubious. I'm not so crazy about people recognizing me this easily. It probably means I won't even be able to use a public bathroom, ever, especially if I'm feeling extra gassy. I should also find a way to pee silently. Otherwise who knows what's going to make it into the tabloids?

The man takes us to a beautifully set table for two. A slim vase of two white orchids with the lightest hint of pink on the ends of the petals sits in the center. Another person comes out to pull out my chair as the maître d' does the same for Kim.

"If you need anything, just let your server know. Enjoy," the maître d' says, then leaves.

I pick up the ivory leather-bound menu. As I read the lunch options, I can sense hives breaking out over me. "The cheapest lunch here costs, like, a billion dollars," I say, squirming at the idea of spending that kind of money. Nate's money. Technically I guess it could be called our money, because we're married, but it just feels really awkward.

"Only a hundred, including two mimosas per person." Kim's tone contains a shrug.

"Um. Wasted on me."

"Why? They use good bubbly for their mimosas, unlike some shitty places."

"Because I can't drink right now." I close the menu. "I'm pregnant."

Kim gapes, then covers her mouth with a hand. "Are you serious?" she asks, her voice hushed. "Is it Nate's?"

"Of course it's Nate's!" How can she doubt me when Nate didn't? Then I remember telling her I didn't sleep with him. Okay, maybe she's a little confused, just like I was.

"Sorry, I thought... I mean, I knew you weren't dating, but you said your marriage to Nate had to end. I thought that meant a clean break."

"It's *really* complicated..." I trail off as our server appears with a pitcher of citrus water.

As if he can sense we're in a rather urgent private conversation, he doesn't spend too much time being chatty. Instead, he introduces himself, asks us if we need more time, pours the water, then takes our lunch order. Kim orders for both of us because I can't even choose from all the hundred-dollar-plus options.

"She's pregnant," Kim tells him. "Can you prepare something special for her, non-alcoholic, instead of the mimosas?"

"Certainly. It'll be our pleasure." He turns to me. "Any allergies?"

"No," I say. "But I really like kale and broccoli."

"Lovely. I'll make note of that."

Meanwhile, Kim looks at me like I'm an alien queen occupying her friend's body. "Who are you? Or more like, what's happened to you? You hate broccoli."

"Yeah, but now that I'm pregnant, I love it. And kale."

"Oh wow. So you really are pregnant. I can't decide which is worse: craving canned tuna, or kale and broccoli."

"Canned tuna?" Just the thought... *Ugh*. "Who craved that?"

"Some dumb kid in high school," she says, her voice suddenly cold and edged. It's her "I want to rip somebody's face off" tone, and I can never be sure if she's going to be okay with me probing too hard when she uses it. Best not to go there.

"Anyway, I even had the same shake Nate had this morning," I say.

Kim shudders. "That's beyond gross. I'm sure he enjoyed it, though."

"He did. I was pleased about that. Do you think I'll get used to the taste and continue to drink it after the baby's born?"

Pure horror crosses her face. "Good God, I hope not...but I don't know. I've never had a baby." She props her chin in her hand, her elbow on the table. "So. This baby means no divorce? Barron didn't pressure you or anything, did he?"

"No, no need to worry. It's just Nate's and my decision. We're going to work things out. And, you know, he really is a great guy."

"Uh-huh. That isn't the only reason you're staying with him," she says. "I bet he looks even better totally nude."

My cheeks flame as my mind conjures up what he did to me in the shower.

She points and giggles. "Oh my God. Look at you blush. So adorable!"

"Oh, shut up." Thankfully, our server brings a mimosa and a green smoothie, plus our salads and an appetizer platter of white fish, smoked salmon, pâté and minced olives.

She picks up her mimosa. "To your happy life with Nate."

We clink glasses. "Thank you. To a happy ending for you, too."

She gives me a warm smile, and we drink. As I down the refreshing shake, I remember the thong incident. I put my glass down and lean closer. "Okay, something totally crazy happened at work. Tell me what you think."

"Sure."

I go through the story of how I lost my thong in Vegas, and then magically had it delivered to me via one Miles Wellington today. "What do you think it means? This guy actually mailed the thing. Weird much?"

She takes her time before answering. "I think you're lucky it didn't get lost in the mail, because that would've been really awkward."

"How?" I ask, slightly annoyed she's latching on to the most pointless aspect. "I wouldn't have known he sent it, so there wouldn't have been any problem."

"Yeah, until he asked you about it."

Huh? "Kim, I don't know this guy. We've never met."

She gives me a perplexed look. "Sure you do. I mean, okay, maybe not in person, but you know who he is."

"I really don't."

"Evie, come on. He's Barron Sterling's personal assistant."

Thank God I don't have anything in my mouth. Even so, I gasp, feeling like I'm choking. Finally I recover. "Are you kidding?"

"Not even a little. How can you not know who he is, especially if you're working for Sterling & Wilson?"

"But why does Barron need an assistant?" I demand, utterly scandalized. "He's retired!"

I put it together. The only way Miles could have ended up with my thong is if it somehow got stuck to Barron's butt in Vegas. Talk about embarrassing! And I was wondering if he wrapped my thong around his junk when he was...doing the thing. My mind starts painting images I can't un-see. I think I'm going to throw up.

"Because he doesn't like to do things himself when he can simply delegate."

Makes sense. Barron's too rich to do anything himself. But that doesn't mean all is fine. "Why didn't anybody tell me who Miles was?"

"Did you ask?" Kim says, arching an eyebrow.

"Of course not. I'd never heard of the man until today."

"Well, there you go."

I give up. Her logic is circular. "All right. Well, anyway, now that you know all about my married life and undergarments, tell me about what's going on with you. I remember you saying you were setting up some special getaway for your boss. Did he finally accept your proposal?"

The moment I ask, I know I've made a mistake. Her face goes

glacial, eyes flashing evil intent. What did Salazar do? Make her redo the proposal yet again?

She attacks a hapless little leaf on her plate viciously. "I did, and he *loved* it. So he decided to give me a month off."

"Paid, right?"

"Yes."

"Well, that's great, isn't it?"

"No, it's not. I'd rather swim with sharks in a vat of acid."

"Why not? You're getting paid to binge-watch Netflix for a month!" It's one of her favorite activities.

She stabs the fork in the air like a knife. Salazar's lucky he's not here because she might just skewer him. "Because he *lent me* to someone. And now I have to put up with the Greatest Asshole in the World!"

"Who?" I ask, shocked at how furious she is.

She grinds her teeth. "Wyatt Westland!"

I flip through my mental contact list. Wyatt Westland doesn't ring a bell, even though she's saying the name like I should know it. Maybe she mentioned him before, but I just don't remember.

Since I can't wing my way through this, I ask, "What did he do?"

"What did he not do?" She pushes her hair back, showing me the scar on her jaw. "See this?"

I nod, surprised. She's never, ever talked about the scar, and I never dared to ask, assuming it might be a sensitive topic. "Yeah."

"He and his buddies used to call me Scarface in high school."

"Ouch." Although Kim seems cool about the scar now, and nobody would make fun of her about it, the situation had to be terrible when she was younger. The teen years are pure hell. Mine were awful too, all because my family was poor.

"Every time he and his idiot friends saw me, they'd yell, 'Say hello to my little friend,' in bad Cuban accents."

I laugh, but I'm thinking, *Douchebags!* I wish I could go back in time and hug the younger Kim. "And they lived?"

"Only because it isn't worth going to jail for. And there were the popular kids." Her expression turns ugly. "You know the type."

"No way," I say. "You had to be popular in school, too. You're gorgeous."

She gives me a small smile. "Let's just say I was a late bloomer."

Still. She had to have been pretty underneath the gangly awkwardness of puberty, which her immature peers were probably too stupid and shallow to notice. "So why did Salazar lend you to him?"

The knuckles around her fork whiten. "Somehow he's friendly with Dane—ugh—and he convinced Salazar he really needs a fake date to his ex-wife's wedding."

"Do people actually go to their exes' weddings? I mean, seriously? I thought that only happened in romance novels."

"Of course not. I mean, yes, I might consider going to an ex's wedding if I wanted to warn the bride. Or to poison him so he's permanently impotent."

My mouth parts. I can totally see Kim doing it. "There's a poison that does that?"

"I don't know...but Google does." She winks.

Our server appears, interrupting our bizarrely morbid conversation. He takes away our appetizer plates and replaces them with our entrées—slow-roasted duck with berry and mushroom sauce. It smells amazing. He also refills our drinks, then leaves. Maybe he caught a whiff of Kim's plan to find erectile-dysfunction-inducing poison and doesn't want to stick around a second more than he has to.

"Anyway, back to the topic." Kim cuts into the duck with more zeal than necessary, apparently not realizing that it can't fly away. "Wyatt has a child. And it's this child who needs closure after the divorce, and this wedding is supposed to give it to her. So she knows it's over between her parents."

Sympathy stirs for the girl.

"I'm actually thinking about murdering Wyatt. It can't be that hard to get away with. There are lots of people—potential suspects. Like his ex."

I let out a shaky laugh at how serious she sounds. "Don't tell me you're going to frame his ex."

"Why not? Serves her right," Kim mutters.

Oh wow. What's the story there? "At least do it behind the girl's back," I say, unsure how to calm Kim down. "Otherwise you'll traumatize her."

Kim nods vigorously. "Sure. She's better off without her asshole dad." Then she mutters, "Or her bitch mom."

"Um... Right." I can't think of anything else to say to her angry plan. I know she doesn't really mean that thing about killing him. At least...I don't think so. But there's part of me that disagrees with her assessment about not needing a dad. I wish I'd had one growing up. Even though Mom said he was a great guy who would've loved me if he'd known me, the tiny bit of consolation I get from that isn't enough to make up for the fact that I only had one parent, when everyone else had two.

As we finish lunch, I wonder if I should look for him again. Bradley Brown is going to be hard to locate, even starting with the fact that he was in Dillington over twenty-seven years ago before Facebook and Google tracked people everywhere. But Nate has connections. Maybe he could help...?

I sigh. I probably shouldn't impose on Nate like that. We just normalized our relationship and decided to make our marriage work. I don't want to shake things up by asking him to do this and that, making him feel like I'm using him or taking advantage of his network.

Maybe if this were a normal marriage—where he and I were both madly in love and had gone through the entire dating, proposal and wedding process—I might feel different. But for the moment, I should be careful. Trust isn't love, and it could easily be damaged if both parties aren't mindful.

38

EVIE

AFTER LUNCH, KIM DRIVES ME TO THE APARTMENT WE USED to share. We drop by a bookstore on the way to get some cardboard boxes so I can pack my things.

"Classier than trash bags," she says. "How come Nate isn't hiring movers for you?"

"I vetoed the idea. I don't have that much stuff, anyway."

She nods as she parks her car in the apartment lot. "That's true." She takes the boxes from the back. "I'll be carrying them. You're pregnant."

I roll my eyes. "Pregnant, not crippled."

"I'm racking up points with Nate in case I ever need a favor from him."

"If you ever need a favor, you can just ask me." I know she'll never do it unless it's a matter of life and death. Besides, her boss is the more likely choice for her to turn to. Salazar Pryce is just as powerful as Nate, and he's supposed to be pretty mean when the situation requires it.

As we walk along the hall to get to our unit, a black cat trots toward her. It's a gorgeous animal, the fur sleek and glossy. Aside from a crown-shaped white mark on its forehead, it's as black as the back of a penguin.

"Hello, Princess," Kim says with the kind of warm, sweet smile a man would give up a kidney for.

"Princess?" I ask, watching the cat mewl and wrap itself around Kim's leg.

"Yeah. A new cat from next door."

"She seems so friendly." I crouch to pet Princess. She lets me scratch her behind an ear, and as I do so, her eyes turn to blissful slits. *So adorable!* I always wanted a pet, but Mom and I could never afford one.

"She's a great cat. The name could've been better, though."

"Why?"

"She has a crown." Kim points at the white mark. "She should've been named *Queen*."

The cat mewls as though it totally agrees with Kim.

"I know," Kim coos. "It's just a total lack of imagination, isn't it?" She turns to me. "Princess, indeed."

I feel like there's a story somewhere here. Maybe somebody called Kim a princess or something.

Kim unlocks and opens the door to our unit. A light brown furball shoots out, tail wagging. I gasp and take a step back in surprise. It's not really a furball. More like a furry cannonball. The breed is one hundred percent indeterminable. The face is slightly foxy, the tongue hanging out of its mouth in a doggy smile. The tail sort of looks like a golden retriever's, but the fur around its head is a bit odd. I can't place it, even though it's somehow familiar.

Kim moves inside, backing the dog into the apartment. I follow her in.

She bends down and rubs his head. "Hey, Champ, you good boy! Did you miss Mommy?"

Mommy? I stare, stunned. She never said anything about getting a dog.

He licks her hands and cheeks, not caring about eating her makeup.

"Wow. You got a dog?"

"Well, I do now."

"I've been replaced," I joke, even though it hits me suddenly that a chapter in my life is closing, and a new one is starting. A tinge of nerves entwine around excitement. I can't believe that I'm not only married to one of the most eligible bachelors in the country, but with his child.

She laughs. "Don't be silly. Nobody can replace you. But he keeps me company."

"What is this?" I ask, gesturing at the dog.

"Champ." She lets him lick her fingers, then pulls back to dump the boxes on the dining table.

"Yeah, but what is he?"

"A mix of many things, including golden retriever and Pomeranian."

I blink once. Then twice. That explains the fur around the head. But... "Can a golden retriever and Pomeranian..." I make a circle with one hand and stick an index finger on the other hand in and out of the loop.

"Apparently." Kim gestures at Champ.

"Wow. How does that work?" I ask, trying to imagine the deed with that size differential.

"I don't know, and I didn't ask."

I squat down so I can run my hand along his soft body. "I didn't know you wanted a dog."

"I didn't. Annie—you know, the building owner—asked me to keep him and take care of him. He's her mom's dog, but she passed away last Thursday. Annie told me she just couldn't deal with the dog because it reminds too much of her mom. She's devastated."

"Oh no, that poor woman," I say, my heart aching as I imagine what it must be like to suffer such a loss. I don't know if I'd be able to cope in that situation.

"She says she can trust me to be good to him."

"She's right. I can't think of anybody more responsible than you."

"Anyway, so I'm stuck with him."

Champ wags his tail and gives her another doggy smile. Meanwhile, Princess wraps herself around Kim's ankles, while mewling loudly and—unless my imagination is being overactive—*possessively*. Did she follow us in? I didn't even notice.

"So I guess that narrows your roommate search to people who like dogs. You know what? I'll continue to pay for my portion of the rent until you find someone."

"Nah. Annie gave me a break on the rent for taking care of Champ. So I'm good. I actually think it'll be good for me to have the place to myself for a bit."

"Oh. Well, cool. That's great," I say, relieved she's all set. I've been feeling a bit guilty about abandoning her before the lease is up.

We go to my room. Kim helps me pack up my things. We avoid stuffing each box, since I'm not sure if lifting heavy things is okay or not. As we go through my stuff, Kim asks me if I want to throw anything out. We find a bottle of expired lotion, aged hair product samples that I'm certain aren't good anymore and a couple pairs of worn-at-the-heels socks, so I toss them. The rest gets organized into boxes and labeled, while we gossip about people, TV shows and movies. Kim's been plowing through so many on Netflix.

"You want the vase?" she asks me suddenly.

Pausing in the middle of writing *shoes* on a box flap, I lift my head. "What vase?"

"The one that one of your online dating guys gave you."

Ugh! The pink-and-green monstrosity looks like a bloody snot tower. "I thought you threw that out."

"I didn't, just in case."

"Don't want it."

Her eyes gleam. "Perfect."

"Who is that slightly evil expression for?"

"No one."

"You planning something?"

"Nope."

She's definitely planning something, but it doesn't look like I'm the target. So okay.

I carry a small box with my shirts to the living room and almost drop it when there's a sudden black streak right in front of me. "Does Princess hang out here a lot?" I ask, curious why she isn't in her own place and left to wander around the building's halls.

"She likes to be with me when her home's empty."

Aw, that's cute. The cat's just lonely. Champ is wagging his tail and looking happy in a corner, while panting like...well, an excited dog. And that makes me realize...

"He hasn't barked even once," I say.

"He doesn't bark. Trained not to. Otherwise I would've never been able to take him in. The other people in the building would've gotten upset."

"Does he make any sound at all?"

"He whines when he wants something. But otherwise he's a very nice, quiet dog."

I prop the door open, and Kim and I move the boxes one by one.

"Just one more left. I'll grab it," Kim says, going back to my room.

I stretch my back, then my sides. Who knew packing could be so labor-intensive? I didn't think I had that many things, but I've accumulated quite a bit since moving to L.A.

"Hey. Need some help?"

I turn and see a guy standing at the door. Wow. I've never seen him before, but he's a hottie. Not as hot as Nate—nobody's hotter, obviously—but he's got that nice, strong face with a square jaw and bright, deep-set blue eyes. The dark hair's cropped short and slightly messy, like he's run his fingers through it a few times. And when he shifts, I can see muscles moving underneath his shirt.

Definitely a winner.

When I continue to stare, he gives me a warm smile. "Sorry, I should've introduced myself." He starts to gesture at the unit next door with his thumb. "I'm—"

"Just leaving," Kim cuts in with a fake-polite voice. "And no, we don't need any help. Evie, let's go."

Wow. She isn't generally rude to people, so what did he do to get on her shit list?

The man's mouth tightens. "Kim—"

"We're very busy. Oh, don't forget to take your cat."

Ah-ha. So this is Princess's owner. The cat makes a protesting growl when he picks her up. I raise my eyebrows. Doesn't she like him? Is he an abusive dick? He doesn't look like one, but then, most Capital Dicks don't have *I'm a dick* written on their faces.

Shooting him a look cold enough to keep mint chocolate chip ice cream frozen, Kim picks up all the stacked boxes except a couple and starts toward the elevator. The sight of her holding four is impressive, especially if you don't know that the boxes hardly weigh anything. I take the remaining two and follow, stealing another look at the man. His lips are tight. He definitely did something he shouldn't have. He's probably sorry he has no chance with Kim, who is a babe.

Kim pretends like he isn't staring at her hard enough to make her back tingle and steps into the elevator. After the door closes, I take a good look at her face.

"You okay?"

"I'm fine," she says. "I just don't like it when jerks move in next door."

"When did he move in?"

"Two weeks ago."

Wow. The man must've made a terrible first impression. There must be a good story to this, but before I can ask, the elevator stops and Kim steps out purposefully. We walk toward her car.

She gives me a small grin. "I know it sounds silly, but I'm actually excited right now. I've always wanted to see the inside of Nate's mansion. I've never seen his home featured in magazines!"

I nod. He gets a few requests for those things from architectural or lifestyle magazines, but turns them down every time. "He doesn't like strangers in his home, taking pictures and stuff. Says it's rude because he lives in a residence, not a museum."

"Exactly. But if I'm helping you he'll let me in, right?"

"Kim, you can just visit me. He knows you're my friend."

She brightens. "That's true. And friends help friends move."

When we're in the car, I ask, "So. What's the deal with that guy? I honestly thought you found the jackpot when I saw how hot he was at first—"

Kim makes a strangled noise in her throat. "That shithead is Wyatt Westland."

"The asshole you have to put up with during your month off?" I say, stunned. "The jerk who called you Scarface?"

"Yes." Her jaw tightens.

"You didn't tell me he was your new next-door neighbor!" Poor Kim. It must suck to live next to a bully from her past.

"Because he's going to move soon! He sold some fancy-schmancy photo app patents to Sweet Darlings Inc. for a *lot* of money. And what do newly minted billionaires do with their new cash?" She snaps her fingers. "Spend it! He's bound to upgrade his car, his home and his furniture. Which means he's going to be gone—to some overpriced, eye-gougingly gaudy mansion located someplace very far from here. This is just him slumming until he finds something 'better.'"

"Wow." She's probably right. I've read about lottery winners spending money like crazy. Why would this Wyatt guy be any different?

"He's already sending his kid to private school. So soon I'll have a nice, normal, non-douchebag neighbor."

"Hey, do you think he abuses his cat?"

"I don't know. Why?"

"The cat doesn't seem to like him much. She was complaining when he took her away."

"Oh." Kim shrugs. "Princess loves me more than him or his daughter for some reason." She smirks. "Probably because even an animal with a brain the size of a walnut knows I'm not a dick."

39

EVIE

KIM SLOWS DOWN AS WE DRIVE THE LONG, QUIET ROAD AND approach the wrought-iron fence around the mansion. The design is complex and elaborate, and I'm pretty sure any determined crazy could drive through it with an SUV or a truck, but Nate told me that even a flimsy barrier tends to discourage people from approaching.

The car stops at the gate. I turn to tell Kim the security code to put into the number pad, then stop as a man moves slowly toward her side of the car.

He doesn't look like a vagrant or loiterer. He's in his mid- to late fifties, with his stubble half white and half light brown. The skin's tanned and weathered, and his shirt and jeans are both old and faded. The sneakers on him are black-gone-gray and as weathered as his skin. There's a firm purpose to his gait, and in his steady, clear gaze. He knocks on Kim's window.

She lowers it, just enough to talk, but not enough for him to stick his fingers in. "Look, we have no cash, and the owner won't be back for a while," she says.

"I'm not looking for cash. I was wondering if you know when

Evie Sterling is coming back. You might know her, if you're working here."

I snort-laugh at the man's assumption, until it suddenly registers that he's looking for *me*, not Nate.

I shift until I can peer at him better. "What do you need to see her for?" Maybe it's about one of the medical centers. But then, why not just go to one directly, or come to the office?

He dips his head and stares at me hard. Then he puts a hand over his mouth for a moment and starts blinking hard and fast. "Oh my God. It's you," he says finally, his voice thick. "You're more beautiful in person than in the pictures."

His over-the-top reaction makes my face hot, and I squirm in the passenger seat. I'm not anything special, and I resent the fact that strangers can now recognize me because of the tabloids.

"I'm Bradley Brown," he says.

For a moment, I can't even speak. It's as though somebody dropped a bomb in my psyche. It's like all my birthday and Christmas wishes came true.

"I just..." He wipes at his eyes. "It's enough to know you're okay. I didn't mean to... Sorry." He starts to turn away as though realizing he's revealed too much.

I jump out of the car.

"Don't!" Kim says, getting out of the car herself.

I put a hand up toward her, then call, "Stop!" I start after him, with Kim following half a step back.

He keeps walking, and I pick up the pace. Kim reaches for me.

"What if he's a *kidnapper*?" she says. "Do you know what you're worth to criminals now?"

I ignore her because I know he's not. He's—

He spins around, his eyes flashing. "I'm not a criminal, and I'm not trying to hurt her!" he yells. Dull red blooms on his face, and he looks away for a moment. "I... I just wanted to see her, that's all." He runs a hand over his cheek, sniffling.

A golden ring on his finger flashes, and I move forward to look at it more closely. I squint and realize it has a flower motif like Mom's.

Suddenly my legs are unsteady and trembling. Someone

might be able to pretend to be my dad, but the golden band? That's different. "Can I see your ring?"

He pulls back, hiding the hand behind his back. "No."

"Please! It's important."

He hesitates and seems to debate with himself.

"I swear I won't steal it. I just want to see it." I need proof. Even as my heart says this is my dad, my head says I have to be absolutely sure. Kim's right about my new station in life and what that could mean to the unscrupulous.

After three beats, he reluctantly pulls it off his finger and gives it to me. The metal's warm from his body heat.

"I don't know why you're so interested," he grumbles, looking at his shoes. "It's just a cheap ring. Not even real gold."

I don't care about the cost. I only care about the design. The flower motif is just like Mom's. It's gotta be the same set that my mom's came from. My hands shaking I tilt the band to see the inside. Mom's says *...till death do us part*. This one says *To love and cherish...* in the same swirly script.

Tears spring to my eyes as my hand clenches around the ring.

He shoots me a glance, then sighs. "Aw, don't cry like that. I'm sorry. I didn't show up to cause any trouble or anything..." He shakes his head, then looks at Kim beseechingly.

Kim puts a hand on my shoulder, shifting to put herself between me and him. "Evie, hey. Are you okay?"

I nod, touched that she cares even though the gesture is wholly unnecessary. "Yes. It's my..." I pause as I realize what I'm about to say. "It's my dad." Another wave of longing and joy sweeps over me, and my chest feels tight. I wasn't sure if I'd ever get to see my father, much less introduce him to any of my friends. But now I get to do both.

"Your *dad*? I thought he wasn't around anymore." Kim takes another good look at him. "How did you find her?"

"I saw articles," he says. "I only wanted to see her, that's all. I'm embarrassed I fumbled around like a fool."

"You didn't." My voice is shaking hard. "Do you have any idea how much I wanted to find you?"

"Evie..."

"Mom said you were a great guy. And I...I was hoping you'd

come find me one day, because I wasn't sure if I could find you. We lived in Dillington for so long. I think Mom secretly wanted you to come back," I say through the tears that keep welling and falling, my heart overflowing with emotions I can't begin to identify.

Dad steps closer...

40

NATE

I LEAVE THE OFFICE EARLY. THERE ARE STILL A FEW THINGS to review, but I can do that at home. My office feels oddly empty without Evie around. It's as though she's what makes everything complete.

As I approach the gates, I notice a couple of women and a man off to the side. Weird. We don't have many pedestrians around here. I do a double take when I realize it's Evie and Kim with a guy I don't recognize. Rage fists around my heart at the sight of tears on Evie's face. What the hell is going on? Is the guy hurting her?

He starts to move toward her.

Oh no you don't!

Fear for Evie and our unborn child slams into me, along with fury and an overwhelming need to protect her. I slam on the brakes and jump out, my hands clenched into fists. I leap between Evie and the man and point a finger at his chest. "Stay away from my wife!"

The man flinches, blinking like *I'm* the bad guy. The gall!

I turn to Evie. "Are you okay? Is this guy harassing you?"

She swipes at the corners of her eyes, then sniffs. "No. It's my dad, Nate."

She isn't making any sense. She's been crying, so maybe she's too emotionally overwrought to speak coherently. I glance in Kim's direction. She looks tense, not happy and relaxed like a woman who just met a friend's parent. I turn my gaze back to Evie. "What?"

"My dad. I thought I'd never see him again, but he came looking for me." She shoots me a teary smile.

Alarms start to go off inside my head. *Keep an open mind. This might actually be Evie's dad.*

I turn to this alleged father of Evie's. He looks at me with a small, uncertain smile. "Hello. I'm Bradley Brown. Nice to meet you."

I'll bet it is.

I take an inventory of the man. He's tall, attractive under the stubble. The features aren't classic, but nicely arranged. His nose is slightly crooked, probably broken at some point. The clothes are shabby, but not so much that they're embarrassing. Just enough to make him appear like a friendly, normal guy, the kind of man who's down on his luck—an underdog you might want to root for.

Except I don't quite buy it. Maybe I've become skeptical over the years because of too many douche burgers trying to take advantage of me and my family. Women aren't the only ones who approach us, and I just can't believe this man's motives are all that pure.

Besides, how can Evie be so certain he's the man he claims to be?

But she's smiling, her face glowing like her fondest wish just came true. I can't bring myself to ruin that, especially when I have no proof that this Bradley Brown is a scammer.

So I school my features into warmth and congeniality and put on my most charming smile. "Nate Sterling. It's a pleasure to finally meet Evie's dad. Sorry about that just now. I didn't know who you were."

Sniffing, Bradley scratches the tip of his nose. "It's all right. If

I were you, I might've done the same." He turns to Evie. "Sweetheart, can I have the ring back?"

She starts. "Of course. Sorry. I forgot I was holding it." She hands over a golden band to him.

I look at it curiously. Is that the proof he offered?

As though he senses the question, Bradley says, "It's the part of the set I gave Mari. I had it designed myself."

"Ah." A DNA test is a better option and more conclusive. I wonder if he'll agree to one.

But I don't think he's going to be the real problem. It's Evie. She's looking at the man like he single-handedly discovered the Holy Grail. Obviously she wants him to be the person she thinks he is. And she'll be upset if she thinks I don't believe him—not even a little.

But something about him feels off. I can't quite place my finger on the precise issues I'm having, but there's something about him that's trying a little too hard.

Sighing, I remember that Kim is still standing there. "Hey, Kim."

"Hi, Nate." She gestures at a car parked at the gates. "I was just driving Evie home."

"Thank you," I say.

"She also helped me pack my things, and I wanted to ask her in for coffee or tea," Evie says quickly, her gaze darting to Kim, then back to her dad.

Kim also looks at Bradley, but her eyes are still more polite than friendly. *Interesting.* Is she getting the same vibe I am?

"I can take a rain check on that," she says, her voice sweet as she turns to Evie, although her gaze is slightly guarded. Evie doesn't seem to notice. "I don't want to intrude on your time with your dad, especially when you haven't seen him in forever."

"Thank you, Kim," Evie says. "You're such a good friend."

"I know, right? Don't you forget it."

My car isn't designed to haul two extra passengers, so Bradley and Evie climb into Kim's car. I want to object, since I don't trust the man at all, but there's no good way to do it without looking like a jerk.

That guy isn't going to do anything crazy. He's looking for a bigger score, I tell myself, not that it's much comfort as I swing in behind Kim, so I can keep an eye on the three of them.

During the drive along the long, winding road to the mansion, I assemble a list of things to do. First, I need to offer to feed Bradley dinner, since I can't quite kick the man out, no matter how uneasy I feel. Second, I need to figure out how to get rid of him graciously. Maybe put him up at a hotel. There's no way I'm inviting him to spend the night. Third, I need to get Pattington to do a thorough background check on this guy. If the family detective clears him—and only if—I can let my guard down some.

My mind made up, I dictate a text asking him to look into Bradley Brown, a.k.a. my wife's father. He confirms the new assignment, and I let out a soft breath. Pattington's good at his job, and he's been working for my family for years. He'll not only be quick but discreet.

Kim pulls to a stop in front of the main door. I park my car behind her and go up to the three of them.

I put a hand on Evie's shoulder, squeezing gently. "I'll get your things with Kim."

"Do you need help?" Bradley offers.

I give him my warmest smile. "It won't be necessary. Why don't you go ahead and catch up with Evie over there?" I gesture at the small porch.

He nods and walks off with Evie, a hand at the small of her back. I narrow my eyes, but keep my mouth shut.

Kim pops her trunk open as I join her. She breaks the silence first, her voice quiet. "Good thing you showed up."

"You don't like him either?" I ask.

"Nope. I feel bad because it's obvious Evie's excited, but..." She shrugs. "There's something about him. I'm pretty sure I'm just being paranoid, though. It comes with the territory of being Salazar's assistant. He gets his share of...leeches." She wrinkles her nose.

As much as I hate it, part of me is relieved Kim and I are on the same page. I'm not just being paranoid for no reason.

She continues, "I could be wrong, because I'm protective of Evie and don't want to see her hurt. Maybe he's just a genuinely nice guy but super nervous. I mean, it makes sense, right? And some people are just awkward, terrible at making a good first impression." She gestures at the boxes in the trunk. "All her stuff."

"Thanks." I pick a couple up. They're surprisingly light. "I owe you one."

"You and your whole family." She winks.

I let out my first genuine laugh since seeing Bradley step closer to crying Evie. Salazar isn't just Kim's boss, but Justin's father-in-law. She does a lot to smooth things out between the families when opinions clash, and Salazar can be very stubborn.

"Keep an eye on them while I take the boxes in, will you?" I ask, not wanting Bradley to move off the porch or try to get into our home.

"Sure." She smiles, then walks toward the porch.

I take Evie's things, put them in the foyer and lock the door again. When I come out, Kim's hugging Evie. When she notices me, she shakes hands with Bradley.

"I should get going and let you get to know each other," she says.

Evie looks torn. "Are you sure? I'm dying to invite you in."

"Next time. You owe me a complete tour." Kim winks, then turns to me. "Bye, Nate."

"Bye, Kim," I say.

She drives off, and I start toward Bradley and Evie. She's laughing softly at something he said. At least he knows how to entertain her. That's a point in his favor...but only a small one.

"Why don't the three of us go out for dinner?" I say, putting an arm around Evie's waist, wanting to ensure Bradley understands he better not hurt her.

He hardly bats an eye. As a matter of fact, he seems pleased. That should ameliorate the unease in my gut, but it doesn't.

"That sounds like a great idea," Evie adds hurriedly when Bradley doesn't immediately agree. "You don't have anything to do tonight, do you, Dad?"

My jaw muscles tighten at the affectionate way she calls him Dad. How in the world can she bond with him so quickly? If I were in her place, I would be suspicious.

She isn't cynical like you.

But she'll learn, I think with a bit of sadness. People who treat you the same regardless of the size of your bank account are rare. I wish I could shield her, but it's simply not possible.

He gives her a paternal smile. "Of course not. I'd love to spend some time with you and get to know you better. So where are we going?"

"Virgo," I say.

Bradley smiles. "I've heard great things about that place."

I'll bet. "Did you drive here?"

"I parked my car a few blocks away from where Evie and her friend stopped."

"Okay. Why don't we go get it and then go to the restaurant?"

"Sure," he says, and I grab my Beamer SUV to take him to his car and wait for him to get behind the wheel.

As I drive to Virgo with Evie sitting next to me, I can see Bradley's car in the rearview mirror. It'd be nicer if he got lost. On the other hand, maybe not. Evie would probably freak out.

"Thank you," she says softly. "I know the visit is a total shock to you."

"Wasn't it for you?"

"Yeah, but in a different way. It's my dad, someone I always wished I could meet some day. You didn't even know you had a father-in-law."

I grin. "Your mom didn't have you all by herself. I just didn't think I'd ever meet the guy." Was hoping I wouldn't, if he was enough of a dick to leave her only to come back when she's married to a rich man.

She and I both know we're together because we care about each other. I adore her, want the best for her. But to a lot of people out there, she's just a lucky girl who managed to snag a super-rich boss. Some assholes are probably calling her a gold digger, and might even think she deserves to be fucked over. It's my job to ensure those douchebags don't get to hurt her.

"I know the timing looks bad," she says. "Him popping up like this. But please just understand I've been wanting to find him for a long time. Mom said he really loved her. He's a good man, just bad luck and timing separated them, you know?"

"I get it. But how did you know he's really your dad, and not some imposter?" This is the question I didn't want to ask in front of Bradley. I didn't want his presence to affect her answer.

"That ring he showed me? It's really the same one as my mom's."

"He could've copied the design." I would if I were a con man.

"Yeah, but my mom's ring has half a sentence engraved on the inside. His is the other half. And Mom *never* takes off her ring. So that's how I knew he was my dad for real."

Hmm. That does sound pretty genuine. But it isn't enough to totally calm my suspicions. My instinct is telling me something's wrong, and I need to tread very carefully.

I pray Pattington works fast, hoping my gut feeling is wrong for Evie's sake.

41

Nate

The food is great, which is to be expected. Virgo is a perfect restaurant. Unlike the other places that Vanessa's older brother Mark owns, the dress code is slightly more relaxed, so Bradley's outfit doesn't get us kicked out.

We could've gone to some other place, but I chose Virgo, especially because I want Mark to see Bradley and give me an impression. Unfortunately, he isn't there. Damn it.

Once we're seated, Bradley defers to me for wine and menu options, saying he doesn't know much about fancy sit-down meals. I merely smile, since it isn't *that* fancy, and he could just pick his own food and drink. I can't decide if he's worried that I'll judge him if he selects the wrong wine or if he's trying to ingratiate himself somehow. There's no need for him to play up the "poor relative" role to this degree. Until Pattington clears him, I'm not letting my guard down.

Still, I do my best to put Bradley at ease. After all, he hasn't done anything wrong...yet. And I'm good at hiding how I really feel when necessary.

Bradley is a pleasant conversationalist, and he tells Evie stories of how he and Mari met, fell in love and so on. I don't believe much of it. If he loved her so much, he would've stayed. He would've made it work even if he was embarrassed to go back to her because his business failed and had nothing to show for it. He would have found a way to provide for his woman and the child she carried. He acts like he's sorry he never went back to Dillington, swears he would've gone back if he'd known about Evie. But he doesn't seem to realize the problem was always him leaving. If he'd stayed, he would've known about her.

I've seen Mari, the signs of the hard life she led in the lines on her face, the calluses on her hands. Even if she doesn't seem too crazy about me being with her daughter, I respect her for having done all that she could for Evie. She really deserved better than Bradley.

"So what do you plan on doing now? Stay in L.A. for a while, or...?" I ask over our main course of steak and lobster tail, keeping my tone friendly.

"Uh. Yeah. I'd like to get to know Evie. Maybe go visit Mari together, you know?" he says a bit sheepishly.

"Have you spoken with her recently?" I ask.

"Not yet."

I nod, but I'm thinking, *Why the hell not?* Does he have something to hide? Maybe he doesn't want Mari to know?

He adds, "I don't have her number anymore."

"I do. I'll text and let her know you're in L.A.," Evie says, pulling her phone out.

Bradley's expression tightens for a moment. I catch it, but Evie, busy with her phone, doesn't.

"And why don't I give you her number so you can call her tonight?" she asks.

His eyes brighten. "I'd love that."

He seems sincere when he speaks, but why do I have a feeling he's not going to do any of that? And unless I'm mistaken, he doesn't want Evie contacting Mari either.

"Where are you staying?" Evie asks, texting quickly.

"At a motel for now. I'm looking for a small apartment."

Concern crosses her face as she lifts her gaze from her phone. Time to step in before she does something she shouldn't—like invite this man into our home.

"Why don't I put you up at the Aylster?" I say. "It should be more comfortable, and you'll be closer to our place." That part isn't necessary an advantage, but it's for Evie's benefit.

Bradley laughs, waving his hand like I'm just too much. "I can't. And you don't have to. You don't even know me."

"Ah, we'll get to know each other as the time goes on. But I just can't have you staying at some motel. Really, you're practically family." God, I'm laying it on thick. He better not insist I call him Pops or something.

"Listen to Nate, Dad. He's right. We'd normally offer you a room at home, but..." She clears her throat. "It's a little complicated."

It is? I didn't know that, but I'm glad she thinks there are enough complications not to invite Bradley to stay with us.

Evie calls the Aylster. It's just pro forma, though. Of course the hotel always has a suite for a guest of the Sterlings. Of course they'll be more than happy to make his stay comfortable.

And now that she has her phone out, she exchanges phone numbers with her dad. Although I don't want him having her number, there's no socially acceptable way to prevent it. I don't bother giving him mine, since I don't want him to have direct access to my personal mobile. Mari earned my respect or trust when she came to visit; this guy hasn't. Evie taps a few more things on her phone, then puts it away.

After dinner, Bradley says he's tired from the excitement of the day.

"Of course," I say. "Besides, you have to pack your things to move." *Let's not linger, because I've hit my acting limit for the day.*

"I know, right?" He laughs heartily. "Thank you for that."

"My pleasure. Anything for Evie's dad."

Something sparks in his eyes. It's so quick, I wonder for a moment if I imagined it.

Bradley's expression returns to a mix of mild shyness and joy. "Anyway, I should get going. Get some sleep and have a good evening, Evie." He nods at me. "Nate."

We leave the restaurant together. He whistles, then waves at Evie before getting into his car. The tension that's been gripping me since I laid my eyes on him loosens a bit, but I know this is just the beginning.

~

EVIE

When we're walking into home from the garage, my phone rings. It's Mom. I smile, my heart swelling with joy. Bet she wants to know all about Dad's visit!

"Hey, sweetie," Mom says.

Nate looks at me inquiringly, and I mouth, *Mom*. He nods and goes upstairs. I stay below, taking a seat on the couch facing Barron's X-rated art and toe off my shoes. It's good thing Nate offered to put Dad up at the hotel, because I'm not sure how I'd explain the statue.

"So what's going on? You said to call as soon as possible," she says.

I suppress a laugh, trying not to give away the big news. I was going to text her Dad was here, but decided not to, wanting to share the moment when I tell her. "You're not going to believe this, but I actually have something fabulous to tell you. Dad's here!"

I wait for Mom to say something. She doesn't. In fact, the line is so quiet that I wonder if we got disconnected.

Maybe she's too overcome to speak. I mean, I could barely process it when I saw him, and he's not even someone from my memory. Mom actually knew him, and they spent a lot of time together. She still loves him and misses him.

"Mom?" I say. "Are you there?"

A soft clearing of her throat. "Yes, baby. I'm here. I'm just... shocked. I never thought he'd return to our lives."

"I know, right?" I literally can't sit still. "He saw me in some articles and decided to get in touch. If I'd known the publicity would bring him back, I would've done something to attract the paparazzi's attention a long time ago."

"But you hate being in the spotlight."

"Yeah, but it's *Dad*! I've always wanted to see him. This is a dream come true." I've always wanted to have a dad, and now I do. Unlike some terrible dads, mine loves and wants the best for me. He only stayed away all these years because he thought he wasn't good enough for me and Mom. That resonates in an odd way, because I've felt like an imposter too.

"Oh. Well, I'm very happy for you, hon."

"I wish you were here," I say wistfully. "Then we could be a complete family."

"So do I." Her words are full of feeling. "How is he? Is he doing well?"

"I think he just moved here. He's been staying at a motel, but Nate moved him to the Aylster. Nate couldn't have been more polite or nice to him, and Dad was really sweet, too."

"I wish I could be there with you and your dad, baby, but Betty needs me."

The reminder puts a damper on my excitement. Of course. How selfish am I not to remember Betty? "How is she doing?"

"She's hanging in there. A fighter."

"You know, if she needs anything—anything at all—Nate can probably make it happen."

There's a pause. "I'd...rather not."

"Don't say that. He'd never turn his back on someone who genuinely needed help," I say, wanting Mom to understand she can trust Nate the way I do. "Normally I wouldn't ask, but this is something his family's foundation *does*. He'll be happy to help. He's all about making a difference, one sick person at a time."

"Thank you, Evie. And tell Nate I said thanks. Oh my goodness, my break's almost over. I need to get back to my floors."

I sigh. Her janitorial shift is in the evening. I hate it that she works so late at night when she's a morning person. But I also know that if I offer to help her financially so she doesn't have to work at night, she'll absolutely be insulted.

"We'll chat more," she says.

"We will." I snap my fingers as an idea occurs to me. "You know what? I'm going to see if he and I can visit Dillington to see you. I know you miss him." It's going to be awesome for them reunite, especially after all these years. Seeing Mom wearing the ring he gave her is going to let him know he is still loved, and always part of our family, no matter what.

"That'll be lovely, but don't put yourself out to do it. Remember, you're pregnant, so you should take it easy and rest instead of worrying about me. Just let Nate deal with it if anything unpleasant happens."

42

NATE

I change out of my work clothes, while Evie's downstairs talking with Mari. I put on my favorite boxers and a white T-shirt and am walking out of the closet when my phone buzzes. I lunge for it, praying it's Pattington with some news, even though it's still too early for him to have dug up something on Bradley.

You shooting blanks?

I stare at the text from Court. What the hell is this about?

The only thing blank is your mind, I reply, then sit on the bed, my legs stretched out. Court needs to check who he's texting first. I don't need to know about his friends' issues. Or maybe he meant to text his brother Edgar.

A few seconds later, I get a call from Court. "You didn't see the article?"

"What article?" There's so much crap written about me that if I tried to keep up with all of it, I'd never have time to sleep, much less take care of the medical centers.

"It says you're shooting blanks and Evie's kid isn't yours. Oh, and the marriage isn't real because you weren't supposed to marry her." Court pauses for a moment. "There's also some stuff about her. Greedy, gold digger... You know, the usual."

My jaw muscles clench. Murderous rage pours through me as I sit up straight. "Who wrote this shit?"

"Tom Brockman."

That asshole. Nothing's sacred for that bottom feeder in his quest for clicks. Every piece of dumb gossip and speculation he hears about turns into an article. He went after Court's family earlier, then attempted to ruin Court's fiancée's as well.

"Should've run him over when I had the chance," Court mutters.

"You think a lot of people saw it?" I ask, praying the article's buried under something juicier.

"I don't know. It got published this afternoon, and it's trending now."

Fuck.

"Lots of comments. All bullshit. Don't even bother looking."

"I gotta go," I say, hanging up because now I *have* to see the comments.

The online trolls are out in droves. Many mock me, calling me impotent, among other things. I don't care about that, though. I've been judged and attacked before because of my family's position and wealth. Normally I just laugh it off.

But this time they're dragging Evie into it, and she isn't used to this. She won't understand. I remember how uncomfortable she was with all the reporters and photographers after the auction...how much she didn't like the idea of public exposure when we had to go to Vegas together for our date.

"Gold digger" is the kindest term people are throwing at her. It enrages me that the woman I adore—the mother of my *child*—is under attack because of her association with me. Because vultures like Brockman won't leave her out of it.

Brockman is going to pay for this. I'll make the motherfucker bleed. He's going to wish he never wrote that article. He'll wish he never learned the goddamn *alphabet*.

My phone vibrates in my hand. *Barron.*

"How's Evie?" His voice is tight, which means he's read the article. Miles undoubtedly showed it to him.

"As far as I know, she hasn't seen it yet." She's still downstairs, which means she's still on the phone with her mom. Then it hits me. *Has Mari seen it? Shit.*

"But she will." It's a flat statement. People always notice articles about themselves, unless they're living in a cave somewhere.

"Most likely."

"Stress is bad for pregnant women. Ethel almost miscarried once because of it."

I've heard that story, and although I've always felt sympathy before, now my emotions veer into fear. I can't have Evie lose our child because of this. It isn't just that I want the child—because I do. But the emotional and physical trauma a woman experiences from miscarriage is something that can never fully heal. "I'll take care of it," I say firmly.

"The family will respond," Barron says, quoting the phrase we use to show unity against outsiders. "Evie is one of us, Nate. Nobody hurts one of our own."

I finally rein in my own emotions and hear the cold rage radiating from Barron.

"They think this article will disgrace Evie or make us turn our backs on her. It will not. If they want to come at us, they can strike at me directly. Everyone involved will pay."

"Tom Brockman is mine," I say before Barron decides to drop a nuke on his apartment building.

"Fine, but I can't promise he won't feel some collateral damage. Give Evie my love, and tell her she has nothing to worry about. Next time, they'll think twice before publishing this type of trash." He hangs up.

I get a text from Justin next. *Is Evie okay? The family will respond. This will not go unpunished.*

Vanessa. *The bastard is going down. Tell Evie to ignore the haters. We have more lawyers than anybody and a war chest big enough to destroy them all.*

More texts are pouring in. All showing support, asking after Evie because they know just like I do what this is going to do to her.

I wonder if there's a way I can prevent Evie from seeing the article. Maybe I can just whisk her away on a long honeymoon to

Thailand. Bora Bora is pretty, too. Then I can keep her busy in bed—shouldn't be too difficult, and a hell of a lot of fun—and Tom Brockman and his article will both be history by the time we return.

Except is she going to want to leave the country when she just reunited with her dad?

Fuck. Talk about timing.

I get another call. Shit. It is Mari. She probably saw the article too and is furious I let this happen to her daughter. I brace myself for an ass-kicking. "Hello," I say.

"Hello, Nate. This is Mari. If Evie's in the room with you, would you mind going to another one? I'd rather not she overhear anything I'm about to tell you."

That bad? Maybe I should get a shield, like Captain America. "She's still downstairs," I say.

"Okay." She sighs heavily. "She called saying that she met her dad."

"Yeah, she's very happy." I don't tell Mari that I have suspicions about Bradley, because she must obviously still love the man to wear his ring.

"Get rid of him."

Whoa. "Excuse me? Could you say that again?"

"Bradley Brown is bad news."

O-kay. "I'm sorry, but didn't you tell Evie that her dad was a nice guy?" I say slowly, making sure there's no miscommunication.

"Well, of course. I didn't want her to know her father is a... piece of crap. He's a cheating, uncommitted, worthless con man. Mark my words, he's only there to weasel some money out of her."

So my instincts were right. But mixed with vindication is annoyance that Mari lied to Evie all this time. If she'd just told Evie the truth from the beginning, Bradley would've never been able to approach her. "Why don't you tell her? It'll ensure she stays away from him."

"She doesn't need to know what kind of man he really is. It isn't good for her."

"It isn't good for her to be taken advantage of out of ignorance. She's thrilled to be around him because of what you told her," I point out, stunned at Mari's non-logic. I thought she was more sensible than this.

"She isn't like you." Her words come out like slaps, almost accusatory. "She has so few good memories, don't you get it? She never got to go to homecoming or prom or any of the things that normal kids do. We never had *anything*. The only thing I could give her is that her parents loved her, even though that good-for-nothing son of a bitch never stuck around. He was just slick, and I fell for the gloss because I didn't know any better."

"I understand she had a hard life." And I plan to make up for that and spoil her rotten, now that I know how badly she's been deprived. "But how is keeping up this lie going to make it better for her?"

"Do you love your father?"

The question pierces my heart like a lance, and an old ache spreads through me. "Of course. He was a great man."

"Then how would you feel if somebody said he was a terrible person? If some woman showed up and claimed he cheated on your mother and had babies with her? Or if someone said he swindled people out of money? How would that make you feel?"

I shove my fingers through my hair, then clench them until my scalp hurts. The possibility of that happening is nil, but if it *did* happen... I'd be furious, betrayed...

I don't even know all the things I'd feel, honestly. Dad was the man I looked up to, the kind of person I wanted—still want—to become. The devastation of that would be too painful to bear.

"Would you be mad enough to shoot the messenger?"

Possibly. *Most likely.*

Shit.

"You have everything, and she has nothing. Let her have this one thing. You're a powerful man with a lot of money and rich friends. Make Brad go away. Do it for Evie. I'm counting on you to keep her safe and happy." She clears her throat. "I need to go back to work. Thank you, Nate." She ends the call.

Oh fuck. Frustration swirls inside like a tornado, and it's all I can do to not hurl my phone at the wall. This day started out perfect, with Evie climaxing against my mouth, the doctor's visit, her moving out of her old place and into mine.

But the collection of bullshit that just hit me, starting with Bradley Brown's appearance... What the hell.

"Nate? Is everything okay? You look really tense."

I turn around and see Evie coming into the room. *Tell her the truth. She deserves to know*, my mind whispers.

Let her have this one thing. I'm counting on you to keep her safe and happy. Mari's voice is in my head like a harbinger of doom. *Would you be mad enough to shoot the messenger?*

Would Evie? I look at her beautiful, expressive face. It was glowing not too long ago, as she basked in the pure joy of meeting her dad. The honest words stick in my throat like fish bones. I swallow the pain.

"It's fine. It's just..." I let out a heavy sigh. Then, like a coward, I settle on the easier choice. "Some tabloid writer published a bunch of crap about us."

Her brow furrowing, she takes out her phone and starts tapping. When she lets out a gasp, I know she found the article.

"This is ridiculous!"

"I know." I go put a soothing hand on her shoulder. "It's just the usual bullshit."

"What does your family think?" She scans further down the screen. "Oh my God, they're basically saying your dick is defec—! How dare they! It is so not defective!"

Even with everything going on, I have to laugh. "Clearly not. There is *nothing* wrong with my dick."

"It's an amazing dick."

"Celestial. Transcendent. Olympian, even."

Now she's smiling. "But seriously, where are they getting this kind of crap?"

"Obviously they don't need proof to publish. They wouldn't be in the tabloid business otherwise."

"Oh my God. This is..." She looks at me.

I brace myself for some anger over people calling her a lying, gold-digging whore who's passing off somebody else's kid as mine.

"Are you upset about it? Them saying that you're, you know...sterile?"

This is what she's worried about? "Why would I be, when you and I both know it's not true? And really, I've heard worse. I'm more concerned about you."

"Me?" She blinks, then looks down at the screen. "Oh. Right." She reads a little more. "Well, to tell you the truth...meh. Like you said, we both know all this is untrue. It's actually funny how hard they're trying to create drama out of nothing."

They're not going to think it's so funny when Barron and I get through with them. But she's not done.

"Where do they get these clichéd scenarios?" She laughs. "I mean, a fake baby? Gold digging? That's the best they can do? Don't they have any editors with creativity?"

The vise around my heart eases a little, and emotions start swelling. "I thought you hated this kind of publicity. You threw up on that reporter after the auction."

"Well, yeah. I *don't* like being the center of attention like that, and I was stressed." She flushes. "But this article isn't even true..."

She takes a moment and breathes in deeply. "Look, my life hasn't been always pretty or rosy, but I was able to get through it because I had my mom, who's always been my pillar and family." She reaches out and takes my hand. "Now I have you—another pillar. More family. And that makes me feel stronger, safer and protected. The article sucks, but I'm not going to give it the power to affect our relationship, Nate."

Something hot and tight swells in my chest as I gaze at her lovely face, eyes shining, cheeks rosy and mouth soft. I kiss her like her lips are the elixir of life.

Love.

I love this woman.

I love this woman who can laugh at the world. Who cares about what's important. Who overcame so much to be where she is now.

Evie is the kind of woman who would still stand beside me even if I had no money, no connections, nothing.

I touch her, my hands urgent and greedy, craving all of her, needing all of her. I pull her blouse over her head, unclasp the bra and cup her soft breasts, my thumbs over the hard, rosy tips.

She moans into my mouth, her fingers digging into my hair.

Lust roars through me like a raging beast. I kiss her jaw, nip her earlobe. Hear her sharp gasps, feel the slight rocking of her hips against my hard dick.

Yes.

I push at her skirt, yank away her underwear. She's soaking, hot and slick.

"My God, Evie," I say.

"I want you, Nate. *Now*," she demands, unbuttoning my shirt.

I rip the rest of the buttons, unable to wait, then kick my boxers away.

"I love it that you're so impatient." Her pink tongue sweeps over her lips. The sight is more erotic than any pornography. She could be blinking like an owl and I'd still think it was erotic.

"I'm always impatient to have you, always horny for you."

She spreads her legs, her eyes shiny with excitement. Trust. And something else soft and sweet that I can't quite name but makes my heart ache anyway. "Then I'm all yours."

My mouth around her nipple, I push into her in one smooth stroke. She cries out, the sound hot and urgent. Her fingers dig into me, and I spread her even wider, pulling out and surging into her again.

She wraps around me like molten gloves, and I feel it like a hand around my heart. Sweat pops over my forehead, and lust thrums in my head. There's pressure gathering at the base of my spine. I'm too close, but I refuse to go over the edge alone.

Gripping her pelvis, I tilt her so that with every thrust I'm grinding against her clit. She's panting, her breasts rising and falling, and pleasure twists and unfurls over her.

She screams my name, her spine arching. Her inner muscles spasm around me, and I drive into her one more time, as deep as I can go, then follow her into the blinding abyss, where nothing matters but us.

43

NATE

"How's Evie doing?" Court asks as we sit down at Virgo for lunch the next day. I gave Evie a bullshit excuse about my best friend needing some guy-talk time and came alone. Yuna is also able to come, taking a break from her all-important baby shopping. Court's sister-in-law isn't even close to her due date, but Yuna is apparently sweeping through stores like there's going to be a massive shortage of baby things next week.

"She's all right," I say. "Taking it better than I thought."

"You know that means she's a keeper," Yuna says. "So, is he dead yet?"

"Who?" Court asks.

"Not yet," I say, knowing exactly who she means. "I can't decide if he should be made never to publish again or worse."

"Why settle for one?" Loathing seethes in Court's voice. He has a history with Brockman because the asshole used to date my friend's candy-bar fiancée and write trash about *his* family. Brockman gets around.

"If you need anything, just ask," Yuna says. "Happy to help crush him. I swing a mean wrecking ball. Well, I know people who can."

Yeah, like her ridiculously wealthy and overprotective parents. "Appreciate the offer, but I'm okay. I can handle him on my own."

"But you're worried," Court says, barely looking at the menu.

"You shouldn't be," Yuna adds. "If you fail, I'll avenge you."

I laugh, my shoulders shaking at her overly serious expression. "Thanks, but really, I don't need any help to squash that bug. It'll be a pleasure to make him squeal."

"Then why did you ask us to meet you? If it's not about that shitbag, and you aren't going to introduce us Evie..." Yuna grows thoughtful. "You *should* introduce us. I'm dying to meet her."

And I should. She'll enjoy my circle of friends, and most importantly, I want her to feel more included. "You can all come over this weekend to see her, but I've got a delicate situation on my hands."

Yuna leans closer, propping her chin in her hand. "Ooh. Tell me. I love delicate."

I chuckle in spite of myself. "You can't tell anybody."

"Of course not," Court says.

Yuna raises a hand. "Scout's honor."

It makes me pause for a moment. "*You* were a Girl Scout?"

"Of course not. Don't be silly."

"It's Evie's dad." I tell them my dilemma. The waiter interrupts a couple of times to take our lunch order and bring the food, but otherwise leaves us alone.

When I'm done, Court says, "Wow."

"It's like a scenario from a Korean mak-jang drama," Yuna says.

"Mak-jang?" I ask.

"Yeah. A totally fucked-up drama with your typical clichés—secret births, dark history that nobody knows, messed-up connections that began even before you were born...you know." She shrugs.

I don't like that definition at all, even though I have to admit it sounds about right. "So how do I fix this?"

Court shakes his head. "You can't."

"I have to. I have to make Bradley leave, and without Evie knowing I'm behind it. And the sooner the better, so they don't start to fake-bond or anything." Court is a great guy, but he can be a little slow when it comes to women. Him being engaged to the love of his life is nothing short of a miracle. Proof that God does care about everyone, including the most clueless among us.

"That's the problem. You can't...unless you run him over," Yuna says.

"She deserves to know the truth about her dad. She isn't a little kid who needs coddling," Court adds, his expression dead serious, waving his fork around as though it's a wand that makes people understand him better.

"Dude, she's pregnant. She fainted at the family welcome party, and the doctor told her to avoid stress," I say, annoyed that Court doesn't understand the delicacy of the situation.

"My brother's wife fainted a few times when she was pregnant. It's normal," Yuna says. I'm not sure if she's trying to console me or freak me out. "I mean, it's obvious people like him would want money, right?" she continues. "But if you give him any now, he'll come back for more. You'll be turning yourself into a sucker. It'll only upset her when she finds out."

"What if she doesn't?" I say, even though I'm getting a sinking feeling. It's so damn hard to let her keep her pristine image of the guy, especially since it's all a lie, but Mari's right. Evie has so little. Maybe she should have this, even if I'm contorting myself to give it to her. Why can't I be just a little Machiavellian? Like Dane?

"Secrets always come out," Court says, growing serious. "Always."

I sigh. Court's family had a secret too—one so explosive, it tore his family apart when it came out. I bury my face in my hands. "Fuck."

Yuna pats my shoulder. "You'll figure it out and do the right thing, Nate. I know you will."

44

NATE

AFTER THE LUNCH IS OVER AND MY FRIENDS HAVE LEFT, I SIT in my car and ask the question: What would Barron do?

That old man is impossible, but he knows what he's doing when it comes to things like this. The man's also unsympathetic enough that he'd be telling Mari to shove her lies, but I can't quite do that. She isn't his mother-in-law, and Evie loves her. It'd be devastating enough for her to discover her mother lied, on top of realizing the dad she's idolized in her mind is a parasite.

Low stress. That's the way to go with Evie right now. So it's best for her not to have a huge argument with her mom, as well as keep that unjustifiably rosy perception of her dad—so long as Bradley stays away from her.

So. My plan is a slightly modified version of what Barron would do.

I contact the Aylster and ask the front desk to connect me to Bradley's room. He answers, and I tell him I'd like to see him in the next half an hour. And to throw him off, I make sure to keep my voice affable—the naïve son-in-law who doesn't suspect a thing.

"Sure," he says with such sweet warmth that I feel like honey is pouring out of the phone. "Is Evie coming with you?"

"No. It's something I need to talk to you one on one about."

"All right. It's not like I have anything to do today." He laughs.

Uh-huh. All you have to do is sit tight until you squeeze money out of me or Evie.

I text Evie to let her know I'm taking some personal time off.

Now? You never take personal time off, she texts back. *Is everything okay?*

Nope, but I'm not telling her that. *Just shopping. Even a billionaire needs to buy some things himself.* I add a wink emoji, hoping she won't ask too many questions.

Putting the phone away, I drive to the hotel and go up to the suite I reserved for Bradley. He answers quickly. He's dressed in a faded button-down shirt and slacks, the image of a guy who's been fighting his entire life to make something of himself but couldn't quite do it. But I'm not as trusting and stupid as he thinks. I can finally put a name to the bright light in his eyes—greed. Pure, unadulterated greed to score some easy money.

"So. To what do I owe this pleasure?" he says, gesturing me inside.

I step into the suite. The door shuts behind me, and I move into the living room. A room service table has been left with a half-empty bottle of superb Bordeaux, and the air smells of peppercorn steak. The fucker probably cleaned out the minibar, too.

I sprawl in the couch like I own the world. Bradley follows and stands awkwardly by the armchair. The man isn't dumb. He can probably sense something's wrong.

"Sorry about the mess. Housekeeping hasn't come by to clean up," he says. "Want a glass of wine?"

"No. I'm driving," I say, not wanting to touch anything he offers, even if I'm the one footing the bill.

He sits in the armchair. Smart. At least he knows he should have a clear head for what's to come.

"I'm here to talk about you." There's no point in sugarcoating it.

"Me?"

"Yeah. You need to leave."

"Leave?" He tilts his head, all innocence. "Am I being moved to a different hotel?"

I almost snort. I live in Los Angeles, and nothing annoys me like bad acting. Especially when somebody's trying to fuck me and my family over. "No. You're going to move to another state and never get in touch with Evie again."

The faux-affable air slowly fades. "Is that a fact?" His eyes go narrow and mean, leaving a rodentlike expression. "And why would I do that?"

"Because it'll prove to be in your best interests."

"You can't make me." He braces himself physically, holding on to the arms of the chair.

Oh, for God's sake. Does he think I'm going to have security drag him away? I could, of course, but that's a bit too unrefined for my tastes. Besides, people like him don't go away that easily. They're like a cancer that keeps coming back. "Don't force my hand. You won't like it."

"Don't force mine. Evie loves her dear old dad."

"She doesn't know what kind of money-grubbing scum you are."

"Did you already look into me?" he demands with a smirk. Then he slowly shakes his head. "No. That's too fast, even for you. It must have been Mari."

I don't answer.

He rolls his eyes. "She's such an idiot. Never had the guts to do what's hard, but always had the nerve to bitch and moan when something didn't go her way."

"Shut up. At least she stayed and took care of her child."

He gives me a level look. "And? I told her to get rid of it. What does she want now, a goldfish or a jellybean?"

Outrage bubbles up, ugly and toxic. What kind of monster is this? He's talking about a world without Evie like it's no big deal.

"Did she think I'd give up everything to be with that dumb whore? For fuck's sake. Any woman can get pregnant like that." He snaps his fingers. "She never had to act like a fucking saint. This is the least I deserve for having put up with her whining."

Suddenly all the hot rage inside me turns icy as I know exactly what I want. I give him a long, hard stare. "You will leave town, Bradley. You will never contact my wife again, and you won't even breathe of your connection to her."

"Or what?" he says, still full of bravado and not getting it.

"I'll show you what the Sterlings do to people who cross one of their own."

"You wouldn't dare."

I smile coldly. "You won't even be able to spit on the street without a cop chasing after you. Every time you try to get on a plane, you'll be set aside for extra security and questioning. You forget to signal before you turn, you'll be ticketed. Trust me. I can make your life very unpleasant in every aspect, no matter how small and petty. Death by a thousand harassments. And that's just an appetizer. How'd you like to be unemployable for the rest of your life? I mean, it doesn't look like you're used to working a nine-to-five as it is—so much easier to just take some mark's money, right?—but you'll be reduced to begging on the streets. Bradley Brown, the first male bag-lady."

"You fucker!" His complexion turns red, purple veins sticking out in his forehead.

"'Fucker'? Really? I thought you con men were more creative."

Shaking, he glares at me. Then finally, he says, "Fine. But I want to see Evie before I go."

"No."

"Don't you think she'll find it weird if I just disappear without a word?"

"Well, let's face it, Bradley. It isn't like you've never done it before."

His lips tighten until they look like hyphens on his face. "It'll be better for her if I tell her I have to go and that I love her. That way she doesn't wonder if she did something to upset me and make me leave or whatever. She's pregnant. Pregnant women are impossible—I know from experience, trust me"—he rolls his eyes—"and it'll give her closure."

My instinct says to hell with his proposal, but he has a point. Evie might very well assume it's got something to do with her. I don't want her beating herself up over a piece of shit like Bradley.

"Fine," I say despite a small voice in my gut saying, *Noooooooooooo!* "You can see her, once, but after that, you need to go."

"Don't worry, I will."

45

EVIE

WHEN NATE FINALLY COMES BACK TO THE OFFICE, HE'S carrying a box of Belgian chocolates and a bright bouquet of carnations and daisies. He hands me both.

"This is what your shopping was about?" I ask, a big grin splitting my face.

"Yup. I couldn't ask you to get them for me, now could I?"

"You didn't have to."

"Every man is entitled to spoil his wife without her protesting. Just enjoy them."

I smile. "Thank you."

"My pleasure." He runs the side of his index finger along my cheek.

I duck my head, suddenly embarrassed. I don't think anybody is staring, but...

Regardless, I've been very lucky. My coworkers are slowly accepting that I'm the boss's wife. Actually, some of them were furious about the tabloid article. Haruka even said, "I'm going to stuff blowfish ovaries down that so-called writer's throat."

I laughed, thinking it was cute how she wanted to make him choke on tiny ovaries.

"Don't laugh. They're toxic and will kill you. Make you stop breathing and you die. In agony, and with bad-trip hallucinations."

Note to self: do not mess with Haruka.

Kim also volunteered to off Brockman in gruesome fashion. All I have to do is say the word because she knows a guy who knows a guy.

Mom texted me to be careful, concerned that the notoriety of being Nate's wife isn't good for me. I reassured her we're both fine, and that it's only bringing us closer.

I get a text from Dad as well, asking me if he can talk to me at a Starbucks near the office. I say okay, since Nate doesn't have a meeting, and I don't have anything pressing this afternoon. I'm guessing he read the article and is concerned. That's sweet of him, but totally unnecessary.

Half an hour later, I tell Nate I'm heading to Starbucks.

"What for?" he asks. "Did we run out of decent tea?"

"Dad wants to chat. I think he saw the article." I wrinkle my nose.

"Ah, okay. I'll come with you. Let him know we're as strong as ever and there's nothing for him to worry about."

"If you don't mind." I smile. "That'd be great."

Nate and I walk to the Starbucks together. Dad's already at a booth with his drink, checking something on his phone. When he sees us, he starts, then waves, placing his phone on the table.

I wave back and grab an iced tea, while Nate gets a shot of espresso.

"Hi, Dad," I say.

"Hey, sweetheart." He searches my face. "You look good."

"I'm fine." I look at Nate, who sits next to me. "We're fine."

Nate gives him a warm smile, and Dad smiles back. "I'm glad to hear that. I saw the article and thought it might have upset you."

Nate holds my hand on the table and squeezes gently. "Well, Evie and I both know the truth. That's what matters."

Dad leans back in his seat, his shoulders lowered. "Wow. Now I feel like a silly old man, panicking over nothing." He laughs softly.

"Don't. We just trust each other," I say, not wanting Dad to feel bad. Any parent would be concerned.

"That's good," he says. "Honestly, you can't have anything if you can't trust the other person. And I know it's hard. Especially when he has so much power over you."

Over me? What an odd choice of words. Nate's fingers shift a little around mine, but he still seems relaxed. "How do you mean?"

"You know. He's a wealthy, well-connected, influential man." Dad's gaze flicks to Nate. "And you aren't any of those things. It can be hard to balance that out."

What he's saying pokes at one of my old fears. It's true that such a power imbalance would normally be a little scary...even dangerous. But the faith I have in Nate makes it inconsequential.

"Evie is my wife. Everything I have is hers, including my wealth, connections and influence." Nate's voice is as cordial as ever, but I swear there's a hint of steel underneath. "Everything."

Dad nods slightly. "I heard things were hard for you in Dillington," he says, turning toward me.

That's a sudden change of topic. "Mom told you?"

"Something like that." He shrugs, looking slightly uncomfortable. "She didn't want to burden me with old stories, but, you know, when you've been away from your child for so long, you want to know everything about her, hoping it will bring you closer."

"I'm sure." Nate smiles, then brings my hand to his lips and kisses in a gesture that's both loving and protective.

"Oh my God! What the *fuck*!"

I turn, looking up to see the furious face of Georgette. *Holy mother of God.* What is she doing here? And why does she look like somebody crapped all over her favorite cake?

Nate is sitting between us, and turns in his chair to face her. I look at her over his shoulder. At least she's dressed like a normal person this time. A Yankees cap is on her head, her T-shirt says, "Bow to This Goddess," and the jeans are super tight and studded with faux jewels, but for her, it's a sedate look. Regardless, embarrassment and annoyance mix together, as she's interrupting our time with Dad.

"Nate, why are you still keeping this ho around?" she demands loudly.

"What are you doing here?" Nate says.

"I wanted to make sure you saw the article! And kicked this bitch out! She's supposed to be crying and shit, not sitting here sipping on a latte."

"Are you *stalking* us?" I ask, disturbed by the possibility.

"This is a public place." She puts her hands on her hips. "Didn't Barron try to kill you? He tried to when my pregnancy went bad."

Oh geez. I vaguely remember the story Nate told me. "You mean when you faked a pregnancy to marry Nate, but got caught?"

"I didn't fake shit!"

I'm not going to argue this, because she's obviously going to believe whatever fantasy she wants to believe in. I can almost hear Nate grinding his teeth, while Dad just looks shocked.

"I don't care what that old man thinks!" Georgette waves her index finger, a hand on her hip. "He should've tossed you out on your ass! I know your baby isn't real. Nate can't get anybody pregnant, okay? That's why I couldn't, even though I did everything to have his baby."

Nate has obviously had enough, because he gets up and starts to push her away. *Go, go, Nate. Dad doesn't need to hear this.*

Suddenly something clicks in the back of my mind. "Are you the source for that article?"

"Of course!" she says triumphantly. "Who else knows the truth? If it weren't for me, you would've never married him, you skank. Do you know how hard it is to slip something into a drink at a casino? *So* many people watching. I had to dress up like one of those loser waitresses and learn the ordering system!"

I can't believe it. We were drugged in Vegas, and Georgette was behind it all? Holy shit. I wondered how we ended up not remembering what happened the night before, but wow.

The back of my neck begins to prickle, and I realize people are staring. Of course, Georgette's drawing everyone's attention. She might as well have shown up in hooker heels and that mink bikini.

And Dad is still looking stunned. How am I supposed to explain all this to him?

Georgette isn't finished. Nor does she care that people are pulling out their phones to record her crazy antics. "And then I had to practically drag him over to the chapel! But you...you wouldn't leave! No, you had to tag along like a leech! You stole my wedding!"

She was going to drug Nate into marrying her? Who goes this far? It's not even love. It's insanity.

Her eyes glow with manic intensity. "The stupid security donkey thought you were with him! *You!* Who in right mind would want to be with you?" She's yelling now, spittle flying everywhere.

"Enough!" Nate says between his teeth, and yanks her arm.

"You know she's a lying little bitch!" she pleads with him, trying to shove him away to continue this mad confrontation.

Dad's phone buzzes on the table, but he doesn't check it. He's too busy gawking at Georgette. Hard to blame him—that was my reaction when I first saw her.

"Admit it! Tell everyone whose baby that really is!"

Nate picks her up of the ground to separate us, and she kicks wildly. One of her legs sweeps everything off the table as Nate, cursing under his breath, forcibly carries her away. Georgette screams as she goes, her nails clawing at his back.

"Oh, shit!" I bend down to start cleaning up the mess around our table. Dad's phone is on the floor, right next to a spreading pool of coffee. I pick it up, noticing the screen is still intact. Letting out a soft breath, I start to hand it to him until I see a text he missed.

We don't have all week. Is your daughter gonna give you the 100k or not?

For a second, I don't understand. What is this about? I read it again. This time, each word sinks into my head, etching its meaning like acid on metal.

"What is this?" I whisper.

He snatched the phone out of my grip, the movement adder-quick. "Are you all right?" he asks, ignoring my question. "Who *was* that? Nate's ex?" He shakes his head. "I hope he takes care of that woman. It's humiliating for you."

"The text, Dad."

"Ah, it's nothing. Just some business stuff. That woman, though. Whew! It's been a while since—"

"Tell me the truth. What's that about?"

Dad looks at me, and slowly his eyes change. "Well, you read it. What do you think?"

I don't know what to think. Does he owe money to some nasty people who might hurt him if he can't pay it back? Or is it something else? But how could it be? I can't seem to process anything right now. "Mom said... She said you're a good guy. She told me so just yesterday."

His eyes turning heavenward, he heaves a huge sigh. "Mari could never just admit it when she screwed up. *Never*. She has to hide the truth, make excuses. She knew everything. She knew she made a mistake with me, but didn't want to tell you the truth. Probably too embarrassed. I'll tell you, she's sure got a lot of pride for such a pathetic girl. Always did. It was easy to manipulate her. All you had to do was poke it."

"But—"

"But what? You thought your mom was perfect? That she'd never lie to you? People always lie." He tilts his chin. "Even your knight in sterling armor Nate isn't entirely innocent."

My palms are slick with sweat. I look around the Starbucks in search of Nate, and see he's outside with Georgette and a couple of baristas, blocking the door so she can't get back inside. He's defending me, shielding me from that lunatic woman. How could he be anything like what Dad is saying?

Still, I feel slightly queasy, and it has nothing to do with morning sickness.

"He came by earlier today to threaten me. Told me he wasn't going to give me anything, and that I'd leave town if I knew what was good for me. He even said he'd sic the cops on me, which he could easily do. He has the money. The power. They'll do whatever he asks," Dad says bitterly. "He knew what I wanted from the beginning. Men like him always know." He looks at me. "Guess he didn't tell you that, huh?"

"No," I rasp, realizing that Nate lied about why he took personal time off after lunch. It wasn't to get chocolate and flowers. Why didn't he just tell me the truth?

"You see, everyone lies when it's convenient. Or maybe he doesn't think you need to know. Or maybe he was going to use it against you."

Against me?

"How easy will it be to take the kid away from you when you come from a seed like me? Maybe he'll claim your background makes you an unfit mom. He might have the money, but not all judges are kind to daddies. They still love moms more. He must love that kid in your belly. Doesn't he?"

What Kim said pops into my mind. Kids are precious in Nate's family because Barron lost two grandsons when they were young.

"Just because he fucks you at night and sleeps next to you doesn't mean anything. I did the same with your mom. And look how that turned out. The difference between me and him is I couldn't make her do what I wanted, and I didn't want her brat."

It's a good thing I'm sitting down, because my knees are trembling. Are we having an earthquake? It sure as hell feels like the entire foundation of my life is shaking underneath my feet.

"Anyway. Tell your husband I'm leaving, just like he wants me to. But make sure to let him know it would've been easier and cheaper if he'd just coughed up a couple hundred grand."

Dad puts the phone in his pocket and leaves.

I stare at nothing. Then finally I stand, toss the tea in the garbage and walk out onto the sidewalk. The sun from the sky lights on me. I'd never felt this cold in the Los Angeles sun.

46

NATE

FUCK. THE COPS TAKE FOREVER TO RESPOND TO THE CALL, and by the time they haul Georgette away, Bradley walks out. A nasty smirk is on his face, and I have a bad feeling.

"What happened?" I ask.

"Nothing. I told her I'm leaving. Ask her." Shrugging, he trots away.

Shit. I should've never left him alone with Evie. I wasn't planning on it, but fucking Georgette...

I start to step into the Starbucks, but Evie comes out, her face pale. "He's gone," she says in a wooden voice.

That prick probably didn't even tell her he loves her. Bastard. I should've listened to my gut and never let him talk to her in the first place.

I sigh, guilt pricking at conscience. "I'm sorry to hear that. It's too bad he had to leave so soon. And I'm so sorry about Georgette. I didn't know she'd do that. She won't be a problem anymore. I promise." I'll make sure of it.

Evie looks at me, searching as though she's waiting for something. Since I'm not sure what more I can say, I just smile. Although Court and Yuna made sense, I'm still debating if I should tell everything to Evie. Does she really need me to unload more junk on her after what just happened with Bradley and Georgette? "You know what? Why don't we go out tonight? Maybe meet my friends? You haven't met Court and his brother yet, have you? And Yuna also."

"Is that all?" she asks me, her voice listless.

An internal alarm goes off. "You feeling okay? Should I call Dr. Wong?" I ask, even though my gut is telling me something's very, very wrong, and it's not something the good doc can fix.

"No, I'm fine." Evie starts walking toward the office, and I go with her, wondering what's making her act so strangely.

Maybe she's upset her dad had to leave so suddenly. Or embarrassed about the scene with Georgette. People were recording it, and I'm sure it's going to make a splash on more than one tabloid site. For all I know, the incident is already all over social media.

A night out will be a good idea. It should cheer Evie up.

I take her to her desk, then go to my office. I text Court and Yuna, asking them if they're free for dinner with me and Evie. Court says yes, and wants to bring his fiancée. Yuna says fine, but warns me her mom's assistants are going to tag along, and hopes Evie won't mind them too much. I tell her not at all. I ask Court about Tony, but he says Tony has a date night with his wife. It's okay. Court and Yuna are fun. And Skittles is nice too. Maybe it'll help Evie forget Bradley and get her mind off my sociopathic ex.

At five, the office is emptying out like a beach at low tide. I go to Evie's desk. "Ready for a fun night out?"

"Actually...can we talk?" she says. "It's just the two of us here."

"Sure." Something must've happened between her and Bradley while I was occupied with Georgette.

"A lot of people want your money," she starts slowly. "So you're naturally suspicious."

I shrug, feigning nonchalance even though I immediately know Bradley yapped. *Fuck.* "Not all the time, but sometimes, yeah." I should've just slugged Georgette back at the café, knocked her out and never left that con man alone with Evie. "I don't generally make myself available to most people. You know that."

She nods. "Yeah. I block them for you."

"Exactly."

Evie looks away, making fists, then opening her hands and curling them back into fists again on the desk. Suddenly she jerks her chin up and faces me. "Nate. Do you trust me?"

"Of course," I answer without hesitation.

"Enough to tell me the truth no matter what?"

Shit. I feel like the floor underneath my feet has just turned into a sinkhole.

"Or does the trust only extend to some convenient line you've drawn without telling me about it? Or maybe you never meant for this"—she gestures at us—"to last long enough to matter."

Okay, this is bad. My brain starts working overtime to figure a way to pull myself out of the hole I'm in. "Evie, it's just... You can't... I didn't want you to worry about it," I say, not wanting to throw Mari under the bus. I don't agree with her decisions, but that doesn't mean I want to screw up her relationship with Evie to save my own ass. "What Bradley did or didn't do has nothing to do with us."

"Doesn't it? Or maybe you just didn't want to tell me the truth. You were hoarding the little nugget in case you ever need to use it against me," she says like she's reciting something somebody told her. Or maybe it's something she's been thinking for a while.

The blow couldn't be more devastating either way.

"Evie, no! How could you think that?" Most importantly, what made her think that? Haven't I done everything in my power to reassure her I'll keep her safe?

"I don't know," she says, her chin trembling for a moment before the muscles in her jaw start to bunch. "I'm just... I thought you'd always tell me things. You said you trusted me. How can it be trust when you lie?"

Desperation pierces through me. I have to make her understand or I'm going to lose her. "I didn't want to hurt you."

"How did you think I'd feel when I found out?" Her voice is thick with hurt.

"I was going to..." I can't even complete that and say I was going to tell her, because I was merely *thinking* about it, and not even that seriously. I don't want to add new lies to what I've done. I clear my throat.

"You weren't going to tell me until it was convenient for you, is that it?" she says, tears shining in her eyes.

"Evie..." I rake my fingers through my hair. I don't know what to say to fix this. The longer I stay silent, the more she slips away, but if I say the wrong thing, it'll be the end of us...

"You know... Let's just go back to the house," she says after a while.

"Okay." Dread is spreading through me. I notice she didn't say "home."

I text Court and Yuna to cancel the dinner, telling them I'm sorry. The drive is silent. The urge to say something is strong. However, I know from experience that this is the time to shut my mouth and come up with a plan. The wrong words can dig an even deeper hole. But what's the right thing to say? This is uncharted territory, and all my negotiation and management skills are useless.

When we're home, Evie goes straight to the bedroom. I follow, but then stop when she turns to me. "I need to rest. I'm tired."

I search her face and note the tightness around her mouth, the sadness in her eyes. "Evie... I'm sorry," I say, because it's the only thing I can say.

She raises her eyes to me for a moment, but nothing changes in their depths. "Okay." She looks away and walks inside.

My hands flex and unflex, but ultimately, I can't stop her. Or even reach out and hold her hand. This feels like a richly deserved punishment, and maybe forcing things would only make it worse. I remind myself Evie's also pregnant, and she needs the time to process and regroup.

Instead, I go to my home office and call Pattington.

"Yes, Nate?" he says, his voice inflectionless.

"You remember that Bradley Brown I wanted you to look into?"

"Yes."

Anger surges. "Make sure he can't even get on a highway without getting pulled over."

Pattington grunts. "It's a serious step to take."

"Yeah, well. I warned him." The motherfucker knew what I wanted. He might've followed the letter, but not the intent. So fuck him.

"Got it," he says, and hangs up.

I stare at the phone. The satisfaction I hoped for doesn't come. No matter how much I punish Bradley, the damage has been done. And I know I need to do something to fix what's broken.

47

EVIE

SINKING SLOWLY ONTO THE EDGE OF THE MATTRESS, I COVER my face in my hands. Nate didn't follow me into the bedroom, for which I'm grateful. I need time alone.

My father is a fraud. Always was. Although Nate didn't say it, it's clear Mom's been lying to me all this time. And underneath the hurt, an ugly, angry recrimination is simmering.

Why?

There's a small part of me that says I can't believe everything Dad said. It also says the text could've been a setup. How could someone who's driven to squeeze money out of me be stupid and careless enough to show his hand so soon?

But does it matter? It doesn't change the fact that I've been lied to, especially by the two people who I've had such faith in...

I think back on my time with Nate. He told me he trusted me. But Dad's right. You don't lie to people you trust.

I'm an idiot. I started to open up to Nate because I thought we could build a beautiful life together. But that isn't going to happen, is it? How am I going to be certain of him now? It goes beyond trust. His treatment of me proves he doesn't consider me his equal, just someone he has to shield with lies and omissions. What happens when he gets tired of that? Or he decides he needs somebody strong, not some weak, pathetic thing he has to protect all the time?

The thing is, I will never be as powerful and influential as Nate. So where does that leave me? And our child? I place a hand over my belly and try to think…

I can't come up with a single answer.

Finally, I pull out my phone and call Mom. I need to talk to her, hear her voice. *She owes me an explanation.*

"Hello, Evie," Mom says after a few rings. She sounds warm and affectionate, just like always.

But I'm no longer overcome with love for her and all that she's done. The knowledge that she weaved a stupid illusion about Dad all my life bubbles up like poisonous gas. "You lied to me about Dad."

A moment of silence. "Did Nate tell you?"

I blink at the question, ugly emotions churning in my gut, my sense of betrayal growing a hundred-fold. "You told Nate something you never told me?"

"What?" she says, now sounding utterly flustered, a liar caught in her own lies.

"He never said a word about you, and I thought he figured it out himself. But I guess not. I guess everyone talked about it behind my back. Did you laugh too?"

"Evie, hon—"

"Don't *Evie, hon* me."

"What did you expect? You had so little, and I couldn't give you much as a child."

"What does that matter?" I demand, confusion and anger tearing at me.

"I wanted you to have the idea of a nice father at least."

"So you lied when I called you and said Dad found me? You couldn't tell your full-grown adult daughter that he's really a jerk I should stay away from?"

"Evie, I'm sorry. I just wanted you to have some good memories. Why is that so hard to understand?"

Disappointment drips into me like drops of ink, dirtying my view of my life and people around me. Suddenly I'm exhausted. "I had good enough memories, Mom. You were enough for me. You didn't have to lie," I say quietly, then hang up, not wanting to deal with her excuses. I don't have the energy right now.

48

Nate

The rest of the week is sheer torture. Evie and I are living together, for which I'm eternally grateful. She doesn't select my outfits, but she still makes me the shakes like usual. She even makes me coffee, goes to all the meetings and organizes my work schedule as efficiently as ever.

But there's the Great Wall. It isn't made of pillows this time —because I burned them all—but it's just as solid. And this new wall is sandwiched between two gulfs the size of the Grand Canyon. Evie doesn't smile, and she's often pensive. I tell myself it's going to work out, because she isn't the type to hold a grudge and time will make it better. But if I'm honest with myself, I don't know if that's really true. There are times when I'm tempted to just hold her and tell her sorry I am, but she looks so fragile and brittle that I'm afraid she's going to shatter if I touch her wrong. And I'm not confident I'll be able to put the pieces back together.

Fuck. I call myself a thousand kinds of moron for causing the damned wall to come between us again. The worst thing is that I don't know how to smash through it. When I look at things from her point of view, she's right. I fucked up. I just don't know how much longer I can stand this punishment or deal with the anxiety building inside me.

I've rarely had things not go the way I want in the end. Hell, I was born lucky. Only the most ungrateful bastard could complain about being born into a family like mine, with billions of dollars, loving parents and relatives. That alone puts me ahead of ninety-nine percent of the world population.

And no matter how it might look to outsiders, I'm happy to be married to Evie, I couldn't be more ecstatic about our baby. But I know that unless I do something, I'm going to lose them both.

And that is unacceptable.

So on Friday, I ask Yuna if she can see me.

You need to buy me lunch. I'm still peeved you canceled on me and Court, she texts. It's fine. I'll buy her whatever she wants.

We meet at a cute American bistro of her choice. She comes with two women tagging along—her mother's assistants. Yuna calls them spies, but I think it's sweet of her mom to be so protective. Yuna is a wealthy heiress, single, a perfect target for an unscrupulous man like Bradley Brown or some other fortune hunter.

I groan when I see Court walk in. I didn't realize she invited him. I only wanted her opinion. Court is not female, and therefore, can't possibly understand exactly how Evie is feeling or know a way to fix this. He's the friend I'd turn to when I need someone to drown my panic in twenty-thousand-buck-a-bottle whiskey.

"Hey, man, what's up?" he says.

"What kind of greeting is that? Can't you see something's wrong?" Yuna tells Court, sitting down.

I raise an eyebrow. "What are you talking about?"

She makes circles with her index finger around my face. "It's all over. Your expression says, 'Something's seriously wrong.'"

I pull back, surprised I'm wearing my feelings so obviously. I'm harder to read than this...aren't I?

Then I think, *Who cares?* My life is a fucking mess. I run a hand over my face.

"So she's right?" Court says.

I nod. "Let's order, then we can get down to business."

She gets a cheeseburger. Court gets the bacon cheeseburger, since, according to him, life is better with bacon, while I order the day's special because I don't care that much about food. What good is bacon if I lose Evie and our baby?

"So tell us what's wrong," Yuna says.

"Not yet. I don't want the server interrupting." And I need a moment to suppress my panic over all that I stand to lose. Also to gather my courage before admitting what an idiot I've been.

Giving me a dubious look, she chats briefly about her shopping for Ivy's baby and Court's grand plan for his honeymoon, which Yuna's been advising him on. She's all for an overwater bungalow in Bora Bora or the Maldives, and a private waitstaff.

Finally, our lunch arrives. Yuna sets aside the top bun. "Gotta do this if I want to have fries."

Court steals the discarded bun. "More for me, then."

I push the food around on my plate. It's a whole fish, and it looks baleful, as though even the dead fish is thinking, *Dumbass. Liar. Screw-up.* I stab its head with the fork. *No more judgment from you.*

"Okay, so what's wrong?" she asks, squeezing extra ketchup on her melted cheese. "We can talk now, right?"

I nod. "If you were a woman, what would you require to forgive somebody?"

Court chokes on Yuna's extra bun.

She gives me a bemused look. "Uh, I *am* a woman. And that depends."

"Sorry. Too much distraction and too little sleep."

"What did you do?" Court asks.

He's going to think I'm a fool after I tell him I ignored his advice and got into trouble. So will Yuna. Hell, *I* already think I'm an idiot. "You remember the thing with Evie's dad?"

"Yeah."

"Yeah. Well...she found out."

"Ouch." Court winces.

Yuna sighs. "Guess you didn't tell her like Court told you to?"

"She found out before I could," I say.

"Were you *going* to tell her?"

I press my lips together, slightly embarrassed that the answer isn't going to be affirmative. "I was thinking about it..."

Court slowly shakes his head. "Dude..."

Yuna heaves a sigh. "Not good enough. Nate, really, you should've just come clean from the beginning. Then none of this would've happened."

"I know that now. But can't you give me some advice? I can't ask Vanessa, because she'll drag Justin into it."

"Why would she do that?" Yuna asks.

"Because she tells him everything. And then he'll try to fix it, but he's a man, so he's going to botch it. And God forbid Barron gets wind of a problem with my new marriage."

"Just make a grand gesture, like I did," Court says. "Chicks dig that shit."

"You mean like crash a wedding and kidnap the wrong person?" I ask.

My sarcasm apparently flies right over his head. He grins. "It worked, didn't it? I got the girl."

"Not because your plan was smart."

"Hey, genius, what counts is the ending. I got the girl I wanted."

True that. Court one. Nate zero.

Yuna is staring off into the distance. "I honestly don't know, Nate. I'm not Evie, and I don't know her well enough to tell you. You have to find somebody who knows her better."

Shit. Evie is close to her mom, but I can't ask Mari. She's probably pissed Evie knows the truth, and she's never seemed that crazy about me. So who?

"And you better choose this somebody wisely," Yuna continues. "Do you know why we talk about second chances but not third ones?"

"No."

"Because there are no third chances."

My mouth dries. My appetite vanishes too. "How...cheery."

"I know. I'm an optimistic type." She grins. "Now tell me what you'd like for your baby. The tabloids say you're shooting blanks, but I don't believe that for a second."

49

NATE

Yuna has a point. Back at the office after lunch, I make slow rotations in my chair, thinking. Who knows Evie really well and can help me out?

Kim.

She's been Evie's roommate and friend since Evie moved to L.A. She's actually the one who referred Evie to me when I was looking for a new assistant. They've got to be close enough.

I check my calendar. No meetings. I grab my car fob and leave the office. As I do so, I walk by Evie's desk. She's working on her laptop...probably drafting a memo we need for the children's hospital in Chicago. She looks pale, her eyes distant. The determination to fix our marriage firms until it hurts my chest. I'm going to make her smile, going to make her *happy*, if it's the last thing I do, damn it.

"Nate, where are you going?" she asks, her voice remote.

"I have a personal meeting," I say, because that part is true. "I'll be back soon." I'm going to fill in the Grand Canyon-sized valleys between us, then demolish the Great Wall.

Filled with anticipation and hope, I drive to Salazar Pryce's downtown office, but Kim isn't there. The receptionist says Kim's on a long paid leave, courtesy of Salazar. *Damn it.* Should've called first, instead of rushing out.

I call Kim, praying she didn't take advantage of her time off to explore the Sahara or some other place with no cell phone reception.

"Hello?" Kim says in a dulcet tone of a master assistant.

Thank God. "Kim, this is Nate." Then, in case she knows lots of other Nates, I add, "Sterling. Where are you? I need to talk to you, and it's very, very urgent."

"I'm home, but I don't know if I should," she says.

"So she told you."

"We texted, yes. And I'm going to see her later today to talk about the situation."

"Look, I know I screwed up, but I want to fix it."

Silence. She's probably debating. She's Evie's friend, but she also works for my brother's father-in-law, which means she's sort of stuck in a bad place.

"Come on." *Rein in your desperation. Desperation is never persuasive.* "You're the only one who can help me. Just a few minutes."

"I'm not going to plead your case to her," she says finally. "I'm not your friend. I'm hers."

My shoulders sag with relief even as I spin the car around. "I know that. In fact, I'm *counting* on that. I'm coming over right now."

I drive to Evie's old apartment. I already know the unit number from the HR file, which I read back when I was trying to learn everything I could about her.

As I walk through the hall, a black cat trots over and mewls. I look down at the little thing, wondering whose cat it is or if I'm supposed to alert somebody in case it's lost. Do they do Amber Alerts for lost felines?

The door to Kim's unit opens, and a guy comes out, jaw set and looking upset. I nod to him, sharing a bit of sympathy for his obvious frustration. On the other hand, I'm not going to get in the middle of it in case Kim's having an issue with her boyfriend. Nothing ever good comes of that.

I grab the door before it closes. The man glares at me with

open hostility and the outright territorial instinct of a guy ready to defend what he deems his.

"She's not interested," he says.

"Great. I'm not interested either."

"Who are you?"

Despite my current crappy situation, I can't help myself. "Her potential roommate," I say, and walk in, shutting the door in the other guy's stunned face.

"What were you two talking about?" Kim asks from her dining room, arms crossed.

"He wanted to make sure I knew you weren't interested."

She shakes her head. "Ugh."

"I told him I was your potential roommate."

Her eyes widen, then she laughs. "Good. For that, I'll spare you some time."

"Great. Because I *really* need to talk to you."

She gestures me toward a chair. "Want something to drink?"

"No, thanks. Actually...yes. Some water."

She brings me a glass of ice water and settles in the seat to my left with a glass of wine. "So. Tell me what happened." Her tone says, *Tell me what you did.*

So I do, leaving nothing out, because if I do she won't be able to give me the advice I need. Besides, Yuna's rather dire comment keeps circling in my head. Only second chances, no thirds.

I can't fuck this up.

Kim leans back in her seat, half her wine finished. "You shouldn't have done that."

Everyone around me thinks that. And I wish I'd listened Court earlier. "Yeah. I know that now."

"Do you know Evie was attracted to you before, too? But she was never going to give you a chance."

"Really?" I would've never noticed from her behavior back then, although a small part of me is happy that my topless act and drinking all that green goo weren't in vain. "Why not? Because I'm her boss?"

"No. Because you have everything; she has nothing. Comparatively speaking, I mean. She was afraid—probably still is—that you were going to use your power against her."

"She has my heart in her hands!" I protest, stunned and outraged. I don't come across that badly, do I? "That means she has everything of mine."

"Does she? Did you tell her?"

That makes me stop. I look down at my hands. "I...can't remember."

She sighs. "Nate, there's this thing called timing. If you tell her now, how will she know it's real?"

I shake my head. She won't.

"You blew it. She's had men tell her 'I love you' before, only to betray her in the end. You heard about her previous boss, right?"

I start to seethe. "That Chadwick guy?"

"Yeah. That Chadwick guy." Kim's smile is thin and humorless.

Maybe I should just murder him for hurting her. Would his figurative head soothe Evie?

"He totally messed her up. I'm actually surprised she decided to stay married to you, baby or not."

"I'm glad she did," I say.

But is she glad? *Look how you screwed things up.*

"I think you're sincere. But you have to convince her. And I don't know how you can do that. Because if you can't find a way to allay her fears, whatever you have with Evie is over."

Jesus. The magnitude of what I need to do sinks in, making my lungs tighten until I can barely breathe. But Kim has a point. I'm the one who lied, so why would Evie believe me now?

But how can I find a way to convince her?

Time stretches, with neither of us breaking the silence. Finally I say, "Thanks, Kim."

Her expression grows sympathetic. Maybe I look as terrible as I feel.

"I should probably get going. Figure this out," I say.

She gives me a small nod. "Good luck, Nate."

I leave her apartment, processing what she said. Fucking Chadwick, and all the men like him. Ruining good women with their careless, selfish douchebaggery.

My heart aches. I know that Evie was once hurt so badly that she can't even believe me when I tell her I love her. And I've been an idiot. I didn't even fucking propose to her after our Vegas wedding. I should have. She deserved that. I also should've considered what else she deserved—a real wedding, a real honeymoon, the works.

How do I convince her what I feel for her is real? How do I let her know I'll never do anything to hurt her, that everything at my disposal is hers?

A grand gesture, man, Court's voice says in my head.

I need something so big, so unequivocal, so *final* that it'll make her really understand that *she's* the one with all the power in the relationship. And there's only one way to do that.

My mind made up, I call Ken Honishi, the partner at the law firm Sterling & Wilson has on retainer.

It's time I make a grand gesture.

50

EVIE

NATE DOESN'T RETURN FROM HIS SUDDEN OUTING EARLIER. I wonder what he's doing and what the personal meeting is about. Is he talking to Barron about my dad? Or is it something else?

I hate it that I'm continuously second-guessing him and wondering about his motives now. I hate it that the life I thought I could have with Nate was just an illusion, like Mom's lies about Dad.

My hand rests over my belly. The baby...

I thought Nate and I could have a loving marriage, raising our child—or children—together. I thought our children would never know the piercing longing for a dad who was never around, or the ridicule from other kids, or miss out on common experiences kids have—school dances and field trips and more.

Maybe I'm just doomed to repeat the mistakes I made before. Chadwick seemed like a great guy too, even told me he loved me, only to betray me and make sure I would never find a decent job in Dillington. Los Angeles isn't a small town, but Nate's family is terrifyingly well connected and wealthy. It's frightening what they could do if Nate turns his back on me.

Focusing on that isn't helping you focus on your job. One thing at a time, Evie.

Shoving my churning emotions aside, I keep working until five. A few of my coworkers give me odd looks. They probably suspect something, but they don't want to get in the middle of their boss's personal issues. And if there's a falling out between me and Nate, they'll all side with him. They'd be stupid not to. And I'll have to... I don't even know what I'm going to do then.

Move back in with Kim? Will she want to have a roommate with a baby? Her boss is tight with Nate's family. In fact, they're in-laws.

Go back to Dillington? *No.* I can't go back, since Chadwick's still there and I'm probably still unemployable. Actually, it'd be so much worse now. Everyone in town who tsked and wagged their fingers at me would feel vindicated if they saw me tossed aside after having married my boss.

I grab an Uber to my old place and text Kim that I'm on my way. I feel like I need an impartial third party to help me process everything. I'm too close to the situation to be objective and logical, and everything that happened with Dad, Mom and Nate is spinning around in my head without offering any clear conclusions.

Kim's waiting for me with a couple of fruit smoothies. "I figured you'd want this rather than wine."

"Thanks," I say as I walk in and plop down in a chair in the dining room. "You're a goddess." I suck down half the glass, then feel my eyes sting with tears. *God.* I told myself I wouldn't cry like an idiot.

"Come on." Kim sits next to me and rubs my back comfortingly. "What happened?"

"Dad happened, then kind of...unhappened. Then Nate. And then *Mom.*" I tell her how everyone lied to me, turned me into a fool. How happy I was that Dad came to see me, then the emotional crash when I realized he only wanted to use me. That Nate knew everything but *didn't tell me* in order to help Mom perpetuate a lie she should never have started.

"Are you angry at Nate?" Kim asks.

I shake my head. "I don't know. I wish he hadn't lied. I don't know why he felt like he had to keep things from me, like I'm some idiot who can't handle real life."

"You told him how much you love your dad." Kim's voice is soft and gentle. "He probably couldn't find a good way to tell you."

"So what?" I say, suddenly pissed off that she's taking his side. Shouldn't she be telling me to kick Nate's ass?

Kim shakes her head, but her dark gaze is far too understanding. "Don't be angry with me, Evie. I'm trying to help you be happy. Answer me this before we go any further. Do you love Nate?"

My face crumbles, piercing pain radiating from my chest. "Yes." More tears fall. "I do." I wipe them away impatiently. "And that's the problem. I'm in love with him. Why can't I be in love with some normal, ordinary guy, the kind you see on streets all the time?"

"Because nobody falls in love with someone they think is just...ordinary." Kim places her elbow on the table and props her jaw in her hand. "You fall in love with someone *extra*ordinary. And in your case, that's Nate. You have to overcome your fear of the power he has if you want to be with him. I mean, he's a *Sterling*. He's always going to be rich and powerful."

I cry harder because she's right. And I don't know what to do about it. It's so hard to think. I'm somehow more emotional. I wonder if it's the pregnancy, but surely nobody becomes this overwrought because of a little hormonal fluctuation, do they?

Kim looks off into the distance. "Think of it like a Chinese emperor and his harem."

"What?" Why are we going from Nate to some old Chinese emperor?

"I've been watching some Chinese historical dramas. The emperors in China held all the power, right? And the girls in the harem didn't, of course...*unless* they could make the emperor fall in love with them. Then *they* had all the power, because the emperor loved them and would do anything for them."

"What does this have—"

"Nate cares about you deeply," she says. "He may even love you."

I shake my head. "He just wants the baby. His family loves children."

"Evie. No matter how much he cares about pleasing his family and wanting the child you created together, he wouldn't stay married to you if he didn't care about you."

"But you said Barron's traditional. And he's still the head of the family, at least for social stuff. The baby—"

"Evie! We're not back in the eighteen hundreds. None of that matters if Nate doesn't want you, and he wouldn't have stayed married to you to please Barron, either." Kim purses her mouth. "No matter how much influence Barron might have, Nate doesn't do everything the old man wants. He just goes along with Barron because they both want the same thing."

That seems unbelievable. On the other hand, I've seen the steel in Nate when he dealt with the people who stole from the hospital in Houston. The contrary and mulish part of me says, "He lied."

"Yeah, he did. But let me put it to you this way. If you found out that his mom was a horrible person, would you tell him immediately?"

"But she's not."

"Hypothetically. I'm saying *if* she... Let's say she was unfaithful to his dad, and she embezzled some family funds set aside for charity. Would you tell Nate immediately or would you hesitate, wondering how it was going to impact him and his relationship with his mom?"

"Of course I'd tell him," I say, feeling stubborn.

"Really?" Kim arches an eyebrow. "You wouldn't hesitate? Even a little?"

"Well..." I squirm under her no-nonsense gaze. "Maybe I'd think about a good way to approach it."

"Come on, Evie. Hesitation would be totally normal. It isn't easy to shatter somebody's world."

I hate it that Kim has a point, even though I want to insist she's wrong. "You're supposed to be on Team Evie."

"I'm on Team I Want to See Evie Happy." She squeezes my hand. "I hate to see you drive yourself crazy like this. It can't be good for your baby, either."

I rest my palm over my belly. "I know."

"Only you can decide what you're going to do. I'm not telling you to forgive Nate if you can't make yourself do it."

Kim's right. I need to find a way to let it go if I want to be with Nate. It's just that it's so hard to make that leap when it isn't just me who might be hurt, but the baby as well.

51

EVIE

BY THE TIME I GET HOME, IT'S A LITTLE PAST NINE. I toe my shoes off in the living room and lie on the couch, exhausted. I know Nate isn't back yet because I checked the garage on my way in. What could be keeping him away for so long? Should I text him? I start to reach for my phone, then change my mind, not wanting to look like a needy, clingy wife.

I keep thinking about what Kim said. She has a point, even if I don't like to admit it. The thing is, it's easy to pretend I'm brave when it's just talk. But when it's for real? Risking everything is hard.

Love.

She's right that I still love him, and Nate will always be powerful and wealthy. So my course is clear: I have to overcome my hang-ups if I want to be with the man I love.

Do I really think he's going to be another Chadwick?

The deepest part of my heart says no. Chad never put my needs above his. Nate has done that more than once. And he probably couldn't find a good way to destroy my illusions about my dad. To be honest, it's partly Mom's fault, too. She should've said something a long time ago. Or—at the very least—when I called to let her know Dad had reappeared. A petty part wants to lay all the blame on her, even though I know it's unreasonable. She did what she thought best out of her desire to make me feel good about my parents when I was growing up. I can't really stay angry at her for too long about it.

What do you want, Evie? To cling to your fear or to live your life with the man you love?

I hear the roar of Bugatti. Nate's home. I sit up, my palms sweaty, my heart racing.

The door opens, and Nate walks in. I inhale deeply.

"Evie," he says.

"Nate." I gesture awkwardly in the general direction of numerous seats we have in the living room. "We should talk."

He nods. "We should." He comes to me, then crouches in front of my chair. He reaches out and holds my hands in his, his eyes bright and determined.

My pulse throbs hard with anticipation and a tinge of uncertainty.

"I've thought long and hard about what you said, and you're right. I should've told you the truth. I should've treated you like an adult who deserved to know the real deal, no matter how unpleasant it was."

"Thank you," I say, touched he's saying this, especially since I can tell he's sincere. It soothes the frayed edges of my nerves.

"And I understand your fear of the power I have—what my money represents."

I bite my lower lip. I didn't know he understood, not really.

"So..." He takes a deep breath. "I decided to take it out of the equation."

What? How can he just remove something that's been part of him since he was born?

"I had a long meeting with Ken Honishi."

"The lawyer?" I ask, my nerves growing taut. *Is he talking an annulment? Custody of the baby?* But how do either of those relate to—

"I signed everything I have over to you, Evie. All the money and the power it represents are yours."

I stare. His words penetrate, my brain is translating them for me, but somehow they don't compute. Nobody gives away billions of dollars!

When I don't respond, he adds, "Literally everything. This house. The cars. All my clothes." He gestures at his own outfit. "Technically I shouldn't even be wearing these because they're yours. Even my underwear."

"Oh my God." I'm shaking all over. Even my heart feels jittery. How could he do this? It's crazy. Maddening. Humbling. And I know this is the man I'll always love, till the moment I draw my final breath. "Take it back, Nate!"

He shrugs. "Can't. You know Ken. He does impeccable work."

"Tell him no."

"It's a done deal." He takes my hand between his palms. "Evie, I love you. All that I have means nothing without you in my life."

"But Nate, I didn't... I never wanted this. I didn't do it because I wanted your money."

"I know, but that's why I love you. You don't care about any of that."

He goes on his knees.

My heart is thundering, and it's a miracle I can hear anything over the roaring in my head.

"I'm doing a terrible job of this, but I want you to know I love you," he says. "Will you marry me?" He pulls out a four-leaf clover. "I made a loop. YouTube had a tutorial on how to make a clover ring, but I wanted to get one with four leaves for luck. Just in case. Took me friggin' *hours*. I thought about a Tiffany ring, but then I realized spending your money to get you a ring would be wrong."

Laughter and hot emotions swell like a tide. "You silly man. You didn't have to do this."

"I did, and I do. I want you to have peace of mind." He smiles. "I also wanted to make sure you take me back. In case you didn't know, I don't draw salary for the work I do. So if you don't take me back, I'm going to be homeless."

"You won't be homeless!"

"And naked."

"That's—"

"Left swinging in the wind. Like, literally. Because I'm naked. You getting an image...?"

"Shut up." Tears sting my eyes and nose. "You're crazy, you know that?"

"Crazy in love with you. Evie, say you'll marry me."

"Of course I'll marry you. I love you too much not to, and there's no way I'm letting any other woman see you naked." I extend my hand. "Put that ring on me."

He slides the four-leaf clover on my finger. It fits perfectly. And I couldn't have asked for a better proposal.

52

Nate

It's our wedding day—with the proper ceremony Evie deserves.

No expense is spared. Well, she tried to spend some of the billions that are rightfully hers now, but Barron overrode her and decided to pay for it—with the attendant garish ice swans and fountains. He insisted on a yacht wedding, and I told her to just go with it because that's easier than fighting, unless she really doesn't want the ice swans and fountains.

Barron also included Mari in the planning. Evie and Mari's relationship is slightly strained, but they're working it out. Evie's slowly accepting that her mom did what she did to protect her, even though part of her still resents the deception.

Although I could only afford the four-leaf clover ring, Evie gave me a stunning platinum band with onyx stones around it to cement our commitment. I admire the ring as I drink a celebratory brandy in my cabin. The sunlight reflects just so, making the band sparkle brightly.

Dane gives me a look. "What's that ring? You aren't even married yet."

"We *are* married. We're just doing the ceremony. And it's from Evie. She gave it to me." I grin. "She's so good to me."

Pure disgust crosses his face. "You're pathetic. Pussy-whipped."

"Wow. I don't know if a guy who drives *a pink car* has the right to say stuff like that to another man."

"That's not my car." He bristles.

"Uh-huh. Keep kidding yourself," I say, taking half a step back. Dane has a mean right hook. I like my nose exactly the way it is, thank you very much.

Court steps between the two of us. "Just hold back until the ceremony is over, and the photographer got his pictures," he says to Dane.

Wow. "Whose friend are you, man?"

"Yours...but he looks mean," Court says in a stage whisper.

Dane makes a noise of annoyance and stalks off toward the bar. Justin appears, sticking his head into the cabin. "It's time," he says.

This is it. I finish my drink and check my appearance in the mirror one last time, smoothing my hair and running my hands over my stomach.

"Try not to puke while you wait for your bride at the altar. It makes for a singularly poor photo," Dane says.

"Colorful, though," I say as I walk out.

The slight buzzing in my belly isn't nerves—it's excitement and anticipation. I walk up and out onto the deck with Justin and Court as my groomsmen. The sky is crystal clear, a cerulean plate broken only by a few distant seabirds. White satin-covered chairs are laid out with geometric perfection, almost all of them already occupied by friends and family. Thousands of orchids and lilies stir in the gentle breeze. Mari looks at me and nods with a small smile. *A win,* I think. She's finally warming up to me, especially after learning that I did my best to keep her out of the Bradley Brown drama.

The quartet is set and ready next to the altar. Barron wanted a small orchestra, but he lost at rock scissors paper, so Evie got to have her quartet.

I gaze down the long aisle and wait until the most beautiful woman I've ever seen in my life appears—Evie. The white empire gown creates gorgeous flowing lines, and she glows, holding a bouquet of pink, white and blue flowers. Barron, resplendent in a crisp black tuxedo, offers his arm to her, and she lays her hand in the crook of his elbow.

The quartet strikes up the beginning notes of "Here Comes the Bride," Evie takes her first step down the aisle and it's the most perfect overture to the wonderful life we're going to have together.

∽

THANKS FOR READING *MARRYING MY BILLIONAIRE BOSS*! I hope you enjoyed it.

Would you like to know when my next book is available and receive sneak peeks and bonus epilogues featuring some of your favorite couples? Join my VIP List at http://www.nadialee.net/vip.

TITLES BY NADIA LEE

Standalone Titles

Marrying My Billionaire Boss

Stealing the Bride

∼

The Sins Trilogy

Sins

Secrets

Mercy

∼

The Billionaire's Claim Duet

Obsession

Redemption

∼

Sweet Darlings Inc.

That Man Next Door

That Sexy Stranger

That Wild Player

∼

Billionaires' Brides of Convenience

A Hollywood Deal

A Hollywood Bride

An Improper Deal

An Improper Bride
An Improper Ever After
An Unlikely Deal
An Unlikely Bride
A Final Deal

∽

The Pryce Family

The Billionaire's Counterfeit Girlfriend
The Billionaire's Inconvenient Obsession
The Billionaire's Secret Wife
The Billionaire's Forgotten Fiancée
The Billionaire's Forbidden Desire
The Billionaire's Holiday Bride

∽

Seduced by the Billionaire

Taken by Her Unforgiving Billionaire Boss
Pursued by Her Billionaire Hook-Up
Pregnant with Her Billionaire Ex's Baby
Romanced by Her Illicit Millionaire Crush
Wanted by Her Scandalous Billionaire
Loving Her Best Friend's Billionaire Brother

ABOUT NADIA LEE

New York Times and *USA Today* bestselling author Nadia Lee writes sexy contemporary romance. Born with a love for excellent food, travel and adventure, she has lived in four different countries, kissed stingrays, been bitten by a shark, ridden an elephant and petted tigers.

Currently, she shares a condo overlooking a small river and sakura trees in Japan with her husband and son. When she's not writing, she can be found reading books by her favorite authors or planning another trip.

To learn more about Nadia and her projects, please visit http://www.nadialee.net. To receive updates about upcoming works, sneak peeks and bonus epilogues featuring some of your favorite couples from Nadia, please visit http://www.nadialee.net/vip to join her VIP List.

Made in the USA
Columbia, SC
29 May 2020